WE ARE NOT LIKE THEM

WE ARE NOT
LIKE THEM

CHRISTINE PRIDE
AND JO PIAZZA

THORNDIKE PRESS
A part of Gale, a Cengage Company

GALE
A Cengage Company

Copyright © 2021 by Christine Pride and Jo Piazza.
Thorndike Press, a part of Gale, a Cengage Company.

ALL RIGHTS RESERVED
This book is a work of fiction. Any references to historical events, real people, or real places are used fictitiously. Other names, characters, places, and events are products of the author's imagination, and any resemblance to actual events or places or persons, living or dead, is entirely coincidental.
Thorndike Press® Large Print Basic.
The text of this Large Print edition is unabridged.
Other aspects of the book may vary from the original edition.
Set in 16 pt. Plantin.

LIBRARY OF CONGRESS CIP DATA ON FILE.
CATALOGUING IN PUBLICATION FOR THIS BOOK
IS AVAILABLE FROM THE LIBRARY OF CONGRESS.

ISBN-13: 978-1-4328-9129-9 (hardcover alk. paper)

Published in 2021 by arrangement with Atria Books, a Division of Simon & Schuster, Inc.

Printed in Mexico
Print Number: 01   Print Year: 2022

For our friends

The only trick of friendship, I think, is to find people that are better than you are — not smarter, not cooler, but kinder, and more generous and more forgiving — and then to appreciate them for what they can teach you, and to try to listen when they tell you something about yourself, no matter how bad — or good — it might be, and to trust them, which is the hardest thing of all. But the best, as well.

— *A Little Life,* Hanya Yanagihara

Maybe she and I failed each other by allowing each other the freedom to be ourselves, and maybe that was the inevitable consequence of true friendship.

— *Trouble,* Kate Christensen

PROLOGUE

When the bullets hit him, first his arm, then his stomach, it doesn't feel like he'd always imagined it would. Because of course, as a Black boy growing in this neighborhood, he'd imagined it. He'd thought it would feel hot and sharp, like the slice of a knife; instead, his entire body goes cold, like someone has filled his insides with ice.

The blood is a surprise too, not how much — he'd pictured it pooling around him — but how little, a warm, sticky trickle flowing from under his jacket where he fell to the ground.

He hears heavy footsteps and voices coming closer, two of them. One is calling for an ambulance. They're talking loud and fast, not to him but to each other.

"Check his ID."

"No, don't touch him."

"Fuck!"

And then: "Where's the gun? Get the gun!"

One of them says this over and over.

There's no gun. He wants to explain, but no words come out of his mouth.

He was wearing his headphones — Meek Mill blasting in his ears — when he thought he heard shouting, felt footsteps pounding in the alley. He turned and instinctively reached for his phone in his pocket to turn off the music. That was stupid. He knew better. *No sudden movements. Don't be a threat. Do what they say.* His mom had drilled this into him since he was old enough to walk. He didn't even have a chance though; his mind moved so much slower than the bullets.

An image comes to him — his face on the news. He knows exactly which photo his mom will choose: his school picture from last year, eighth grade. She was happy he'd finally smiled in it; he usually tried to keep his mouth closed to hide the gap in his teeth, even though just last week he'd overheard Maya in line behind him in the cafeteria call it "cute." He pictures Riley Wilson, the pretty one on Channel Five, with her bright red lips, her voice smooth as melted chocolate: "Fourteen-year-old Justin Dwyer was shot tonight by Philadelphia police officers. . . ."

He looks at his phone on the ground next to him, screen shattered into a spiderweb of cracks. For a split second, he's seized with panic — his mom had made it clear when he lost his last phone that she wouldn't buy him another one. Then it hits him just as suddenly: it doesn't matter. In the backpack lying beside his phone there's a brand-new polo — one he bought with his allowance, ten bucks a week for good grades and doing the food shopping and making dinner the nights his mom works double shifts. He's scared he's never going to get to wear that shirt. He vibrates with nervous jitters like when time is running out on a test. There are so many things he still may never get to do now — drive a car, see the ocean, have sex. As he hears the sirens growing louder, he starts to shake uncontrollably.

He tries to stop himself from thinking about his mother. He knows what her cries will sound like, because he heard them when his dad died four years ago. He won't be able to comfort her as he did then, rubbing her back, telling her, "It's okay, it's okay," even though it wasn't, even though he was terrified that he now had to be the man of the house.

It's okay. It's okay. He whispers the words

to himself because there's no one else to do it. The officers are close, their scuffed boots eye level; their voices float far away, jumbled with the shrill sirens and the chatter from their radios. One of them kneels near him. "Hang on, kid. You're gonna be all right. Please just hang on." He wants to tell them his name. If they know his name he'll be less alone. Worse than the pain or even the fear is that he's never felt so alone in his life.

A single star is visible in the hazy sky above, like the light in the fish tank in his room. It's something to focus on, something to hold on to until whatever comes next.

CHAPTER ONE

RILEY

You can't trust white people. My grand-mother's voice is in my head out of no-where, her Alabama lilt still honey-thick despite almost a lifetime of living in Phila-delphia. I swear I can even feel her hot breath in my ear. It's been happening more and more lately, ever since Gigi passed out two weeks ago on her faded corduroy La-Z-Boy, where she faithfully watched *Judge Mathis* every afternoon. She may be over at Mercy Hospital on round-the-clock dialysis, with a prognosis the doctors call "grim," but she's also in my ear with her no-nonsense advice and favorite sayings on random rotation. *Always keep some "run-nin'" money in your pocketbook. Don't kiss a man with dainty fingers. Never drink more than two glasses of brown liquor.* Sometimes she's a little more direct, like this morning when I stopped by the hospital and she

13

clucked, *Baby girl, that skirt's a little short, ain't it?*

I glance down at my skirt, which probably *is* a little short for work. I tug at my hem, then force it all out of my mind and bust through the station's double doors, as giddy as a kid playing hooky. Back upstairs, everyone is still in the middle of the 6 p.m. broadcast. For the first time in weeks, I was able to arrange it so I don't have a package running or a live shot so I could leave at a decent hour and finally meet up with Jen. I'm still running twenty minutes late though. I pull out my phone to text her that I'm on my way and see she's beaten me to the punch.

You're even pushing CP time. Get over here already!

Funny, Jen . . . real funny. I roll my eyes, amused. Why did I let her in on the concept of "colored people" time?

I wait at the WALK sign at the corner, in the shadow of a giant billboard featuring the KYX Action News anchor team. As I look up at Candace Dyson's face, the size of a small planet, the gloss of her toothy grin catching the setting sun, the usual thought runs through my head: *One day.* Candace was the first Black weeknight anchor at KYX. I idolized her growing up and told her as much on my first day of work five months ago. "I loved watching you as a kid. I dressed up like you for two straight Halloweens," I gushed.

Instead of her being flattered, I was met with a chill that still hasn't thawed despite my repeated attempts to ingratiate myself. Maybe she could sense how badly I wanted her chair. Maybe she sees me as a threat. Maybe I am.

When the light finally turns, I charge across the street, beads of sweat dripping down the back of my neck, my hair getting frizzier and frizzier by the second in the steamy humidity. It's almost seventy degrees, which is just plain wrong considering it's a week into December. It feels like I'm back in Birmingham, which makes me shudder despite the heat.

I bound through the entrance and slam into a throng of happy-hour revelers — a sea of Crayola-colored J.Crew sheath dresses and blue button-downs. I only suggested this place because it was close to the station, but I'm barely through the door before the crowd, the faux-farmhouse decor, the waitstaff in plaid suspenders, all combine to radiate an instantly irritating pretension.

Not long ago this street was all liquor

stores and check-cashing places, the kind of block a woman knew better than to walk down after dark. It's like this now all over the city; gentrification creeping into every corner, as relentless as water finding its way through every crack, the grit and grime replaced by sleek lofts and craft breweries. I barely recognize my hometown.

It's the same feeling when I spot Jen sitting at the bar. It takes me several double takes to recognize my oldest friend. She's chopped off her long hair so it ends right at her chin. In the three decades I've known her, she's never once had short hair. She looks like a stranger. Without even quite meaning to, I edit the scene to a more familiar sight — Jen's long dirty-blond hair, streaming down her back, smelling like the lavender Herbal Essences shampoo she's faithfully used since middle school. She and I haven't seen each other as much as we promised we would when I moved home, and it's all my fault, the new job has consumed me, but seeing her now, I'm hit with a rush of love. *Jenny.*

I stop to watch her for a moment, a habit from when we were little girls. Back then, I thought if I studied her enough, I could train myself to be more like her — breezy, outgoing, fearless. But that never happened

— turns out you don't outgrow yourself.

Jen leans into the man sitting next to her, whispers something to him, playfully slaps his thigh, and then laughs so loudly other people look over. He's mesmerized, basking in the attention like a fat lizard on a sun-soaked rock. This is what Jen does, draws you in and makes you believe there's something uniquely interesting about you, even when you're completely ordinary and boring, prying personal information from you that you aren't even sure why you're sharing. She probably already knows whether he gets along with his mother, the last time he cried, and what he'd rather be doing with his life besides going to happy hour at pretentious gastropubs. It's her gift, her aggressive friendliness, and it's why it was always Jen who charged into parties, or the first day of school, or the first track meet, with me trailing behind, counting on her to be our emissary, to make friends for the both of us. It was easy for Jen, who, unlike me, fits in everywhere, with everyone.

And though she's not classically pretty — she once joked that she was "trailer-trash hot . . . a poor man's Gwyneth Paltrow" — men have always been drawn to her. Like this guy who's now leaning a little too close despite Jen's wedding ring I can see even

17

from here. Not to mention his.

I take a few steps in her direction and stop short when Jen turns ever so slightly. There, poking out from her black tunic, her round stomach. Like the hair, this startles me, though it shouldn't. The last time I saw her, for brunch right before Halloween, she wasn't really showing. Seeing her belly now, almost as big as the soccer balls we used to put under our shirts when we were little to *pretend* we were pregnant, makes it all too real. This pregnancy may not have even happened without my help, but I'm still getting used to the idea that Jen is having a baby. As if sensing me, Jen turns around and shouts, "Leroya Wilson, get your butt over here!"

I'm startled hearing my given name, which I stopped using years ago and for a second I wonder why she's yelling it across a crowded bar. Then I see the look on her face and can tell she's offering it as a term of endearment, a signal of our connection. *I knew you when.* It's funny that I can't even remember exactly how I came up with my new name, but I do remember how emphatic I was about changing it. It was after a field trip to the news station in eighth grade. Standing in the control room, watching the energy and action of live news, seeing Candace sitting at the anchor desk with her stiff helmet of curls and her Fashion Fair coral lipstick, gave birth to a dream.

I leaned over and whispered to Jen right then and there. "I'm gonna be her, Jenny. I'm going to be the next Candace Dyson."

For weeks after, I spent every day after school staring in the bathroom mirror, wearing the plaid blazer Momma had bought me for mock trial and a mouthful of metal braces, practicing my sign-off. "This is Leroya Wilson, for Action Five News." But it never felt quite right. It was rare enough to see someone on TV who looked like me, and when they did, they definitely didn't have a name like Leroya. And so I became Riley.

By the time I've elbowed my way to the bar, Jenny is standing, waiting to greet me.

"Whoa, mama!"

"I'm huge, right?" Jen arches her back and cups a hand under the bump to exaggerate its size.

"Well, I meant your hair!"

"Oh yeah! Surprise! I did it last week. I wanted something shorter and easier, but not a mom cut." Her hand floats up from her stomach to run through what's left of her hair. "It doesn't look like a mom cut, right?"

"No, not at all," I lie. "It's very chic. Come here." I pull Jen into a hug and flinch a little at the odd sensation of her hard belly pushing against mine. When I press my face into her hair, the familiar smell of lavender is so strong I can taste it. The nostalgia is like a warm blanket. Thank God I didn't cancel. It *had* crossed my mind more than once today, but standing here in Jen's embrace and a haze of memories, the stress about Gigi, work, my never-ending to-do list, the exhaustion — all of it recedes and there is only Jenny, exactly what I needed. I'm already more relaxed knowing that for the next few hours I don't have to try so hard or impress anyone. Sometimes you just need to be around someone who loved you before you were a fully formed person. It's like finding your favorite sweatshirt in the back of the closet, the one you forgot why you stopped wearing and once you find it again you sleep in it every night.

The press of Jen's belly against mine does remind me of one thing I need to do: call Cookie back. I'm supposed to be cohosting Jen's baby shower with her mother-in-law, a brunch on New Year's Day, and Cookie has left me three messages this week. But every time I pick up the phone to call her back, I find a reason to procrastinate. Mainly because Cookie — a woman who uses "scrapbook" as a verb, constantly references her Pinterest boards, and refers to Chip and Joanna Gaines by their first names — keeps saying things like, "It's the Year of the Baby!" as if "Year of the Baby" is a thing people say. Her last voice mail was an agonized two-minute monologue about what color balloons we should get, since Jenny "refuses" to find out the sex.

"Isn't it so selfish that she won't find out?" Cookie asked in the recorded rant.

Well, maybe it's selfish for you to demand to know, Cookie. It's what I want to tell her, but of course I won't. My tongue may well fall out with all the times I'm going to have to bite it with her. I guess that's the price I'll have to pay, because Jenny deserves a fun shower, and if the tables were turned, I know Jen would be on the phone with my mom every night trying to convince her that rum punch served in baby bottles would be *hysterical*!

If there's one thing Jen loves it's a party, but she also always goes out of her way to be thoughtful, which makes you feel adored when it doesn't make you feel undeserving.

Case in point: The day I moved back from Birmingham this summer, anxious and bone-tired from driving thirteen hours straight, there was Jen bounding out of the coffee shop next to my new building, where she'd been waiting for me to arrive for who knows how long. Her hands were full with not one but two housewarming gifts — a spiky houseplant and an eight-by-ten framed picture of us from when we were kids.

"You can't kill a succulent," she insisted, hugging me tightly before thrusting it into my arms.

I *did* kill the plant in record time, but the picture is still there on my mantel. It's one of my favorites, taken when we were six or seven. We'd spent the afternoon running through the Logan Square fountain with a hundred other sun-drunk kids and the camera caught us lying on the wet cement, side by side in matching pink polka-dot bikinis, clutching each other's hands.

While we waited for the super to get my new keys, we sat on the curb in the sticky heat. Jenny reached out to wipe my face. "You're here," she said.

I hadn't even realized I was crying. I was just so . . . happy, or maybe it was more relieved. After everything that had happened over the last year, my fresh start was real. Sitting there together on the warm concrete, it was one of those rare times when, for a brief, glorious moment, the pieces in your life fall into place. I was home.

Jenny gestures now toward two stools to her left. "Here, sit." She removes the denim jacket she'd spread across the top, oblivious that the man next to her is irritated to have been so abruptly robbed of her attention. She's already forgotten him. "I saved three seats. One for you and two for my fat ass."

"You *wish* you had a fat ass," I joke. "You look great; you're glowing," I tell her.

"You too. But you always look camera-ready, so no surprise there. Your bangs are growing out. That's good." She reaches over to touch them. Jenny is the only white woman in the world I would let get away with that. Or talk me into cutting bangs.

"You know, I used to think you were such a weirdo for getting annoyed when people want to touch your hair, but now that I've got this" — she places a hand on either side of her stomach — "I get it now. I'm like Aladdin's lamp. No one asks. They just rub."

It isn't the same thing at all, but I let it go.

I finger my bangs, which look even frizzier next to Jen's smooth bob, which is now starting to grow on me. "So why did you talk me into this again? Chopping these two days before a brand-new job?"

"I know. My bad. We thought it would be

very Kerry Washington in season two of *Scandal*."

"Yeah, but it ended up more like Kim Fields in *The Facts of Life*. All I need is roller skates."

"This'll make it all better, Tootie." Jenny slides over one of the sweating glasses. She doesn't need to tell me it's a vodka tonic.

"That's why I love you." A long sip sends the cool liquid flooding into my stomach, reminding me that, once again, I've gone the whole day without finding time to eat.

"I'm jealous." Jenny raises her glass. "Ginger ale for me."

"Oh, come on, have a glass of wine with me," I beg her, because it's not as much fun to drink alone. Now that I'm here, all I want is to get buzzed with my oldest friend.

Jenny looks down and clutches her belly protectively. I feel like I'm intruding on something private.

"I don't want to chance it, Rye."

I shouldn't have suggested the wine. Not after all those years of trying, then the miscarriages, and all those rounds of IVF. Jen shakes her head. "I just can't."

"I understand." It's true, I do, but the role reversal *is* ironic given that it's been Jen's mission all these years to loosen me up, to get me to "live a little."

24

I make a show of downing another gulp. "Then I'll have to drink for the both of us."

"I'm so glad you're here. God, I've missed you so much!" Jen grabs my hands as soon as I set down my drink.

I don't know why I'm suddenly self-conscious in the face of her effusive affection — and guilty too. "I'm sorry I've been so MIA. Work's been brutal."

Even with a top-of-the-line "miracle" concealer, I can see the dark circles and deep lines around my eyes in the long beveled mirror above the bar making me look closer to forty than thirty. So much for Black don't crack. Clearly, the twelve-hour days, the six to ten packages I'm producing a week, and the almost nightly live shots are taking their toll. It's the work of three people, but I'm used to that by now. *You gotta work twice as hard to get half as far as them, baby girl.* It was a mantra most Black kids were all too familiar with, as ubiquitous as reminders to lotion up ashy knees.

"No worries, I get it. And you're totally killing it. I loved your story last night on how the city needs to invest more money in the West Philly school lunch program. I had no idea how many kids went without lunch every day because they couldn't afford it."

"You caught that?" It had taken several

weeks to convince my boss, Scotty, the news director, to let me do the piece, and then when all the positive emails started rolling in, he'd conveniently forgotten that he'd said, "Not sure anyone's going to care, Wilson."

"Are you kidding me? Of course I did. I always catch your broadcasts, Rye! You're the only reason I watch the crappy local news. And soon you're gonna be anchor!" Jen raises her soda and clinks my glass so hard I'm worried she cracked it.

"We'll see." I half-heartedly toast, scared that I'm going to jinx it somehow. *Don't go counting your chickens before they hatch.* Jen was the first and only person I'd told when I heard Candace might be retiring soon. I always assumed Candace was the type to be carried out of the studio in a coffin, but sure enough, when Scotty took me to lunch last month, he confirmed the rumors that she may "soon be exploring other opportunities," and that he'd probably be looking for someone "internal" to replace her. It was clear from the way he said it that she, a woman just past sixty, was being pushed out after more than two decades at the station. I should have been outraged by that, but I was too focused on what it could mean for me — a chance at the anchor desk.

Given that I've only been at the station a few months, it's a long shot, but ever since Scotty dangled it as a possibility, it's a shiny prize that I'm reaching for, greedy as a grubby-handed toddler grabbing for candy. The more Jen acts like it's a done deal though, the more anxious I feel about the fact that it might not happen.

"Trust me, it'll happen," Jen continues. "I know it. Anchor by forty! Right? You always said that was the goal. You're gonna get the job, and your bangs are gonna be a mile high on that billboard. You'll be so famous, and then I can tell everyone that I knew you when you used to practice French kissing on a pillowcase with Taye Diggs's face on it." She looks down and rubs both hands over her belly again. "It's all happening for us, Rye. All the things."

"God, remember how many games of MASH we used to play? I feel like I was somehow always living in a shack with Cole Bryant from algebra."

"OMG, you would have been thrilled to live in a shack with Cole. You loved his dirty drawers!"

It's funny to think of just how many hours — endless — that Jen and I devoted to imagining our future lives: where we would live, what we would do, who we would love, how many kids we would have. All we wanted was for our lives to hurry up and happen already. And now here we are. It was supposed to be the happily-ever-after part; what we didn't understand is that adulthood would be a relentless series of beginnings — new cities, new jobs, new relationships, new babies, new worries. Which is probably why I can't escape the feeling of always being on the cusp of the next thing.

"Here's to us, all growed up." This time, I clink my glass to Jen's more enthusiastically. My head spins from downing my drink too fast and my stomach growls. "I really need some food."

"Me too, we're starving." It takes me a second to figure out what Jen means by "we."

The menu is a long strip of parchment affixed to a piece of leather and printed with the day's date on top like a newspaper. Each dish has a gag-worthy "origin story." Steak tartare from Bucks County, farm-fresh burrata from Haverford described as "barnyardy," and honey procured from hives on the restaurant's roof. It's a long way from the Kool-Aid, Stouffer's pizza, and boxed mac and cheese we grew up on.

"Everything is crazy expensive," Jenny

says, staring at the menu as if it's a problem to solve.

It's true, the prices for "the array of small plates" are as absurd as their descriptions. I should have picked a cheaper place, considering how much Jenny and Kevin are struggling. But the subject of money is something I try to avoid with her entirely, so she won't be reminded of the reason it looms between us, the loan I know she'll never be able to pay back. I didn't have a choice though. I had to give her the money. When I was home for the holidays last year, and she stopped by my parents' place as usual on Christmas Eve, she was a desperate wreck. It had been more than six weeks since her final round of IVF, her third try, didn't work.

"What can I do?" I'd asked, as we passed a bottle of warm red wine between us, and then wondered what I would say if Jen wanted me to carry her baby in some sort of Lifetime-movie-of-the-week scenario.

"Nothing." Jen lay down on my childhood bed. I stretched out beside her, wrapped my arms around her bony frame, and buried my face in her hair. It smelled like it hadn't been washed for days, not a trace of lavender.

"You can try again, right?"

"No. We can't." Jen sighed.

"You can. You *will*," I insisted. "What will it take for you to try again?"

There was a long stretch before she spoke.

"Money. We're already, like, thirty grand in debt."

"Thirty grand," I repeated, taking in the staggering number. It was more than my annual salary in my first job out of college, working as a scrub reporter in Joplin, Missouri. And it was an insane amount of money to spend on something that didn't seem to be working at all. They still didn't have a baby. But I made up my mind not to judge. Besides, I'd never seen Jen like this. It was painful to witness someone you love want something so desperately, and to watch as each miscarriage fundamentally altered her — made her more fragile and bitter. Gigi said it was like Jen's spirit itself was withering like forgotten fruit. There was only one thing to do.

"How much do you need?" I braced myself for the answer.

Jen didn't respond right away, which made me think she might say no, and maybe that's what I wanted. Finally, she said, in as small a voice as I'd ever heard her use, "Maybe five thousand? That could help us . . . if it's not too much."

Again, I tried not to react to the number and just wrote her a check, instantly wiping out more than half my hard-earned savings. The way she couldn't stop saying, "Thank you, thank you," as she hugged me and wouldn't let go made it all worth it. So did her scream — so loud I had to hold the phone away from my ear — when she'd called to tell me the next round of IVF had worked. Still, sometimes the money feels like a little pebble caught in a shoe; you're not going to stop walking, but you always know it's there. We both look down at her belly now and silently come to the same conclusion — any awkwardness between us is a small price to pay.

"Don't worry. I can expense dinner. We might do a story on this place." I lie again to make us both feel better. "Order whatever you want. It's on me . . . on the station."

Jenny's visibly relieved as she turns back to the menu. "Well, in that case let's get it all. We fancy. We've come a long way from Chef Boyardee, huh?"

The bartender finally tears himself away from a gaggle of blondes who barely look of drinking age and pays us some attention. I can tell when he does a double take that he recognizes me. It's embarrassing how much I like this, how it never gets old. I offer him a sheepish smile, but he's all business, with a brisk "What can I get you?" and even then, he only addresses Jen, as if she's the one footing the bill. I order $100 of overpriced small plates to prove a point, though what exactly that point is, I have no idea. The bartender walks away before I can even set down the menu.

"We're gonna feast! Kevin's been picking up all the shifts he can until the baby comes and doing overtime working the Eagles games on Sundays, so I've been eating a lot of cereal alone on the couch bingeing *Fixer Upper.*"

"The glam life of a cop's wife."

Jen bites the edge of her bottom lip, a lifelong nervous habit that's left her with a tiny white scar. "I wish. It's been hard. The holidays are such a shit time to be a cop. Thanksgiving and Christmas are supposed to be, like, the happiest time of year for most people, but there are way more calls, more domestics, and a lot more suicides. Kevin had to go to one last week — day after Thanksgiving, guy hung himself in the backyard from his daughter's swing set. So awful, right? He left a note taped to the swings that said he couldn't fight the demons. It messed Kevin up for days. He doesn't say anything, but I can tell. It's too much for the cops . . . to be the social workers, the therapists. . . . Anyway, enough about that. God, so depressing. How's Gigi?"

For as long as Jen has known her, she has called my grandmother by the same nickname my brother, Shaun, and I use, the one I gave Gigi when I was first learning to talk and couldn't say "Grandma." Of course, Gigi loves this, since Jen is basically her granddaughter too. I tease her that she loves Jen more than me and vice versa. Ever since the very first day Jenny came to the day care that Gigi ran out of our house, the one she started when she moved in with us after Grandpa died and she retired from thirty years at Bell Atlantic, she took a special shine to Jenny, calling her "my little firecracker."

I always rib Gigi about this. "But can we trust her, you know, her being white and all?"

To which Gigi responds with the utmost sincerity: "Oh, baby, you know Jenny is different. She isn't like the rest of them." It was too funny since I can bet on the number of times people have said that about me.

"I overheard my mom talking to Pastor Price about needing to think about 'the arrangements' for Gigi and I got so angry.

33

Like Mom was acting like she was already gone."

Jen puts her hand on my arm. "Gigi's a fighter, Rye. She's still got a lot of life in her."

"I don't know. . . . The dialysis isn't cutting it anymore, and there's just not much else the doctors can do." I pause for a moment, worried I'm going to sound crazy, but then I tell her anyway. "Gigi's been haunting me. I hear her voice everywhere, Jenny, and it makes me feel like I'm losing my mind."

"Is she reminding you that nice girls wear pantyhose?" Jen scrunches up her face and cackles, so loudly people look over again. She's clearly thinking about the time Gigi insisted Jenny borrow a pair of her stockings to wear to church one Sunday after she'd slept over, even though the Hanes Her Way were two shades too brown for Jenny's pale legs.

"It's not funny!" I say. "Maybe I'm losing it."

"Shut your mouth. You're not crazy. You're worried about her. You love her. And you got a lot going on." Jen rubs the knot between my shoulder blades. "I should go see her."

"Yeah, she'd love that. She was asking

about you, and I told her I was seeing you tonight. She'll want to rub your tummy and tell you the baby's future. Who they're gonna marry, when they'll be elected president . . ."

"You know because of Gigi I grew up thinking all Black people were psychic."

"It's not psychic. It's the tingles."

Gigi always claimed that the women in the Wilson family had a touch of the "tingles," a sense of knowing the future.

I'm about to remind Jen of the time we tried to convince Gigi to let us charge the kids at school for her psychic readings when I see the moment has taken a turn. Jen is staring off into space, brows knitted. "Don't you wish you really could see the future, Rye? I just want to know everything's going to be okay. He, she . . . it's all going to be okay, right?"

Jenny and I were always making wishes together as kids — for our crushes to notice us, for Juicy sweat suits our parents couldn't afford, for boobs. She'd offer a fallen eyelash on the tip of her finger and tell me to blow. She would get annoyed when I wouldn't tell her my wishes, the ones I was too embarrassed about or most wanted to come true; I didn't want to risk ruining my chances.

I grab Jen's hand to reassure us both.

"Is this the hormones? A second ago we were toasting to all our dreams coming true. Of course the baby's fine. Little Bird is healthy and happy and can't wait to make fun of their mama with me."

When Jenny first starting calling the baby "Little Bird" after the Philadelphia Eagles mascot, it sounded like the corniest thing I'd ever heard, but over time I've decided it's sort of cute. I even found these adorable onesies on Etsy with baby birds and bought twenty of them that I'm planning to string up at her baby shower. Also, a shirt for her that reads, "Momma Bird." So I have done *something* for the shower, even if it was without Cookie's approval, which I suspect isn't going to go over too well.

"I'm just freaked out, you know. The closer I get . . ." Jen stops and looks down at her stomach again. "The scarier it is. There are so many things that can go wrong. You know what I mean?"

I know exactly what she means — the biting fear that everything you've worked for can disappear in a second, that you can bust your butt, do everything right, and it won't matter one bit. I know it all too well.

"It's going to be fine, Jenny. Better than fine. I'm so, so happy for you." Granted, it's a complicated happiness. I want to love this new part of Jenny's life, but there have been times when I've secretly indulged a stupid, petty, and selfish line of thinking: What does all this mean for me? How will this change everything? But in this moment none of that matters. It all gives way to a pure and bone-deep joy that Jen is about to get the thing she's always wanted, her version of the anchor chair.

I wrap my arms around my friend and hug her tightly and hope the physical re-assurance will penetrate more than words. When she pulls back to look at me, she's so close I can count the constellation of freck-les that dot her nose. I still don't say anything. Instead, I touch my index finger to the middle of my left eyebrow, and this does the trick — the memory chases the worry from Jen's face.

We were twelve when I decided to experi-ment with plucking my bushy brows for the first time. I wanted to give them a fierce arch like Posh Spice. But I was too excited and overplucked and then overplucked some more until half my left eyebrow was gone. No one could make me come out of my room, not Gigi, not Momma. I had finally opened the door for Jen, who promptly fell on the floor laughing, which only made me howl even louder. Then, while I stood there blubbering, Jenny marched right into the bathroom, grabbed a pink Bic, and shaved off half of her own left eyebrow. On the rare occasions I get annoyed with her, this is what I think of to calm myself down, the time Jenny shaved off half an eyebrow for me.

"You're right, you're right. I'm sure everything is gonna be fine. And guess what? I have some news." Jen brightens, her dark mood passing as quickly as it arrived. "I officially gave notice on Monday!"

"Oh, really?" I'm so caught off guard, it's hard to keep my voice neutral. It's not like Jen loves being a receptionist for a dentist on the Main Line, but given their money situation, I didn't think quitting was an option.

"What?" Jenny asks, clearly expecting a happier reaction.

"Nothing. I'm just surprised. I guess I didn't see you as the stay-at-home-mom type."

"It's not forever. Kevin's schedule is nuts. It changes all the time. He's four days on, then four nights, and that's when he doesn't pick up the overtime. One of us needs the flexibility. It's best for me to stay home. He's on track to make sergeant soon, and that'll mean more money coming in. And

I'm going to throw myself into raising this little one and making French toast every morning, and packing healthy lunches every day just like Lou."

There's a beat before we crack up at how far this is from the truth. The only thing Jen's mom, Louise, has ever been good for are dirty jokes, dirty martinis, and dirty looks. Her idea of a home-cooked meal is a Lean Cuisine.

As if on cue, our food arrives, and we turn our attention to appetizers that live up to their description of small plates. The farm-raised-beef sliders are no bigger than a half-dollar. Jenny pops two into her mouth back-to-back like popcorn, errant globs of mustard dribbling down onto her belly. I dip the corner of my napkin into my water glass and reach over to dab at the stain. There's a reason I stopped sharing clothes with her.

"God. I was starving," Jenny says, scooping up a bacon-wrapped date. "So listen. More big news. Kevin has a man for you."

Jen likes to give the impression that Kevin is much more invested in my life than he actually is — I suspect she's always had this romantic idea that we would be the Three Musketeers or something. But I can't say Kevin and I instantly clicked when we first met all those years ago, despite Jen's assurances that I was going to *love* him. My first impression when I saw him though was, *This guy?* It was hard to pick him out from all the other identical-looking white guys in plaid at the Irish pub on Walnut Street we'd met up at on one of my rare visits home. Kevin wasn't what I was expecting based on everyone who had come before him — the tattoo artist, the professional poker player, the guy who lived on a rickety houseboat and grew hydroponic weed. The evening was pleasant enough, and I could see how much Kevin adored Jenny, but he clearly didn't feel he had to work particularly hard to earn my approval even though I was the *best* friend. Later I'd overheard him talking to Jenny. "Yeah, she's cool, you guys are just so . . . different." Which was fair, and I felt the same about him. Kevin — simple, basic, vanilla, chinos-wearing Kevin — was just not who I'd always imagined for my friend.

He's not enough for you. It was my first thought when Jen announced they were engaged a year later. And then: *Please don't settle.* But I swallowed those doubts with a gleeful scream and a promise to throw myself into maid-of-honor duties immediately. I have no idea what Kevin thinks about me beyond how "different" I am, but I don't believe for a second that he's the driving force in any setup. It's Jen who, like every married woman with an unattached best friend the world over, has a single-minded mission to find me *someone.*

"Oh yeah?" I can guess the reason Kevin thinks this guy and I would make such a great match.

Jen takes a big bite of a crab cake and talks as she chews. "His name is Kayvon Freeman."

And there you go: a fine upstanding brother.

"He just came onboard as detective at the Twenty-Second District with Kevin. Moved here from Delaware . . . I guess he wanted to work in a bigger city or something."

A cop? No way in hell would I ever date a cop. But I obviously can't tell Jen that.

"And he's hot. And tall, we know that's a must! Kevin says you two would hit it off. We should double! I mean, Kevin/Kayvon. It's too perfect."

"I have zero time to date right now, Jen." It's my stock response — offered reflexively as a defense and an excuse. "I'm so busy. I need to —"

Jenny stops me with a raised palm. "Riley. It's time. How long has it been since you've

41

had sex? Your vagina probably has cobwebs by now." She playfully makes as if to lift my skirt, but her tone is laced with concern.

"I'm focused on other things. And I've got time." Though some days it doesn't feel like that at all. Some nights I'm wrenched awake at 3 a.m. with the unsettling sensation that time is speeding past me and I'm so behind I'll never catch up. I know what Jen's going to say before she opens her mouth. Because it's a lecture I give myself at least once a week.

"C'mon Rye. You can't be single forever. It's time to move on. To get back out there. You need to —"

I put my hand up to stop her before she gets to the part about how all the "good ones" are going to be taken.

Even though she may have a point. At Jen's urging I went on two dates since moving back to Philly, with people she'd swiped for me on Tinder. One guy talked about himself the whole time and then when I called him out about it said, "I'm just trying to help you get to know me." And the other one told me I must think I'm "bigtime" when I told him about my job and then just eyed the check when it arrived, waiting for me to pick it up. I had little faith third time would be the charm.

"I can't take the idea of getting back out there, Jenny . . . starting from scratch with someone new, letting someone see me naked for the first time. . . ."

"So you're just going to be celibate forever? No way. Here, give me my bag so I can get my phone. Let me show you his picture. You'll want me to make this date happen tomorrow." Jen goes to grab her purse and then winces sharply.

"Son of a bitch."

"Are you okay?"

"Fine, fine, this happens all the time," she says, waving off my concern.

"You sure?"

"Just a kick. Right in my ribs. You want to feel?" Without waiting for an answer, she grabs my hand and places it to the left of her belly button. There's a series of little jabs, quick and insistent. I fight against pulling my hand away from the little alien boxing in my friend's belly.

Jen finally finds her phone and pulls it out triumphantly.

"Ugh. Kevin's texted a bunch." Her stubby fingers swipe the texts away and scroll through her photo album. "Here, I found him. Kayvon. Hot, right?" Jenny holds up the screen.

Kayvon *is* attractive, with his buffed bald

head and sprinkle of stubble. In the photo he's dressed in his buttoned-up blues and wearing a sly kind of smirk, like he could be up to trouble. I see him giving me that smile across the table in a dimly lit restaurant and then I see him slapping handcuffs on teenagers and wrestling them to the ground. I chase both images away with a swig of my drink.

"Okay, true story. He is good-looking. So maybe . . . we'll see." I'm hoping Jen just drops this, even though I know better.

"No, no maybes. This is happening. It's been like a year since Corey."

Actually, it was fifty-six weeks to be exact. Hearing his name out loud, my stomach turns over on itself. I should be over this by now. It makes me crazy that I can still have this reaction to just hearing his name. Or finding one of his socks tucked in the back of a drawer, like I did last week, which threatened to wreck my whole afternoon, until I marched out on the balcony, threw it into the air, and watched it flutter onto the hood of a delivery truck.

I hold my breath and wait for Jen to ask me again about what happened between us. She's never been satisfied with my vague answers. But she seems to register the pained look on my face and switches gears.

Corey is a bear we do not poke.

"We need dessert," Jen says, and we let the subject dissipate like smoke after fireworks.

"Okay, you have to get the bartender's attention though; he's not giving me the time of day. Look pregnant and hungry and sad."

"I can do that." As Jenny juts out her lower lip and bats her eyelashes at the bartender, her phone buzzes and "Hubby" lights up on the screen.

"Seriously? It's like I go out one night and he can't stop texting me." She rolls her eyes, but I know she loves this about Kevin, that he needs her so much.

"Oh, text him back. You're pregnant. He's probably worried about you."

She swipes to open the message. "Or he's bored. He always texts when he's on patrol and he's bored. I told him to start playing one of those games where you kill birds —"

In almost thirty years I've seen about every expression Jenny can make. I know her face like I know my own. But the look she has right now, as she reads Kevin's message, is one I've never seen. I grab her arm. "What's wrong? Is Kevin okay?"

She doesn't respond, too focused on opening the Uber app. "I have to go."

"What? What happened?"

"I have to go." She's in motion, gathering her bag, her coat, knocking over her purse, picking it up by one strap. A tube of Chap-Stick falls and rolls across the floor.

"Wait. Jen. You have to tell me what's going on."

"Something happened . . . to Kevin."

It is these four words that will haunt me, how she phrased it: *Something happened. To Kevin.*

"My Uber's pulling up," she says. "Look, I'm sorry, I just need to find out what's going on. I'll call you tomorrow, okay?" She's already standing, buttoning her coat. She moves in for a quick hug.

I'm worried, but also a little pissed at being inexplicably shut out like this.

"Okay, then." I probably sound bitchy but she's not listening anyway. She's halfway out the door.

When the bartender appears, I order a second drink, which is noticeably stronger than the last one, practically a shot. Maybe he saw Jenny rush out. Maybe he thinks I was dumped by my pretty, white, pregnant girlfriend, which makes me laugh a little. The liquid singes the back of my throat as I drain the glass and then search for my phone, calculating that it's been at least an hour since I've checked it, a record these days.

Adrenaline pricks at my skin when I see I've missed three texts from Scotty.

We need you tonight.

Where are you?

Get here, now.

He also sent two emails. As I open them, my whole body buzzes, the tingles. A Black teenager shot by a Philadelphia police officer, in critical condition. I make the sickening connection. I know exactly why Jenny had to rush home.

CHAPTER TWO

JEN

In my dreams I never see it happen: never see Kevin get shot, never see my husband splayed out on the pavement, bleeding out. The nightmares always begin in the morgue, a scene straight out of *Law & Order,* a freezing room with puke-green walls. He's lying on a metal table when I arrive. No matter how hard I try, I can never touch him. My arms are glued to my sides, and I can only stare at his dead body. I've had that dream once a week since he started at the academy.

The truth is, I never wanted to be a cop's wife. When I met Kevin, he sold Internet ads for a living — good, safe, stable, boring. Thinking back on it now, I should have known better. The way Kevin had told me, so proudly, on our very first date that he came from a long line of police officers. Even Kevin's younger brother, Matt, had recently joined the force. But in the next

48

breath Kevin insisted he liked it at Comcast, and that if he left it would be to become an entrepreneur, maybe design an app or something, the type of vague grandiose shit you can get away with saying when you're in your twenties and have bright blue eyes and a headful of floppy curls that I kept wanting to run my hands through.

I wanted to be something bigger back then too, whatever that meant. My number one goal was to get the hell out of waitressing ASAP. I was so sick of working at Fat Tuesday, slinging watered-down margaritas to drunk sports fans who grabbed at my ass. I wanted to get a degree or start some sort of business, or maybe get my real estate license so I could flip houses. The details didn't matter so much. My single goal in life could be summed up pretty simply: whatever you do, do not turn into Lou. And then there was Kevin, banner-ad-selling Kevin, who had his own apartment with framed pictures on the walls and a real couch (not some stained futon), a good salary, health insurance, and all I could think was: *This. I want this.* I'd always had this feeling that the life I wanted was out there and I was just waiting for it to arrive, like a bus. Or waiting for someone like Kevin to arrive. A year later we got married, and life was going to be stable and safe and maybe even a little boring, just like I wanted.

Safe and boring went out the window a year after our wedding when Kevin turned to me out of the blue and said, "I wanna be a police officer, Jen. I'm joining the academy. I don't want to look back on my life and say the best thing I ever did was convince more chumps to sign up for Xfinity." His dad had recently retired from the force after suffering from a severe stroke, and my brand-new husband was suddenly all about carrying on his legacy. Being a cop became Kevin's "dream," and once he said that, used that word, what could I do or say? I wasn't going to stand in the way of my husband's dream.

And now, here were are in this nightmare. As far as I know, Kevin has only ever even pulled his gun once. And now this. Not that I know any details yet, beyond Kevin's text: I shot someone. But there's nothing to do now except wait. I'd raced home from the bar so fast, leaving Riley there all worried and maybe even pissed at me, but Kevin still isn't home yet. He's probably being grilled in some dark room at the station.

I pace the kitchen, waiting for the microwave to beep, while terrifying thoughts tumble round and round like socks in a dryer. Administrative leave. Investigations. Lawsuits. Hell.

When I grab the mug of hot water, my hands shake so badly that steaming droplets splash onto my bare feet, burning tiny sparks. I yelp and so does our dog, Fred. I scratch the wiry fur behind her ear to hush her. Then I return to my cup, bobbing the tea bag, willing it to release all the magical "calming" ingredients promised on the box. It hasn't even had time to steep, but I take a sip anyway, and the liquid scalds the tip of my tongue, making it go numb. If only the same thing could happen with my mind. I carry my steaming tea to the living room and am settling back on the couch when Fred yelps again. This time it's a happy sound, the one she makes when Kevin's key turns in the lock. The door slams, and my husband's voice carries through the foyer. I think he's talking to me until I realize he's on the phone with his brother.

"I don't know, Matt. We just have to wait. He's alive; they took him over to Jefferson Hospital. No one will tell me anything. I hope . . . I don't know if he's gonna make it. I'm meeting with my union rep in the morning. I'll call you after, okay? I just got home; I gotta go." He lets the phone fall to the carpet as he collapses beside me on our

51

worn sectional.

"Oh God, Jenny." His head drops like a heavy weight onto my shoulder. I smell old sweat and something musky, the acrid scent of adrenaline lingering on his skin. He's back in plain clothes. Where's his uniform? I picture a bloodstained pile.

I cup his chin in my hand and tilt his face toward mine. "Babe, tell me what happened. Start from the beginning."

He turns away from me, silent. This is nothing new. He shuts down all the time when it comes to work, especially when shit goes bad. I grab his hand, trembling and ice-cold. "Kevin, I need to know what happened."

"It was all so fast, Jaybird. Cameron shot, so I shot."

"Wait, who's Cameron?"

"Travis Cameron. New kid. I was matched with him at roll call this morning for the first time."

I can tell Kevin and I are having the same thought: We both miss Ramirez. Kevin missed his partner of five years because they'd become best friends, close as brothers, and had each other's backs at all times. I missed Ramirez because he was the only person I trusted to keep Kevin safe out there. It was a shock to both of us when

Ramirez announced that he and his wife, Felicia, were moving back to Felicia's hometown outside Topeka to take care of her mom, who was battling cancer. In the couple months he's been gone, Kevin's been noticeably grumpier when he comes home from work, full of complaints he didn't have with Ramirez. Ramirez calls Kevin throughout the day to vent about the new force he's on in "this nowhere town with no action." I bet Felicia loves the fact that there's no action. We'd spent how many dinners together talking about how much we worried about our husbands — their safety, their mental health — while they swapped years' worth of their greatest hits of stories and memories from the streets on a loop.

Kevin takes a deep breath, as if willing himself to continue, then starts talking so fast I can barely keep up.

"We got a call for an armed robbery, guy shot a convenience store clerk when he wouldn't open the register. Plugged him point-blank in the chest. From the description it was this guy Rick, who robbed another bodega last week. Cameron and I were first on the scene, and we saw him running down the street. We started pursuit in the car. When he pulled up on Ridge, we got out and ran after him. Cameron is hella fast — he actually ran track at Kutztown — so he's a few yards ahead, turning into an alley. I hear him yell, "Police, stop!" and I'm there at his heels when he yells, "GUN!" and fires. I stop and fire too and the guy goes down." Kevin suddenly stops talking and stares into the empty fireplace across the room, like he's watching the scene play out on an invisible screen.

"It was so fast. I didn't have time to think. I should have — FUCK." He's digging his nails into my thigh so hard they leave a mark.

I don't even feel the pain because I can only focus on one thing: My husband is alive. All the talk about armed robbery, chases, and gunshots, and Kevin is still here, right here with me.

I've gotten used to a lot in eight years as a cop's wife — the erratic schedules, the bullet casings in the laundry, the missed birthdays and holidays — but I will never get used to the constant, relentless fear. Every day Kevin puts on his uniform and walks out the door is a day I wonder if he's going to make it home. It doesn't help that he works in one of the most dangerous districts in Philly or that his bulletproof vest expired two years ago. He's supposed to go out there and face down men with guns with nothing between his heart and a bullet except an expired vest. He doesn't know it yet, but I've been saving up to buy him a new one for Christmas, the best on the market. I put it on layaway last summer, and the final payment's due in a couple of weeks. I keep telling myself that once he's wearing the vest I'll stop having all these nightmares.

I reach for him with both hands, desperate for the reassurance of his body, his breath, his presence here before me. *You're alive.* The fact of it makes me weak with relief.

"He was a bad guy. You did the right thing. He's in the hospital? I heard you tell Matt. He'll recover?"

Kevin stands so quickly he almost knocks me off the couch. He paces the room without answering, a wild, terrified look on his face, like a scrawny cheetah I once saw in a cramped cage at some janky wildlife park in the Poconos. That's what Kevin reminds me of now, a caged animal. In nine years of marriage, I've never seen him like this.

"He's alive, yeah, but . . ."

"But what?" I want to go to him but I'm rooted to the couch, paralyzed with dread, just like in my nightmares.

Kevin talks to the wall instead of to me.

"It wasn't our suspect — it wasn't Rick. He didn't even match the description. Rick was tall, like six foot three and wearing a dark jacket. Cameron never should have . . ." His voice trails off. "Christ, Jen, this is bad."

How bad? A question forms. I can't make my mouth produce the words though; something about the look on my husband's face stops me. *Was there even a gun?* This opens the door to other questions I'm also too scared to ask. *Was the guy Black? Did you shoot an unarmed Black guy? Is this going to be the headline?* In my gut, I already know the answer. I also know what that will mean for Kevin, for us. Maybe that's why I don't ask. Maybe that's why my heart won't stop pounding.

"I need to sleep, Jay," Kevin says when he finally looks at me. "I keep seeing him." His voice wobbles. "I keep seeing him there on the ground. I don't want to see him anymore tonight."

I don't say another word. I grab Kevin's hand, lead him upstairs, and give him two Tylenol PMs. He lies down in our bed, and I crawl under the sheets beside him, listening as his breathing slows. He's almost asleep when I decide I have to ask after all; the need to know for sure is a weight on my chest.

Turning on my side to face him, I scoot close enough for my lips to graze the back of his neck and speak softly into his musky skin. "There wasn't a gun, was there? The guy didn't have a gun?"

Kevin barely shakes his head by way of answering, but it's enough.

We don't speak again. I breathe into the back of his neck, matching my breaths to his until he slips into jerky snores, and then I flip onto my back, an act which takes a shocking amount of effort these days, and watch the electric blue numbers on the cable box tick forward minute by minute.

"Kevin is a good cop." I whisper this out loud, trying to reassure myself. I remind myself of his commendations. Two of them so far — a medal of valor and one for bravery. And that time he was called in to arrest a woman for shoplifting in the Walmart. At the hearing she struggled through broken English and hiccupping sobs to explain to the judge that she was stealing food because she was desperate to feed her kids. When the woman was let off on a misdemeanor, Kevin bought her a pantry full of groceries and quietly left them on her stoop.

People know his name in the neighborhoods where he does his foot patrols. He carries treats for their dogs, for Christ's sake. And talk about dogs. What about smelly, snaggletoothed Fred, who Kevin rescued from Philly Salvage last winter, where she had been left padlocked to a chain-link fence in below-zero temperatures. I reach for her now, curled up as usual in the tangle of our feet, and remind myself: *My husband is a good man.*

But I'm not getting any calmer; instead, I'm sweaty and clammy in a knot of sheets. I rip them off and head to the kitchen. Maybe more tea will help. When I get downstairs, I see my phone, forgotten on the kitchen table. The screen is filled with missed-call alerts from hours ago — all Riley. Without thinking about it, I call her back. By the fourth ring, I don't think she'll answer and then she's there, on the line, sounding winded: "Are you okay?"

She knows. "You know, don't you."

"Yeah, I'm . . . I came into work."

Of course she's there. She's always there.

"Scotty called me in. The shooting to-night . . . Kevin was . . . involved." Riley is measuring her words, like she's finding one at a time and slowly stringing them together.

I don't know much about what's happening, but I know enough to be careful with my words too. Still, I can't help it. "I'm scared, Rye."

"Do you know what . . . what happened?"

From upstairs, I hear Kevin cough. Or it could be a sob. I should be with him.

"I've gotta go. I'll call you tomorrow."

"Okay, I love you, Pony." I already have my finger on the button ready to hang up when Riley says it, the nickname from back when we were kids, one she hasn't used in years. Pony for me, for my long blond ponytail I wore every single day in elementary school — the only style Lou could manage no matter how much I begged for French braids. And Puff for Riley, for the trademark Afro puffs she wore atop her head from grades one through five. Riley's mom wasn't much more creative.

I love you, Pony.

I love you, Puff.

I love you, Pony.

I love you, Puff.

The end of a million sign-offs until one day we'd just stopped.

"I love you, Puff," I say now. It reassures me better than any stupid tea, and I try to hold on to that comfort as I trudge up the stairs and climb back into bed with my husband.

Lines of light shine through the venetian

blinds covering our bedroom window to form shadowy stripes across our navy bedspread. I throw my arm over my eyes to shield them from the light, and pat the bed beside me. It's still warm, but Kevin is gone. That's when I hear the loud retching from the bathroom. Fred leaps off the bed, nails scratching across the tile, as if heading to Kevin's rescue. My own stomach roils in solidarity, and I swallow a gag.

I need to call into work, before anyone gets in this morning. It's crazy to even think I could give two shits about confirming that Steven Frye's X-rays are covered by insurance or calling Maureen Wyatt to remind her about her cleaning. As the phone rings, I frantically debate what the hell to say. Do I go with the flu, or fake a few pathetic coughs? When the answering service picks up, I settle on a quick "Something came up, and I'll be in on Monday."

By the time I hang up, Kevin's returning from the bathroom, his face the color of wet concrete. My phone vibrates against the bedside table, the glow of the screen bright in the dim room. I don't move to answer it.

"It's probably Riley. I'll call her back after you leave." I don't tell him I talked to her last night. It's not a lie. I just don't say it. "She's worried after I ran out of the restaurant so fast."

"What did you tell her when you left?" Kevin snaps, his sharp tone catching me off guard.

"Nothing, Kev."

"You can't talk to her about this, you know," he says.

"What are you talking about? Why not?"

"Come on, Jen. She's media. Our names haven't even been released yet. The department is going to handle PR and stuff. Until then."

"But Riley is not 'media,' Kevin. She's my best friend."

She was my first friend. And *best* still feels true even though we've lived in different cities longer than we've ever lived in the same one. Over the past sixteen years, ever since Riley left for college, there have been moments when she didn't even seem real, more like the main character in a favorite movie that's always on TV. I got used to the distance — we had FaceTime, texts, visits a couple of times a year — but now she lives right across town. It stings a little that we haven't seen each other as much as I'd hoped we would. It's one thing to feel distant from your best friend when you live in different states; it's another when you're a few miles apart. But she's only been back a few months; we have time to reconnect. Besides, she's always, always been there for me when it mattered. Like when I was fired from Fat Tuesday for refusing to sleep with my married boss and Riley banged out a fiery two-page, single-spaced email to him demanding that he pay me severance. The first time I miscarried, she flew home and held me on the cold linoleum of my bathroom floor as I sobbed until dawn. And, of course, there was the money for the IVF, for our miracle baby that's flipping over in my stomach right now.

Kevin sits down heavily on the bed; the springs in the cheap mattress groan. "Look, Jen, I know, okay? But the union rep, the captain, everyone made it clear that we can't talk to anyone right now until they decide the story we're gonna tell. That's what they said. They need to figure out the best way to 'present' this to the public. I don't totally know what that means. But you know how these things blow up. We can't risk it. We need to see what happens today after my meetings. This is my life, Jenny. Promise me."

Our life, I want to scream. *Our life, Kevin.* But my husband, my sweet husband, looks so scared and broken that I bite my tongue and promise. Satisfied, Kevin lumbers around our bedroom, getting dressed, slamming drawers, yanking clothes off hangers, all the while talking me — and himself — through what's going to happen today, the meetings with his union rep and officials from OIS. I struggle to recall what that is . . . the Officer Involved Shooting department, I think, one more of the many acronyms to keep track of in the police world. Being a cop, or a cop's wife, is like living in your own country, a parallel nation to the US, one with its own language, own rules, own secrets.

Kevin grabs at things on the dresser — his wallet and keys, which he drops, twice — and then crosses over to the bed.

"I'll call you later, okay?" His lips rest on my forehead for the briefest of moments.

I grab his arm and make him stop and look at me. "I love you, Kev." It's different from the breezy "I love yous" I usually send him off with, and I can see in his eyes that he knows it. I watch him walk out the bedroom door, listen to his feet pound down the stairs, and then the front door slams.

I should get up and get something in my stomach, not for me but for Little Bird, even though I have zero appetite. I force myself out of bed and down to the kitchen to make some toast and more disgusting tea.

Even though I burn the bread, I sit at the table and choke it down. Little black crumbs fall onto the workbook for the Realtor's license exam I'm taking in a few weeks. I haven't told a soul except Kevin that I'm taking it, because if I don't pass, I don't need anyone feeling sorry for me. I should try to study or catch up on the mountain of laundry or cut my raggedy toenails, but I can't seem to move. Then again, the alternative — sitting here all day, waiting and listening as the silence of the house grows louder and louder — is also unbearable. I scream at the top of my lungs just to fill the void, to have something to do.

"Fuuuuuuuuuuuuuuck!"

It helps — a little, even if Mrs. Jackowski next door hears and wonders if I've gone insane.

I want to call Riley again but remember my promise. Instead, I go to the fridge and grab my favorite picture of the two of us, held to the door by a magnet shaped like a cheesesteak. I blew it up and framed it for Riley for her fancy new loft. I never got around to framing mine. There we are in those cute little bikinis. I'd blown a huge raspberry into Riley's ticklish ear seconds before Mrs. Wilson took the photo, which is how the camera caught Riley — usually so serious — laughing out loud, her grin wide enough to reveal two missing bottom teeth. This has always been the best thing: making Riley laugh.

It's funny to me how our friendship, so obvious to us, has always confused other people. They see a tall, elegant Black woman and a short, scrawny blonde and think, *These two?* If it hadn't been for Lou's desperation to hand me off, we probably wouldn't have become friends. I can credit a flyer in a Laundromat for one of the most important relationships of my life. Lou, barely twenty-two at the time, was tending bar in Center City at McGlinty's for the lunch shift and happy hour and working the ticket counter at the Trocadero at night, when the old lady who lived upstairs and usually watched me up and died. That's how Lou always described it, all bitter, "She up and died on me," as if Ms. Landis did it on purpose to screw with her, and it did, since Lou didn't have any other child care options. It's not like she could drop me with my dad. I'd never met the guy who knocked up my mom her junior year of high school. "You were an immaculate conception. I'm essentially the Virgin Mary," Lou said whenever I asked about him, satisfied that this was a sufficient explanation. Which it wasn't, obviously. I had a right to know who my father was. No matter how many times I demanded an answer, she never budged. "You're all mine. That's it." End of conversation. Finally, I gave up. Her stubborn possessiveness made me feel loved, in a screwed-up kind of way, and burned my fury away.

I wouldn't have put it past Lou to leave me alone with some dry cereal and a tightly locked door, but a few days after Ms. Landis died, she came across the ad for Gigi's day care, Sunshine Kids, a place that specialized in taking the scrubs, the kids whose parents worked odd hours or late nights.

"I got such a kick out of it when we showed up at the Wilsons' and I saw all these little Black kids," Lou told me, years later. "You were like a snowflake in a coal mine! I thought maybe you'd all form a little rap group."

I don't remember noticing that I was the only white kid at Gigi's, at least not at first; I was too focused on Riley, though then she was Leroya and I thought her name sounded so fancy, like a perfume. She was sitting at the kitchen table biting her lip in concentration as she practiced writing her name. Her hair was braided into intricate cornrows that

66

I wanted badly to touch. When I did, Riley swatted at my hand, and I knew I had done something wrong even if I didn't know what it was. I tried everything I could think of to convince her to play with me that day. She kept blowing me off until the other kids started holding relay races in the backyard and, out of nowhere, Riley walked over and challenged me to one. She might have had longer legs, but I knew I was faster. I took off across the yard, pumping my skinny legs as fast as I could. Then, at the last second, I slowed down and Riley won, but she wasn't happy about it. She accused me of letting her win. I only did it because I wanted her to like me. We argued about it, faces red, little fists balled at our sides, until Gigi marched across the yard and turned the ice-cold hose on us. "That'll keep you from fussin'." We fell to the ground, sopping wet, in shock, and then looked at each other and started laughing. That was when we knew we'd be friends. Even with that rocky start we became inseparable, the sisters we'd always wanted.

I only went to Sunshine Kids for a few years, until Lou decided I was old enough to stay home alone after school and at night. "That's what I did," she said. "And see how I turned out." Then she laughed, and I did too, because it was always better to be in on the joke. But by then I'd already laid a ferocious claim to the Wilsons as my adopted family and Riley as my best friend. The Wilsons seemed like an ideal family, with their nightly dinners together at a real dining room table and calendars on the fridge with dentist appointments and soccer games and a mom who read fairy tales to you at bedtime instead of *Rolling Stone* alone in the *bathtub*. Even as young as I was, I understood they were one of the best things to ever happen to me. I've said as much to Lou over the years. Like that time in high school when she accused Mrs. Wilson of having a stick up her ass. I had a primal flash of rage then, like *How dare you insult my family,* which was confusing, considering who was doing the insulting here. I'd screamed at her. "If it weren't for the Wilsons, I'd probably be a stripper or a drug addict."

Lou was unfazed. "There's still time, baby girl."

Lou should have been as grateful for the Wilsons as I was, since she always had a place to park me for her getaways, work concerts in New York or Atlantic City, or when she needed some "grown-up time" with a new man.

Like the summer before fifth grade, when

she disappeared for more than two weeks to follow her roadie boyfriend, Blazer, to Summerfest in Milwaukee. It was the longest stretch I'd ever been away from her, and my feelings when she knocked on the Wilsons' door to pick me up afterward were as confusing as ever. With her golden tan, sun-streaked long hair, and new tattoo of a mermaid running the length of her forearm, Lou was as wild and beautiful as ever. She never looked more beautiful than when she was returning after time away from me.

I gathered my things and climbed into the back seat of Blazer's Ford Escape, a stomachache already beginning to form. Blazer glared out the window at Mrs. Wilson and Riley waving goodbye from the porch and turned to Lou with a look of disgust. "I can't believe you let your kid stay with them niggers."

Riley and her mom continued smiling and waving from the doorstep, oblivious, and this made it all the worse.

Blazer winked at me in the rearview mirror, mouth open just enough so I could see the pink flesh of his tongue. I wanted to spit in his greasy hair, say something to make him slam on the brakes and toss me into the street. *White-trash bum.*

Lou just smirked. "Why do you shave your

balls, Blazer? You ask me a stupid question, I ask you a stupid question. Mind your business. They're nice people."

I slunk down in the ripped vinyl back seat, burning with shame that I hadn't spoken up. It was the first but it wouldn't be the last time someone would spit out the N-word or some other awful joke or comment over the years while I said nothing, the same shame rearing its ugly head, knowing I was betraying Riley with my silence.

The shock of my phone buzzing against the table makes me jump, sending my mug to the floor, where it shatters into pieces.

It's too soon for Kevin to be calling with news. I know who it is without looking — and I promised I wouldn't talk to her, so I let it go to voice mail. When I pick up the phone to listen to the message, I see it wasn't Riley after all, and I don't know if I'm relieved or disappointed. The voice on the other end is my sister-in-law, Annie, speaking in a fast whisper. "Hey, Jen, it's me. Matt told me. I'm thinking about you and praying for everyone. Call me. Let us know what's going on. I'm working an overnight, but call anytime."

Annie probably knows more than I do at this point about what happens now. Even with her crazy job as an ER nurse, she makes time to be involved in all the LEO groups. Yet another acronym — LEO, for law enforcement officer — and LEOW when it came to the wives. A close-knit group who organized volunteer committees, prayer circles, and gathered to drink margaritas and bitch about their husbands' crazy schedules on a Tuesday night. They're a club, a kind of sorority. I don't know why I've held them at arm's length — too much pressure to be a joiner, maybe. But now I wish I hadn't because I'm sure there's someone from the LEOW Facebook group I could reach out to for insight and support. But I'm not ready yet. Instead, I text Kevin:

What's happening?

I know he won't respond anytime soon — he warned me these meetings could take hours — but that doesn't stop me from staring at the screen, willing it to light up until I can't stand it a second longer. I should avoid the news, but I move to the living room anyway and turn to Channel Five out of loyalty, half expecting to see Riley's face even though she isn't on in the mornings. If it weren't for Riley, I wouldn't watch the news, period. None of the officers' wives do. It's impossible to listen to the crime reports when you have a man on the streets.

Gayle King appears on the screen announcing that *CBS This Morning* will be right back. After the commercials, they switch to a local news break. Riley's perky colleague, Quinn Taylor, comes onscreen, looking every bit the Texas pageant queen Riley told me she once was.

It takes a second for what she's saying to make sense, as if my brain is on a time delay.

"Fourteen-year-old Justin Dwyer remains in critical condition at Jefferson Hospital after being shot by police yesterday evening."

Fourteen? I'm falling through a trapdoor, my iron grip on the armrest of the couch the only thing keeping me tethered to the room. *He's only a kid.* Never once did Kevin say that he shot a *child.*

The face of a young Black boy fills the screen. He's right there in the living room — handsome with a gap in his front teeth that makes him look younger than his age, light hazel eyes that remind me a little of Riley's brother, Shaun's.

The screen cuts to a shot of a woman — the mother — covering her head with a plaid scarf, hiding her face as she walks toward the hospital. When she reaches the glass double doors, she stops abruptly and lets the scarf fall away before staring directly into the camera, her face the very picture of heartbreak.

"That's my baby in there. Please pray for him."

Her baby. I reach for my swollen stomach.

It takes me a minute to realize I'm crying. I'm not a crier. Lou always said tears were like pets and men, useless and needy, and made a point of ignoring me whenever I cried. By six, I'd learned not to bother.

Don't die, little boy. Please don't die.

Quinn's voice floats across the room again. "Sources close to the police department have confirmed the identities of the officers involved as Kevin Murphy and Travis Cameron."

No. No. No. The room spins. *Everyone knows.*

When the doorbell rings it sounds like it's coming from far away, like the voice on TV.

Please be her. Please be her.

I'm dizzy as I wobble to the front door. It has to be Riley, the person I need the most right now. The phone in my hand buzzes as the doorbell trills again.

"I'm coming, I'm coming," I yell, wiping the snot off my face with the back of my hand, drying it on my sweatpants.

A white light blinds me as I throw open the door and stumble backward; a barrage of questions assaults me.

"What did your husband say about the shooting?"

"Did he see a gun?"

"Is your husband going to be indicted?"

A white man in his fifties with a complicated comb-over breaks from the pack of reporters to climb the porch stairs and thrusts a microphone in my face. I bat it out of his hand and try to step back inside. A cameraman has already wedged his foot in the door.

"I'm pregnant, goddammit!" Both of my arms wrap around my middle, and I push my shoulder as hard as I can into the guy who has his foot stuck in my door. Adrenaline pumps through my veins. I need to calm down. This is bad for Little Bird.

"Is your husband here?"

"Would you care to comment on the shooting?"

"Has your husband had problems working with the Black community before?"

A lanky Black kid pushes his way forward. He's wearing a Temple T-shirt and a Black Lives Matter pin. It's small, but I notice it as he thrusts his iPhone in my face.

"Are you a racist?"

He pointedly repeats the question. "Are you a racist?"

Am I a racist? You're a teenager who writes for the school paper and knows exactly nothing about nothing and you come here to my house and ask me something so insane? I think of Riley, of all the nights I spent at the Wilsons', of helping Mr. Wilson organize his fishing rods, and of rubbing Gigi's feet when her corns were "acting up."

"Fuck you." I regret it the second it leaves my mouth, but I can't stop now. "You don't know anything! My best friend and god-mother of my future child is Black. How dare you, asshole!"

I finally manage to slam the door shut and slide down the other side until I'm a heap on the floor. Fred licks the sweat that's turned cold on my arms.

I remember my phone buzzed right before I answered the door. A text. From Kevin.

Meet me at our spot after work. It's bad.

My nerves are so frayed, like guitar strings pulled too tight, it's hard to get my fingers to cooperate. I finally type three words: *I'll be there.*

With reporters practically barricading our street, I have to sneak out the back-patio door and trek through Mrs. J's yard, where I step in a mound of fossilized poop on my way to meet an Uber three streets over. I gulp air from a crack in the window to escape the noxious mix of strawberry air freshener and dank weed in the car. The cold wind in my face does nothing to help the nausea or the nerves. I'm a mess by the time the guy drops me on Kelly Drive.

I trudge to "our spot" — a little azalea garden sandwiched in between the Victorian dollhouses of Boathouse Row and the looming burnt-orange columns of the art museum. In the summer, hot-pink flowers burst from every bush like confetti. Today the branches are bare, gray, and gnarled like an old woman's hands. A flock of bored Canada geese that forgot it was time to migrate gnaw on bits of trash at the river's edge.

Kevin chose to meet here so we could be alone, and sure enough, it's empty — the temperature nosedived into the low forties this morning and it's drizzling. As I walk along the river, I'm taunted by the happy memories we've had here. Like when Kevin dropped down on both knees to propose.

"I think you're only supposed to be on one knee." I laughed.

"I'm begging," he'd replied, grinning like a fool.

Kevin didn't notice there was a split second I hesitated, faltered before I gave him my hand. The proposal wasn't a complete surprise, but the sudden panic that came with it was. This was the moment when everything in my life would change, and it was more terrifying than I thought it would be, the permanence, the "ever after," all the other doors closing. I wasn't used to getting what I wanted, and when it finally happened, this momentous thing, I didn't know how to feel anything else other than confused fear. I never told anyone about that moment, not even Riley. And when I remember back to how we got engaged or when I retell the story, I gloss right over the part where I didn't answer right away. In fact, I never answered at all. I just thrust out my hand for Kevin to slip on the delicate diamond ring and assumed he would think it was shaking from excitement and not from nerves. I falter again now, for a different reason this time, as I spot Kevin's broad figure hunched over on the bench. I worked myself up on the way here, imagining what I'll say. *A child, Kevin. You killed a child. You shot a child. He was a boy, a kid.*

But when I see his face, ashen and vacant, I can't say any of those things. I can't break down, can't attack him. I have no choice except to be the strong one.

"Tell me everything," I say as I ease myself

down beside him.

Predictably, he doesn't answer right away. I wait as patiently as I can, rubbing his back in a slow figure eight.

"Cameron and I are on indefinite administrative leave while they investigate."

"Okay." I'm not surprised. There has to be an investigation. But what else? I brace myself.

"The union rep told me this was going to be bad, Jen. Like they were going to make an example out of us. He said they had my back and blah, blah, blah, but he just 'wanted to prepare me.' And we have to get ready to 'fight like hell.' Fuck, Jen. This is not on me. This is on Cameron! He shouldn't have shot. I mean, the kid didn't match the description at all! And he just . . . he just fired on him. He kept saying, 'The shot was good, the shot was good, right, Kevin?' " Kevin slumps back on the hard bench.

After a few minutes, he starts talking again, and this time he's grabbed my hand but still isn't looking at me: he stares out at the fast-moving current.

"They said to prep you too — it's all going to start soon: the protests, the media hounding us. . . ."

I don't have the heart to tell him about

the reporters banging down our door. It's already started.

"They're even sending over a media rep to talk to us. I can't believe this is happening."

When Kevin speaks again, his voice is barely above a whisper. "Am I a monster, Jenny? Do you think I'm a monster?"

"Kevin, look at me." When he turns to me, finally, he has such intense torment across his face, I summon every ounce of my conviction and speak clearly and slowly so that he knows I mean every single word.

"Kevin Murphy. You are not a monster. It sounds like this was an awful mistake. But you are not a monster. And I am going to be here with you every step of the way, and we are going to figure this out. Do you hear me? It's all going to be okay."

I'm saying it as much to myself as I am to him. But I'm not sure either of us believes it.

CHAPTER THREE

RILEY

If there's a sound more magical than the Ebenezer AME church choir, I've never heard it. They're opening with an exuberant medley of gospel, funk, and some Broadway-style riffs that feels more like a stadium concert than a church service. A sea of golden robes sways like flags in a brisk wind as the notes of the organ bounce off the stained-glass windows and course through me. The choir calls everyone to their feet, and I rise, limbs loose, eager to abandon myself to the invigorating rhythm. It's a packed house today, with some three hundred people filling the cavernous space, the energy palpable. There's nodding and swaying, spontaneous shouts and murmurs. You don't need an invitation to hug a neighbor, burst into tears, or sing along as loudly and proudly as Mahalia Jackson herself.

It's been a while since I've been to church, but exultation is like muscle memory. For a blissful moment, I don't feel stressed or self-conscious; I feel *rejoiced.* One of those rare moments when I understand what people mean when they say they're filled with the Spirit. The sanctuary of this church is as close as I've ever been to feeling God. Back when I was a little girl, my insides wound up so tight I felt like I was suffocating, these gleaming pews on a Sunday morning were a kind of escape, from thinking about tests and grades and the kids who called me "Oreo" and said I talked so white when I used the SAT vocab words Mom had been drilling me on since kindergarten. I need this now, a cocoon from the outside world, even if only for an hour. A respite before I have to return to work, and to covering the story for which I'm now the lead reporter, the one about how my friend's husband shot an unarmed Black kid.

By the time I arrived at the station Thursday night, after downing two espressos to counteract the vodka, Scotty was already huddled with a crew in his office, desk strewn with Burger King wrappers, the smell of grease and the anticipation of a big story charging the air. As soon as I walked in, his focus shifted to me.

"I want you front and center on this, Riley."

I must have given him a look, because his next question was, "Is that a problem?"

No, of course it wasn't. Of all the beat reporters, the rest of them white or Asian, I knew exactly why this was "my story." I'd take it too; I had to, I wanted to — it was going to be a big one, maybe national. "No, Scotty, no problem at all."

My first call was to a sergeant in the Twenty-Fifth District whom I've been cultivating since I started at KYX.

He finally called me back after midnight and confirmed what the tingles had already told me: "You didn't get these names from me, but everyone's gonna have them by morning. Kevin Murphy and Travis Cameron."

When Jenny called a few minutes after that, I froze. Finally, before the last ring sent her to voice mail, I dashed into a conference room, slamming the door behind me. I didn't know what I was supposed to say, but I needed to know she was okay.

We only talked for two seconds. But last night, as I reported live in front of the Twenty-Second District — Kevin's district — I kept picturing her watching, her reaction, her biting furiously on her lip, as I spoke into the camera. "If Justin Dwyer doesn't wake up from his coma, the officers involved — Kevin Murphy and Travis Cameron from here at the Twenty-Second — could be indicted for murder."

Jenny was calling again by the time I reached my car to head home after the broadcast. Of course she'd been watching. She said she always watches my broadcasts. I couldn't bring myself to answer this time. She'd know if I sent it straight to voice mail, so I stared at the phone as it rang and rang and then waited for a message that never came. I spent the rest of the night pacing my apartment.

So when Momma called last night, as she's done every single Saturday since I've been back, to ask if I was finally coming to church, I gave her an answer that surprised both of us.

"Yep, I'll be there." I needed church. I needed something.

Momma reaches over and takes my hand in hers, warm and papery. "I'm so glad my baby's here." It's not always this easy to please Momma, and the thrill of it makes me happy. Shaun, though, not so much. I lean over to my brother behind Momma's back as she sways and swings to the music. Shaun is standing, stiff and sullen, like he's determined not to let the music get to him.

"I'm surprised to see you here."

He shrugs. "Wouldn't be if I had my way. But you know, 'house rules.'"

Shaun is always railing against Momma's ironclad mantra, "In my house, you'll do as I say;" he hates that he's a twenty-seven-year-old man living at home, hates everything that's gone wrong in his life to lead him here.

We're whispering, but of course she hears. Momma always hears and then has the last word. "Don't act like God is punishment, boy. God is a gift. And that's exactly why you're here. To remember that." She starts clapping and singing even louder, as if she can channel the spirit to Shaun.

As the choir winds down, everyone is flushed and primed for Pastor Price, who lumbers up to the cherrywood pulpit. The imposing figure of Christ looms behind him, but even Jesus himself is no match for Pastor Price. He's divinely exultant in his vibrant purple robes, his dark skin gleaming against the rich fabric, the lines of his strong jaw clenched as he prepares to give his flock the holy word.

"It's a beautiful morning to praise the Lord, ain't it!" Pastor's baritone thunders up to the rafters. He hasn't aged a bit since

I was a kid, even though he must have rounded seventy. He's led this church for more than forty years, and in that time has become the de facto leader of all the Black churches in Philly.

Daddy sometimes grumbles that Pastor likes the limelight a little too much. Momma will counter that even outside of the church, he's doing God's work, and so what if that means he doesn't mind a crowd or a camera. He's earned his stripes as a civil rights crusader and still has the scar up his arm from being beaten with a baton during Freedom Summer. Then she'll remind us about how he's "friends" with Obama. I don't know about that, but Obama did visit one Sunday when he was on the campaign trail in 2012. Of course people here still bring that up every chance they get. Gigi loudest of them all. Apparently, our future president complimented her hat. When she'd told him he should get Michelle one just like it, Obama had winked and said he didn't know if his wife could pull it off nearly as well. Or so the story goes.

As Pastor calls on the crowd to accept the Holy Spirit, my phone buzzes in my pocket.

"Don't you dare," Momma murmurs, barely moving her mauve-painted lips. Suddenly I'm seven years old again and about to get a slap on the thigh for not paying attention to the word of the Lord. Back then, when she scolded me, I'd bury my face deep in her armpit to hide my shame but also to be as close to her as I could. I fight the urge to do this now, to remember what it felt like.

I allow myself the quickest peek at the phone. Jenny. Again. I wish she'd leave a voice mail. I need to know what she's going to say first, to figure out how I feel. Especially after she went on TV shouting that her best friend was Black. On one level, it's such a laughable cliché — *Me, a racist? Some of my best friends are Black* — but, on a deeper level, it gnawed at me. Here I was worrying that I was the one betraying her by covering this story, and then she goes and uses our friendship and my "Blackness" as a shield, a defense. It brought back something she'd said years ago that I'd decided to let go since we were having such a good time and I didn't want to rock the boat. I was home from Northwestern on my first winter break, and she and I went club-hopping on Delaware Avenue. We were beyond excited to be together again following our first and longest time apart since we were five years old. I wanted Jen to notice that I was different — three months at college and I already felt more sophisticated and grown. But I was also scared she wouldn't notice, and that that would mean I was the same ole Riley after all. But Jen was too busy gushing about two new friends she'd made, fellow waitresses at Fat Tuesday. She talked about these girls with the breathless infatuation of someone with a new crush. "They think it's so cool that my best friend is Black." Jenny rolled her eyes as she said it, but it was still clear that it was some sort of weird badge of honor for her, like I was a trendy accessory — otherwise why mention it at all?

That first semester away, I had met more than a few white girls who were too eager to claim me, who were proud of themselves for going to college and getting themselves their very own Black friend, checking off all those freshman-year experiences — get a tattoo, hook up with a senior, meet people "different from you."

I'd been thinking about this when I'd called Gaby last night. Ironically enough, she and I had become instant best friends in college by bonding over "these white girls" our first week on campus. We'd been in an endlessly long line at the bookstore when Gaby caught my eye and smirked at the girl in front of us whining loudly on the phone to her mom about how she should have been allowed to bring her car on campus and how her roommate said she didn't like the matching comforters she'd picked out and wanted to "do her own thing." It was the first thing Gaby ever said to me, leaning in with a stage whisper. "Man, oh man, these white girls with their tears and flat asses and rich daddies." Never mind that Gaby comes from one of the wealthiest families in Jamaica. She told me that point-blank within five minutes, without even a sliver of humility. "Oh yeah, I'm hella rich, but it doesn't matter, you watch, everyone here is going to think I'm a poor little island girl." They did. As we inched forward in line, she went on an animated tirade about how she wasn't going to get fat in America like all the tourists she saw spilling out of the cruise ships in Montego Bay. It was clear from the jump that this girl had a lot to say about everything, and she'd warned me, proudly, that she was "one of those people who tell it like it is."

Our entire college experience was four years of her telling me about myself, recognizing some unrealized potential in me to be cooler than I was. I showed up at Northwestern a shy, nerdy brown girl from Philly who'd never had sex, wore hideous khakis (cuffed!), and knew exactly one reggae artist: Bob Marley — and Gaby made it her mission to change all that. (The khakis were the first thing to go, my virginity next.) I didn't mind being Gaby's project at all. Actually, I loved it; I was all too happy to have someone else be responsible for turning me into the adult version of myself. So I latched on to her, right then and there, and she became — and still is — my anchor, the person I can count on to tell me how I feel even when I'm not sure myself. That's exactly what I hoped she'd do when I called her last night. She'd cursed and muttered in patois as I told her every detail.

"So Jen's husband just mowed this kid down? Here we go again with this shit. What does she have to say about it?" She sucked her teeth dramatically when I told her I hadn't really spoken to Jen about it yet and related the comment Jen had made to reporters.

"Excuse me. No! 'My best friend is Black'? That's some Don't Do 101 shit. You've got to call her out on that BS, Riley. How could she not know that's a fucked-up thing to say?"

Good question. But I didn't call Jen out, just like I hadn't all those years ago. I didn't have it in me — the thought of opening this door was overwhelming. I'm just relieved

Jen didn't mention me by name on camera. If Scotty knew I was friends with the wife of one of the cops involved, he likely would have taken me off the story. For a split second I had considered telling him, but I couldn't risk it — there was too much at stake.

I should have known better than to think I could escape Jen and the shooting while in church, because of course Pastor Price opens the service by talking about it.

"Our hearts are heavy this morning. One of our young brothers is fighting for his life over at Jefferson Hospital." Each syllable vibrates with emotion, conjuring a somberness that permeates the air, as thick as the scent of White Diamonds, the perfume all the older ladies favor.

"What has become very clear to me is that Black lives do not matter. Not in 1719, not in 1819, not in 1919, and not right now in the year of our Lord 2019 either. Black lives do not matter when a little boy is lying there bleeding out on the street for doing nothing more than walking home from school. What do we do? What can we do? What is the purpose of this church, this congregation, our community, in the face of this slaughter?" He lets the word sink in; the congregation responds with urgent murmurs: "Tell us what to do. What do we do? What does the Lord want us to do?"

He answers his own question. "We can't be silent. We will speak. We will not stop speaking. We will march. We will not stop marching. We will no longer let our babies be cut down in the streets. We will demand justice. For each and every boy and girl unfairly and unjustly slain. Michael Brown, Eric Garner, Tamir Rice, Freddie Gray . . ." He counts each name with a knobby finger, a roster that's too long and hauntingly familiar. At least to some people. I wonder who holds these names in their memories, a reminder and a warning. Does Jen? Does she know all these names? Does she carry them with her as I do?

"We will make our voices heard. We demand to be treated with dignity. I hope you all will join us and our brothers and sisters all over town for a March for Justice in Justin's honor. Next Saturday, right down Broad Street. And in the meantime, we're going to pray for that boy, aren't we? We're going to pray with our hearts that he pulls through. Now we need some inspiration today, don't we, church? We need a reminder that God calls us to turn our faith into action, for He surely does. Please turn to James two verse fourteen and let us read."

I grab the Bible in front of me, its burgundy leather cover worn soft as cloth with age, and turn dutifully to the appropriate verse, but my mind isn't there. I'm already thinking about how I'll cover the march Pastor mentioned and how to reach Tamara Dwyer. Scotty made his orders clear: "Get the mother, Riley. We need Mrs. Dwyer."

So far, Tamara has given only one comment, in front of the hospital Friday morning: "That's my baby in there. Please pray for him."

When Pastor calls for us to bow our heads in a closing prayer, I do so reflexively, respectfully going through the motions. I rarely pray anymore — it feels selfish and disingenuous given my shaky relationship with God, the fact that I've been to church only a handful of times in the last ten years. The last time I prayed, I did so without even meaning to — when I was crying my eyes out, pathetic and hopeless, on my bathroom floor last fall in Birmingham. I didn't have the right to ask God for much then, but in my desperation, I did it anyway. I'm surprised when I find myself doing it again now, offering up sincere, fervent pleas, for Gigi and then for Justin. *Please don't let him die. Not another one.*

The choir starts a rousing rendition of

Kirk Franklin's "My World Needs You," signaling the end of the service.

"Well, that was a blessed sermon," Momma says as we file out and join the long receiving line.

Here we go. I plaster a smile across my face, knowing that despite the tragedy hanging in the air, Momma wants to show me off on my rare church appearance, perfect Riley, with the perfect grades and the perfect manners and the perfect education and career. The thought of it is exhausting, but I ready myself for showtime, standing a little straighter, remembering never to say "yeah," always "yes," and to make sure I look everyone in the eye and ask after their family. In other words, I'll do Momma proud like I always do. I'll uphold Momma's carefully maintained image that we are a model family, basically the Huxtables, only with a lot less money. Though the irony of the Huxtables as the epitome of Black success is not lost on me. I look behind me and see that Shaun, too, has transformed his scowl into a polite smile as we follow Momma down the aisle.

Momma doesn't walk, she glides, her hat angled just so over her fresh roller set, her backbone so straight she appears at least three inches taller than her true five feet, a strutting peacock mindful of a roomful of onlookers. For sure, she already has a list of accomplishments and updates running through her mind like ticker tape. Normally, she'd be arm in arm with Daddy, whispering gossip under her breath. But he was called in this morning for a plumbing emergency on Penn's campus, where he's worked for twenty years as a janitor — or "Ivy League custodial engineer," as Momma calls it — so she forgoes the gossip in favor of pointing at me and loudly exclaiming, "Look at my baby girl here today," to anyone whose eyes she catches. "You know she's on TV, right? Channel Five News. Every night."

I'm not on every night, but I don't bother correcting her. My role here is to follow obediently and smile manically. I reach up to smooth my hair, which I flat-ironed to within an inch of its life this morning in preparation for church and to pass muster with Momma. I have a flash of getting ready for church as a little girl and Momma pressing my hair with an ancient metal comb she heated on the fiery red stovetop burner and inevitably gave me singed ears no matter how still I sat.

When we reach the vestibule, Pastor Price's voice parts the crowd around us.

"Well, well, well, I'd like to say a mighty prayer for the prodigal daughter returned! If it isn't Leroya Wilson right here in my church. Now there's a miracle!"

This time, I'm not surprised to hear "Leroya," and I glance over at my mom guiltily, reminded of how upset my parents were when I announced — emphatically — that I was changing my name, the wounded looks on their faces. But Momma is all smiles now, beaming up at Pastor like she's presenting a prize.

Stepping into Pastor's embrace, I feel like a little girl, like Leroya again. I'm happy that he's teasing me as he always did back then — like when I would press him with questions about why Jesus looked so white in the storybooks.

"People need to see themselves in Jesus, Leroya," he'd said. "When you see him, maybe you should see a whip-smart little Black girl."

He stands back, placing both his hands gently on my arms, holding my body away, appraising me. "You're all grown up, ain't you, and as beautiful as ever. Just like your mother here." This is another thing about Pastor Price: he was always a flirt.

"You're doing good work, God's work, on the news. I watch you all the time. Don't I,

Sandra?"

"You do, you do." Momma grins so hard her face might crack. Shaun looks bored and small. Gone are the days when our parents stood right here in this vestibule gushing about his soccer talent, his game-winning goals, his scholarship to Temple, his big future. My little brother used to cast a large shadow. That was before. Now he hardly takes up any space at all.

Pastor Price leans in and lowers his voice. "So this is some mess with Jenny." Growing up, Jenny used to come to church with us. I always had a strange sense of pride that Jenny could hang, that she could be one of us, so comfortable being the only white person in the crowd. It was ironic given I was the one who had plenty of practice being the "only one" in countless places and situations, including ending up at one of the whitest high schools in Philly, but it had never come quite as easily for me — in fact, some nights I fell into bed depleted from the effort of it all.

Before I can work out how to respond to Pastor's comment, he's moved on. "We'll talk more this week," he commands. "God sent you to us, Leroya. And right on time. We need your voice, your power, your influence. They're going to cover for their own.

They always do. We won't let them get away with it this time. We need you to tell our story. Call my office tomorrow, you hear?"

His tone of collusion doesn't feel right. I'm a journalist, not an activist. But then again, I may need his help and connections to get to Justin's mother, and I know better than to try to parse the nuances here anyway, so I just smile.

Pastor Price grabs Momma's hands in his. "I'm praying for your mother, praying hard. And the ladies' prayer group is headed to the hospital to see her this afternoon. Sister Marla's a strong woman."

We nod in agreement and gratitude, and Momma gives an overly detailed update about Gigi's condition. Meanwhile, I watch Shaun duck away to the other side of the lobby, where he discreetly drops a $20 bill in the tithing box. The gesture pinches my heart. I know full well that he doesn't have twenty to spare. I gave him a hundred bucks last week so he could pay his phone bill.

"How's he doing?" Pastor Price has followed my gaze, his concern plain. "He doing okay with the moving job?"

After a year of struggling to find someone who would hire him, Shaun finally landed a job with a local moving company, thanks to Pastor Price, who knows the owner.

Momma stands a little straighter. "He's fine, fine." She's quick to remind everyone of this and then move the subject along. She does it whenever anyone dares mention what happened to Shaun. It's "family business," akin to an NSA document stamped CLASSIFIED. But we never discuss it with one another either. We don't talk about why Shaun lives at home, or the crushing debt, or the fear and resentment that cling like a shadow to our entire family.

"We'll see you next week, Pastor," Momma says. I can tell she's happy for us to slip away.

There's a sharp chill in the air as we step outside; the temperatures have plummeted even since this morning, so now December feels like December, cold and gray like it should be. It's a comfort when things are as they should be, which is why I don't mind when my ears turn numb almost instantly. Momma dashes off to a women's auxiliary meeting in the annex next door, while Shaun and I, compelled by good manners, are forced to linger on the vast stone staircase, flocked by people I haven't seen in years, showering me with praise.

"Look at you, beautiful girl. You've done so well. Ms. Sandra is so proud."

"I watch you all the time."

"You're the best thing on the TV."

It's overwhelming to be in their favor like this.

Shaun shifts restlessly next to me as Ms. Nettle, whose mothball smell nearly bowls me over, is delivering a lecture about how I need to do a story on her grandson's new business, a mobile barbershop he's started in a converted RV.

She clearly knew better than to talk to me while Momma's around, let alone ask for a favor, since Ms. Nettle is Momma's sworn enemy after she blackballed us from getting into Jack and Jill when Shaun and I were younger. Ms. Nettle, who's descended from one of the first Black families to settle on the Main Line and the original members from when the organization was founded in 1938, held sway over who was worthy of being admitted into the local chapter back then. When word got back to Momma that Ms. Nettle said she and Daddy weren't "professional enough," Daddy's response was, "Who cares, why do you want to hang around with those bougie folks anyway?" But Momma's pride never recovered from the slight.

"Can I steal her away, Ms. Nettle? I'm taking my big sister to lunch." My brother rests his skinny arm on my shoulders. Shaun's polite in a way that makes me wonder if Momma is watching, listening.

"Well, this is a first!" I tease, in mock surprise. Then I lean over and murmur a thanks for the rescue.

"No, seriously, I want to take you to lunch. Let's go to Monty's Fish Fry. Old time's sake."

It's been at least ten years since I've been to Monty's, even though it used to be our Sunday place, all the Wilsons starched and shined, and packed into a booth after church before heading to the Broad Street soup kitchen to serve Sunday dinner to homeless veterans. Suddenly, there's no place I'd rather be. The comfort of cornmeal-breaded mackerel and four-inch-deep dishes of mac and cheese beckons.

"Let's do it."

Once we're situated at the yellowed Formica table, plates piled high after serving ourselves at the buffet, greasy fingers pulling at fish bones, I take Shaun in, searching for a sign that he's okay. Of all the worries I have on a constant loop — Gigi's health, Momma and Daddy's finances, the end of democracy — I worry the most about my baby brother. He'll always be that to me. He arrived two days after my seventh birthday and I just knew he was my present — a doll come to life. I carried him everywhere. I used my allowance to buy him his first Lincoln Logs and LEGO sets, and when he decided his freshman year at college that he wanted to major in architecture and design skyscrapers, I was so proud to have inspired his dream.

Shaun's okay, baby girl. He's gonna be a-okay. Gigi's voice is a whisper in my ear.

Shaun is dousing his plate in hot sauce, oblivious.

"Did you hear that?"

"Hear what? The music? Yeah, this is the jam."

Shaun starts snapping his fingers and shaking his head along to "Return of the Mack," which blares from a speaker bolted into the corner of the restaurant. "Seriously, I love this song, man. The nineties! Those were the good old days."

"Rodney King? O. J. Simpson? That wasn't the greatest decade for us. There was also your Arsenio Hall haircut. We don't need to go back there."

"Ah, man, you tell me what decade *was* good for Black people. I'm talking about the music, sis. Biggie. Tupac. Wu-Tang. And besides, my haircut was fresh. Why you tryin' to clown with your Tootie bangs anyway."

I flick a piece of cornbread at him. "So how was the Landry move yesterday?"

"It was fine, if eight hours of backbreaking work carrying boxes down five flights of stairs is your thing. The woman watched us like a hawk, like we were going to make a run for it with a forty-pound box of her precious china. What really kills me is you show up in work gloves and sweats and these people treat you like you're a moron. I swear she was talking to me extra slow like I have two brain cells. I wanted to be like, *You want to see my SAT scores, bi-atch?* But whatever, it's a paycheck, man. And with Mom and Dad at each other about money all the time . . ."

"Dad still on Mom about selling the house?"

A dark cloud passes over Shaun's face, and I'm sorry I pressed the issue.

"Yeah. She's in denial about it," he adds.

Of course she is, that's Momma's way. How can she face losing our *home,* the house that has been in our family for three generations? Great-grandpa Dash bought it in 1941 with $8,000 cash he carted to the bank in a brown bag and handed to a banker who said, "Look at this Negro with a bag full of bills. How'd you get all this money?"

" 'Did I ever tell you about how I would deliver the *Philadelphia Tribune* door-to-door at five years old?' " I do my best Gigi impression, attempting to lighten things.

He picks up on the joke with his own Gigi impression. " 'I was a newswoman before you were, Leroya.' "

Gigi has only told us this story a thousand times. How she earned enough money as a child to contribute a full $100 to the house fund. She joked that the front door was all hers.

We laugh for a minute before we remember that Gigi is in the hospital, and our worries catch up to us.

"Anyway, it's my fault if they lose the house. If they hadn't had to help me . . ." He takes an aggressive bite of a drumstick, working his stress out on the chicken.

Hearing the pain and guilt in his voice makes my heart hurt. "It's not your fault, Shaun. It was always only a matter of time before they'd have to sell."

Never mind Shaun's legal bills — property taxes were skyrocketing with all the white people who'd fled for the suburbs fifty years ago wanting back into the city. Even with me helping as much as I can, their modest salaries as a janitor and nursing home manager, with all they'd borrowed against the mortgage, mean it's a lost cause, the coming heartbreak inevitable.

The weight of Shaun's struggle is obvious, like he's carrying a backpack of bricks. Every time I ask him how he's *really* doing, he says the same thing. "It is what it is." But it's clearly taken its toll. I hurry to change the subject. "Did you and Staci meet up last night?"

Staci, with an *i,* and Shaun have been off and on since high school. I give her credit for sticking by him when he had to leave college, but that's about it.

"Nah, we broke up . . . again." He becomes all too focused on slathering butter on every square inch of a biscuit.

"Oh, man, that's too bad." This pitiful attempt at sympathy isn't winning me any Oscars.

"Ah, come on, you've never liked her. You think she's a ditzy white girl who's not good enough for your little brother."

Truer words had never been spoken. Staci's always gotten on my last nerve with her skimpy crochet crop tops and her insistence on endlessly discussing her vegan diet. But it's not really about Staci so much as it's about the fact that Shaun almost exclusively dates white women, has preferred them since he was little. When he was five years old he told me about his first crush — a girl named Hannah, a wispy blond thing in his kindergarten class.

"Why don't you like one of the Black girls in your class?" I asked him.

"White girls are prettier," he said, like it was a fact of life, or common sense, an obvious conclusion everyone agreed with.

At twelve years old, this hit way too close to home. It was hard enough having braces and that stubborn patch of acne across my forehead, but on top of that, bushy hair and dark skin? How could I argue with him, when everything around me, including the mirror, whispered that he was right? It took many years and a lot of hard work before I could understand and argue confidently about the influence of patriarchy, false standards of beauty, and how centuries of toxic history have conditioned Black men to see white women as the ultimate prize — angles I've tried on Shaun over the years, but never the one that cut me the deepest: If Black women aren't good enough for my brother, then what does that say about me?

"Y'all need to stay away from these white girls, ya hear?" Gigi told Shaun over and over when we were growing up.

Shaun being Shaun, he always tried to turn it into a joke, only Gigi never laughed.

"I mean it. You be careful," she'd say.

"Well, maybe you can find a nice Black girl," I say to him now, my glare countering the sarcastic tone. "How about that?"

"You sound like Grandma. And you kill me with all your little lectures about finding a nice Black girl. I mean, hypocrite much? Like you never dipped in the cream." He snickers. "Whatever happened to that dude, anyway? We all thought you were gonna marry him."

Two mentions of Corey in four days is two too many.

"Not going there."

Shaun has no idea the role he played in the end of my relationship with Corey, and I'll never tell him. Momma's not the only one who doesn't air her dirty laundry.

"Fine, fine. You talked to Jen yet?"

"No. I have to call her back. I don't know what to say."

"I mean, it's crazy we actually know this dude. All those other cops who do that terrible shit all the time are strangers, but I know Kevin."

Kevin. He's Kevin, not Officer Murphy. And we do know him. In fact, I know intimate details about him, ones that would horrify him if he realized. Like how he makes a noise like a yeti when he comes, or that he can only poop if he removes his pants completely, or that his low sperm count was the reason they couldn't get pregnant and that he punched a hole in their bedroom wall when he found out. Kevin and I may not be close, but there's still an intimacy by proxy.

"I don't know how you're ever going to talk to him again, Rye. I mean, he killed a kid. A Black kid. How do you get past that?"

"Justin's not dead. He's in a coma."

"That kid ain't waking up. I'm sorry, but he ain't. We can march and pray and march again, but it won't make a difference. Also, he didn't have a gun. Imagine fucking up in any other job like this. Imagine you work in McDonald's and you serve someone fries you've accidentally covered with rat poison instead of salt and that person dies right in front of you. No one's gonna say that ain't murder. But this . . . these cops murder someone and their bosses just go, 'Ooops, we did it again.' Every single time." He accentuates his point by waving a chicken bone in the air.

Shaun's voice is loud, but so is Mark Morrison's on the speakers and the baby crying at the next table over, and no one seems to be listening. All the same, my head swivels like an owl's to see who can hear him.

Momma always got on us for being too loud in public.

I start to shush him, and then remember all my promises to never turn into my mother and stop myself. I bite my tongue even as my brother gets louder, more riled up.

"If you shoot a Black kid and that Black kid doesn't have a gun, then that police officer should go to jail. Screw you. You have failed in your job as a cop. You remember when I got fired from Kinko's in high school for putting the wrong toner in the color printer. Sure, the printer broke, but no one died. I swear some of these dudes decide to be cops just so they can bust heads — Black and brown heads — and be on a power trip. I mean, maybe that's not Kevin necessarily, but it's a lot of them. You hear about their text messages with nigger this and that and leaving nooses in locker rooms and whatnot and people have to wonder why we're suspicious of the police? They need a racism-screening test before people join any police force, man. Like, if we're going to find on your Facebook that you've been posting jokes about Black people being monkeys, or describing us as 'savages' or 'filthy animals,' do not apply."

"You're right. Everything you said. It's

messed up."

"I mean, it could've been me."

We're both quiet for a beat; we've cut close to the bone, too close.

"You gotta interview Justin's mom. Tamara Dwyer," Shaun says. "She needs her story told. We gotta keep the mothers of the movement in the spotlight. The mothers are what hit people. He killed someone's *child*."

Shaun's militant fire never fails to focus me. "Exactly, I have to get to her. I need to talk to Tamara."

"I can connect you."

"Really?" I'm relieved to hear that I may have a way in that doesn't involve Pastor Price.

"Bet, my boy Derek lives over in Strawberry Mansion. He knows her people. He used to mess with Justin's cousin Deja. Her dad, Wes, is one of Tamara's brothers. She's got a slew of them."

Justin was shot only a few blocks from his row house in that neighborhood.

"You'll ask for me?" This is why I love being back on my hometown turf, a network of sources I can easily tap.

"Yeah, I got you, sis. She ain't gonna wanna talk to any of those white people anyway. Quinn Taylor? No way is Nancy Newscaster doing this interview. You got this. Now I gotta go tear up some more of this mac."

Shaun's got the same chip on his shoulder that I have about Quinn, ever since I told him what she said on Halloween.

"You should all come to my house in Society Hill," she offered the news team. "Our whole street is decorated, and we get kids from all over the city. Their parents drive them in from the ghetto. It's cute."

Shaun gets up to grab seconds from the buffet. He's a grown man, but he eats like a teenage boy in the middle of a growth spurt. He looks like one too, with the carriage of a gangly adolescent, a puppy who hasn't quite grown into his paws and ears. It's why the girls have always flocked to him: he looks like someone you want to save. Gigi always calls him tenderhearted, and it's true.

Someone approaches from behind me, and I reach for my purse, assuming it's the waitress coming to fill our iced teas. I want to pay for our meal while Shaun's at the buffet.

"Hi?"

It's not the waitress.

I turn around and I'm face-to-face with Jenny, who, once again for a disconcerting split second, seems like a complete stranger. She's wearing an extra-large Phillies sweatshirt commemorating their World Series win. It's peeking out of a puffy coat that doesn't quite fit around her middle. Her glow has been replaced by scarlet splotches.

"Sundays is church and Monty's." She offers a tentative smile.

An unfamiliar awkwardness charges the air between us.

"I haven't come here in forever."

Jen's face flushes pink. The redness of her eyes makes me think she's been crying, only Jen never cries.

"Shaun posted on Facebook that he was taking his sister to Monty's. I had to see you. You didn't answer my calls."

I can't explain why my heart is racing. I take a deep breath, but before I can respond, Shaun returns and, when he sees Jenny, almost drops his slice of apple pie.

"Oh . . . hey, Jenny."

"Hey, Shaun." She tentatively steps forward to hug him, and he lets her, even though he stiffens up, a contrast to his usual bear hug.

He clearly doesn't know what to do or say once they're apart. He reaches out like he's about to touch her stomach, then thinks better of it. "You're so big. You having triplets or something?"

No one even attempts to laugh, not that it

was particularly funny, or maybe even meant to be. Instead, there's a beat where we all stare at one another like actors who've forgotten their lines.

Shaun breaks the spell by doing what I wish I could do: he leaves.

"I'mma let y'all do this. I'll catch an Uber back, sis." He leans down and kisses the top of my head like a dad sending his daughter off to school and then nods at Jen. He's a few feet from the table when he turns back. "Kevin fucked up, Jenny." He says it loud enough that heads swivel toward us. And then he's out the door.

Jenny visibly cringes at Shaun's words, and I do too. But what else was he supposed to say or do right now? Flirt with Jenny like he normally does, or make some lame joke about her haircut? She looks like she's going to call out to Shaun, and then she stops herself; instead, she turns to me, helpless. I want to reach for her, but my hand doesn't move.

"Can we please talk?" Jenny's not asking, she's pleading.

And whatever tornado of emotions is swirling through me right now, about what Kevin's done or the things she may have said or not said, there's only one answer to her question. I motion for her to sit.

CHAPTER FOUR

JEN

Shaun's words are a sucker punch to my gut. It takes everything I have not to turn and bolt out the door. Coming here was a mistake, I see that now, but I can't leave. I can't do anything except slink into the booth across from Riley, who stares at me like I'm a stranger. She's waiting for me to say something, face as blank as an empty canvas. I have no idea what to say. *I'm sorry?* But what am I sorry for exactly, and why am I apologizing to Riley?

Finally, almost like she's taking pity on me, she says, "How are you?"

I didn't know what to expect; she hasn't returned any of my calls this weekend, but her concern is such a mercy that I feel a flicker of hope.

"I'm okay, I guess. But . . . it doesn't matter how I feel." I sound like a martyr, but there are more important things I want to explain. I plant my damp palms on the table, ready to launch into the speech I practiced a thousand times on the way over.

"Listen, Rye, Kevin thought he was chasing a guy who had just shot someone. He thought there was a gun. He feared for his life." I stop short of saying it was Cameron's fault, even though I'm completely convinced of that. *He* shot first, so Kevin had to open fire. *Cameron* was inexperienced; *he* made the bad call. If Kevin had been with Ramirez, this never would have happened. Maybe I'm being overly defensive, but it's just that I want — I need — Riley to know.

I search her expression for any trace of understanding, trying to gauge the likelihood that she'll say what I so desperately need her to say: *I'm here for you.* There's a hard glint in her eyes — it passes in a blink, but it's enough for me to know that I'm probably not going to hear those words.

"This is all so awful, Rye," I manage. "What's going to happen to him?"

"The doctors say they're going to operate tomorrow and try to dislodge the last bullet, to stop the bleeding."

Shame burns my cheeks. I pretend that's what — who — I meant.

"Yes, he's going to be okay," I say with conviction, or, more truthfully, desperation.

I can't get the boy's picture out of my head, can't stop thinking about his mother, sitting next to his hospital bed, waiting for him to open his eyes. I haven't even seen or touched my baby, and I already know I'd die for him or her.

"Let's hope," Riley says. "There are a lot of prayers for him, that's for sure."

She looks at me as she says this, really looks at me — and I slide my hands forward on the greasy table, close enough that she could grab them. She doesn't.

There's no graceful way to change the subject, to turn it back to Kevin and me, but I don't have a choice. It's the reason I came here to Monty's in the first place. "So you saw that I called last night?"

"Yeah, I did. You didn't leave a message."

"Since when do I have to leave a message for you to call me back?"

Riley doesn't answer. It's suddenly like I'm at a job interview or in the principal's office — formal and furtive. I'm at the mercy of her judgment, and it makes me feel like I'm trying to run on solid ice.

"Well, I wanted to ask you in person. For a favor." I clench my fists, gather my nerve. "I was wondering . . . you know how the media can be. No offense." I was trying to go for a joke, at least I thought I was, but it doesn't land that way. I quickly continue on. "I was hoping that maybe you could do a piece about Kevin, his side, you know? I saw that you're covering the story. You could talk to him and he could tell the viewers what really happened?"

Kevin and I came up with the plan over the weekend, or rather I did. He was still wary of Riley as "media," and didn't think there was any way the department would let him talk publicly, but I convinced him that maybe she could actually help us. It was worth a try. But Riley's mouth twists like she drank something sour. She shakes her head even before she answers. "I can't . . . I can't interview Kevin. It wouldn't be . . . right. What I mean is, I couldn't be objective, and that's my job. Professional objectivity." The words she mutters are white noise; it's the tone that hurts, so distant, robotic. She's wearing the Riley mask — that's what I call it when she shuts down her emotions like this. She's an expert at it. After Corey dumped her, or whatever happened between them last year, she acted like she was a-okay. Same responses every time I asked about it: "I'm fine." "It wasn't meant to be." "We were never that serious." The mask. But I know better. Corey was good for Riley. He made her way less uptight. She loved him in a way that I'd never seen her love anyone, and as much as she may think she has people fooled, she's never fooled me.

"It's just . . . I get it. I don't want you to do something you're not comfortable with, Riley, but it's already starting, everyone saying terrible things about Kevin. We need his side of the story out there. It was a mistake, an awful mistake. It would help for people to understand that he isn't a bad guy, which he isn't. I mean, you know that."

But the way Riley is looking at me, it seems she doesn't know that. It seems like I have to allow for the possibility that she thinks my husband is a bad cop or, worse, a racist. Surely she can't think that? It's dawning on me that she expects me to be ashamed of my husband. And that, more than anything, starts to piss me off.

"Well, let me ask you this: Would you do the interview if Kevin shot a white kid?"

"Jen . . . I don't . . . it isn't just . . ."

I've seen Riley lock words away and hide behind silence; I've never seen her at a loss for them though. Why did I have to bring up race? It's never mattered between the two of us.

Finally, she meets my eyes. "I don't know, maybe, Jen. Maybe." It was like admitting that cost her something. "And, well, it's not

117

usually white kids being accidentally shot by police, is it?" This time there's no stammering: the question glides out of her mouth and slices like a knife.

"Look, I don't want to turn this into a conversation about what kind of lives matter. This isn't even about race, Riley. It's about Kevin."

"How can you even think this isn't about —"

I cut her off. I hate where this conversation is going. The anger that's been simmering beneath the surface since I sat down is building into a furious blaze. It's the only reason I say what I do next. "You never liked Kevin. That's the real reason you won't do the interview. Admit it."

I don't even know if I believe that. It's more like an idea I'm trying out in the moment, and the accusation, being on the offensive, it feels good. Or maybe it *is* true. Maybe Riley tolerated Kevin all these years but never really liked him, and that's why she won't help us. I'll always have to wonder, because I'm out the door before she can even open her mouth.

Ever since I was little, I've loved cramped, claustrophobic spaces. I would nestle into Lou's closet, cocooned in the familiar scents of faux leather and stale cigarette smoke; it made me feel safe somehow. At the moment, this closet-size powder room in my mother-in-law's house is the closest I can get to squirreling myself away. I know better than to hide in Cookie's closet.

I sit on the lid of the toilet and replay the conversation at Monty's, trying to make sense of it. It's been five full days since Riley and I have spoken. It's the longest we've gone without talking or texting or emailing that I can remember. I do some deep breathing. That's all I do these days: deep-breathing exercises. There's a basket of cinnamon-scented potpourri on top of the toilet tank, and I can almost taste it with each inhale. I stare at the peeling floral wallpaper in front of me, fight the urge to grab the loose corner and tear it all off. It would be so satisfying to do that, to destroy this one little thing.

Cookie's voice travels down the hall. I can't make out what she's saying, only the shrill cadence, the soundtrack of my life since Kevin and I moved in with his parents last Friday, the night after the shooting. We're hoping the reporters and protesters won't follow us all the way out here to Bucks County. But every so often, I peek through the curtains in the living room and expect to spot a news van. It's probably only a matter of time. They're still camped out at our house, round the clock, waiting for someone to arrive or emerge so they can swarm like flies to a carcass. I know this because Mrs. Jackowski from next door texts me updates.

"Where did Jenny get off to? Is she okay? She's got to keep it together." Cookie's voice fills the bathroom now, loud and clear, as if that's her intention, which it damn well is.

Cookie's had this song on repeat over the last week, that I'm checked out, that I'm not doing enough to help Kevin. It's so obvious Cookie is projecting her own powerlessness onto me, but that doesn't make it any easier not to scream at her, *What the hell am I supposed to do exactly? Tell me and I'll do it!*

I keep swinging wildly back and forth between a manic adrenaline rush — *How can we fix this, what do I do?* — to shutting down, pretending this is all happening to someone else, until I can't pretend any longer. Like now.

I splash cold water on my face and take yet another deep breath. "Come on, Little Bird, we got this," I whisper to my stomach before forcing myself to open the door. I

120

find Kevin and Frank exactly as they have been for the last hour, father and son sitting at the built-in banquette in the corner of the kitchen, which has essentially become a war room.

"There you are!" Cookie looks up from chopping celery as I slide in beside Kevin on the upholstered bench. I rest my head on his shoulder; he leans his own down to rest atop mine. We fit together like puzzle pieces. His thigh brushes my leg, and I shift to keep us close. We used to touch all the time, back when we were dating and first married, our various body parts finding each other like they were magnetized. But somewhere along the way — maybe when we started scheduling sex on a Google calendar — we stopped reaching for each other. Now I find myself seeking him out whenever I'm near him, a hand squeeze, a shoulder rub, anything to say, *I'm here.* Whatever Cookie might think, I am. I'm trying.

Fred spots me through the patio doors and offers a pathetic whine. She's not happy either, being exiled here at Cookie and Frank's house, especially since Cookie keeps her locked in the backyard.

"Julia Sanchez will be here any moment, you know."

121

Cookie's accusatory tone makes me clutch the table so hard my knuckles turn white. Of course I know the media consultant sent by the union will be here any moment. Cookie's only reminded us like a hundred times, which is pretty hilarious because she didn't even know what a media consultant was until two days ago, and now she thinks this woman can magically make the world stop hating her son.

"We know . . . ," I say.

"You keep telling us," Kevin finishes my sentence, another habit we fell out of since we were first married.

My mother-in-law wipes her hands furiously on a tea towel. Cookie is somehow always wiping her hands on a tea towel. She has an absurdly large collection of them.

Now she waves a plaid one in the air. "I could use some help here." She looks at me pointedly, which is unnecessary. We both know she's not drafting Kevin or his dad, Frank, into kitchen duty. I learned the rules a long time ago. When Cookie says, "I'm getting started on dinner," it means "we're" getting started on dinner. And by "we're," she means any women in the house better snap to attention and start chopping.

It's not like I was a big feminist or anything before I married Kevin. At least, I wasn't until I started coming to dinner at the Murphys' and found myself filling deviled eggs to Cookie's exacting standards while the men — Kevin, Matt, and Frank — watched the Eagles in the sunken living room, even though I'm the biggest Eagles fan in the whole stupid house. Our baby's womb name is Little Bird, for God's sake! I was at the Linc in 2005 when Chad Lewis scored that two-yard touchdown against the Falcons to send them to the NFC championship. But I've never been able to sit and enjoy a game here. Kevin will wander in every now and then to report the score while offering me a commiserating look that says, *This is just how it is with my mom.* Easy for him to say as he stuffs his face with Cheetos in front of the TV.

I trudge to the counter, and Cookie thrusts a plastic sack of celery and a knife at me.

"Three-inch slices," she commands, like an epicurean surgeon.

Along with Julia, Matt and Annie are coming over. Cookie has demanded that we all circle the wagons; she, for her part, will make sure we're well-fed while we do.

"Do you think we should have invited Brice over this afternoon too?" Cookie asks before answering her own question.

123

She's notorious for these animated conversations with herself, which is fine by me. I'd rather silently chop.

"No, no, I suppose we got what we needed in yesterday's call. I know we have to hold tight."

Brice Hughes is the lawyer Kevin's parents hired to represent him. Kevin insisted his union lawyer was enough, but Cookie wouldn't hear of it.

"You need a *real* attorney," she'd said.

Brice is the son of a woman Cookie knows from her bridge group, and he comes "highly recommended." I have no idea if these stellar reviews are from anyone besides Brice's own mom. He seemed fine on our initial call, even if he sounded like he was throwing around words from a legal dictionary to impress us. I don't want to think about the money Frank and Cookie are spending on this. When Brice told us his rates — $300 an hour and a $10K retainer — Cookie looked like she'd swallowed her tongue. Living on Frank's police pension doesn't leave room for many extras, like, say, a legal defense fund. But it doesn't matter. Cookie will sell her last possession to help her son. For all her faults, I love this about Cookie.

During the call, we'd all hovered around

Kevin's cracked iPhone on the kitchen table, as Brice explained that the boy, Justin, is the real key to everything, and that we're waiting for him to regain consciousness so he can tell his version of events. "As you probably know, they've moved him over to CHOP — the children's hospital. Maybe so he can receive better care . . . but also the optics, to remind everyone that he's just a kid. And you know, of course, if he dies, we're talkin' a whole other ball game. The DA, Sabrina Cowell, I don't know if you're familiar with her, but she's a real tough-ass, power hungry. Her whole agenda is police reform, so . . . it's possible she could go after serious charges here. Assault with a deadly weapon, manslaughter, or even second-degree murder."

Murder. Cookie audibly gasped and fanned herself with a towel. The word made its home in the room like it would be there forever.

"My son is no murderer," she spat, actual drops of spit flying out of her mouth and onto the tabletop.

"Well, we just have to hope the kid pulls through. That'll make this a whole lot better," Brice said, his tone so shockingly matter-of-fact I wanted to reach through the phone and grab him by his throat.

A boy could die.

"In any case, everything here will depend on two words." He paused, and I pictured him holding up two meaty fingers. "Reasonable. Threat. In order for Kevin and Cameron to be convicted of any crime, the prosecutor will have to prove that they didn't believe there was a reasonable threat to their lives. You thought this kid pulled a gun, right? You feared for your life?" The way Brice posed the questions, there was only one answer. But Kevin didn't say anything.

I didn't dare turn to look at Kevin, but I felt his hand land heavy on my thigh beneath the kitchen table. I squeezed his fingers, willing him to respond.

"I followed my training." His voice was robotic.

"I gotta say, that seems like a dodge, Kev. That's not going to work for the prosecutor or jury. We need conviction."

Kevin tried again like he was rehearsing lines. "We were in fast pursuit of a dangerous offender we knew was armed and had already shot someone. It all happened so fast. Cameron yelled, 'Gun!' and fired, and in that split second my training kicked in and I fired to protect myself and my partner."

126

"Exactly, exactly. It was a dangerous — *deadly* — situation. And it happened so fast. All leads to reasonable fear for your life. And there's something else here — sounds like Cameron was the instigator. He's the one who supposedly spotted the gun. So technically it was Cameron who shot the wrong guy. I mean, you had no choice but to back him up? You had to, that was your training, but it was on Cameron to identify the right guy and properly assess if there was a weapon. Yeah, yeah, that could work. . . ." It was as if we weren't even there and Brice was working out an entire defense in his head. "And Cameron is young, inexperienced?"

"He's pretty fresh out of the academy. But I don't know if that —"

"Feels to me like this is our strategy," Brice continued. "Cameron is the bad guy here; he's green, out of his league. He made a bad call. Sounds like you didn't know him all that well, but did you ever hear him say anything against Blacks? Maybe he had a bias there. Some buzz around the district about him being a bad apple? Anything like that?"

"I don't know. We didn't talk that much." Kevin shook his head; he clearly didn't like where Brice was going with this.

127

"Okay, okay, well, we can dig into that more. But whatever the case, this could work. Cameron guilty, you innocent. You'd have to testify though."

Kevin's father had been silent until that moment, so we all jumped when he raised his voice. "No way!" The stroke had left half of his face and his right side completely limp, and sometimes his cheek twitches when he wants to say something, his jaw muscles straining to get his mouth to cooperate with his brain. Kevin's told me stories about Frank's extreme mood swings when he was growing up. One minute he was the most fun dad on the block, playing kickball with the kids until the sun went down, the next he was whipping off his belt and lashing Kevin for back talk. But since I've known him, Frank's always seemed docile, like a bird with its wings clipped. Not in that moment, though: he was fired up, and his words flowed as forcefully and as easily as I'd seen.

"That's not gonna happen. We don't turn on our own. When we draw our guns we do it for a good reason, and we shouldn't have to defend ourselves for defending lives. You have no idea what it's like out there. I spent forty years on the force. I've been shot at, punched in the jaw. Some crazy son of a bitch tried to run me over with his car after we tried to arrest him for beating the hell out of his pregnant wife. When you're on the streets long enough, deal with the criminal element long enough, you have instincts, and you can't explain those instincts to anyone. We do what we do to protect ourselves and our partners. There's a thing called loyalty in the force, and Kevin would never turn against another cop. Right, Kevin?"

My husband looked at me instead of looking at his dad. "I should tell the truth." I watched the muscles in his back tense. All he'd ever wanted to do was make Frank proud of him. It was why he put on that uniform in the first place.

"I hear you, Frank." Brice changed his tone when he addressed the man who was ultimately paying his bills. "We just have to figure out the best case for your son. And yeah, yeah, of course you need to tell the truth, Kev, it's just there can be different versions of that, you know?" He paused here. "We also have to consider what the video's going to show."

I was already holding my breath as Brice threw all of that at us, and then a video? This was caught on camera? I didn't know if that was a good thing or a bad thing, same as I didn't know if it was good or bad luck that neither Kevin nor Cameron had body cams. Because of the limits of the department budget, they're doling them out in waves, like the new vests, outfitting one unit at a time. Kevin's wasn't scheduled for a few months yet.

"There's video?" Kevin asked, clearly just as surprised. It was hard to tell how he felt about this possibility.

"Oh yeah, yeah." Brice seemed pleased that he was the one delivering this information, like he was already earning his absurd fees. "Pakistani guy who owns the liquor store on the corner rigged cameras in the alley after someone tried to break in through his back door. I'll get it as soon as I can. Hopefully before it leaks. Without a body cam, this is a big deal. If a video does surface, it's going to show exactly what you describe, right?" Brice asked. "No surprises? 'Cause if there are, I need to know up front."

"No surprises," Kevin echoed him, sounding like a toy that had run out of batteries.

Beyond that, Brice was spare on specifics. He gave us a rough sense of the timeline, but also said that it was impossible to understand what exactly would happen next and how fast it would happen. In the meantime, our future hangs in the air like a slow-motion coin toss.

The doorbell rings, and it's time for yet another person to tell us what we can and can't say, do, expect, hope for. I pick a piece of celery out of Kevin's front teeth as Cookie walks to the front foyer. We sit in silence in front of the mile-high platter of vegetables and listen to her exaggeratedly enthusiastic greeting.

"Oh, look at you. You're so pretty. Like a movie star. I didn't expect someone so pretty. Come in. Come in."

I glance from father to son. They look so much alike, especially as Kevin's gotten older. The same dimpled chin, steel-blue eyes, and thick curly hair, though Frank's is entirely gray now. They also have the exact same expression: beleaguered and exhausted. Particularly Frank. Julia Sanchez rounds the corner into the kitchen, a pint-size woman in sky-high heels. She wears a pin-striped suit and carries an expensive-looking bag, as if she's headed to a sleek corporate boardroom and not sitting in a suburban kitchen with rooster wallpaper. Cookie clucks around her, making introductions, pouring sodas, arranging and re-arranging the platters on the table. As usual, she nudges a basket overflowing with potato chips toward Kevin. She's always thrusting snacks on him like he's a toddler.

Julia looks a little overwhelmed by the aggressive hospitality as she settles on the banquette. But she doesn't get much further than, "I'm sorry, I know you've been through a lot," before the front door opens, bringing in a fury of noise.

"That'll be the rest of the family," Cookie explains, as Annie and Matt's four-year-old son, Archie, comes tearing into the room pretending to shoot a plastic bazooka at everyone. I wonder if I'm the only one who sees the irony in this. When I catch Julia's quick cringe, I realize that I'm not.

Cookie scoops up her grandchild, weapon and all, and pecks at his neck like a mama lion licking her young cub clean. Matt and Annie, my favorite Murphy besides Kevin, are close behind. They line up to kiss Cookie hello, and she puffs up at the attention. Nothing makes Cookie happier than having both her sons in her kitchen, even under these circumstances.

Julia waits patiently as drinks are poured and Archie is settled with a snack in front of the TV. When she finally has everyone's attention, she clasps her hands on the table and begins. "So I'm here to help advise you. You've been thrust into the public spotlight, and I'm sure the attention is intense for everyone. I'm sure it's been . . . challenging."

"It's been absolute hell," Cookie says, wringing her liver-spotted hands.

"I can imagine. And I'm afraid it's going to get worse before it gets better. You need to prepare yourself. You know the story is getting national attention already. And the local media is rabid. I'm sure you saw the piece this morning?"

"Of course we did," Matt says about the viral op-ed in the *Inquirer* about how Philly's racist police force needs to be rebuilt from the ground up. "All these cocky Ivy League assholes with their opinions on police and guns — I bet none of them has even met a cop."

Julia eyes Matt warily. "I know it's a lot to take in. I'm here as a resource to help you through this. The first thing you need to do is deactivate your social media accounts. You can't give the trolls a platform, and you don't want to be tempted to say anything yourself that could influence — or damage — public opinion. That's really the key, no public commentary. Period. Your best bet is to wait until things die down."

"It seems like an impossible dream that

this will ever die down," I say, almost to myself.

Julia nods at me, compassion in her eyes, compassion I wish I'd gotten from Riley.

"I understand. And it's not fair to any of you, but the press and the public have already made up their minds that Kevin is guilty. Unfortunately there's a lot of anti-police sentiment out there right now."

"Who do they think is gonna come save their ass next time some junkie snatches their Prada purse or someone breaks into their Bimmer?" Matt says. "Not every cop is a racist asshole, but that's what you'd think from watching the news, the way they spin the stories with half-truths and hyped-up headlines," he finishes, drawing a long sip from his beer.

Annie nods in agreement. "I remember how when I first married Matt, I was wary of even telling people he was a cop — all the stupid assumptions they would make about him."

"And now they're protesting us like *we're* bad guys," Matt snaps.

"Julia, do we have to worry about this protest tomorrow? What can we do about that?" Cookie asks. "I hope it rains, a big old downpour so they have to cancel it. It's absurd that the mayor thinks it's okay to talk to them. He's supposed to be on the side of law enforcement. I mean, for heaven's sake, show some support. He keeps bending to those *activists*" — she spits the word as if she'd said "puppy killers" — "when he should be standing up for the people who are doing their jobs."

I've lost track of how many times Cookie has delivered this rant. She's been in a perpetual tizzy over the mayor and the police commissioner and how she thinks they're bowing to media pressure instead of protecting the officers, and her son. The mayor issued a statement in support of the police department twenty-four hours after the shooting. Then, a day later, after the protests began, he dialed it back, saying, "The city will do everything in its power to make sure justice is served."

"It's a betrayal!" Cookie slams her fist on the table. "Those people trying to make my child out to be some devil just for doing his job. I won't have it!"

"Come on, honey." Frank's jaw gives the telltale twitch. When Cookie gets worked up, her husband is the only one who can calm her down. "We know the truth. Kevin had to do what he did to protect himself and his partner." Frank's words ooze from the side of his drooping lips, but they don't

135

have their desired effect, judging from the red streaks across Cookie's sallow cheeks.

"Exactly. He was protecting himself. It's a jungle out there. A war zone — right, Frank? We know. You remember." It seems to soothe her to say this again and again. "I mean, there are animals out there."

For her part, Julia doesn't seem fazed by Cookie's outburst, or at least she hides it well, probably a necessary skill for her job. "I understand your frustration, Mrs. Murphy. I do. One of the things I need to remind you of is that you should feel free to express these really difficult emotions here in your own home. You should — you need to. But you also have to be very careful about whom you share your opinions with and the language you use to share those opinions. Everything you say can be misconstrued, and that is the last thing Kevin needs."

Julia lets this sink in. I can tell she doesn't want to have to say the obvious: *How about you don't call people animals?* When Cookie nods, she continues.

"We have to count on the fact that both sides of this story will come out. When it comes to the march, try not to take it personally." Julia pointedly says "march" instead of "protest." "People are marching

136

about an issue. It's not about Kevin per se."

"Well, it sure feels personal. They want to send my son to jail. For doing his job."

"They're gonna riot, you know they are. Set fires, break windows, punch a police horse. That'll be good for us." Matt again. No one reminds him that the one time someone punched a police horse in this city, it was a drunk white guy celebrating an Eagles win.

"Oh, shut your mouth, Matt, it's a peaceful event," Annie says, ever the diplomat and always quick to put her husband in his place. But he's too worked up and skulking around the kitchen. Like mother, like son.

"First of all, whose side are you on, Annie? And mark my words, those people are ready to riot. They riot. That's why they do. Hello, Ferguson? They're going to turn Broad Street into Ramallah."

If one more person says "those people," I might lose my shit. Besides, I'm willing to bet Matt can't locate Raleigh on a map, let alone Ramallah.

I try to catch Kevin's eye, but his are squeezed shut. He leans his head back against the wall as Matt blusters on.

"March for Justice, my ass. How come they can't see that? You asked him to drop his weapon. He went into his pocket. Better to be tried by twelve than carried by six, man. If you have to take the shot, you take the shot. You did the right thing Kev-o. You've got a baby on the way. Your job is to get out alive."

I have a flashback to last May, standing in a hot banquet hall in Passyunk at the wake of a cop named Jamal who got shot Memorial Day weekend while trying to stop three guys from breaking into an ATM at the Navy Yard. Kevin hadn't known Jamal all that well, but it had hit him hard; any officer's death anywhere does. It hit me too, and again when Matt says it now. *Your job is to get out alive.* At Jamal's wake, the officers stood in tight clusters, stiff and formal in their dress blues on one side of the room, while the spouses, mostly women, clucked over sweaty deli platters at the buffet on the other and passed around an envelope growing fat with cash — including the $100 bill that Kevin slipped in that we really couldn't spare. One of the LEO wives set up two weeks of meal delivery for his widow, Denise, and three kids and I did my duty by dropping off a chicken casserole on my designated day. I left it on her doorstep though. I couldn't face her knowing I was going home to my husband. That very night, I started researching bulletproof vests.

"I just wish I was on duty tomorrow," Matt says. "If Annie wasn't working, I'd happily volunteer for overtime and keep the knuckleheads in check."

Matt's normal beat is Rittenhouse, safest neighborhood in Philly; the other cops call it Hollywood, but you'd think he was battling ISIS to hear him tell it. As I watch him fume, a thought that has always hovered just out of reach crystallizes, like a camera lens clicking into focus: I hate my brother-in-law. He and Kevin are close, so I tolerate his bullshit, but suddenly, after all these years of stomaching his mansplaining tirades and moody tantrums, I can't ignore the simple truth: Matt is spoiled, immature, entitled. And now that I've allowed this thought into my mind, the door slams behind it and I won't be able to deny it any longer. I wonder, not for the first time, how Annie — lovely, funny, smart Annie — can be married to this man. They've been together since they were kids though, and in that time Annie got sober, lost her parents, had a baby and a miscarriage. Matt was her rock, her person, even if he's an asshole to everyone else.

"Fuck you, Matt." I say it under my breath. It's not as satisfying as saying it to his face. I might as well be ten years old in the back seat of Blazer's car again, when that dirtbag called Riley and Ms. Sandra the N-word and I stayed silent.

Annie does speak up. "You can be a real asshole, Matt, you know that?" And I secretly cheer.

"Please stop. We have company." Cookie shoots daggers at both of them.

Julia waves a hand in the air to dismiss the concerns, and my eyes catch on her giant diamond ring, a sparkling boulder on a ridiculously skinny finger. I hide my own hands beneath the table, finger my sliver-size diamond.

Cookie leans over to Julia as if taking the woman into her confidence. "Listen, we know someone who's a reporter. Don't you think it would be smart if she interviewed Kevin so that people could see he's a good guy? She's a personal family friend — Riley Wilson."

This was inevitable; still, it blindsides me, especially Cookie's ownership of Riley when they've barely met. In fact, it was right here at this kitchen table that Cookie tried to talk me out of having Riley as my maid of honor. She leaned into me as we were flipping through inch-thick copies of wedding magazines, her breath sweet with chardonnay. "Are you sure you want Riley to be your maid of honor? You and Annie have gotten so close. It would mean so much to her, and wouldn't she look beautiful up there at the altar with you? She's going to be family, after all."

Clever the way she'd couched it, but I knew what it was really about. Riley had once tried to explain this particular mind-fuck to me: you could never be sure what was about race and what wasn't, so you always had to second-guess yourself (*Was that because I'm Black?*). In that moment, I got it — in Cookie's mind, Annie made for better wedding pictures.

"You're friends with Riley Wilson? She's the *Black* friend?" Julia turns to me, putting the pieces together.

"Best friends," Cookie stresses.

The mere mention of Riley's name makes my insides burn. There's no way Riley is going to do the interview, but I haven't told anyone about what happened at Monty's or that we haven't spoken since, least of all Cookie. They all stare at me, waiting for a response.

I can't lie or dodge, as much as I may want to. "I really . . . I don't think Riley will do the interview with Kevin."

"Well, I don't see why on earth not. Would she do an interview with you at least, Jen?"

Cookie claps once, as if she's found the magic solution. "*You* can tell our side of the story."

Before I can respond, Julia jumps in. "I really don't think that's a good idea, Mrs. Murphy. Jen isn't the center of the story. It's bad optics."

"Bad optics. Pffff."

"Yeah, I can only imagine all the white-tears memes that would come as a result of that," Annie says, earning a disapproving stare from Cookie.

"What on earth is a meme?" she asks.

"Never mind, Mom, the point is, Jen is not the focus here. Even with her connection to Riley."

I shoot Annie a grateful half smile.

Matt abruptly gets up and walks out of the kitchen and into the sunken living room and turns on the Sixers game, as if announcing that the meeting is finished. He calls out over the play-by-play. "None of this matters. It's gonna be fine. We don't need an interview with Riley or any of those vampires in the press. It's not like Kevin's going to get indicted, man. These investigations are all for show. No cop ever serves time."

Julia interrupts him. "That was true. But things are changing. Public sentiment *is* against you. We are here to protect you, but you have to work with us."

She makes a point of looking at her watch. "I think we've covered what we need to for now. I'll be in touch as things progress. You can call or text me anytime, day or night, in the meantime. Remember, the most important thing is to stay quiet. If anyone from the media reaches out to you, send them to me." She drops a business card on the table, ring glinting in the fluorescent light, and then turns to me.

"Will you walk me out, Jen?"

At least it's an excuse to leave the kitchen. I follow Julia down the hall like a dog. I wish I could follow her right out the front door. We could go see a movie or wander around the mall, and I could pretend I have a different life for a few hours.

Julia stops at the door, places a hand on my arm. "Please don't talk to your friend Riley about this case. I'm sure you think you can trust her, but you never know about people."

She's wrong. I do know Riley, and I would trust her with my life.

I only nod, and Julia pauses, hesitant to say whatever comes next. "I have to ask. Does Riley have any personal information about Kevin that she could use against you?"

"What do you mean?"

"Oh, things you've confessed to her in the past as a friend, about Kevin or his job? Any trouble he's gotten in . . . ?"

Even as I say, "No, of course not," my mind races. Is there something? The truth is I hardly know anything about the inner workings of Kevin's job. He's almost always stopped himself when he starts telling me: "Never mind. . . ." "I shouldn't. . . ." "It wasn't that bad." There was one night when we both got shitfaced and he started in on a story about a couple of cops who would threaten people for arrests for stuff like jaywalking or loitering or traffic stops just so they could shake them down for cash.

"Made him give him everything in his wallet and a bag of weed that was in the glove compartment and let the guy go. Hazard pay, he called it." The next morning Kevin was mortified he'd told me. "Never tell anyone I told you that, okay? I need to keep my mouth shut."

"I'm your wife, Kev. You can tell me anything."

"That's not how it works, Jenny. What happens at work needs to stay there. My dad always said that, and I never got it until

I became a cop, but it makes sense to me now. Not with that dude stealing the weed. That guy was an asshole. But sometimes we need to break a few rules, especially this new DA's rules, to get the job done. No one but a cop understands the kinds of things we see, the messed-up people we're trying to help every day. They punch us, shoot at us, tell us they'll kill our families, and we're supposed to just read them their rights and give them a hug. It doesn't work like that. It never actually works like that. Shit happens and sometimes we have to do things. If another cop has your back, then you need to convince yourself that you would have theirs, because the alternative is that you stop trusting anybody."

I told myself over and over that Kevin didn't — wouldn't — behave like some of those asshole cops. And besides, even if I ever told Riley anything, she would never . . . but then the tiniest sliver of doubt creeps in. It's Julia's fault. I need the woman to leave, need to close the door against her and this crazy line of thinking. Riley may sometimes be distracted and distant, but she would never, ever betray me. There aren't many fundamental truths you can count on in life, but this is one of them. If I don't believe that, then I don't know what I can believe in.

Kevin isn't in the kitchen when I return. Annie's playing solitaire with an ancient deck of cards that is for some inexplicable reason always sitting on the table. There's friction in the air. It wafts toward me like the smell of spoiled food.

"What's going on?"

"I was telling Cookie that just because cops usually get off, that doesn't make it right necessarily," Annie says, adding to the row of cards laid out before her.

"You're talking about your brother-in-law." Cookie glares at her from the sink, where she's washing dishes. Annie can get away with saying the kinds of things that I could never say to Cookie, because she grew up down the street, literally six houses away. Cookie's known her since she was in diapers.

"I knew little Annabel Myers when she was still wetting her pants," is how Cookie opened her toast at Annie and Matt's wedding. At which point my sister-in-law leaned over the table and whispered to me, "Yeah, because she scared me so bad, she made me wet my pants."

"I'm not talking about Kevin. I'm saying in general. You know we had to do this bias training at the hospital, all the nurses.

'Unconscious bias,' they call it. Like a white nurse not listening to a Black patient tell her they're in pain or judging them for being overweight. We all do and think these things subconsciously. Like I realized that I'm way nicer to the Black store clerks because I feel like they probably don't like me, or how I call them 'honey' or 'girl.' "

"That's all baloney," Cookie scoffs. "Everybody wants to make everything about race. Calling everyone a racist right and left! I'm so sick of it. Sometimes things just happen."

I remember Annie telling me about this training. We'd had drinks that night, our standing monthly date over dim sum we always used to catch up or, mainly, to complain about Cookie. She said they'd done an activity where the facilitator asked people what came to mind when they thought about race. Apparently, one of the nurses, a white woman named Stephanie who often works the same shifts as Annie, had blurted out, "I feel lucky I'm not Black."

"Can you even imagine?" Annie said, horrified, blowing her indignation into her hot broth.

I shook my head, mustering all the shock I could, except the truth was, I *could* imagine thinking that. I've maybe even had the same thought pass through my mind before, quickly, like a dark shadow. Not that I would ever, ever admit it to a roomful of strangers, or my sister-in-law. Or even myself. It's way too awful. What if Riley ever knew I thought that?

Annie sets down the cards and looks up at Cookie. "All I'm saying is, would Kevin have been so afraid of a fourteen-year-old white kid that he would have shot him?"

The air evaporates like the room itself is holding its breath. How did she dare to ask that question, the one I can't even ask my own husband? Riley's words from Monty's echo in my mind. *Well, it's not usually white kids being accidentally shot by police, is it?*

"Shut the hell up, Annie," Matt hollers from the living room.

"Language," Cookie yelps, as if "hell" is the worst thing happening here.

"Where's Kevin?" I look into the living room, at the empty seat next to Matt on the couch, desperately hoping he didn't hear this exchange.

"Bathroom, I think," says Annie.

"Please don't say that in front of him, Annie. Please," I beg.

My sister-in-law nods. She loves Kevin like her own brother and would never want to hurt him.

I go off to look for my husband and find him in the narrow hall, charging out of the bathroom.

"Look at this!" His normally easygoing expression morphs into disbelief and then something even uglier: rage. He shoves his phone in my face.

It's a screenshot from Twitter, a tweet with a cartoon drawing of a Black body on the ground and cops brandishing giant machine guns standing above it. Someone photoshopped Kevin's real face over one of the cartoon cops'. Floating above their heads are large block letters: KILLERS BELONG BEHIND BARS.

"Julia literally just told us we can't look at stuff like this, Kevin. You've got to try to block it out. It isn't helping anything."

He bangs his head against the hallway wall a few times. The row of family photos shudders. Cookie in her wedding dress, a replica of Princess Diana's, but even bigger and more sparkly; four generations of Murphys in their dress blues, years of school portraits — Kevin with a bowl cut, Matt with a rat tail.

Kevin speaks into the wall. "I'm a good cop. I'm not an asshole. I'm definitely not a racist. All the things I've done for people . . ."

"I know, Kev. I know." I run my fingers through his hair.

This is the most emotional Kevin's been in five days. Hearing him break down is a relief, better than the "I'm fine" he's given me every time I've asked him if he's okay.

When we were first dating, I loved that Kevin was so quiet, such a mystery. It was, and it still is, a challenge to try to unlock what he's thinking or feeling. He's similar to Riley in that way. They both require effort. I decided I was the only person in the whole world who could get him to open up, and every time he reveals something — the first time he found a body on his beat, the night he spent in the NICU with a baby whose mom was high on oxy — it's a victory. Sometimes in the middle of breakfast, or a run, or once through the bathroom door while he was taking a shit, I would ask him, "What are you thinking *right* now?" Usually the answer was, "Er, nothing," but it became a thing between us.

I try it now. "What are you thinking?"

He sighs and bangs his head yet again. "I don't want to do this, Jen."

I look at him, waiting patiently. It usually does the trick.

"Okay, fine, I'm thinking about the baby.

I'm thinking I don't want to be in jail when you give birth."

This is what I get for wanting him to be honest and open up. "Don't even say that."

"You asked."

"Here, feel him." I grab Kevin's hand, bring it to my stomach, where Little Bird is kicking.

"You mean her?" Kevin smiles. It's barely there, but I hold on to the slight twitch of his lips like a kid clutching her favorite stuffy.

From the very beginning, Kevin has been convinced the baby will be a girl. I know it's a boy though. The other night I dreamed about him. I pulled him to my breast, his eyes opening and staring up at me. They were greenish-brown like Justin Dwyer's. I woke up then, swells of nausea overcoming me. I screwed my own eyes shut and prayed my baby's eyes would be a boring mud brown like mine.

"We'll know soon enough."

Too soon. I'm so ready for this pregnancy to be over, though I know it's easier with the baby inside me. I can't have a kid in the middle of this, when everything is in chaos.

A wave of fatigue hits me. "I'm going to go lie down for a while. Why don't you go watch the game with Matt. Try to relax for a bit if you can? And no more Twitter." I kiss his cheek, my lips catching on sandpaper stubble. He hasn't shaved since the shooting.

Despite the rest of the house smelling like a Yankee Candle shop, the scent of pubescent boy still lingers in Kevin's room. There's an old aquarium that used to house a snake called Hoagie and, next to that, a box filled with faded yellow CliffsNotes and a stack of CDs. On top is a scuffed plastic case that calls to me, Nirvana's *Nevermind*. I put it in the three-disc changer on the ancient stereo and press play, stare at the chubby naked baby on the cover.

Come as you are, as you were
As I want you to be

I can barely remember to brush my teeth in the morning or where I left my keys, and yet each and every word of this song comes rushing back to me like I'm fourteen again.

The faded glow of the stars still glued to the ceiling are like dozens of eyes watching me as I lie back on the itchy quilt covering the bed. It's too much: our life is never going to be the same. I have to remind myself of this again and again. The last five years have been so hard — all the miscarriages,

152

the failures to get pregnant, the all-consuming fear I would never be a mother. All the times I lay in bed like this, blinking up at the ceiling, thinking the worst thing that could ever happen to me was not having a baby. It was like driving down a stretch of highway that disappears into nothing. That's what my life would have been like, no children, no degree, no great career . . . *nothing.* On those long dark nights, I used to bargain with the universe: *If you just give me this, I will never ask for anything else.* And it worked, I got pregnant. The worst was over. But that seems so stupid now. Of course life can get worse. It can always get worse. I was so focused on one thing, there wasn't room to consider all the other terrible things that could go wrong. Like my husband going to prison for the rest of his life, or the lawsuits that will bankrupt me and my kids and my kids' kids. And that poor little boy. Every time I let myself wallow, I come back to that poor boy and remember what my husband did. Will I ever be able to look at Kevin and not think about that boy?

I fumble around the bedside table for the tiny, dusty remote to the boom box so I can play the song again. Instead, I land on my phone, abandoned since this morning. It's been so long since I had that heart-quickening sensation of waiting for a boy to call or text me, and I experience that same jolt of agitated anticipation now: Has Riley been in touch? But when I look, the only text waiting there is from Lou.

You hanging in there kiddo?

Never mind that her message is more fitting for someone home sick with a cold. At least she's checking in. It's something.

I close the text and scroll to my favorite pregnancy app, the one that tells you the size of your baby from week to week. At thirty weeks, our baby is the size of a large jicama. I look up what a jicama is — this whole fruit-and-veggie thing comforts me. It helps to picture the glob of cells growing inside my belly. I've already lost a baby the size of a blueberry, and one the size of a plum. I scroll through the next few as if looking into my future: a butternut squash, a pineapple, a pumpkin, then a baby.

I drift off dreaming of vegetables.

It could be minutes or hours later when Kevin comes into the room. His voice, its urgency, wrenches me from a rare deep sleep. "Jen, Jenny."

Kevin makes a kind of choking sound like the words are caught in his throat.

"He died, Jenny. Justin died."

CHAPTER FIVE

RILEY

Gigi's eyes flutter behind paper-thin lids. Otherwise, she doesn't move. I swipe a damp washcloth across her cheek, skin so smooth it should belong to a baby, not to an eighty-nine-year-old woman.

I'm happy to lose myself for a moment in this simple act of caring for Gigi, especially considering all that she's done for me over the years, patiently teaching me how to play chess, sewing my Halloween costumes, giving me swimming lessons while keeping her head above the water so she wouldn't mess up her roller set; painting my toenails Berry on Top, even when Momma told me no because that color was trashy.

It's not enough though, this piddly washcloth. I would do anything — walk through fire, give any organ or my last dollar — if it would help. But nothing will. Yesterday the doctors told us she's too weak to continue on dialysis, which wasn't really working anyway. Her blood is essentially poisoning her day by day. They hinted to us that she only has weeks, rather than months. We're all desperately hoping for time: one more Christmas. *Just give us one more Christmas. Please, God, one more.*

This early in the morning, it's blissfully peaceful in the small hospital room. The TV perched in the corner is muted. I look up and catch my face on the screen. Yet another thirty-second promo for my live interview tonight with Tamara Dwyer, set to air at the top of the five-o'clock broadcast. The banner on the bottom of the screen reads: A MOTHER'S ANGUISH. The station's been teasing the segment hard, and each time I see the ad, my jangly nerves ratchet one level higher because I'm still not even sure it's going to happen now. I change the channel to CNN. The news about Justin's death has been making the rounds of the cable networks. #JusticeForJustin began trending this morning on Twitter.

Beyond Gigi's soft snores, I can hear laughter from the nurses' station. Their trivial conversations waft down the hall to fill the rooms of those watching their loved ones waste away. This morning they're twittering on about a new royal baby.

Yesterday, I overheard one of the nurses complain about the overflow of flowers in this room, as if that was really something to be irritated about. Granted, the bouquets from Gigi's church friends are taking over the place, covering every available surface, their sickly sweet scent strong enough to stick to your clothes, but no one has the heart to throw them away. Even if Gigi doesn't care much for flowers.

"They should be in a field somewhere, not in a vase," she's grumbled more than once.

I close the door a few inches to block out the noise. With the blinds drawn, it's dark in her room, a liminal space. Hospitals are like casinos that way, free of the constraints of climate or time. There is only here and now. I try to embrace the calm, but it's hard when Justin's face appears on the screen. The headline reads: UNARMED TEENAGER SHOT BY POLICE IN PHILADELPHIA DIES. I watch the anchor's lips move, the sad nod she exchanges with her coanchor, a Black man who just landed his own show on the network focused on race and politics. They're probably trotting out the same grim statistics I've been researching: *Philadelphia ranks fifth in the nation in Black homicide. Black kids are ten times more likely to die from gun violence than white kids. The police fatally shoot an average of one thousand people per year nationwide.* And now another one: Justin, an innocent fourteen-year-old.

I'd just gotten home from work last night when I heard. Arriving within seconds of each other: a text from Scotty — *Kid didn't make it* — and one from my source at the hospital who'd been sending me confidential updates. I slumped on the couch, precariously close to crying, as if Justin were my own brother. Maybe because it *could* have so easily been my own brother bleeding out on the ground.

My phone pinged with another text from Scotty not ten minutes after his first:

I hope the interview is still on. Find out. Make it happen.

It was obnoxious to intrude on the Dwyers at a time like this, but I needed to know if the interview was still happening, as crass as that was, which meant reaching out to Justin's uncle, Tamara's brother. Wes was serving as the family's de facto media liaison, a role he was thrust into and clearly found overwhelming judging from his anxious tone whenever we spoke about the interview. I was trying to come up with the right words to text to Wes when my phone buzzed yet again. I assumed it was Scotty, but it was Wes's number that came up, and the first words I saw as I frantically scanned were, *I'm sorry.* I was already strategizing as I read the entire message.

I'm sorry. I don't think Tamara's gonna be able to do the interview. She wants to — she's just overwhelmed. You understand.

No, no, no . . . was all I could think as I fumbled to come up with a response that was polite and thoughtful and not overly desperate. If I could meet Wes face-to-face, I might be able to persuade him of how important this was. I remembered a time in Joplin when I'd convinced grieving parents to go on air hours after their daughter was murdered by her boyfriend. I was all of twenty-four years old, barely older than their daughter, and I felt dirty even as I pleaded my case. But they did it. And that interview led to a Kickstarter that raised $50k for domestic violence charities in the county. As I texted Wes, I reminded myself that as intrusive as it might seem, what I do can make a difference.

I do understand and I'm so sorry for your loss. The entire team at KYX is thinking of you. Is there a chance we could meet tomorrow morning to talk? Anywhere that works for you?

After pressing send, I checked my phone every thirty seconds for a response. I told myself that my agitation and eagerness were entirely noble, not self-serving at all. The interview *was* important for Tamara, and for the community, even if the exclusive would also be huge for my career and might help get me one step closer to the anchor chair.

When my phone buzzed an hour later, I almost pulled a muscle lunging for it.

Okay. Can you meet me at the funeral home, Morgan & Sons, on Girard? I have to be there at 11, so maybe right before . . . 10:30?

There's an opening, a window, a crack I could squeeze through. I knew the reason they agreed to the interview in the first place was because of Pastor Price. The first time I spoke with Tamara, her voice was so soft I could barely hear her over the machines beeping and whirring in the background, the ones keeping Justin alive . . . at least until they didn't anymore. I could picture her, one hand on her cell phone, the other holding on to her unconscious son.

"Thanks so much for taking my call. I'm Riley Wilson, a reporter for —"

"I know who you are. I've seen you on TV. And Pastor Price called me about you. He said you're good people. Local girl?"

"Yeah, Northeast. Close to where Roger's Diner used to be."

"Oh yeah, I loved that place. Best crab fries." A lightness crept into Tamara's voice.

"I'm the lead reporter on this story, Ms. Dwyer, and —"

"Call me Tamara."

"Okay, Tamara. What's happening to you and your family is . . . tragic. And you have my full assurance that I will do it justice. I want you to know that —"

She interrupted again, gently. "The pastor said I can trust you, so I will, but let me talk to my brother Wes first," Tamara said.

Pastor Price obviously didn't tell her about Jenny. He knows better, of course, like I do. We both want me on this story. Never mind the unease that coated me like a slick film when Tamara said those words. *I can trust you.*

I have the same apprehension about not being completely honest with Scotty. I still have it. The resignation letter I'd written to my old boss at work. I don't know why I keep it — maybe it's a reminder that sometimes prayers do get answered. I needed out of Birmingham. It was supposed to be my big break — a top-fifty market after years in the minors — but as soon as I arrived in town, I sensed I'd made a mistake. All the Confederate flags — on houses, cars, buildings, the bronze monuments of vainglorious white men and wholesome plantation tours. I took it as a bad omen when I saw a newborn baby in a MAGA onesie. And the giant hand-painted sign in the apartment next to mine that said, IF YOU DON'T LIKE IT HERE, GO HOME. I'd only been in town for forty-eight hours, but it seemed like good advice, if not exactly what the sign painter intended.

It didn't get better when I learned I was one of only two Black people in the entire news operation, my counterpart a cameraman who was about to retire after being at the station for forty years since he started out as an "errand boy" for the affiliate's owner.

When the news director took me to lunch for our interview — after he took it upon himself to explain what a croque monsieur was — he'd said, "We need someone like you," I assumed he meant hardworking, talented, resourceful. I later realized that my hire likely had more to do with the fact that the station's parent company had issued a diversity quota, and I was their check mark. Especially with Harold on his way out.

So I shouldn't have been surprised when I overheard him on the phone complaining about me. I'd pushed back, respectfully, about a story, and he'd made a comment about my "attitude" and then called me "uppity." And there it was, its coded meaning clear as the glass panel in his office, through which he occasionally sneered at me like he was mad I wasn't more grateful to be graced with a job in "his" newsroom. So I decided to shut my mouth and try to practice patience and gratitude, put in my time and get out once I could build up my clips, but it got worse.

I reported a story I thought was heart-warming, about a local Black woman who'd found an abandoned baby and was trying to adopt her. The woman was Black, the baby white. I should have been prepared for the online comments, or avoided them altogether, which I usually have the good sense to do. I know better. But that day I read them, each one worse than the last, as bad as I'd ever gotten.

A nigger doesn't know how to raise a white child right. That baby would be better off dead.

And, of course:
Riley Wilson is an ugly ape who doesn't deserve to be on our TV.

Even the same tired insults hurt — hate doesn't have to be inspired to cut you. I was twelve the first time I was called the N-word. Even though Ryan DiNucci, the seventh-grade boy who left the note in my locker, spelled it wrong, the drawing of the monkey that accompanied it was pretty clear. I crumpled the paper, threw it in the trash, and never told a soul. Just like I didn't about all those comments. But they still ate away at me, especially on top of everything else that was blowing up last fall, everything with Shaun, and Corey — it all threatened to swallow me up. I could barely keep it together in front of my colleagues. I don't know what was worse, the comments themselves or the fact that when I mentioned them, my colleagues dismissed them entirely with breezy eye rolls and oh-so-helpful advice: "Just ignore those assholes."

It had been a few years since my last serious bout with depression, long enough for me to believe that maybe it wouldn't happen again, but I was wrong. That night, I could feel it coming on like the first hint of a tickle in the back of your throat before a cold. The coils inside me wound tighter and tighter, the obsessive thoughts beginning to churn, whispers that could turn into screams. *What's the point? You're not built for this place. You're an impostor. You're never going to be good enough.*

I drank an entire bottle of wine, wrote that resignation letter, and spent the next week working up the nerve to turn it in. Maybe if I could get out of Alabama, away from the cloying civility cloaking casual racism, from all the memories of Corey and a job that was going nowhere, I would be okay. That was the moment I found myself, bare knees on the cold dingy tile, talking to God, praying for a miracle. And wouldn't you know it, I got one. Scotty called, out of the blue, at the end of that week. He was a fellow Northwestern alum. He had kept in touch ever since we met at a J-school event right after graduation. He'd said he wanted to hire me at KYX, and now he had a spot.

Life doesn't give you many miracles or second chances, so I promised myself I'd make the most of this one. It's not like I'm lying to anyone outright about my friendship with Jenny, and if asked point-blank, I wouldn't deny it. So the omission feels defensible, even if by degrees. It could all blow up, of course, which is terrifying, but what choice do I have? Besides, I haven't spoken to Jen since Monty's last week, and I don't know when I will again.

I try to recall the last time I was truly angry at her, how long we've ever gone without talking. Once, in high school, she called me a "goody-goody" and didn't speak to me for a week after I refused to cover for her when she wanted to go to New York and meet up with some guy she'd met online — or those first few months after she married Kevin, when it felt like we might be drifting apart. But somehow, we always come back together, the ups and downs eventually balancing like a seesaw. Maybe it's because we've had the benefit of distance all these years being in different cities — our text exchanges and once-a-year visits haven't allowed a lot of opportunity for any serious drama beyond her getting annoyed that I don't call her back fast enough sometimes, or my irritation that she constantly interrupts me. But nothing heated, nothing like her yelling that I hate her husband. Or her asking me for a favor that could compromise my job, and saying, "This isn't even about race." *Are you kidding me? It's always about race, Jen.* That's what I'd wanted to scream back at her. She may have the luxury of pretending that it isn't, but I don't. Her naivete was stunning. Or was it worse, was she really *this* oblivious? And how did I not realize this? I once thought I could never know another human as well as I knew Jen, but it's possible that Jen has changed and I didn't realize, or I did. Jen *is* different these days. She used to dream about traveling the world, but when I suggested a trip to India last year she worried it would be too dangerous. She used to collect new friends like scarves, cool interesting people she met at weird music festivals, and now her social life seems to revolve around Kevin's coworkers' wives. She used to have a not-insignificant shoplifting habit, and now she's married to a cop, for heaven's sake. On good days, I chalk it up to adulthood — this is what it looks like when you settle down, you evolve, your dreams and beliefs and desires are more conservative. On bad days, I blame Kevin: he changed Jen, made her world smaller, made her less open and curious. On very bad days I'll think, *After more than twenty-five years, how well do I really know her anymore?* And vice versa?

Given this spiral, it's a relief when Gigi's eyes, cloudy with cataracts, slowly flicker open and focus on me, her cracked lips breaking into a smile. "My baby girl's here."

"I'm here, Gigi. I'm sorry I haven't been able to come more often this week; it's been hectic."

"You here now, that's what matters."

Gigi gets irritated when anyone fusses over her, so I ditch the washcloth and move to sit in the chair beside the bed.

"How you doing, Leroya?"

My grandmother's never going to call me Riley. For a full month after I changed it, I refused to answer whenever she used my given name, a bratty act of defiance, a protest as shameful as it was futile.

"Your parents gave you the name Leroya — after my darn fine husband, I might add — and so that's what I'm gonna call you. Period," Gigi said. And that was the end of it.

"Forget about me, how are you?"

"Oh, you know, these old bones have seen better days. But I've seen worse too." She looks up, over my shoulder, at the TV. "That march is today, ain't it, for that boy? And your interview?"

She doesn't miss a beat.

"Yeah, it's this afternoon. And then I'm supposed to sit down with Tamara, his mom, right after." *I hope.* I glance at the clock on the wall to see how much time before my meeting with Wes.

"How's the boy doing? It's Jesse, right? How is he? He ain't in this hospital. He over at CHOP. I asked if he was here. I woulda liked to see him, woulda liked to hold his hand."

The thought of my grandmother being wheeled down the hallway to hold the hand of a boy she never knew when she can't even get out of bed for a bath touches something deep inside me.

"His name is Justin and . . ."

"What, girl, what happened?"

"He died. Yesterday."

Gigi lets her lids fall closed, lies still for a long moment. Then a tear leaks out of her eye and falls onto the pillow. That single tear is quickly followed by others, chasing to catch up.

I scoot myself closer to her frail body, rattled by her emotion. "I know, Gram. It's so sad. He passed away in his sleep." I try to reassure her. "He didn't feel any pain."

I have no idea if this is true, but I say it anyway. For Gigi's sake and also my own. It's what I want to believe, though who knows how he felt in the moment. Or when he was lying on the cold concrete, bleeding. Did he know he was going to die? Did he cry out for his mother? That's what I keep imagining: Justin wanting his mother so badly, begging for her.

Gigi reaches out a hand dotted with moles, swipes at the tears that spill over. "They just keep killing us, don't they?"

What is there to say to that? I'm at a loss. Maybe what we need is some light. I stand and go to open the curtains; a golden glow peeks around the fabric. She stops me.

"No, leave it closed. Leave it be."

I turn back, sit on the edge of the bed. "It's awful. I know. It's just awful." God, can I manage anything more than these empty platitudes?

"I can't believe it. I can't believe Kevin killed that boy."

"I know, Gigi. I can't believe it either."

"He killed that baby." Gigi's facing the same struggle, saying it out loud, processing it, trying to figure out how to feel and what it means.

"Just like Jimmy," she adds softly.

Does she think Justin's name is Jimmy now?

"Who's Jimmy, Gram?"

"They left him hanging from a tree, full of holes."

I still don't understand, but the imagery instantly conjures a cold dread.

170

She pulls her hand from under the sheet to grab ahold of mine, like she's steadying herself.

"Jimmy was my aunt Mabel's eldest boy. You remember Aunt Mabel, my mom's older sister."

I do, vaguely. I remember her as an impossibly ancient woman I met a few times as a child. She always had a butterscotch candy in her mouth and would point to her prune-like cheek and say to me, "Come give me some sugar," which I resisted until Momma ushered me forward with a jab in the back that said, "Or else."

"Jimmy was my cousin. Mabel's oldest. Eleven years older than me. Lord, did I worship him. He loved his woodworking, and sometimes he let me help him in his little shop. In the afternoons we'd go fishin'. Out there by the stream for hours even though we never caught nothin'. I'd just be so happy he let me hang around." Her lips curl into a gentle smile at the memory.

"Jimmy was only 'bout seventeen or eighteen, still a young fool who didn't know better. Well, he did know better but was too much a fool to stop himself — he took up with a white girl in town, daughter of Roger Wilcox. I caught them kissing once, in his woodshed. He bribed me with a peppermint to keep my mouth shut, and I did, never told a soul. But then Roger caught them one afternoon, and they said he raped that girl and took Jimmy to jail."

I know exactly how this story ends. Now it's me squeezing Gigi's frail fingers inside my own. I ease off before I hurt her.

"They tried to go visit him that night — my parents and Aunt Mabel and Uncle Donny — but they couldn't. The sheriff wouldn't let 'em. Our parents went about gathering money for a lawyer, a good colored lawyer someone knew up in Montgomery, but . . ."

A bout of dry coughs leaves her struggling to catch her breath. I pick up a glass of water, maneuver a long straw to her lips. Gigi takes another full minute to recover, or maybe it's to gather her strength before telling me the rest.

"That night, they got him. Just took him." She's crying in earnest now.

"It's okay, Grandma."

"It's not okay, it's not." Her words drip with anger. I know it isn't directed at me but at everything else. At all the ways it has not been okay. "They dragged him through the town. Roger and his friends. They did terrible things to him. *Terrible.*" I don't need the horrific details; she can spare us both. I can already picture them. I have a vivid memory from my own childhood of coming across a copy of the 1955 issue of *Jet* magazine with Emmett Till's mutilated corpse right there on the cover. I found it in Daddy's desk drawer, tucked away like a keepsake. There was Till's face, bloated beyond recognition, flesh mottled with deep purple bruises, swollen slits where his eyes should be. You couldn't even tell he was a young boy, only a few years older than I was at the time; the savage beating and drowning had left him horribly disfigured. I couldn't tear myself away from the picture, or the article. I read it over and over, like it could offer an answer to the question that most vexed my young mind: *Why do they hate us so much?*

When I learned a few years later, in my sixth-grade history class, during our requisite one-week unit on the civil rights movement — in February, of course — that the white men who'd lynched Emmett Till were acquitted, I'd slumped in my seat in disbelief. I couldn't believe how naive I'd been, how shocked I was to learn this, like I had somehow missed some essential truth, like I should have known better.

The week before, when we'd covered slavery, our teacher had avoided looking at me the entire time — at all the Black kids — speaking about its horrors in this singsongy voice she never used otherwise. Mrs. Trager came from New York, a master's program at Barnard. She was completing a one-year teaching fellowship in the Philly public school district, and even though she tried too hard, I liked her.

As she spoke, I busied myself writing in my notebook ("Dred Scott," "Underground Railroad," "Middle Passage"), hoping to avoid the uncomfortable glances of my white classmates, even Jenny. I knew she wouldn't get it either. Why did I feel so ashamed and self-conscious when I hadn't done anything wrong? A sickening realization had dawned on me: my good grades didn't matter, or the extra credit, the proper English, how faithful I was, how kind. None of it could ever erase the fact that people were going to hate me. My head felt heavy. I let it drop to my desk, hiding from the burden of it all. In that moment, tucked into the dark haven of the crease of my elbow, more than anything in the world, I wanted to be cute and white and blond and have the whole world find me precious. I wanted to be Jenny.

By the time Gigi starts talking again, my jaw has worked itself into a tight knot. "My daddy went to go about cutting Jimmy's corpse down from the tree, but everyone said it was too dangerous. It *was* too dangerous for us to stay. I remember the adults sitting around the table. No one knew what to do. Everyone was so scared . . . and when you're a kid and adults are scared, well, that's the worst feeling. No one cared if we went to bed, so we stayed up all night. We packed what we could, left the next morning in two caravans. Early as it is right now, we set out, my father and uncle driving two cars, with all of us cousins and everything we owned that could fit in the back. We drove all the way to Philly without stopping. Aunt Mabel wailed the whole time. That's what I remember most. And no one could make her stop. No one even tried. Aunt Mabel was never the same. You don't recover from that. Losing a child. Especially like that. Hand me a tissue, will you?"

I jump to grab her a pack of Kleenex, happy to have something to do. I wish I didn't know this story. It's like I'm in sixth grade again. I want to hide my face in my arms on my desk.

"I don't get it; why didn't you ever tell us, Gigi?"

"What's the point? My momma told me we should try to forget about it. The hurt was too much. It was easier to never speak his name again, Jimmy's name, to block out the pain. Better to seal it off, like a room you stop goin' into. And the shame. We all felt so much shame. Ain't that something? We felt bad even though they's the ones that strung him up and left him to die. And he didn't rape that girl."

Gigi dabs at her eyes some more.

"God help him, he loved that girl."

Y'all need to stay away from those white girls, ya hear? All those times Gigi had said this to Shaun. To her it had been a matter of life and death — someone she loved had died because he loved a white woman. That kind of fear follows you for your entire life. I think of Shaun and Staci, and all the Stacis who came before. Every fiber in my body feels flush with adrenaline, a response to a threat I can't quite pinpoint, thinking about all the ways my brother and dad are unsafe in this world. But deeper than that, bone-deep, there's a dark hum, pain like a shadow, the ancestral trauma that lives in me. Meanwhile, Roger Wilcox probably has grandkids of his own walking around somewhere right now. I wonder if they know what their grandfather did, or if they're oblivious to the fact that the sweet old man they remember for giving them crisp $2 bills for

Christmas or for flirting with the nursing-home staff was a ruthless murderer.

"Do you know what happened to them? To Roger Wilcox? To the girl?" They're probably long dead, and I wonder something else too: How the hell did they live with themselves?

Gigi only shakes her head slowly, full of weariness.

"We don't know what happened to Jimmy either. I mean, where they put him. When we left, Mabel said she would never set foot in that state again until she died. She wanted to be buried near her son, even if she didn't know exactly where that was. Uncle Donny too. He died before your time. I'm thinking that's where I wanna be too."

"Grandma, it's not time —"

She cuts me off with a look. A *Don't even try it,* so I don't bother. I can give her that.

"I want to be buried in the family plot too — with them. Y'all make that happen, ya hear? And you bring Grandpa Leroy's ashes and scatter some around me so he there too. God knows why that man wanted to be cremated. I want to be in the ground, dust to dust, like Jesus. Right where I was born. Sometimes you gotta go home. You promise you'll take me there."

"We will. I promise." My heart is screaming.

"And when you talk to that boy's momma today, you tell her I'll take care of him. I'll see him soon. I'll take care of her baby. Me and Jimmy. We got him."

Gigi lies back in bed as if she's resolved something vital. Or maybe the weight of the story has taken something essential from her, as it did me. I never knew my cousin Jimmy, never even knew *of* him until five minutes ago, and yet Gigi has been carrying this grief all these years. And Aunt Mabel — to lose a child in that way. How many Mabels have there been? How many Tamaras?

It kills me how some people want so badly to believe racism is buried beneath layers and layers of history, "ancient history," they say. But it's not. It's like an umpire brushing the thinnest layer of dirt off home plate: it's right there. Only too often the trauma, the toll of it, remains unknown generation after generation. Like how Gigi kept her own awful secret, presumably to protect us from the ugly truth, and I've kept my own secrets, haunted by a similar shame.

I assume she's nodded off, but then Gigi opens her eyes and looks up at the ceiling. "I want the world to be better, baby girl. We gotta do better."

The washcloth is ice-cold now. I pick it up anyway, wipe the wet streaks from my own cheeks. Gigi's nodded off again. I lean over and kiss her forehead, cool as silk. I need to leave — I only have about twenty minutes to get to my meeting with Wes — but I stay rooted anyway, listening to Gigi's steady breathing. When I finally tear myself away and get to the door, I hear my grandmother's voice behind me. "Tell my Jenny to come see me. Never mind all the troubles. I wanna see my firecracker."

When I turn around, Gigi is fast asleep. But I heard it. I know I did.

Jimmy's story clings to me like a scent as I race across town to meet Wes. It's shaken something loose in me, my emotions stirred up like flakes in a snow globe. I need to settle down, focus on what I have to say to Wes. I haven't told Scotty the interview is in jeopardy. Hopefully I won't have to.

I pull into the small parking lot of Morgan & Sons Funeral Home, and there's Wes sitting on the steps in front of the place, under a dark green awning. It's easy to recognize him from his pictures, an older, brawnier version of Justin — light skin, a smattering of freckles across his nose, gap teeth, and his eyes, a striking hazel that lean brown or green depending on the angle. He's wearing a giant pair of Beats headphones and nodding his head.

When he looks up, he slips them off and calls out my name like we're long-lost cousins and not strangers. "Riley Wilson!"

I sit down on the stairs next to him; the concrete is as frigid as a block of ice.

"You ever see *Hamilton*?" he asks.

"No, I wish. I wanted to take my grandmother to see it when it came to Philly last Christmas, but we couldn't get tickets."

"Same. I stood in line at six a.m., but ticket brokers scooped 'em all up and then they were out of my price range. That's what I was just listening to, the soundtrack." He looks at his headphones like he wants to pick them back up and tune out the world again. I don't blame him.

"I can't stop listening. Justin and I knew all the words to all the songs. We would do a full-out performance to 'The Room Where It Happens.' I mean, we got down!" He stops to sit with the memory. "Justin put it on TikTok or Chatsnap or one of them. He showed it to me, but I'll never be able to find it — but then, I probably couldn't even watch it anyway. It would hurt too much. Him singing, laughing. That boy loved to perform — he was always spitting rhymes, writing poems. . . ."

Wes looks down as if shocked by the coffee cup next to him, when really the shock must be where he's sitting and why. "Listen to me going on, before I even offered you some coffee." He thrusts a steaming paper cup at me. "I stopped at the new place over on the corner. Six dollars for a coffee should come with a nip too, but this is just straight caffeine. Could use it though. Haven't been sleeping much. I didn't know how you like it, so here. . . ."

He pulls a handful of individual packets of creamer, sugar, and sweetener out of his pocket. I can't believe he even thought of getting me coffee, much less all the fixins. But I'm grateful to have the warm cup in my hands, and the hit of caffeine. I pour the creamer and sugar in my coffee.

"That's how I like it too," he says. "Light and sweet. Opposite of how I like my women, by the way."

His big laugh makes me laugh too — I'm grateful for our easy rapport. But then he catches himself. "Look at me laughing. It's funny how everything can be awful and then for a split second you can't help yourself, it's normal and you forget. Of course then it's worse when that second passes. Does that make any sense? It's like when I wake up in the morning and remember it all again. Justin's gone. He's gone but he's also everywhere. All over the media. I assume you saw the latest? They want to put that stupid picture of him with a joint everywhere. As if that's some news. Teenage boy smokes weed. What a headline. Guess he deserved to die? The irony is he didn't even like weed, said it made him paranoid. He was just doing that to fit in with his friends. He was a total geek, so the idea that he was some sorta drug fiend? Or a drug dealer?" His laugh is back but with a razor-sharp edge. "Gimme a break, that'll be something, Justin out here selling weed. I mean, this is a kid who named a hamster Neil after some science guy. But yeah, yeah, he must be a gangbanger, right? Because we all are. It's some shit." He shakes his head. "I'm not saying some shit doesn't go down with these little wannabe thugs over here, but Justin wasn't caught up in that. I worried about him for that reason. He was too soft sometimes. This world isn't made for soft types, you know. I wanted to protect him. And I failed. Simple as that. I failed." His head hangs so low, the steam from his coffee fogs his glasses.

"You did your best. You couldn't have known this would happen."

Wes shoots me a look. "Come on, little miss. We all knew this could happen. I've been stopped a dozen times by the cops. I wasn't much older than Justin when a couple of them threw me on the ground and damn near ripped my shoulder right outta the socket. I can't sink a layup anymore. But no one was talking about it back then. No one was making videos. I told Justin all about it though. I told him to shut up and do what they say if they ever stopped him. But he didn't get the chance. They didn't give him a chance."

"My dad gave my brother the same talk. And my brother — well, he's had his own problems with the cops." I almost tell Wes everything, the hell Shaun's gone through, but I don't. He doesn't need my problems. "How's Tamara?" It's a ridiculous question — how can she be anything but devastated? — but I ask anyway, sincerely. He picks up his head slow as a sunrise.

"Not great. She couldn't stop screaming when I carried her outta the morgue. It's hard to watch my sis struggle like this. First her husband. And now her child. It's not right, man. If I hadn't given up on God a long time I ago, I would now, for sure. I just wish I could get her to eat. She's all but stopped, ever since Justin went into the hospital. She's lost fifteen pounds she didn't have to lose. She's gonna waste away like this."

I want to reach out to touch him, this man sitting here like God has forsaken him and helpless to help his baby sister. But I keep my hands folded on my lap. Sitting here hip to hip is intimate enough already.

"I was just at the hospital with my Gigi, my grandmother — she's dying of kidney disease. She told me her cousin was lynched when she was a kid. I had no idea." I'm not sure why I blurt this out.

Wes turns to face me. "Damn, man, that's awful. I'm so sorry, Riley."

"I don't know why — I didn't know him. Didn't even know of him. But it hit me pretty hard."

"Of course it did. It just never seems to end, does it?"

It's more a statement than a question, so I don't answer. Instead, I reach into my bag and fiddle with my phone. I'm risking rudeness, but this will be worth it. Wes is lost in thought for the moment anyway, until he hears Justin's voice. I've pulled up the video of their rap. I found it in my research about Justin. I've spent hours on his social media in the last week, a haunting rabbit hole. That's how I already knew about the hamster named after Neil DeGrasse Tyson and how he died last year after escaping from his cage and getting stuck under the fridge.

"Is that . . . ?" He grabs for my phone like it's offering the gift of life, which it is, in a tiny way.

The phone's reflection captures the tears that have pooled along his lower lids. I worry I've made a mistake, but he's smiling too. Nodding along, remembering. He watches the whole three-minute video, rapt.

"This is why I want to do the interview with Tamara," I say when the song finishes. "So that we can reinforce that Justin was a sweet, gentle young man who loved his pets and Hamilton and his favorite uncle.

"People need to see what she's — what you all have — lost, and what's at stake for everyone in the community."

"Well, if anyone, we'd want it to be you. You're different from all these other reporters and producers hounding us. White folks offering us hotel rooms and trips to New York City like we won the damn lottery. Telling us they can feel our pain. Yeah, Charlotte, yeah, Becky, I bet you know exactly what this is like. They have no idea what 'our pain' feels like and they never will."

The anger in his voice, I recognize. It's an anger that's been bubbling up in me these last few days, an anger I haven't really experienced before and don't know quite what to do with. I prefer my emotions predictable and tucked away. Right now, it's too personal, too raw. How can I be objective when I'm this upset? I have to channel these emotions, allow them to fuel me and my work. *I want the world to be better, baby girl.* Gigi's words linger. "I want to give your sister a chance to talk about all of that. I want her to get to talk about the real Justin. I just want the world to know about her son and to see her pain, to share it."

There's a long pause, and Wes closes his eyes like I'm not there. I don't know what to do with myself but wait.

"You know, he would have been fifteen next week. I managed to get us tickets for the Sixers — third row, cost me a fortune. He'll never go. He didn't even know he was going to go. It was gonna be a surprise. I don't know what's worse — that he didn't know he was going or if he did. I'm not making sense; I'm just wondering, should I have told him? He would have had something to look forward to."

Wes's hands turn to two tight balls in his lap. This time I do reach over and drape my palm over one of his fists, which gives slightly in my hand.

"He was lucky to have such a great uncle."

"I tried, man. I tried to always be there for him. Teach him how to survive in this world. Step up when his own pops died."

"You did. You did." I squeeze his fist now. I don't even care about the interview anymore; in this moment, I just want Wes's pain to ease.

"You're a good woman, Riley Wilson. I feel that. Come by today. Let's do the interview. I can convince her to do it. I think it's the right move. But you be careful with her, okay?"

Instead of feeling relief and excitement that I saved the interview, I'm flattened by weariness. I tell Wes how grateful I am and that I will see him in a few hours, and then I stand up, leaving him to go inside and pick out a casket.

At every stoplight on the drive to Strawberry Mansion, I look in the rearview mirror, tug at my bangs. I shift in my seat, smooth the wrinkles out of my dress. I'd planned to wear a dress that was a deep gold. I'd bought it earlier this week, especially for the interview. But when Justin died, it no longer felt right. Instead, when I got home from meeting with Wes, I changed into this black dress that I've owned forever. I wouldn't

187

normally wear black on camera, but it felt right.

The leafy streets of Kelly Drive give way to seedy corner stores and abandoned lots overgrown with weeds and strewn with trash the closer I get to Tamara's neighborhood. I pass more than a few abandoned synagogues, strange in this predominantly Black section of town. They're vestiges from when this area was a wealthy Jewish enclave, before white flight took off and urban decay followed. On one of the crumbling brick walls, a mural is in process, a portrait of a Black mother holding her newborn baby. I slow down to take it in. The woman has been filled in with vibrant colors; the baby remains a faint outline, like a thought waiting to enter the world.

At the next light, I check my phone for video of the march taking place across town. KYX has a crew covering it live online, and I asked them to send the footage we'll be using as b-roll for tonight's package. I load the clips they've sent over, and it's as though the screen itself shakes with the energy of the crowd. We have three cameras at various points on location. The clips offer snatches of footage from each of them — a close-up of the front of the march, where Pastor Price, bald head gleaming in the sunlight, walks, arms linked, with several community leaders and a woman. It takes me a moment to place her: Rashanda Montgomery. Her mentally ill daughter was shot by a police officer in North Carolina last year. She's wearing a sweatshirt that reads, "M.O.M., Mothers of the Movement," with her daughter's face below it.

There's an aerial shot of the crowd behind Pastor Price, a mass of people, young, old, white, Black, snaking down Broad Street, at least ten blocks deep. I'd suspected the turnout would be strong — local activists have been beating the drum all week, putting up stickers and flyers all over town. And no doubt more decided to come out after hearing Justin died last night. The perfect weather helps too: activism is easier when it's cloudless and fifty-five degrees.

I search for my family, though I know it's pointless given the sheer number of people. Shaun and I got into an argument at my parents' dinner table last night about him attending today. Sure, it's supposed to be a peaceful protest, but plenty of events are peaceful until they aren't. If things get out of hand, the first person the police are going to go after is the six-foot-two Black guy wearing a T-shirt with Colin Kaepernick taking a knee.

"It's not worth the risk. You get arrested and you're screwed," I'd told him.

"Protesting for civil rights isn't worth the risk?" he shot back. "Do you even hear yourself? There's no way I'm missing this."

"You can't go."

"First of all, I'm a grown-ass man. You can't tell me what to do. That's the difference between you and me, sis. They're not going to make me afraid. I'm not hiding. I'm gonna be seen and heard."

"We'll all go together. As a family," Dad chimed in. "And your sister's right, it could get dicey out there. You know there'll be some young bloods out there getting up to no good, giving us all a bad name. I got caught up in all that mess back in the '64 riots — tear-gassed and everything. All I'd hoped was that it would be better for y'all. But here we are again, fifty years later and ain't nothing changed but the music. I swear it's like we're on a damn treadmill set to the highest setting and we just keep trying to climb, going nowhere fast," Dad said, taking a giant bite of his peach pie.

My phone dings now with a text from Shaun. He's sent a selfie from the march, standing in front of city hall with Mom and Dad.

I'm relieved to see that the crowd really is

peaceful, so many faces filled with righteous conviction and purpose. Nonetheless, my cynicism creeps in. *Ain't nothing changed but the music.* All the clever signs and chants, the people who showed up just so they could post it to their social media, what does it add up to? How many marches have there been? How many calls for justice? How many lawsuits? How many "national conversations about race"? But then again, maybe this is something. No one had marched for Jimmy; no one had demanded justice. Instead, terror had chased our family out of town, paralyzed them in silence for decades. So maybe the marching, rallying, showing up, it serves a purpose. It says, *We will not be invisible or afraid. We will not give up.* And that's not nothing. It might actually be everything.

Traffic is light this side of town, and I arrive at Tamara's earlier than I intended. So after I park on the street, I take a detour and walk into the alley, the one behind the liquor store, the one Justin walked down on his way home from school. I expect something more menacing, but it's just a dark narrow alley. There's a pile of candles, sympathy cards, battered teddy bears, and fistfuls of deli flowers that serve as a makeshift memorial. I stand there alone and look left and right, imagine turning around and seeing the barrel of a gun. I open my mouth and scream — I scream for Justin and for Jimmy. I half expect to see the cops show up just then, but the only witness to my moment of madness is a stray alley cat with a nub tail rubbing himself against the brick wall. I trace the path Justin didn't get to take that day, squinting my eyes to read the numbers on the line of crumbling brick row houses. When I see the bicycle on the porch — a blue Huffy lying on its side next to a set of concrete steps — I know it's the right one.

As I climb the Dwyers' porch stairs, my gaze lingers on the bike, the one Justin will never ride again. Before I can even knock, Tamara opens the door. She's wearing a red Phillies cap with dried sweat stains along the rim.

"Hi, I'm Riley."

I extend my hand right as she steps forward for a hug, and then we switch, her hand out, me stepping forward, and end up laughing at our awkward dance.

"I'm a hugger," she says, and pulls me in for an embrace that lasts longer than I expected. Even though Wes warned me, I'm not prepared to feel her bones through her skin. She moves away and leads me across the threshold into the living room. All the blinds are drawn, and shadows fall over the room. It takes me a minute to see that the couches and chairs are filled with people. Three teenage boys sit on the floor, watching a video on one of their phones, the sound turned off.

Sadness casts a pall over the room.

"This is Riley Wilson from the news," Tamara introduces me. "Riley, this is everyone. The entire neighborhood has been coming over and sitting with me. Less people today because of the march."

"I was just watching some footage from the march. It's a really strong turnout for Justin."

"I wish I coulda kept it together to go. But no, it was too much — being the center of attention, having everyone looking at me . . . It woulda broke me."

Wes rises from a giant lounger in the corner that reminds me of Gigi's. He doesn't hesitate before reaching out and hugging me as well. "Riley. Long time no see," he jokes.

I allow his chiseled arms to engulf me, my cheek pressed firmly to his broad chest. Now, standing here in his embrace, our connection feels all the more intense, like he's someone I've known forever.

"Do you need a drink?" Tamara offers. "Water? A Coke? We have plenty of food too; people have been dropping it off nonstop. So help yourself."

I already feel like an intruder; I'm hardly going to grab a paper plate of green-bean casserole. "Thank you, but I'm okay."

Tamara goes over to the small galley kitchen, opens the fridge door, and closes it again without taking anything out. She runs her hands up and down her jeans, looks around as if she doesn't quite know what to do with me now that I'm here. Wes, who shadows his sister closely, puts his hands on her shoulders. "Take it a minute at a time, sis. You don't need to do this right now if you aren't up for it."

"No, no, I can do it."

Wes turns to me. "Do you want to see Justin's room? We can do the interview in there if you want."

I nod and follow the two of them a few steps down the hall. Hanging on the closed door is one of those personalized little Pennsylvania license plates that reads JUSTIN. Tamara prepares herself with a deep breath and then opens the door. She walks a few feet into the room, plops down on the bed. It's covered with a pilly plaid comforter. She grabs a pillow, holds it to her face. "I keep coming in here and smelling his pillow. How long do you think it'll keep smelling like him?"

"We won't ever wash it." Wes leans in and takes a whiff.

I take in the room — half-finished models of dusty dinosaurs perch on the shelves; an iconic, and apparently timeless, poster of Tupac hangs above the bed; a trombone case leans against it; and a tattered paperback, *Of Mice and Men,* lies facedown on the desk next to a small tank with one lone goldfish swimming in lazy circles. Loose socks are scattered around the floor. It already feels like a shrine.

Tamara's red-rimmed eyes are focused on watching the fish in the tank. She doesn't look at me when she speaks.

"I couldn't have made it through the last week without this man, without my brother. Wes was there in the hospital with me when we finally let Justin go . . . when I told them to go ahead and pull the plug."

"I couldn't stay in there when they did it, when they unhooked him," Wes admits.

"I was alone in there when my baby died. And then I couldn't figure out how to leave. I crawled up on that bed and held him tight until the breath went out of his body." She trembles and grips her brother like he's a lifeline.

Then she fixes her gaze on me as if she's remembered I'm there, standing awkwardly in the doorway.

"Do you have kids?"

"No," I respond, trying not to sound defensive. Whenever I get asked this, which is all the time, my answer always feels wrong. I hope it doesn't make her think I can't relate to her loss, even though it's probably somewhat true that I can't.

"I've only got one child." She says it like Justin is still right here, like he isn't gone, wishful thinking, the power of language to keep him alive. "He's the best thing I'll ever do."

"I wish I could have known him." Reaching for adequate words is like trying to grasp at air.

The doorbell rings, and Tamara jumps a little. "No one ever uses the doorbell. I better see who that is. I'll be back." Wes trails her closely like he can't bear to be away from her side.

It's too early for it to be my crew — probably another neighbor with a deli platter. I catch snatches of Tamara mumbling to herself as she walks down the hall. It has the gentle cadence and hushed tones of a prayer.

Alone in Justin's room, I feel even more like an intruder. I remain in the doorway and mentally plan out the interview logistics. I can sit in the desk chair beneath the window and Tamara can sit on the edge of the bed, with Bart, my cameraman, positioned right where I'm standing now. We'll need to hang some lights along the closet, but it's a good setup, intimate and personal. I'm so relieved about how well the staging works that it takes me a second to feel queasy about the direction of my thoughts.

Tentatively, I make my way over to the desk chair for a sense of how it might be to sit there for the interview. My phone buzzes. When I pull it out and see the name splashed across the screen, I jerk my head over my shoulder, worried I might find Tamara right behind me, that she might see Jenny's name. Tupac glares down at me like one of those Renaissance portraits, his eyes following my every move.

It's a terrifying transgression to read this text, from this person, in this room. But curiosity gets the better of me. I take another look over my shoulder and open the message.

I'm so sad about Justin. I didn't mean what I said. I feel like we're fighting. I don't want to be fighting.

Are we fighting? Not exactly. I'm not mad at Jenny. Or maybe I am. I don't know. I need to sort out how I feel before I talk to her, but I can't think about that right now. I need her name gone from my screen. I'll write her back later, from somewhere else. Anywhere else. I look at Tupac again and pick up the book lying on the desk. I remember reading *Of Mice and Men* in ninth grade too. I open to the dog-eared page, scan a few paragraphs. George and Lenny have just arrived at the farm filled with dreams. Lenny's doom hangs over the scene. Tamara startles me when she returns right then. I drop the book in my hands to the floor.

"He was liking that book. I warned him it was a sad story. He didn't finish it, so he'll never know about that. That's good, I guess." She picks it up possessively and places it just so back on the desk. "I need your help with what to wear, if that's okay?"

"Sure, you can wear whatever you're comfortable in."

She fingers the brim of the hat.

"Was that Justin's?" I ask.

"Yeah, his favorite one. Can I wear it in the interview?"

"Well, maybe you can hold it in your lap."

"Okay, come on, let's go look in my closet."

Tamara's dresser is crowded with rows of framed pictures, and I peer at each one. Most are of Justin, as a toddler in an oversize Eagles jersey, an eight-year-old in a white first communion suit. Wes and teenage Justin at a Sixers game mugging for the camera in matching throwback Iverson jerseys, maybe the last picture they ever took together.

There's also a lot of pictures of her husband. It's clear where Justin gets his dimples, same exact one, left side. I know from my research his dad was a bike messenger who got struck by a car in Center City during a delivery. When she sees me hovering over the photo she comes closer. "That's Darrell. My husband. Hard to believe he's been gone four years now. It used to be the worst thing that ever happened to me. I couldn't even have imagined something worse. And now here I am. It's a blessing Dee's gone though. I've been thinking about that a lot. He wouldn't have survived losing his only son. I never thought I'd be grateful he was gone, but at least he was spared this."

How much tragedy can one woman bear?

She sits on the double bed that's so close to the wall the closet door only opens part of the way. "I keep thinking, maybe I should've been home more. Maybe this wouldn't have happened. I was working double shifts at the Amazon warehouse over in Bucks County to save up some money. Justin and I were gonna take a trip to Florida. He's never been on an airplane. Now he'll never ride on an airplane."

I hover over her awkwardly and then decide to take the liberty of sitting next to her on the neatly made bed, even though it feels too close. I wish Wes would come back, but I can hear him talking to someone else in the living room.

"That's what gets me, what stops me right dead in my tracks when I start to think about everything he wanted to do and how he ain't gonna get a chance to do it. If he were alive, he would have gone down to that march and made a big sign and screamed the loudest of all his friends. He saw good in the world. He was just a baby, but I know he would have changed things if he'd gotten the chance."

"Maybe he still can," I say, as much to Tamara as myself.

Tamara and I busy ourselves rummaging

through her closet, both grateful for the temporary distraction of having a mission to focus on. We settle on a pretty navy dress that's too big for her but looks nice anyway.

Five minutes before the broadcast, we're in our spots in Justin's room, facing each other as the bustle of sound checks and lighting adjustments carries on around us. Tamara self-consciously fluffs her hair, which has been covered, until moments ago, by Justin's hat, which she grips in her lap. Her pixie cut suits her face; she looks a little like Halle Berry, and unintentionally glamorous, even with eyes that are dark pools of sadness.

"I'm nervous," Tamara admits. "All these people watching, you know?"

"It's going to be okay. I'm only going to ask you about Justin. All you have to do is talk about Justin, okay?"

"That I can do," Tamara says, soft but resolute.

The control room beeps into my earpiece to count me into the start of the broadcast. I have a surge of nervous anticipation, like someone's about to dump a bucket of ice water over my head. I shift my weight forward, wiggle my toes in my damp tights.

Candace's husky drawl comes through my earpiece, describing the highlights of the day's march. I picture the b-roll playing along, the footage I watched in my car earlier. There's a short clip from Pastor Price's speech, his familiar cadence rousing. It's laced with the haunting quality of a eulogy. The broadcast returns to Candace, who sets up the KYX exclusive live interview with the victim's mother.

Then, my cue from the control room: "You're live."

Tamara and I lock eyes. I give her the faintest of nods to reassure her. *I see you, I got you.*

"Thank you for being with us this evening, Mrs. Dwyer. We appreciate you doing it today, so soon after losing Justin. How are you doing?"

"As best as I can be, I guess. It's a hard day. It helps that so many people marched for Justin today. That makes me feel good, to know people want justice for my son."

"And justice, what does that look like to you? The statistics and precedents show that cops are rarely prosecuted for these types of incidents."

"That's not right. They should be punished. They have to be. My boy did nothing wrong. Nothing. And he was murdered. Something has to be done, or this is gonna happen again and again."

A vivid image flashes in my mind, of a man hanging by his neck from a tree, surrounded by a jeering mob. I stumble over my next question.

"And . . . and . . . what should be done?"

"I want those cops who killed my son locked up. For the rest of their lives. Justin doesn't get to have a life. Why should they?"

Those cops. Kevin.

"Take me back to the night of the shooting. How did you first learn about what had happened to Justin?"

"The neighborhood kids ran in and told me. They were always just running in without knocking. I made it to him before the ambulance, but they wouldn't let me near him. But I needed to see my boy. I needed to touch him. I screamed at them to let me be with him, and they ignored me. Wouldn't even let me ride in the ambulance. I didn't even know if he was dead or alive."

The interview is closely timed. I have exactly five and a half minutes. Still, I pause to let that sit with the audience — a mother unable to touch her own son. Tamara holds the hat in her lap so tightly the bill is pressed in half.

"Tell me more about your boy. What was he like?"

"He was a good boy. I know people want

203

him to either be some sort of druggie thug or a perfect kid. Justin was an excellent student and rarely got into trouble. But all this talk about him being on the honor roll — it seems like they mean he was one of the 'good' ones when they keep saying that. His death would be just as unfair if he was flunking out of school. Or yeah, if he did smoke weed once or twice, then he's a bad kid who deserved to die? He did *not* deserve to die."

"Well, tell us more about your son beyond him being a good student. What do you want our viewers to know about Justin?"

Tamara looks like she's wondering how she could possibly narrow everything she has to say about her son down to a sound bite. Her eyes dart around his room as if trying to absorb everything he *was*.

"Well, one thing is that he never killed ants. Wouldn't even step on them. Would go out of his way to let the ants cross in a line on the sidewalk. And chicken tenders were his favorite food. He had these stinky little feet as a baby. I used to put them right in my mouth and kiss his little toes. His first word was 'duck.' He called pigeons ducks, and we let him do it. How'd he know any better, growing up in the city the way he did?" She stops to laugh, then turns serious again, as if she's caught herself doing something wrong. She speaks more softly now, and I hope the mic is able to capture it. "I wasn't finished with him yet. I had so many things left to teach him, to tell him. I'm never gonna get the chance now." Her eyes glisten under all the lights.

There's a pause. I am about to fill it with another question when Tamara suddenly leans over and takes ahold of my hand, squeezes so hard I'm worried I might wince. "Can I pray for him?"

I freeze, caught off guard, mindful we're on live TV. Tamara starts crying softly and bows her head; her voice is now loud, given she's speaking right into the mic clipped to her dress. "God, I need mercy in my heart and grace in my soul."

As she begs God for strength, my own eyes start to water as I reach out and hold on tightly to Tamara's hand.

"Please, Lord, please help me forgive the men who did this to my son."

I silently echo Tamara's prayer: *Please help me forgive.*

CHAPTER SIX

JEN

Shattered glass crunches beneath my sneakers. The storefronts are still boarded up, their owners desperate to escape another night of violence. Someone has spray-painted BLACK LIVES MATTER across the plywood on the windows of a Sephora. The BLACK has been crossed out and replaced with ALL.

It feels like a war zone, a burned-out newsstand, police tape everywhere, mailboxes toppled over. The peaceful march turned into something much uglier after dark. And all because of my husband. My entire city is in pain and on edge, a powder keg that will only be defused once there's justice, whatever that means. Chants of "Lock them up" from the protests still echo in my ears.

As I dash the few blocks to the doctor's office like a fugitive, I can't shake the thought that everyone I pass is staring at me, sizing me up, judging me. Even the short distance from my parking spot to the door leaves me feeling exposed. I've barely set foot outside the house in the ten days since the shooting, and this is the first time since the march three days ago, and that interview, that painful interview.

I catch my reflection in the elevator doors — greasy hair, faded sweatshirt beneath a stained puffy coat that I can't even zip around my belly, worn black leggings that sag around the butt. I look like trash. My appearance at the moment is an actual liability. Someone could see me right now, photograph me, and send the picture to the *Daily News:* KILLER COP'S TRASHY WIFE. That would be the headline, and the picture would be worth one thousand words. *Obviously that cop's racist,* readers would think. *Look at his white-trash wife.*

The loneliness slams into me as I walk into the crowded waiting room dotted with couples. Meanwhile, my husband is at a therapy appointment this morning. The department required one mandatory session after the shooting but gave him the option to continue seeing Dr. Washington voluntarily.

Matt gave him shit for it. "You're off to

see the Wizard," he teased. That's what the cops call shrinks — the Wizard. "Don't get lost in Oz, Dorothy."

But Kevin surprised us all by jumping at the offer. Naturally, he doesn't tell me anything about it. I can only hope that he's opening up to the doctor. He said he'd try to make it today, but I'm not holding my breath. No one else could come with me either. Annie's on shift at the hospital, and I'd never dream of asking her to find someone to cover. Cookie is watching Archie because day care is closed for some reason, and Frank volunteers every Tuesday morning at the VA.

The regular receptionist is out. Her replacement is a youngish Black woman with long thick braids and a necklace made of giant stones. Normally I would compliment her jewelry, ask where she got it, tell her about this girl on Etsy who sells rings that look similar. But I don't do any of that. I barely even look up as I hand over my insurance card and driver's license. She takes it without smiling and squints as she scrutinizes my ID. I shift from foot to foot as I wait for her to recognize the name, hiss at me, call me the wife of a murderer. She just hands me back my card with a friendly look on her face.

"You don't look much like your driver's license picture anymore."

"I chopped off my hair. And I gained some weight." I point to my belly.

"Pregnancy suits you. The hair too."

Her unexpected kindness makes me want to ask her to come into the exam room with me to hold my hand.

I find the most secluded seat possible, far in the corner. I pull my phone out of my bag so I don't have to make eye contact with anyone else. I already have eleven missed calls. All from "Unknown" or unfamiliar numbers. Reporters . . . or worse. It's escalated since the interview. In the last twenty-four hours alone, I've received multiple messages from crazy strangers saying that Kevin should burn in hell for what he did, or that our baby should be taken away from us. And then there was the woman who'd hissed, "Maybe you'd understand if your own baby was killed." After that I vowed to never listen again. I delete anything that doesn't come from a number I recognize.

My forefinger swipes the screen and presses down to pull up the video again. I don't know why I do it — it's like a car crash I keep rubbernecking. The counter at the corner says Riley's interview with

Tamara has been viewed 437,322 times since it aired Saturday night. I'm probably at least a dozen of those. Riley's face, the size of my thumb, is close to the screen. I watch as she nods along when Tamara Dwyer demands that the officers who shot her son get sent to prison "for the rest of their lives."

I drag my finger along the bottom of the screen, fast-forwarding a few seconds to another close-up of Riley, her glassy eyes, her tight grip on Tamara's hand. If any other reporter did that, I'd think it was an act, turning it on for the camera, except this is Riley, and I can tell she means it, that's what makes her so good. She truly cares. Riley looks so genuinely pained, I want to reach through the phone and comfort her, the grieving mother too. Then I remember: *The man they're talking about locking up for the rest of his life is my husband.*

And maybe Riley *is* just doing her job, so why do I feel like I've been stabbed in the back every time I watch this video? Why does it feel like Riley is choosing sides?

We're fine, Riley had written me yesterday, a full two days after I'd texted her that I didn't want to be fighting, after I'd almost stopped expecting to hear back from her. It's obviously not true, which is why I

210

haven't responded. Besides, after that interview, what could I even say? *Nice job making the case that my husband is a monster.*

As betrayed as I felt watching that one-sided interview, I'd still somehow found myself defending Riley to the Murphys when it aired. "She's just doing her job," I offered meekly as we watched it live in the sunken living room on the too-big TV. That I felt the need to stick up for Riley at all only made me more pissed off about the whole thing.

Matt's voice had thundered through the room, rattling Cookie's Precious Moments figurines. "Are you kidding me? That Black bitch knows exactly what she's doing!"

"Do not call her that!" I spat back.

Kevin jumped to his feet, upsetting the empty beer cans on the coffee table. "She's a traitor. She knows me, Jen. She knows me, and she does this?" He stormed out through the patio doors, into the freezing night. Matt joined him; the two of them paced and passed a vape back and forth for hours, long after I went to bed.

Does Riley know Kevin? Even I don't know my husband right now. Before we were married, when we did our Pre-Cana at St. Matthew (at Cookie's insistence), Father Mike, who'd christened Kevin as a baby, looked across his massive cherry desk and asked us to tell him about the hardest challenge we'd faced so far as a couple. He was dead serious, but it didn't stop our nervous giggles. We were all of twenty-five. We'd only been dating for a year. Life was all sex in weird places and dirty texts.

It was hard to imagine a time when Kevin wouldn't make me happy. I tried to force myself to think of scenarios that would break us and came up blank. Kevin would never cheat, never hit me, never leave me. He had a good job. He'd support our family. I guess everyone goes into their wedding day believing these things, but with Kevin, they were facts, not wishes. I was building a life on the bedrock of these truths.

Father Mike left us with what he claimed was his very best advice. "Try not to stop loving each other on the same day." He let loose an uncharacteristic chuckle. "Or, rather, try not to hate each other on the same day."

It sounded ridiculous at the time. I could never hate Kevin. But when I couldn't get pregnant, Father Mike's advice took on a whole new meaning. That's when I became the worst wife in the world, moody, angry, quick to snap for long stretches of time. Sometimes I blamed the hormones; the truth is that I was miserable and scared and took it all out on Kevin because he was there, a sponge to absorb my hostility. He withstood my outbursts like a tree standing in a hurricane. He remained calm, even when we got into the biggest fight of our marriage, last Christmas Eve, when I came home with the check from Riley. I presented it triumphantly, giddily, ready to call the clinic as soon as they opened after the holiday. Kevin had looked at the check with actual disgust and demanded that I return it.

"I don't want to be in debt to her," he'd shouted.

I should have known how he'd react. He's not a huge fan of Riley under the best of circumstances. He thinks he hides it, but Kevin can't hide anything. So when he says things like, "Riley thinks she's the shit, doesn't she?" or, "You always do what Riley says," I let it go most of the time. He's only jealous. He wants to be the most important person in my life — and he is, but Riley's a very close second, a scenario that doesn't make either of them happy.

And there was no way I was turning down the money. I made this pretty clear by screaming it at the top of my lungs. I hate what I said to him before storming out of our bedroom. "Maybe we should get a divorce and I'll have a baby on my own. I'm not the one with the fucking problem." I can only blame my outburst on the fact that I wanted a child with a longing so desperate and feral it consumed me. It changed me; it was like being possessed. The old Jen, the one who sat in Father Mike's office wild-eyed with love, would never have said those words.

My whole life there's been a little voice inside me, reminding me not to want too much. I used to complain to Lou about how unfair it was that I didn't have a father, or new clothes, or a mother who came to school events. "Life's not fair. Get used to it," she'd bark at me. And I accepted that. But a baby — one healthy baby — that felt like a reasonable thing to want. I couldn't summon a dad, or a new mother, but I could, surely, somehow, make a baby. The more it seemed like Kevin was resigned to it not happening, the more determined I felt. Even if the money from Riley wasn't enough and I had to open yet another credit card to make up the difference. Even if taking her money made me feel embarrassed, exposed. Even if I didn't want Riley to think Kevin had failed me somehow. The only thing that mattered was that it gave me one more chance — and that cycle, our Hail Mary, had worked, thank God. But a part of me will always wonder, *What if it hadn't? If we hadn't gotten pregnant, would our marriage have survived? Would I have?*

Kevin stood by me while I was struggling, and he deserves my patience now during the worst time of *his* life, though it isn't easy, especially when he's sullen and withdrawn and drinking too much. There are moments when I want to tell him the same thing Cookie said to me: "You gotta pull it together." Just last night, a news story in the *Inquirer* sent him spinning. Tamara had made a statement to the paper, pointedly inviting him and Chris to attend Justin's funeral next Saturday. "I want them to see what they did."

"I know what I did!" he yelled. "They think I don't know?" Then he spun even further the implications of being invited ("Does she mean this to be a publicity stunt?"), then agonized about whether he should go, which was a terrible idea. Then he landed in full self-pity: "I'm so tired of this. I wish I'd been the one who was shot. I wish it had been me."

I look back down at my phone screen — Riley's face is frozen in place where I paused the video. *How could you?* I think.

And then, *Where are you? I need you.* I send the last part like a wish into the air before tucking my phone back into my bag. I peek around the waiting room. For so many years I hated to be around pregnant women, people with kids. The envy ripped me apart. Now I crave their proximity even if I have no desire to interact with them. *Look at me. I made it into your club.*

But I'm still scared. I start imagining all the terrible possibilities; excruciatingly detailed scenarios play out in my mind on a loop. I picture myself lying down on the scratchy paper stretched thin across the vinyl exam table, bending my knees, the nurse with a big fat smile on her face spreading the cold goo over my stomach and waving that wand that looks like a sex toy. The nurse's smile droops into a straight line, then further into a worried frown. She busies herself putting away the equipment, tells me to wait while she grabs the doctor. When the doctor enters, she picks up the wand, rubs it against my skin, and then looks at me over my swollen belly.

"There's no heartbeat. The baby is gone."

I shake myself out of the dark spiral and stare at the couple holding hands in the opposite corner. The woman's wearing an elegant wool maxidress from that expensive maternity store that bombards me with ads on Instagram. Her husband has on the shiniest loafers I've ever seen, no doubt off to his job at some big-time law firm after this, but even with his demanding job he never misses an appointment with his wife. I start down the road of imagining their perfect lives when I'm startled by a familiar voice booming across the waiting room.

"Would you look at all these big bellies!"

Seriously?

There's Lou sipping loudly from an over-size plastic Wawa cup, in faded black jeans and a thin black Eagles hoodie even though it's freezing outside. On her feet are the scuffed Dr. Martens she's owned since before I was born. When I was twelve, I begged for a pair just like hers, and Lou bought them for me for Christmas that year. I didn't realize they were knockoffs until the yellow stitching started coming out of the soles after only a couple of weeks.

"What are you doing here, Lou?" I didn't once think about asking her to come to this appointment. When I went through the list of possibilities, my own mother hadn't even occurred to me. "How did you know I was going to the doctor today?"

Lou sits down and places her arm around my shoulders in a strange sort of half hug, and I'm smothered by a cloud of stale smells: coffee, cigarette smoke, last night's perfume. The familiar eau de Lou transports me right back to the floor of her closet. "Kevin called and told me about the appointment."

It takes only a second to work out why Kevin hadn't mentioned it — he was sparing me in case she didn't show.

"I worked an early shift this morning, so it was easy for me to pop by."

Of course, as long as it was convenient, Lou could make it. She's been here for approximately two minutes and my jaw is already locked tight from being on edge.

"You worked at the bar this morning? It's ten thirty a.m."

"Bar's been closed for a month. I told you that. Fire. They gotta redo the whole first floor. They're calling it a grease fire, but you know it could've been a case of Jewish lightning. . . ."

"What?"

"You know, when people burn something down for the insurance money."

I look around to make sure no one else heard her.

"Besides that, that's offensive, Lou, the bar owners aren't even Jewish. They're Irish."

Lou shrugs. "It's just what they call it. I hope they open back up at all. Too many of the old-time bars are selling out to the new hipster places. Places that don't even open at seven in the morning — hell, they don't open until seven at night. Sometimes people need a drink when they wake up, you know? Anyways, I'm unemployed until they finish fixing things, so I'm driving for Uber! I didn't tell you? It's great. You meet so many interesting people. Like I just came from taking this couple to the airport. Indians. From over in India, dots not feathers." She points to her forehead with her index finger. "They had an arranged marriage and are going thirty years strong. Maybe I should have had one of those. He works in the diamond and ruby business. She runs an orphanage. I told her my daughter was pregnant but wants more babies. I got her email address for you. Maybe you can go over there and pick up one of them brown babies."

"I don't understand why they told you all that."

"Come on, I've been a bartender for thirty years. People tell me things." She pokes my belly with the tip of her index finger.

"Ow!" I make a dramatic show of pulling away, even though it didn't really hurt.

"You're getting big."

"Thanks." I glare at my mom, taking in the face that has yielded to a film of wrinkles. She's barely into her fifties, but all the smoking and days down at the shore smothered in baby oil have taken their toll.

She's jiggling her belly now. "It's hard to lose the weight. Harder than you think. I gained twenty pounds with you that I'm still trying to lose."

As usual with Lou, I'm mortified. I peek around and am grateful that no one seems to be listening. The golden couple is gone; they must have been called back already. Thank God they're missing this little spectacle.

"So all's I'm sayin' is be careful, you don't want Kev to go off and find something more like this, do you?" Lou picks up a *People,* pointing to the cover image of a bikini-clad Kim Kardashian. Lou loves anything Kardashian.

The nurse, Rita, couldn't have called me back a second sooner. Lou trails behind us on our way to the exam room like a child accompanying her mother on a shopping trip.

"Aw, look at these little boo-boos," Lou says, taking in the newborn pictures clipped with clothespins to strings that line the entire hallway. "Jesus, all these babies look mixed. I don't see a single white baby up there. Oh, there's one." She points to a smushed-face baby named Maddy, wearing a sparkling pink bow on her bald head to signal she's a girl. "It's true what they say, I guess, we're all going to be one color one day. A lot of little mixed kids. That'll be nice. Like if you and Riley had ended up being lezzies, you could get you one of these mixed kids and it would look like both of you." Lou elbows me and cackles loudly.

Rita cringes, but Lou is oblivious.

After quickly taking my blood pressure, Rita leaves us in the exam room to wait for the doctor. I start to change into the itchy gown, weirdly self-conscious about my mother seeing me naked. She sits in the plastic chair in the corner.

"Speaking of Riley, you talk to her?" she asks as I struggle to tie the gown shut.

"A little."

"You seen her interview?"

"What do you think, Lou?"

"That poor woman, the mother. Riley looked so pretty though. That skin, I swear. I would kill someone for skin like that, wouldn't you? You should ask her for some tips." She pats her pasty cheeks.

This is what we're talking about? This is

221

what's important? Beauty tips?

"Well, however beautiful Riley looked with her flawless skin, you understand that interview was not good for us, don't you, Lou? You're missing the point." I'm practically yelling; the patient next door can probably hear me through the paper-thin walls.

"But Riley was doing her job. She's on the TV. She has to act the part. Like Kim and Khloe."

"Seriously? Riley's not an actress and neither are the Kardashians."

"Oh yes they are. Those girls should get an Academy Award for what they do. And Riley's gotta do what she does with that fancy job of hers, otherwise they're not gonna pay her a heap of money."

"She's my best friend. She should be watching out for me."

"Look, I love Riley, but you girls ain't been around each other much in fifteen years. You're different people now. Rich people don't think about people like us the same way."

"Riley isn't rich! Besides, Lou, maybe you should be focused on me, your *daughter.* How about maybe asking how I'm doing?" At least Lou looks chastened.

"I already asked you that."

"No you didn't."

"Well. How are you doing?"

"I'm fine. I just really wish Kevin could be here today." *Instead of you.* And of course it isn't fine. But I've never confided in my mother and I'm not going to start now.

"Where is he anyway?"

"Just . . . meetings." I'm vague. There's no point in bothering to involve Lou in the details, and I can imagine her reaction if I told her he was meeting with a "head shrinker," as she calls them. The only thing more ridiculous and useless than therapy in Lou's mind is electronic cigarettes.

"Well, you need a good lawyer, that's for sure. Get one of those guys from one of the billboards on Ninety-Five. I wish I had some money to give you." Lou raises one of her thin eyebrows. She's always plucked them to a fine arched line that looks as if it was drawn by a satanic cartoonist.

"That's okay. Cookie and Frank are covering it."

This comment is sure to sting, and I feel a little charge of satisfaction. Ever since Kevin and I got married, Lou's been in a strange competition with Cookie that plays out in passive-aggressive jabs. Lou doesn't like losing at a sport, even if she hasn't bothered trying to be any good at it.

"Well, okay then, great. He'll get this mess

all cleared up, I'm sure."

The conversation careens into a brick wall, and we both just sit there, listening to the clock tick. What kind of person doesn't have anything to say to her own mother? Disappointment washes over me. My mom should be gushing with excitement and advice and plans. When I told her I was pregnant last spring, all she said was, "Well, let's see if it sticks this time, kiddo. Maybe it's not in the cards for you."

"These doctors sure take their sweet time, don't they?" Lou picks up the file Rita left on the counter.

"I don't think you're supposed to look at that." I have no idea if this is an actual rule, but it feels like one.

"Well, I don't see why not. These are your files. You have a right to know what they're saying, don't you? So, let's see here . . ." She holds the paper away from her face like she's having trouble reading. "Baby Boy Murphy. He's cute." Lou holds up an ultrasound photo and continues to talk, unfazed. All I can hear is the rush of blood in my ears.

A boy.

A boy.

A boy.

"Jesus Christ, Lou!"

"Oh, shit." Lou realizes what she's done and has the decency to look ashamed. "I didn't —"

"You didn't remember that we wanted the sex of the baby to be a surprise?"

A pure and perfect rage begins in my gut and rises up to my head with such pressure it might just explode. Of all the shitty things Lou has done, this may be the worst. Leave it to her to ruin what was supposed to be one of the best moments of my life, one of the only happy things I have to hold on to right now.

"I'm sorry, I didn't even think. . . ."

I can't hear another word. I hold up my hand to stop her from talking and fall back onto the table to let the news sink in. *I'm having a baby boy.*

Riley and I initially liked the name Jackson for a boy, Jack for short. For a girl, Adeline, Addy for short. But Kevin has had only one name in mind for a boy: *Chase.* Suddenly, in this moment, I can't imagine my baby being called anything else.

Knowing it's a boy, that it's Chase, makes it real in a new and terrifying way, and all the worst-case scenarios come rushing back. Thankfully, there's a loud knock on the door right then, and Dr. Wu strides in, all warm efficiency and brisk purpose.

"Hello?" she says tentatively. It's clear she senses the tension. She casts Lou a look, unsure of her relationship to me.

"Hi, Dr. Wu. This is my mom, Louise. Kevin had a meeting."

There's no way Dr. Wu doesn't know what's going on with Kevin, but her face doesn't give anything away. She extends her hand to Lou and offers her congratulations.

"Your first grandchild?"

"Yes. Thank God! A boy!"

Dr. Wu looks over at me quizzically. She knows it was supposed to be a surprise.

"My mom looked at the file. She accidentally ruined it."

"Ruined it? I mean, you're still having a baby." Lou sounds like a defensive teenager. "And this way you can plan. Surprises are overrated. You were a surprise, and I cried for three days straight."

Dr. Wu musters an amicable laugh and then trains all her focus and attention on me like I'm the only thing that matters to her. This is why I love my doctor — she looks you in the eye, talks to you like she has all the time in the world, as if there aren't forty other women in the waiting room.

"How are you feeling?" she asks now.

Like I want to murder the woman who

gave birth to me. But that's not what I say; what I say is: "I'm having a boy." As if I'm breaking the news to Dr. Wu.

"Yep, looks like that cat's out of the bag. You are." She sounds genuinely happy for me. "So let's get everything checked out and see how he's doing in there." She pulls out a blood pressure cuff.

"Rita already did my vitals."

"I know. I just want to check them again."

I watch Dr. Wu as she clocks the numbers, the cuff on my arm squeezing tighter and tighter. I swear I see a frown when she slowly removes it and pulls out the measuring tape. She opens the paper gown to expose my veiny belly, holds one end of the tape right under my boobs and wraps it down and across my tummy to measure the growth of the uterus, the growth of the baby. Before I got pregnant, I assumed I'd get an ultrasound at every checkup, that I'd be constantly peeking inside my uterus, watching the baby flip and wave, but they are few and far between. I wonder if there would be more if I had better health insurance. It's pointless to even ask.

"Let's check the heartbeat."

There *is* a frown. I'm sure of it now. Dr. Wu isn't as upbeat as usual. I move from imagining the worst and start praying for the best. *Please be okay. Please be okay. Please be okay.* I squeeze my eyes shut as the doctor rubs the gel on my belly.

"Is it too cold?" Dr. Wu mistakes my cringe.

"It's fine."

There won't be a heartbeat. This is it. The baby is dead. My baby is dead, and this is exactly what we deserve. Revenge. Karma. Justice.

I'm sorry. I'm sorry. I'm sorry.

The room is silent except for the thunder of my own heartbeat; the clatter of the busy office outside the door fades away.

I look to Lou for reassurance. My mom is tapping away at her phone, oblivious to the signs and signals that something is wrong.

And then there it is: that reassuring *whoosh, whoosh, whoosh,* the sound of a racehorse galloping across the finish line.

Little Bird's — Chase's — heart is strong as ever. I try to focus on the steady rhythm, to pay attention to the moment.

He's alive.

Dr. Wu looks confused, and I realize that I said this out loud. *He's alive.*

"Of course he is. He's developing well." Dr. Wu was there for all the miscarriages, so she understands my thirst for reassurance and patiently obliges. I'd maybe even consider her a friend if such a relationship was possible with the medical professional who has such intimate knowledge of the inner workings of your vagina.

The doctor rolls closer on her stool; our knees are almost touching. "How are you feeling, Jen? How are you feeling, really?" Her voice is thick with concern.

"I'm tired."

"Are you sleeping?"

"Not really."

"And you've been more stressed than usual," Dr. Wu says. More a statement than a question.

"Yeah."

"I'm going to be honest, but I don't want you to panic."

"We just heard his heartbeat." My skin feels like it's being stabbed with a thousand tiny needles. "It's . . . he's strong." *Chase is strong.*

Dr. Wu grabs my hand. "Yes, he is. I'm more worried about you, Jenny. Your blood pressure is high. Your feet and fingers are swollen. Have you noticed?"

I nod.

"And you know what that means?"

I do. I've googled every possible pregnancy symptom to find out what's good, bad, or meaningless. I'm aware of all the ailments

229

and disasters. "I have preeclampsia."

"Now, we don't know that yet. But I'm worried. I'm worried enough that I want to check a few more things. We might need to put you on bed rest for the remainder of the pregnancy. When moms have this condition, babies can come early. And we don't want that. We want him to get to at least thirty-six weeks, so let's keep him snug in there until then. Okay?"

"Is it stress? This is caused by stress?" Even asking the question makes my heart beat faster again. It's a vicious loop, stressing about stress.

"Not exactly. Sometimes it's genetic. Sometimes it just happens, but stress can be a factor. It can raise the blood pressure and it can sometimes exacerbate other problems." Dr. Wu goes over and starts riffling through the sleek cabinets. "I'm going to give you a shot of a steroid that will help the baby's lungs develop faster. Just in case."

There's a brown water stain on the ceiling. I zero in on it, trying to decide if it looks more like a palm tree or a pineapple as Dr. Wu pushes the needle into the fleshy part of my upper arm. I'm still pissed at my mom, but I also wish she'd scoot closer to the table and stroke my forehead the way Gigi used to when I was sick. But Lou's not

230

a toucher, never has been. At least not with me. Dr. Wu must be able to sense my need for human comfort, because, after administering the shot, she runs her own hand lightly over my hair, smoothing it away from my face.

"We're going to keep monitoring you closely, okay? I'm going to send you down to radiology for an ultrasound. They should be able to get you in within the hour. Is your mom staying with you?"

We both look at Lou, her already pale skin pastier than usual now that she's been called into action.

"I can stay."

Dr. Wu nods in approval. "I'm going to let you get dressed. Rita will be back in with the ultrasound order, and you can head down."

When the doctor opens the door, I spot the beautiful woman from the waiting room walking out of the bathroom in her flimsy paper gown, runny mascara creating black streaks down her face. When we lock eyes, I get the sense that she sees me as the lucky one today.

Lou hands me my clothes. "It's not fair. All this stress on you while you're pregnant."

"Yeah, well, isn't that what you always told me, Lou? Life isn't fair?" Lou doesn't respond as I slip back into my clothes. But it's true, nothing about this is fair. I've done everything right. I read all the books, did all the stupid breathing exercises, took all the vitamins. I've worked so hard for this, wanted it so badly. I've come this far, and I can't let it be taken from me. In my mind a slideshow plays out — butternut squash, pineapple, pumpkin, and . . . then a baby.

"Look, it's Riley."

I almost lose my balance and topple over with one leg in my jeans.

"What are you talking about?"

"Your phone just buzzed. Here." Lou thrusts it in my face, never mind that looking at my phone is none of her business.

There it is, right on the screen: Riley. The last person I'm expecting to hear from. I finish getting dressed before I swipe at the screen with my damp hands.

Hey — I have on my calendar that your appointment is today. Hope everything is okay.

"What? What'd she say?" Lou asks.

"Nothing, come on, let's go."

Riley's message and the fact that she has all of my appointments in her calendar are a surprise. A nice one. Of course, Riley would have come with me today if — if everything was different. So why am I annoyed? *"Hope everything is okay"? Well, it's not. My stress levels are crazy high, and it could hurt my baby, and you're taking the side of the people who want to lock his daddy up forever.*

"Are you okay?" Lou is racing to keep up as I practically jog to the elevators.

"No, Lou, I'm not okay. Did you hear what the doctor said? I might have pre-eclampsia. It's dangerous, okay?" I snap at her, my voice carrying down the hall.

The other woman waiting for the elevator looks at me like I'm a crazy person. I know I should be embarrassed. But I'm not, and I don't feel bad when Lou takes a cowering step backward like a beaten dog.

"What's that?" I ask, seeing something in Lou's hand. My mom holds up an ultrasound photo.

"What the hell? Did you steal that from my file?"

Lou grins. "What? I wanted it. It's not like you've ever given me one. It's my grandson." She looks down at the picture with such adoration that I'm seized by a fleeting hope. Is it possible, is there a chance that Lou would be a better grandma than she was a mom? I'm angry at myself that I even

233

allow this hope to creep into my heart.

"Give me that." I hold out my palm, and Lou lays the photo in it. I trace my finger over the dark shadows. Now that I know to look for it, I can just make out his little wee-wee.

Chase.

Chase.

Chase.

A mantra and a prayer.

CHAPTER SEVEN

RILEY

There's a boy in that coffin.

Even with Justin's picture blown up poster-size on an easel behind the casket, it's almost impossible to believe there's a child inside, a small body trapped in a wooden box soon to be buried beneath layers and layers of dirt.

Through speaker after speaker, I've tried to make sense of that. I look up to meet Justin's eyes in his photo. This one is less staged than the official school portrait Tamara gave to the media — the one where he looks like he's trying to be grown and serious and not let a smile crack his lips. In this photo, his hair is longer, a fade turning into an Afro. He looks unguarded, happy, with an adorable goofy grin wide enough to showcase the straw-size gap between his two front teeth. Like the coffin, I can't bear to look at the picture for long, or the roomful

235

of sorrowful faces. The only other choice is to stare down at my lap. According to the program, the next speaker, now walking to the podium, is the last one. He's a boy, a little younger than Justin. I recognize him from Tamara's living room. He climbs the few steps to the raised platform, approaches the podium that stands in front of the coffin. In a shaky voice, he introduces himself as Malik, one of Justin's cousins.

"He has a lot of cousins, but I'm his favorite." He giggles nervously at the obviously planned joke, and there's a scattered titter throughout the room, hundreds of mourners happy to grab on to a moment of lightness.

"I dunno what to say. . . . So I'm gonna read a poem Justin wrote for English class." He smooths a piece of paper on the podium with one hand, then the other. His spine grows at least an inch taller as he draws in a breath. His voice wobbles again when he starts to read.

What do you see when you see me?
Have you made up your mind about who
  I can be?
You could get to know me if you tried
You could see what I'm like inside

I am made of blood, bones, and muscles
   too.
So how can you say I am less than you?
I have so many dreams, even at my age.
Let me be free, don't put me in a cage.
Watch what I can do.

I bite the tip of my tongue when Malik
breaks down on the final line, written by a
boy proudly staking a claim on his future,
and who was then so cruelly robbed of it.
Watch what I can do. I do look around now
at the grief-stricken faces, and my gaze
settles on Tamara. Justin's mother grips a
tissue in her clenched fist. Otherwise she
focuses straight ahead, tearless, stoic. I know
that look. I've seen it on Gigi's face and
those of many of the other church ladies,
sometimes even my own Momma's — the
look of women who have weathered so
many brutal blows, whose scars have hard-
ened into an armor of steely resolve. *Now
there ain't no point in crying about it.* How
many times has Gigi said that to me, after
lost races or unrequited crushes? Hasn't it
been the mantra of Black women for generations? What choice do we have except to
get on with it already?

I watch Malik return to his seat, furtively
wiping at his face, and I have to swallow

hard against the wrenching sight. He walks over and practically falls into Tamara's lap for a hug, leaving a dark spot of tears on her blouse. Wes reaches over and envelops Tamara's frail frame. The Dwyers are sitting in a long line in the front row, all touching one another, each holding a hand, leaning on a shoulder, wrapped in an arm. It would be nice to have Wes's strong arm comforting me, or to have a hand to hold. Shaun was supposed to come with me today, but he had a moving gig he couldn't miss. Pastor Price is the other person I expected to know, and he deferred to the family's home church minister, who's presiding over the service.

I remind myself that I'm here to work anyway, and make a few notes in my notepad. The last line of the poem will be the ideal opening shot for tonight's package. I jot down a cue for the edit room later and start a mental list of other b-roll images that might work. This is easier, being a "reporter" instead of a "mourner." Focusing on my job helps me to push aside the complicated sorrow. It's a privilege to be here. Tamara has allowed me access, and I want to be worthy of it. Initially, she'd said she wanted the service to be small and private, and while I'll go to great lengths for a story, convincing a grieving mother to allow a camera crew into her child's funeral would have been too far. Then a few days ago, when I called to see if she needed anything — I swear my motivations were pure — she asked me if I thought it would make a difference if people saw the funeral, if she opened it to the public.

"Will they remember him? Just a little longer?" she wanted to know. "All the hashtags and signs and the T-shirts. T-shirts! I appreciate the support, but it's getting to be so it's not even about Justin anymore," Tamara continued. "And the violence, the looting, the fires. He wouldn't have wanted that."

Protesters have gathered every single night on the art museum steps, and there was another spontaneous march down Broad Street this morning in honor of the funeral. It all remained peaceful this time, but the demands for accountability on the part of the police are mounting, along with the tensions. She's right — it feels so much bigger than Justin now.

"Maybe getting to be a part of his funeral will help people heal. Maybe it will help to refocus on Justin."

"Yes. It feels to me like the entire city is grieving, and I think people would appreciate the opportunity to mourn with you. Justin's story has captured the attention of folks here in Philly and beyond, and people want to join you in honoring him. Your son isn't another victim," I said to her. "He's Justin, and it's important that the public sees that so they're able to care about him as an individual. The only way change can happen is if people care."

After all, it's too easy for people to numb themselves to these headlines until they start to tune them right out. *Yeah, yeah, another Black boy is gone, which one was that one again? St. Louis? Baltimore?*

I couldn't help adding the next part. "I'd be honored to cover the service if that's something you want."

In the end, Tamara decided to open the memorial to the public. A few days later, she even issued a public statement inviting both Kevin and Travis Cameron, but I couldn't imagine they'd dare show their faces. I was mystified as to why she'd invited them. To make them squirm? To be forced into some sort of public reckoning? Despite the fact that the spectacle of their presence would make for good TV, I'm relieved they had the good sense to stay away, and imagine she is too.

I was the only reporter allowed inside,

along with Bart to film. Scotty actually high-fived me when I told him the news, and Candace Dyson offered a "Good job, girl," in our meeting with more warmth than she'd mustered since I'd joined KYX. It was pretty unseemly to celebrate entry into a little boy's funeral, but in this business, professional wins are too often tied up in someone else's tragedy. The get was the get, and you grow used to the blurry lines. I had an old boss who would joke, "Behind every Peabody, there's a genocide."

To accommodate the crowd, the family moved the service from a small funeral home in the neighborhood to the gymnasium at Strawberry Mansion High School, where Justin had started ninth grade in September. It's a Saturday, and the varsity basketball team will play a home game here tonight, sneakers squeaking on the waxed floor, the bleachers filled with cheering fans, the smell of popcorn and Cherry Coke in the air. It will seem like a different place entirely, no longer the spot where a boy lay in a coffin right over the mascot's seal at half-court.

The school band, in which Justin had played the trombone, assembles on the stage. They begin an instrumental of Andra Day's "Rise Up." Three teenage boys, self-

241

conscious and serious, line up on one side of the coffin, and Malik, Wes, and another man on the other. The coffin lists toward the boys. They aren't strong enough to hold it level as the procession moves down the red carpet that's been laid across the shiny gym floor, forming an aisle between rows of folding chairs. The boys are almost as tall as the men, right on the cusp of manhood, like Justin, Black boys about to become Black men, a rite of passage rife with danger. All too soon these sweet boys will be seen as menacing and scary, as trespassers in places that certain people don't feel they belong, as people who deserve to be questioned or confronted, or even killed because of the color of their skin.

No one asks the crowd to stand; we rise to our feet on our own, watch the coffin move down the makeshift aisle to the hearse waiting outside. When the glossy box passes a few feet from me, I fight the urge to reach out and touch the wood. Wes catches my eye and gives me a solemn nod. I nod back and hope that with just a second of eye contact I communicate everything in my heavy heart.

Tamara follows behind the casket, head bowed low, as if it requires all of her strength to place one foot in front of the other. A small group of close friends and family will go to bury Justin in a private ceremony at Laurel Hill Cemetery — away from the spotlight and media glare, a quiet moment to say their goodbyes.

Bart comes up behind me, thirty-pound camera resting on his beefy shoulder. "Where do you want me next?"

"Let's get b-roll of the crowds and close-ups of some faces if you can. That should do it."

The package plays in my mind — opening shot of Malik, then a pan to the audience to show the sizable turnout, the casket being lifted by six pairs of hands. Cut to a close-up of Tamara. As I mentally go through the scenes, ensuring we've covered everything, I look up and into the thinning crowd, a sea of backs slowly streaming toward the two sets of double doors at the gym's exit.

A white woman in big dark sunglasses walks quickly along the back wall. Her hair is slicked back in a wet ponytail.

It can't be. It can't be her. I blink a few times to clear my vision. *It is her.* I know that walk. There's no mistaking, it's Jen. *How long has she been here? Did she see me during the service?*

A lifetime of habit makes me start after her. I stop myself. What if Bart saw me talking to Jen and started asking questions? Or worse, what would Tamara think?

I knew neither Kevin nor Travis would have the nerve to come, but Jen? It didn't even occur to me. Beyond the initial shock, I don't know what to make of it. On one hand, I suppose it's reasonable, nice even, that she wants to pay her respects. It's also brave as hell — if the crowd of mostly, but not all, brown faces had any idea she was here, it could easily "break bad," as Gigi would put it. On the other hand, I can't shake this nagging sense that Jen is trespassing. I try to bat the thought away before it takes root, but there it is: *You don't belong here.*

I fixate on her back as she makes her way down the aisle. Right as she's about to reach the doors, she turns around, pushes her sunglasses on top of her head, and meets my eyes, as if she knew exactly where to find me all along. Her eyes are red and sunken, vacant. We stare at each other for a moment that stretches and stretches. Finally, she raises a hand in the air, something like a wave. She's out the door before I can decide whether to wave back.

Two days later, the image of Jen at the funeral — her naked anguish — still haunts me. It flickers between images of the coffin and dark hands gripping bronze handles, Tamara's fingers shredding a tattered tissue. But I've got to shake it off, I've got to get my head in the game.

When I see the house — the enormous mansion, rather — I remember it. The bright white stone facade and the two iron lions flanking the front door. They scared me as a kid when we came here to trick-or-treat. My parents drove us over here to Rittenhouse after Shaun and I begged them because we'd heard that this neighborhood had the best candy — full-size Snickers. There was even a rumor people over here were giving out actual cash.

All these years later, I'm passing the lions and climbing the marble stairs dressed not in a costume of a news reporter but as one. I didn't know the family who lived here before or if it's the same one now; I just know it's the home of an obscenely rich person.

"Excuse me, miss, could you take my jacket?"

I'm barely two feet into the foyer and am too distracted by the wallpaper that appears to be made of real pony fur, not to mention the Basquiat that looms at the end of the entrance hall, to register what the man is saying.

I turn, and a white guy, my age, wearing a bright pink T-shirt under a suit jacket, is thrusting his coat at me. It clicks.

"Excuse me?" I glare at him, forcing him to admit his mistake.

"Sorry. I thought you were working here. I didn't mean . . . Shit. I'm really sorry. It's the outfit."

Yes, I'd slipped off my coat and I'm wearing black pants and a black sweater. But no, it isn't the outfit.

"It's fine," I say to him. "I'm a reporter." Why am I telling him that it's fine? Why am I justifying why I'm in this room? Because I want him to go away. I want this awkward moment to be over so I can do what I came here to do. He apologizes again and rushes into the well-heeled crowd convened in a living room that's four times bigger than my entire apartment, and infinitely more opulent. I grab a glass of sparkling water from one of the servers. Champagne would be better — to stop myself from turning around and walking right back out the door, back to my house, and crawling into bed — but I don't drink on the job. It would sure take the edge off though, and lately I'm on edge about everything, so close to the abyss, the dark thoughts like hands reaching out to pull me down into the quicksand. This is always the scariest part of depression, the panicked edge where you think, *If I can hold it at bay, stay out of its grip, I'll be okay.* The fear of the fall is so much worse than the bottom, because once you've let go, once you're in the darkness, there's comfort in the dull surrender. It's easier than the fight. But I still feel like I can push myself back from the brink. It's the reason I've been forcing myself to run every morning, why I went to church this weekend again — last week too, much to Momma's surprise and delight.

I look around the room. This is not my idea of a good time — a stuffy fundraising event with a bunch of wealthy people doing their good deed for the quarter. But Sabrina Cowell's assistant insisted it was the only time on her calendar this week and if I wanted to get five minutes of face time with the district attorney I'd need to stop by. And I desperately needed to get in front of the woman if I was going to land a live interview. Coming off the high of my interview with Tamara, I had mentioned, somewhat impulsively, in our daily news meeting that I had my sights on sitting down with the city's new upstart DA. When Scotty turned to me and said, "Get it done," it went from tentative idea to mandate before I even closed my mouth.

"Riley?" I hear my name punctuated by two taps on my shoulder.

"I'm Amina, the district attorney's chief of staff. You didn't have any problems at the door?" The young woman has the tiny frame and energy of a hummingbird, head flitting right and left to survey the scene as her fingers fly over the screen of her iPhone, sending a message, all while also talking to me.

"None at all," I lie, swallowing down the microaggression, as I've done a thousand times.

"Thanks for making the time. Sabrina's work schedule is jam-packed right now."

Not so full that she can't take time to slowly work a room, as I watch her do now across the way, rubbing elbows and eating canapés with Philadelphia's moneyed elite, who will be critical to financing her rumored mayoral campaign.

Amina continues to type words in her phone as fast as they come out of her mouth. "I'm going to introduce Sabrina — share her story. And then she'll talk for about ten minutes. She'll shake hands, take selfies, collect some checks, and then you can have ten minutes with her."

"Does she know I'm here?"

For the first time since speaking to me, Amina finally looks up at me. "DA Cowell knows everything."

I snag another glass of sparkling water as Amina heads to the front of the room and grabs a microphone. After two loud taps to test the sound, she starts speaking.

"When I graduated from Georgetown five years ago, I thought I wanted to stay in DC and be an aide on the Hill. And then I read about Sabrina Cowell and I knew I wanted to work for her, so I wrote her a fangirl letter out of the blue telling her how much I admired her career, and she said, 'Well, then, come work for me.' It was the best thing to ever happen to me, so thank you, Sabrina, for taking a chance on a complete stranger who slid into your DMs." She stops for laughter. "Many of you here tonight have heard my boss's story, but it's a good one, so I'll tell it again. Sabrina Cowell was raised right here in Philly, over in the Tasker Projects. She went to Masterman High School, received a full scholarship to Tulane and then Penn for law school, and became one of the youngest women ever and the first Black woman to make partner at Johnston Caruthers. But corporate life didn't suit her. Too much money, too little time. You all can appreciate that, right?"

Appreciative titters from the crowd.

"She found a home at Gardner and Jones, where she worked on pro bono civil rights cases against the police force with unmatched tenacity. But still . . . it wasn't enough. Change only happens in this city if you're on the inside. And so she challenged the old guard, ran a tough race, and tossed them out on their behinds. Please welcome Philadelphia's district attorney, Sabrina Cowell."

Sabrina jogs the few feet over and takes the mic from Amina after a long and what appears to be genuine hug. A hush falls over the crowd as we shuffle closer to her. It's instantly clear — before she even speaks — that she's one of those people who seem to have a field of energy around them, drawing you toward her like a magnet, all the makings of a great politician . . . or a cult leader.

I take in the full force of Sabrina's hair, which is just that — a force. A massive halo of natural corkscrew curls. If I hadn't started relaxing my hair in the eighth grade, if I weren't addicted to the "chemical crack" and my standing appointment at the hairdresser every twelve weeks on the dot, I'd want my hair to be exactly like hers. I'd also love to be able to pull off a bright magenta lip, as she does, even though Momma would insist this flashy shade was reserved for "hussies."

Sabrina scans the room before she starts talking. "A lot of people don't know that my grandmother used to clean houses here. On this very street. Hell, maybe even this very house. And who would have thought that one day her granddaughter would be here getting y'all to pay me, without dusting or shining a damn thing." A pause. "Not this girl.

"Everyone loves the story Amina told you about me. Poor girl from the hood makes good. It's the all-powerful myth of exceptionalism that people salivate over so they can use it to validate the rags-to-riches possibilities of America. If this Black girl did it, everyone else can too. So if someone doesn't, or can't, it must be a personal failing. Never mind the systemic issues stacked against people — brown people, poor people — all the barriers and disadvantages that keep the playing field in this city and this country about as level as a seesaw with an anvil on one end, and the American dream on the other. We gotta move that anvil, folks, and that's why I wanted to be the district attorney and why I'm considering a run for mayor."

She pauses as the crowd breaks into applause — the guy who handed me his coat whistles loudly — then continues. "Every one of you out there wants to change; you see yourself as social justice champions, am I right? Otherwise you wouldn't have paid five hundred dollars to be here tonight. Thank you for that, by the way." Her laugh is deep, husky.

"But as important as voting is, it's the personal changes and accountability that matter too. You think racism is so awful. You want to level that playing field I mentioned. But are you willing to acknowledge how much you benefit from white supremacy? That every single social, political, and legal system in this country is built and maintained by white people, on the bedrock idea of white power, and that allows you to move through the world with a basic confidence in your sense of safety, opportunity, and respect. That as white people you are automatically associated with everything that is good and right and 'normal,' and everyone else's experiences and value are weighed relative to that. A thousand books and movies and lessons in school have told you this was true, so much so that it's seeped into your very soul. That wasn't your fault, but what you do about it now is. So how will you confront the lie? What will you sacrifice? What are you willing to put on the line? Are you going to send your kid to the public school down the street? Are you going to rent your house to a young Black family? Are you going to hire more eager dark girls with kinky curls to be your junior executive? Because your well-meaning intentions, your woke T-shirts, your Black Lives Matter tote bags, your racial justice book clubs are not going to cut it."

She stands at the front of the room staring out at the audience, letting them simmer in an uncomfortable silence.

It's more than an hour before Sabrina can free herself from the claws of her admirers. I get lost looking for the bathroom and find myself peering into the kitchen — there are two Black or brown faces out there, including my own, but in here, there are dozens of brown people serving and washing dishes who smile at me warmly. As I wander back toward the living room, I'm about to give up when Amina appears, grabs me by the elbow, and ushers me down the hall into a quiet library where Sabrina has already made herself comfortable in one of the host's leather club chairs. I settle into the one across from her in the dimly lit, wood-paneled room like we're about to smoke some cigars and talk about our golf handicaps.

"Nice to meet you, Riley Wilson. Why'd you want to talk tonight?" Her brisk officiousness is intimidating. So much for the girlfriend-to-girlfriend vibe I'd hope we'd cultivate, hashtag BlackGirlMagic.

"Well, I'm new to KYX —"

"I know who you are, Riley. I watch you. You're a good reporter. But what *exactly* can I do for you?"

"I'm glad you think so. Then you know that I've been front and center on the Justin Dwyer story." When she nods, I say, "I want to interview you." I can get straight to the point too. "It would be a special segment like I did with Tamara Dwyer."

"I saw that. It was compelling."

"Her story, Justin's story, the shooting — it's showing the deep divisions in our community. I don't want it to get lost in the news cycle. This is an important moment. Things have to change."

Sabrina nods in agreement. "Well, I'm with you there. As you just heard, I'm all about reform. And you know how these white folks just love to be chastised, like it's their racial penance or something. Makes

254

them feel like they're learning. All they want to do is stay learning . . ." Her eyes roll with the word. "Like that does a damn thing. Let's just hope it gets them to open their checkbooks though . . ." She trails off, then turns to look at me. "Before I decide one way or another about this interview, I have a question for you."

"Yes?"

"How long have you been friends with Jennifer Murphy?"

I should have been more prepared for this, that someone would figure out our connection. The most cursory Internet search reveals it. Before I reached out to Tamara, I'd googled, "Jennifer Murphy AND Riley Wilson" to see what came up. There was one old picture of the two of us holding our medals at Penn Relays. But Facebook was a different story. Jen's profile had a lot of pictures of the two of us, more than mine, because I mostly use it for work. It was a relief when she deactivated her Facebook account a few days later. Then I'd felt gross about being so relieved. The guilt hits like I've been caught red-handed doing something wrong. And if Sabrina found out this easily, Scotty could too. Even with my exceptional talent for denial, I can see it's probably only a matter of time, and then what?

Thinking fast, I shrug like it's no big deal, like everyone knows everyone in Philadelphia, which is a little bit true. It's a city, after all, where people ask where you went to high school before they ask what you do. "Jen and I grew up in the same neighborhood," I offer carefully.

Before the shooting I would have said, "We've known each other since we were babies. We grew up together in the Northeast." But that was before. *Before. Before. Before.*

"Hmm, well, with you working on this story, it must be . . ." Sabrina raises a perfectly sculpted eyebrow as she searches for the right word. "Tricky?"

I almost laugh. *Tricky,* that's one way to describe it.

"Well, I haven't really spoken to Jenny since . . . since the incident."

"Since Justin was murdered?"

"Yes," I say; even though her word choice is meant to be a pointed provocation, it's also true.

Amina appears in the doorway, looks at her watch, and puts up five fingers. I'm sure she's been instructed to give Sabrina an escape.

"I think it's pretty clear that you're going to be the next mayor." I don't have much time to seal the deal, so I go with flattery, a shameless tactic. "That crowd loved you. And the time is right. The city needs you to shake things up."

"From your lips. Isn't it something that we are out here, still chasing firsts? The city's first Black woman DA and first mayor."

"It would be amazing, a game-changer. But I know it's tough, too. Your DA campaign was brutal. All those op-eds that said you were unhinged and unqualified, that questioned your 'electability.' "

"You don't even know the half of it. They kept calling me angry and power hungry. As if that's an insult! Hell yes, I'm angry! Yes, I'm power hungry! That's supposed to be a bad thing? Do they not realize I can't change anything without power, the power to rethink, hell, to upend, our tired policies, our practices, and our policing if we are going to get anywhere close to where we need to be? If I were a man, they'd be celebrating me for that. That's why my philosophy is WWWMD."

"I'm not even going to try to guess."

"What would a white man do?"

"Ha-ha, love that."

"Seriously though, a white man would come into this office, or a boardroom or whatever, and believe he had the duty — the power — to change things, make history, lead a charge. Well, I do too."

If I had half of Sabrina's confidence, I'd already be on the *Today* show. Forget the white man; I was going to start asking myself, *What would Sabrina do?*

"Real talk, it's time for a new day. We can't have the same old, same old. Not anymore. Not on my watch. It's a dangerous combination when we have officers with weapons and all the power, who also feel superior to the people they serve, when they look at our communities as places to control and police rather than protect and serve. The white officers approach white people one way and Black people another way, often with less humanity, less concern, less humility. That's just a fact, whether they even realize it or not. We know how it goes. On my watch, I want our justice system to have a culture of humanity, and that means weeding out the officers who don't and reallocating funds to departments that can provide services our communities need."

I think of the officer in New York who made headlines six months ago for the text he sent his supervisor letting him know that a Black suspect had died at their hands during an arrest. *Not a big deal,* he'd written. Talk about a lack of humanity.

"You can't shoot an unarmed teenager and expect zero consequences. Until people understand that fundamentally, we will have cops that are too cavalier out on our streets. We can't let officers continue to kill innocent kids, or men, or women. Period. The price is too high." Sabrina pauses. "I know we're talking about your friend here. Have you figured out whose side you're on, Riley?"

"I'm on the side of justice. And that's exactly why you should do an interview with me. Will you?"

"Your phone is buzzing," Sabrina says. When I go to switch it off, I see it's Shaun, who rarely calls over texting. Something's wrong. I fumble to press the green button. As soon as I hear his voice, quivering with anguish, I have a childlike fantasy that if I hang up now, the words he's saying won't be true.

CHAPTER EIGHT

JEN

Snow falls in sheets as thick as paste, coating my windshield, hopeless against the wipers. After days of increasingly manic weather reports, the first storm of the season is here. Action News meteorologist Hurricane Schwartz started calling it "Snowmageddon" in his frenzied forecasts, advising the greater Philadelphia area to hunker down and stay off the roads. Everyone seems to have listened. Everyone but me.

My hands are slick on the steering wheel. I push my foot on the brake, and the car fishtails on the slippery road. I haven't driven in weather this bad for more than a decade, not since that time I drove to Chicago to pick up Riley for winter break her sophomore year at Northwestern. I was dying to visit her at college, and driving was cheaper than a plane ticket. So I'd hopped in my ten-year-old Camry and hit the road, only to be waylaid when a record-making blizzard descended on the turnpike right outside Pittsburgh.

I had no choice but to wait it out at a cheap motel. I was sure the place had bedbugs. But I didn't care that it was the drive from hell, not once I saw Riley standing there inside her dorm lobby waiting for me, looking like some model for a college brochure, fresh-faced, hair in a loose bun, wearing a bright yellow Medill School of Journalism sweatshirt. Meanwhile, my hair was a greasy blob and I was covered in orange crumbs from the bag of Doritos I'd plowed through during the final twenty miles. I threw my arms around her anyway, Dorito dust and all. Riley was the RA that year and lived in a single that also looked straight out of a brochure: framed poster of *Starry Night,* bright pink mini-fridge, a photo collage filled with people I didn't know.

If Riley noticed my weird mood during her enthusiastic tour of the beautiful, snow-blanketed campus or lunch at a local sushi restaurant (*Riley eats sushi now?*), she didn't let on. As I fumbled with my chopsticks, she asked where I wanted to go that night: a Kappa Alpha Psi frat party ("It's a Black fraternity," she explained), or karaoke with some of her friends from the college paper. We got ready in the dingy communal bathroom, pregaming with a box of wine, pretending we knew how to contour our cheekbones. It felt like the beginning of an epic night. Until Riley announced that Gabrielle would be joining us. Even though we'd never met, I was convinced that Gaby — the famous Gaby I never stopped hearing about, like she was some kind of celebrity or something — didn't like me. It was silly, but sometimes I convinced myself that Riley had moved on, and Gaby was my replacement, and the two of them sat around talking smack about me all the time. Or worse, that they didn't talk about me at all. If Gabrielle did hate me, she didn't let it show. Still, I tried too hard that night, loudly reminding Riley of our shared history, trotting out our best memories and inside jokes so Gabrielle would see *She's mine.*

In the small room of a Korean karaoke bar near campus with the strobe lights flashing, a giant disco ball floating over the stage, Riley and I belted out the lyrics to "Shoop," "Since U Been Gone," and our go-to classic: "Real Love." It was strange to see how much Riley had come out of her shell — singing, laughing, even grinding her hips against some guy from her Intro to Psych class. She seemed so confident, sure of herself, now that she was out here in the world and basically the model student: editor of the college newspaper, dean's list, treasurer of her class. It made me wonder how Riley saw me now. As a loser who hadn't gone to college? Someone she was outgrowing? I hated all this self-doubt and threw myself into shot after shot of something called a Wild Willie, to chase it away, until my mood finally shifted from gloomy to sentimental. I watched as Riley sang "I Wanna Dance with Somebody," one hand in the air, the other around a bright pink vodka concoction, and I danced right up next to her, our sweaty bodies moving side by side.

"We're always going to be friends, right?" I screamed into her ear.

She turned to look at me like I was a little crazy. "Of course, silly."

I could barely make out the words over the music, but I know that's what she said. Then she grabbed my arm so I'd look at her again, raised her finger to her left eyebrow, and pulled me close to her as the bass pulsed through us like a heartbeat.

I woke up with a throbbing headache the next day, pressed against Riley in her twin bed, staring at the calendar over her desk, the little squares filled with due dates and tests and plans, and thought, *This could have been my life. This* should *be my life.* I tried to blame the bitterness on hangover anxiety. I know it was something else though, something uglier: jealousy. Riley was having the time of her life, while I was waitressing at the Olive Garden, which left me smelling like garlic and was giving me love handles thanks to all the unlimited breadsticks.

It didn't help that every single time Riley had introduced me to someone, they'd asked where I went to college, and all I could say was, "Oh, I'm not in school," trying not to sound defensive about it. I wasn't going to admit that I'd already dropped out of community college.

Their surprised and awkward reactions were humiliating, as if I'd confessed I didn't own a pair of shoes. All those kids assumed college was a foregone conclusion, like breathing. It didn't even occur to them that Riley would have a friend who didn't go. I remember the day we both got into Drexel. I must have stared at the photos on the "Welcome" brochure for hours, imagining myself lying in the grass in the quad, laughing with my new friends, or tapping away on a shiny new laptop covered in cool stickers. Riley and I side by side for everything.

And then there'd be Lou's proud expression when she saw me in my cap and gown and toasted me as the first in our family to graduate from college. Instead, Lou narrowed her eyes when I handed her the acceptance letter and financial aid documents. "I don't do banks, and we ain't gonna qualify for free money, because I don't want the government knowing how much I make. That's exactly why I don't file taxes. Don't need to let those imbeciles waste my hard-earned money. Sorry, Charlie."

I pretended I only applied to see if I could get in and that I didn't care one way or another. And I pretended to be happier than I actually felt when Riley was offered scholarship after scholarship, three total to my none, even though we ran the same relay in high school, got the same times, won the same medals. I celebrated at the Wilsons' with a sheet cake under a giant arc of purple and white balloons when Riley decided to go to Northwestern, but the bitterness was something I could taste, like the too-sweet strawberry icing, every time I thought about how I could have gotten a scholarship and gone to college if I'd been Black like my best friend. Then I hated myself for thinking that. Riley worked hard, harder than me, harder than anyone. And of course she deserved good things. She deserved everything.

This keeps happening to me lately, random memories of Riley popping up, stuff I haven't thought about in years. As if to taunt me, unbelievably, "I Wanna Dance with Somebody" blares out of the speakers. I flick off the radio, shutting Whitney Houston right up. Now there's only the muffled hush of heavy snow falling around the car, broken by the rhythmic swoosh of the wipers. The car fishtails again as I slow at a light on the empty road and curse myself for how incredibly stupid I was to have snuck out of my in-laws' house in this weather, but there's a box of photos I gotta get from our place. I need the pictures to finish Kevin's present — a scrapbook — in time for Christmas. Cookie's got all the supplies in her craft room, and I keep telling myself it's thoughtful and not lame, the tried-and-true rationale for everyone who can't afford a real gift. I have one more payment left on Kevin's new bulletproof vest, and I could have swung it, but what's the point now, with him on leave, everything in limbo? The wheels spin as I accelerate, searching for traction, and Chase does a flip in my stomach as if to remind me of the stakes of my recklessness. If Kevin knew I was out here

266

in this weather, he would lose it — he's seen too many fatal accidents. I snuck out of the house after everyone was asleep. Kevin FaceTimed with Ramirez for a good hour earlier, after I begged and pleaded with him to finally call his friend back. Ramirez has called twice a day since the shooting, sometimes more, but Kevin's been dodging him.

"I can't handle talking to him, Jenny," he told me. "I keep thinking about how if he hadn't left, then I wouldn't have been paired with Cameron, and none of this would have happened. I can't blame Ramirez for moving. That's crazy, but . . ."

Tonight I shoved the phone in his face when Ramirez called. "Just talk to him. He loves you." I needed his mood to be someone else's responsibility and I thought it might cheer him up, but it completely backfired.

"Ramirez kept asking me to go over exactly what happened, like I haven't already done that a thousand times." He was clearly upset about something Ramirez had said to him but wouldn't tell me what it was. When they drove together every day, they might have bickered like two old men on a fishing trip, but I couldn't remember a time when they were actually mad at each other. He stomped off to the basement to play video games, and by the time I slipped out of the house, he'd fallen asleep on the ratty old futon.

I hit the brakes to slow down, and the car slides again, sending a fresh wave of anxious chills through me. *You've come too far to turn around now.* Besides, this late at night, in the middle of a snowstorm, is probably the only time I can get into my own house without being harassed by the media or protesters. Even after nearly three weeks, there are still a few stubborn reporters camped out there, hoping to thrust a microphone in our faces, or protesters who throw eggs at our front door. Mrs. J still texts me constantly with updates, including the fact that other people on our street have been complaining.

Please say sorry to the other neighbors, was all I could send back. What else was there to say? Our neighbors hate us now too. *Join the club.*

I switch off the headlights as I pull into the cul-de-sac and sit in the car, squinting into the darkness. The street's eerily quiet; a few lights dot windows here and there. It feels safe enough to go inside. Still, my heart races as I trudge to the front door, keys at the ready. Between my huge belly and the heavy snow boots, tight on my swollen ankles, I'm about as graceful as a moose in heels, but I move as quickly and stealthily as I can, a thief breaking into my own home.

By the first step of the porch, I spot the streaks of dried egg yolk that dribble down our black front door. As I turn the key in the lock and step forward, something squishes beneath my boot — a white plastic bag that had blended in with the snowdrifts. I know exactly what's inside without touching it: someone has left a bag of human shit on our doorstep.

I choke back a gag and throw open the front door. It catches on a mountain of mail, mostly bills, some catalogs and grocery store circulars. I groan as I bend over awkwardly to gather up the pile. Bending over has become such a challenge that anything I drop on the floor is just dead to me. I tiptoe to the kitchen before I have a chance to wonder why I'm sneaking around an empty house. Am I worried I'll wake the ghosts of our former life?

The pile of mail lands on the kitchen table with a thud; I jump at the sound. I turn on the light over the oven instead of the overhead. No reason to alert the neighbors that I'm back after all this time. Shards of my POCONOS IS FOR LOVERS mug, the one I was drinking from the morning after the shooting, are still scattered across the tile floor. The daisies on the table are brown and wilted.

I glance over at the Realtor's exam book on the counter, its glossy cover dulled by a thin layer of dust. The test is scheduled for next week. I've already decided not to bother; it feels silly now. It's not like I told anyone other than Kevin that I was taking it anyway. I was waiting until I passed — if I passed — to spring the news. Riley would be so proud of me, and maybe even a little shocked. I can still see the look on her face when I told her I was quitting my job. I didn't imagine the judgment there. It's not like I'm dying to be a stay-at-home mom; it's not really a choice. We did the math, and day care costs more than my salary, so we'd essentially lose money if I continued working. But now I'll have to find a way. I have to be prepared to support my family, whatever may come.

I drag the trash bin over to the fridge and open it, holding my nose against the spoiled food that awaits me inside. I pour the rancid milk down the sink, drop the carton in the trash. I walk over to the table, grab the dead flowers, and dump them in too, then drop the vase in the sink after pouring out the thick sludge of brown water. A sharp stab of pain in my back makes me double over and grab the counter ledge. Just a cramp, but it's happening more and more. Everything hurts all the time. My boobs throb like they've been slammed in a vise; my lower back pinches; a dull ache has settled into my hip bones. At least my blood pressure is better. As soon as I left my doctor's appointment last week, I went straight to Walgreens and bought myself a monitor. I take my blood pressure obsessively now, at least a dozen times a day.

When the pain lets up, I ease myself into a chair at the kitchen table and flip through the mail. I don't know why I bother when I know exactly what's inside this stack of envelopes: angry demands for money with lots of red ink. The electricity will be shut off if we don't pay the PECO bill soon. We owe the fertility doctor about ten grand, and our credit cards are maxed out. For now, Kevin still has his health insurance, even though he's on administrative leave, but if something happens before the baby is born and we lose our health insurance . . . I press my fingers to my temples, hard, to shut down the thought.

The stack of bills reminds me that we'll never get out of debt: $36,460. The exact amount flashes in my brain like a neon sign. I lied to Riley that it was $30,000, told myself that I was just rounding down. Besides, at a certain point, it doesn't even matter. It's like a six-foot-deep hole; what's another six inches when you're trying to climb out?

I let the bills fall into the trash one by one. I'd rather set them on fire, watch all these stupid numbers go up in smoke. I settle for the garbage, without even opening them, because what the hell — they'll just send more anyway. At the bottom of the stack of mail are two plain envelopes, hand-addressed to Kevin. At least they're not bills. They're probably something worse.

My index finger catches on the lip of the envelope. It tears a small gash across my skin. I put my finger in my mouth to suck away the blood and examine the paper inside. It takes me a second to register what I'm seeing — an image of a coffin, Justin Dwyer's coffin — and to make sense of the words across the top. *BABY KILLER.* I toss the paper away from me like it's on fire.

Seeing this picture is almost as wrenching as the real-life version. Attending that funeral has to be one of the most terrifying things I've ever done. I'm still not exactly sure why I forced myself to go — maybe to torture myself? To make amends? To prove something? But what was I proving? I have no idea. Maybe it was that I owed them, him and his mother. I owed it to them to acknowledge what happened even if I, we, couldn't take it back — no one could. Obviously, Kevin couldn't have gone. But no one thought I should go either.

"For God's sake," Cookie had said, "what good will it do?"

Nothing. It would do absolutely nothing. It wouldn't bring the boy back. It wouldn't return the bullets to my husband's gun. I went anyway.

In a sea of all those people, Riley was the first person I saw, or the back of her head, really. I fixated on her sleek French twist the entire service so I could avoid making eye contact with anyone around me. The few faces I glimpsed looked wounded or angry.

When the uncle stood to speak, his eyes had been wide with fury. It was like he was speaking directly to me when he asked, "Why, why, why?" in a voice so desperate I had to look away.

The middle-aged Black woman sitting beside me in the back row moaned like she had a hurt deep in her bones. "When will they stop killing our boys?" she said. It was almost exactly what one of the LEO wives, a white woman, had said back at Jamal's funeral.

"When's it going to stop? When are these streets going to be safe for our boys?" Same streets, different boys.

During Justin's funeral, each time I caught Riley glancing over at Tamara, all distressed and concerned, was like being stabbed with a dagger. I get that this is unfair, horrible of me, petty even, but sometimes it's easier to be angry. It's easier to let myself think, *Fuck Riley.*

At the end of the service, as I was walking out, emotionally exhausted, I sensed her eyes on the back of my head. I even had this pathetic hope that she'd call out to me, that maybe we could talk for a few minutes, though I know this was stupid of me — dangerous even — on a lot of levels. I'd hoped to at least see that familiar affection on my friend's face, but there was only her blank canvas stare, her mask, as I raised my hand, a hello and a goodbye at once.

I pick up the picture of the casket and slowly tear it in half, then in half again. I'm furiously ripping it into smaller and smaller shreds. The white flecks litter the floor around me like the snow outside. When I'm done, I reach for the other envelope, ready for something else to destroy. What will it be this time? A death threat? Anthrax? I'm surprised to find a personal check made out to Kevin from something called the Order of Kings. For $10,000. I must be seeing things. I hold it up again, closer this time, and the numbers are right there: *$10,000.* The note is one line in a handwritten scrawl. *We protect our own.*

Who the hell are these guys? I google "the Order of Kings" on my phone. Their website has a hazy description, but its imagery (a skull made of the Confederate flag) and their mission statement ("righteous people, fighting to preserve White Western culture") tell me everything I need to know.

I'm about to click on the menu to learn more about "Our History" when an Instagram notification appears on the screen.

The fact that I've kept my Instagram account is a dirty secret. Julia Sanchez made it clear that we're supposed to be completely off social media. It makes sense to protect myself from the online equivalent of shit on my doorstep. I deleted my Facebook account altogether after it filled up with vile rants. Annie says I should have kept it just to log in to the police wives FB group so that I would have support, but I still haven't been active at all, really, since I posted a couple of cute pictures of Kevin in his uniform back in the early days. Annie sends me screenshots sometimes of the messages, which is nice. A woman named Barb I met at the FOP coat drive last year wrote, *God made strong women police wives, you know. If He didn't think we could handle it He woulda given us accountants or dentists. But He gave you and me cops because he knew we could take it. When other people walk away from danger our men walk toward it. And we have their six. And all of us have yours too, Jennifer.* But the couple of times I logged on myself before I deleted my account, there were a few messages that made me queasy. Like one chick who said, *Hey, they're either with us or against us and we're the ones with guns.*

But somehow I can't quit Instagram. From time to time over the last few weeks — mostly in the middle of the night — I force myself to look. The pain is like pressing on a bruise as I read endless rants about the police, or look at happy carefree families on stupidly gorgeous beaches, or see ads for extensions that make me miss my long hair — the usual terrible but addictive schizophrenic medley. It's all a bunch of empty bullshit, like everyone's just trying to outdo each other for the likes. If only we could keep it completely real. Like, what would happen if I posted right now, bloodshot eyes, ratty hair, a caption that reads, "I give up. We ARE monsters." How many likes would I get for that? My fingers keep swiping. *Don't do it,* I tell myself, even as the app opens.

I navigate to the home feed, the most recent photo, and I'm overcome with that disorienting feeling you get when you see someone out of context, your teacher at the grocery store, your doctor in a public restroom. I know the person is familiar, but I still can't quite place her. It's an old black-and-white picture from the sixties — a tall Black woman leans against an old car, wearing white gloves, a pillbox hat.

Gigi.

But Gigi isn't on Instagram. In fact, one of her favorite things to say is, "Why do they call them smartphones when they're really making you dumb?" I swipe to the next image. It's from her eighty-fifth birthday party, which I know because I was there. Gigi's holding court on the big old red armchair we'd pulled out into the stamp-size backyard of the Wilsons' house like she was a queen. The picture reminds me how much I miss her. I gotta find a way to get to the hospital. Then I see Shaun's caption.

Rest in Peace, Gigi.

No, no, no. It's not possible. Once all this settles down, I am going to visit her in the hospital. She's going to rub my belly and tell me my baby's future. I squeeze my eyes closed, trying to process the news — first that Gigi's dead, and then that I had to find out about it on Instagram. It's like I've been slapped across one cheek and then the other. I pick up my phone, start scrolling through missed calls and texts. Maybe I missed a call from Riley or Mrs. Wilson, a text from Shaun . . . *something.* There's nothing. Nothing but the usual string of unfamiliar numbers. No one bothered to tell me that Gigi died. That fact is devastating, almost as devastating as the death itself.

I return to the first photo, stare at it for a while, Gigi leaning up against the car, full of swagger, an expression like she's discovered all the secrets in life and might share them with you if you're lucky. I start drowning in memories, they just keep coming — all the nights I couldn't sleep, would creep out of Riley's bed and find Gigi, also an insomniac, sitting in her La-Z-Boy crocheting an afghan or watching old movies.

"How's my little firecracker? Can't sleep either?" she'd say as I crawled into her lap, ready for another one of her stories. My favorites were the ones about her "heyday," when she moved to Harlem for a few years in her twenties and got a job selling cigarettes at a jazz club called Bill's Place, and how she almost married a professional boxer named Z, but then she met his cousin Leroy, who was visiting from Tennessee. Leroy grinned at her with a gap in his teeth "as wide as the East River" and told her they didn't make women like her in Kingsport, and the rest was history.

"Chile, he swept me up like a Hoover. Didn't know what hit me."

Leroy was hit too, literally. Z broke his nose. It was never straight again after that, but according to Gigi he'd always said it was worth it. Was there anything more glamorous than the image of young Gigi working in a nightclub, out on the town with Leroy, drinking martinis in smoke-filled bars? Not to me.

It was in Gigi, and only Gigi, that I'd confided when one of Lou's boyfriends pulled me onto his lap, slid his filthy hands under my shirt, and asked if I was "a good girl," if I liked the way he touched me. It had left me with a sludgy, confused feeling oozing through my body.

"Some men ain't kind, sweetie. Some men are. We need to protect each other from the bad ones, because no one else will," Gigi whispered as she rocked me gently. "So if that man ever touches you again, so help me God I'mma go to your mama's house to give him a beatdown he won't forget. You tell him that, you hear?"

The next time he went to tickle me, I looked him straight in his beady eyes and said, "I told my grandmother that you were a bad man. You better not touch me. Or else." I'd never felt so powerful, never mind that he laughed in my face. He also never touched me again.

Some nights Gigi and I would wander to the dark kitchen and snack on string cheese or slices of deli meat. Or I'd convince her to make her famous miracle bread — slices of white bread soaked and fried in butter, a mixture of brown sugar and cinnamon on top, then sprinkled with bacon bits. Suddenly, that's all I want. I'm desperate for some miracle bread. I make my way over to the fridge. *Please, please let there be what I need.*

Thank God. There's a half loaf of white bread frozen in the freezer. I don't even remember buying it or putting it in there, but there it is, and that's a miracle itself. I have plenty of butter and sugar. I've been baking cookies for Kevin's overtime shifts at the Eagles game to make all the extra hours a little more bearable for him.

As long as I'm cooking, Gigi is still right here with me, telling me I need to put some meat on my bones. The bread sizzles in the pan and I dump another pat of butter over it, exactly the way Gigi would've done. It's all brown and bubbly on the edges now. I pull it out of the pan right before it burns and spoon sugar and cinnamon a half inch high on top. There aren't any bacon bits in the house, but this will do. Butter drips through my fingers onto my sweater as I bring the slice to my mouth and shove it in, letting the sweet mixture coat the back of my throat like cough syrup.

I need to find out when the funeral will be. Probably this weekend. I press my fingers on my phone screen, leaving greasy smudges. Gigi once told me she wanted to be buried in Alabama. Can I swing a ticket? Would Dr. Wu even let me fly?

I open one of those travel websites on my phone and do a quick search. Fifteen hundred dollars for a last-minute flight, and it's not even direct. The check from the Order of the Kings seems to glow on the table. Ten thousand dollars would cover a plane ticket — and a whole lot more. I can't though. We aren't those people.

Not having the option to go to the funeral is a relief in a way though. It means I don't have to confront the real question, which is almost too much to bear — would I even be welcome? I mean, no one told me she died. Are they mad at me too? Is everyone mad at me? Shaun's Instagram had pictures of the Wilsons at Justin's march. Mr. Wilson held a sign that said, IT COULD HAVE BEEN MY SON. Shaun had one that read, WHITE SILENCE IS VIOLENCE. I've been thinking about that a lot. *White silence is violence.* I thought back to Blazer again. How I didn't say anything when he called the Wilsons niggers. How I never stop Cookie from saying "those people" or Matt from calling them animals. Was my silence as bad as their slurs? I've always tried to make the Wilsons love me. Whenever I stayed over at their house as a kid, I worked so hard to get on Sandra's good side, carefully washing any dish I used, painstakingly folding my sleeping bag with perfect corners in the morning. I even volunteered for weekend chores. There was no greater feeling than waking up Saturday morning, watching cartoons around the kitchen table — and when Mrs. Wilson mentioned that day's activity and Shaun would say, "Jenny's comin' too, right?" Even if Sandra didn't always look fully enthused to have a scabby-kneed little white girl tagging along to the fountain or the zoo. But I was family. *Right?* And okay, I haven't been by the Wilsons' since last Christmas Eve, when I was a hot mess, and I didn't make it to the hospital to visit Gigi, and I've been slacking when it comes to acknowledging holidays and birthdays, but that doesn't make it less true. Yet here I am, like a dog left on the doorstep when the owners move away to some nice new place that doesn't allow pets.

I don't know what to do. Should I comment on Shaun's post? Should I text Riley? I open our text chain and see her last message, checking in about my thirty-week appointment. I'd been too pissed off about her interview with Tamara to respond. Now I can't find the words. This shouldn't be so hard. I scroll further up and see how long our text chain stretches, a blur of white and blue bubbles. I might never reach the end, or the beginning. The stream is a veritable time capsule of every aspect of our lives — proof of our friendship, our closeness, our connection. There have been moments where Riley has disappointed me over the years, or frustrated me, but she has never, until now, broken my heart. The phone itself is painful to look at. I want to throw it out the window. I settle for turning it off completely, in effect turning off the world of bad news, my bittersweet memories. Maybe I'll never turn it on again.

I hear a rustling outside and instinctively crouch down, move slowly to the back of the house. It's become more of a tap; maybe I'm imagining it. I make my way over to the patio door. The curtains are drawn. I pause, crouched, listening. There it is again, louder this time. I dare to peek behind the curtain into the backyard. A shadowy figure stands less than a foot from the glass. My scream is so loud the door rattles.

"It's just me, hon."

The stranger's features arrange themselves into Mrs. J, bundled inside a long puffy coat, her little yappy dog tucked beneath one arm. Shocks of bright red hair peek out around the fur-lined hood wrapped tightly around her face.

"I was up watching Jimmy Fallon and saw the light and figured it was you," Mrs. J says through the door as I fiddle with the lock.

A blast of frigid air slams into me when I open it, though the snow seems to have stopped. I should take advantage of the lull and get the hell back to Cookie's. Mrs. J hands me a small box. "I grabbed this when the UPS guy came the other day. I opened it. Just in case . . ."

Neither of us needs her to finish that thought. I pull up the cardboard flaps, look inside. Neatly folded on top of delicate tissue paper is the onesie I ordered after seeing it for 50 percent off on one of my mommy blogs. The fabric is as white and soft as a newborn bunny. Across the front it reads, "Hello, World!" in a graceful script. I'd forgotten all about it.

I turn on the porch light so I can show Mrs. J, and accidentally flip the backyard switch at the same time. The adorable little onesie falls to the floor as the sight behind her comes into focus.

Across the back fence, the fence Kevin and Matt spent an entire weekend building, there are three-foot-high letters, in bright red paint that drips like blood: MURDERER.

Mrs. J doesn't even turn to look at the fence — she just stares at me, pained. "I already called my grandson. You remember — Bobby. He's going to come paint over it this weekend."

I can't speak.

"Jenny, don't you worry. We're going to get that painted over, good as new." Mrs. J gently pushes me inside. "Come on, it's cold out here. Let's get you indoors."

I let myself be carried along back into the

kitchen.

"I'm going to make you a cup of tea. Everything's going to be okay. You hear me, Jen? It's going to be okay."

But it's not. Nothing is okay. There's no okay after this. There's no okay after you're the reason someone is no longer alive on this earth. I love my husband and I made a vow to stand by him for better or worse, but never did I think that worse would include my son being raised by a man who murdered a child.

No, Mrs. J, it will never be okay again.

CHAPTER NINE

RILEY

That the grief is so physical, tangible, is a surprise. It's heavy, as burdensome as the overnight bag pressing into my shoulder that I let fall to the ground with a thud in front of the Hertz counter. The clerk, a girl who looks like she's barely out of high school, wears a bedazzled Santa hat over her bright pink hair. She's drawn hearts around her name — Tiffany — on her name tag. Before she opens her mouth, I already know Tiffany is going to be too much, too perky, too cheerful.

"Heya, ma'am."

Ma'am? I haven't been called ma'am since I left Birmingham.

"Omigod, I love that nail polish color! How was your flight?! Ain't it lovely out today?!"

Every single one of her sentences ends in an exclamation point. I don't know what to

287

latch on to first in that overwhelming greeting.

"Yeah, sure is warm," I respond with as much enthusiasm as I can muster. Thankfully, while she's looking up my reservation, she turns her chatter to her colleague at the neighboring counter, a prim elderly white woman with a helmet of blue-gray hair, who's helping an older Black guy, decked out from head to toe in Miami Dolphins gear.

I fight the urge to look at my watch or tap the counter impatiently as Tiffany recounts her Saturday night in excruciating detail. Outwardly, I plaster my face with a polite smile. Inside, I'm screaming. *No one cares!!! How could you possibly think anyone cares about any of this? Someone spilled wine on your new hobo bag. Oh, you poor little thing. My grandmother died six days ago. She's gone, Tiffany. Gone.*

The Dolphins fan shoots me a commiserating eye roll. He takes a step toward me, close enough now for me to see the keloid scars from old acne that dot his chin and smell the cigar smoke on his aqua-and-orange Starter jacket. When he opens his mouth to speak, I catch the glint of more than one gold crown.

"Hey, can you give me directions to the

288

lynching memorial?" he asks in a slow, lazy drawl.

The clerk helping him, the elderly lady, interjects, probably to escape Tiffany's inane ramblings. "I think you mean the National Memorial for Peace and Justice," she corrects him, the patronizing tone unmistakable.

"Well, yeah, same thing," he replies, throwing me a knowing glance. *These white people.*

The woman unfolds a large map and pulls out a plastic pen. "I'll circle it here for you. It's very close. About fifteen minutes from here."

"I hear it's pretty powerful," the man says.

The clerk offers a vague nod. She obviously hasn't been there.

Even grief can't shake my compulsion to fill the quiet, to make everyone around me comfortable at all times. "I've read a lot about it. The memorial and the Legacy Museum down the road from it too. They're supposed to be incredible."

"Well, you're here, you might as well check it out," he says. "I'm Willie, by the way." He extends a hand.

"Nice to meet you." I don't offer my name as he pumps my hand vigorously up and down.

Willie has at least two decades on me, and there's something about his slightly flirty vibe that makes me think he's angling to invite me along. Figures, my only action in ages would be with a man old enough to be my father at a museum dedicated to racial terror.

"Oh, well, I'm already late. I need to get to Perote." I'm not sure why I bother to say the name of a dot on a map no one has heard of like it's New York City.

"Never heard of it. Where's that?"

"A little town, if you could even call it that, about an hour south of here."

I will Tiffany to hurry up and finish with my paperwork so I can escape. I'd forgotten this about the South, the incessant small talk that draws out every errand and interaction twice as long as it needs to be. Sure enough, Willie shifts toward me now, fully invested in our chat. "And what brings you down here?"

It's a reasonable question — a predictable one — and yet the answer doesn't want to come out of my mouth. "Oh, uh, it's actually my grandmother's funeral." The convivial mood is ruined as everyone suddenly looks at me with sympathy. The upside is that introducing death into the conversation might make Tiffany get me the keys already.

"Oh, well, I'm sorry for your loss," Willie says with genuine compassion. "My moms died last month. It, well, it's tough."

My back stiffens when he turns to me; I'm irrationally afraid he's going to hug me. Then I feel bad for tilting backward and force myself to lean into the conversation again. He nods and tells me to be strong as he walks toward the exit.

Be strong. God knows I'm trying.

His words have me slipping right back to the night Gigi died. Momma said the same thing when we were gathered around Gigi's bed. "We have to be strong. We have to be strong." The doctors had stabilized Gigi after she'd suffered a stroke. She was unconscious but looked peaceful. You almost wouldn't know her organs were shutting down, even though the doctor had explained that was exactly what was happening. I made it to the hospital in time, which will always be one of the things I am most grateful for in this life. When I arrived, the first person I saw was my dad, staring vacantly into a vending machine down the hall.

"Daddy?"

He jumped a little, coming back from wherever he was. "Oh, hey, baby, come here." He reached over, pulled me close. In the glass of the machine, I could see our reflection, how much we look alike, same round eyes and large forehead, same sadness.

"How you holding up, Daddy?"

"I'm fine. It's your mother we need to worry about. You know this is — this is it, right?" He looked at me solemnly. He wanted me to be prepared. If there's one thing my dad always wants, it's for me to be prepared, for anything, everything in life.

But I wasn't prepared for this, for losing Gigi. I nodded anyway. I knew that was what he needed to hear.

"How's Momma holding up?"

"Oh, you know how she is. She's making unreasonable demands of the nurses and of Jesus . . . going on about miracles. I keep trying to tell her that she has to let Gigi go, but I know that's easier said than done. She should be grateful it's so peaceful."

The look on his face made me wonder if he was thinking about his own parents. They'd died before I was born, on their way from Baltimore to Philadelphia on a Greyhound bus that crashed. "Here one second, gone the next," was how Daddy always put it. The modest settlement from the crash helped pay for my education, which makes me feel connected to the grandparents I never got to meet.

I reluctantly pulled myself out of his arms. "We should get in there. I want to . . . I want to say goodbye, I guess."

It was the last thing I wanted to do.

And now we're here, about to bury Gigi at sundown, and again it's the last thing I want to do.

I glance down at my watch. It's 11 a.m. If I leave now, I'll still arrive in plenty of time for the service. I can spare an hour to visit the memorial. And the man had a point: I'm here, I might as well. When else am I going to be in Montgomery?

By the time Tiffany hands me the packet of papers and keys to my economy rental, I've decided to make the detour. I shoot a text to Shaun, letting the family know I'll be a little later than expected. I want to be with my family, but the pull of the memorial is stronger, a need I can't explain or ignore. *Jimmy.*

Turning into the parking lot itself brings on a sense of reverence and dread, as if this patch of asphalt is already hallowed ground. My breath grows shallow as I approach the entrance, almost like I'm afraid, which I am: afraid of how this place might affect me. I already feel fragile, like I'm walking around with an open wound.

Don't fight the tears. I haven't cried once

since Gigi died, even though crying may be exactly what I need. Maybe that explains this weight I've been carrying around with me, all the unshed tears.

I arrive at a sign near the entrance and stand next to a heavyset white woman who reads it with one hand over her mouth, an apprehensive grimace on her face. I need to move past her before she makes eye contact or looks to me for some sort of reassurance or says something like, *God it's so awful,* and I'll be forced to comfort her. The words on the sign have hit me hard too.

For the hanged and beaten.
For the shot, drowned, and burned.
For the tortured, tormented, and
   terrorized.
For those abandoned by the rule of law.
We will remember.

A little boy, maybe four or five, runs toward me, wearing a shirt that reads, "I Am My Ancestors' Wildest Dream." His giggles carry through the air, both welcome and out of place. Otherwise, the small crowd dotting the grounds is quiet, reverent.

I make my way toward the pavilion, where enormous red stones hang from the ceiling.

Each is engraved with the names of victims, thousands and thousands of lynching victims, county by county. The crushing weight of the stones, of history, the pain of my ancestors, feels like grief. A group of people — probably a tour — huddles together, but no one speaks, as if they're all stunned into silence, reckoning with the atrocities, presented as they are with such unflinching honesty.

I spot Willie standing with his head bowed, chin to his chest. I move closer and see two wet streaks down both of his cheeks. Before I can stop myself, I walk over to him, so we're shoulder to shoulder, in wordless communion. Something about this man's presence, about not being alone here, comforts me.

"My granddaddy," he says finally. "William Franklin. That was his name." He points a long finger at the etching in the burnt-red stone. There are four other names too. Five men tortured and killed.

I whisper the names to myself, adding another: *Jimmy.* I have no idea if Willie has more to say and decide to wait as long as it takes. When he finally speaks, I have to move closer to hear him.

"It was '44. Granddad just back from the war. Fought with the Ninety-Second over in

Italy. He'd opened up a little shop in town, was doing well for himself. The war gave him a sense of dignity, you know? But the white boys didn't like that too much. Especially when he was cutting into their business. A posse of them came one night. Hit my grandma Thelma on the head when she asked what they wanted with her husband. She was pregnant with my moms. Grandpa didn't even know yet. She was waiting until she was sure. They left her there bleeding on the floor while they ransacked the place. Grandpa had a few bottles of hooch that they drank, and then they dragged Willie out the house. Grandma says they talked about how they were going to rough him up, but he started fighting back. So they shot him. Shot him like a dog in his own yard." He takes a quick inhale, almost like he's catching a sob, before he gets to the last part. "He never even knew he was going to have a daughter."

I'm not sure when I grab Willie's hand, but I'm holding it when he stops talking. Much to my surprise, it feels like the most natural thing in the world.

There's a part of me that wants to tell him about Jimmy. But I can't. It's too much. This air, already heavy around us, doesn't need any more tragic stories. He squeezes my fingers like he knows there's meaning here for me too. Without speaking, we make our way over to the pristine grounds, the grass a neon green, the sun a radiant yellow ball against a sea of blue, all of it incongruous to the bloody history all around us. It's hard to imagine that people were lynched on bright, beautiful days like this, but surely they were.

"Willie. You have the same name as him." I make the connection.

"Yeah, quite the legacy, I guess." His tone, bittersweet. "What about you? You never told me your name."

"Riley. Riley Wilson." I could tell him I was named after a relative too, but it would require too much explaining.

"Well, it was nice to meet you, Riley. You were good to keep me company today, sweetheart." A smile touches my lips for the first time all day. This man reminds me of my dad, someone who calls every woman under the age of forty "sweetheart" and can't seem to understand when I try to explain that it's just not cool anymore.

His defense: "Get outta here. People need to stop being so sensitive. It's a term of endearment." And it does feel that way when this man says it, as comforting as a warm bath.

Willie pulls a yellowed handkerchief from deep in the recesses of his coat pocket and blows his nose. "I came here today for my moms, you know. Felt like something I needed to do for her. She wanted to come herself and never made it."

I understand completely. We're both here for someone else and for ourselves and, strangely, now for each other. Willie looks to the ground. There's a sense of panic that I'll never see this stranger again, our brief friendship as sweet and fleeting as a summer rainstorm.

"Could I give you a hug, young lady?"

By way of answering, I open my arms wide, and the two of us embrace. We're standing in front of an iron statue of human beings chained together. When we part, Willie takes a minute to look at the sculpture; his gaze settles on a figure of a woman with a heavy iron chain around her neck, a baby in her arms.

"What a world." He shakes his head and ambles down the path; his words echo even as he recedes. *What a world.*

I don't have much time, and I'm already emotionally depleted, but I decide to make a quick stop down the road at the Legacy Museum too. I need to see the jars of dirt I've read about, each one filled with the soil from all the locations in America where there was a known lynching, emblazoned with a name and date, commemorations of the victims lost to history. It's such a simple, powerful tribute, a way to honor their lives and ensure that people aren't allowed to forget this particular legacy of violence, the toll it took.

Jimmy was lynched right here on this soil too. Even though we'll never know the exact location, his remains are somewhere in this state. His name, the dirt stained with his blood, belongs on a shelf. We — I need to remember, for Gigi.

I'm hurrying back to the parking lot now, but the walk to my car feels longer than the one to the museum, like history is dragging me down. The first thing I do: reach into my overnight bag to make sure the box is still there, buried at the bottom. It was foolish of me to leave it in the car. I breathe again when I feel the smooth vinyl, pull the box out of my bag, snap it open. Nestled in a bed of plush red velvet — a pearl necklace and bracelet. "Real pearls!" Gigi took great pains to emphasize when she gave them to me.

It was the day after she told me about Jimmy. Gigi had directed Momma to a safe-deposit box that no one even knew existed and told her to bring the contents to the hospital. In the safe, Momma found a black Hefty bag containing the jewelry box with the pearls, ancient Pan Am stock certificates, a bundle of letters from Grandpa Leroy, and, the kicker, about $3,000 in small bills.

"Been working the pole, Gigi?" Shaun teased. Momma smacked him on his head even though the joke was lost on Gigi.

Instead, she reminded us for the umpteenth time about how we shouldn't keep all our money in banks. "Too big to fail? Yeah right! Y'all need to squirrel away some cold hard cash, a little at a time and then you got yourself a nest egg." Then she handed me the box of pearls and two notes in her shaky scrawl. I've read them both, even the one that wasn't meant for me. Of course, I'll do what Gigi wants and give this bracelet to Jen. Eventually. But it all feels — how did Sabrina put it? Tricky.

The night Gigi died, I called Jen from a hard bench in the only corner in the lobby of the hospital where I had reception. I kept obsessively retrying, even though I knew it was futile. It was obvious her phone was turned off. I was so desperate to hear her voice. I just wanted to cry with her and miss Gigi together and maybe even beg her to come over and climb into bed with me and tell me every funny Gigi story she could remember. It didn't matter what else was going on. But she didn't answer, and I couldn't form the words to leave in a voice mail. I needed to find another quiet moment to talk to her, one where it would be okay to break down. But it never came — this week has been insane with all the planning and arrangements. I will though. I want to. I need to give her this bracelet. The box closes with a loud snap. I place it carefully on the passenger seat next to me as if it's a talisman, a companion, as if it's Gigi.

All I want is to hear my grandmother's voice again. I haven't heard it since she spoke her actual final words, delivered in a ragged whisper the day before she died, the last time I saw her conscious. "You're a good girl, Leroya, but you gotta let other people help you. You ain't gonna get any brownie points for doing everything all on your own." I should have known it was goodbye. And now it's a too-cruel irony that Gigi passed on and *then* stopped haunting me, like she's twice gone.

Come back, Grandma. I need you. I can't hear you. I wait, listening for another minute, just in case, before starting the engine and turning on the radio. "River" by Leon Bridges is playing, a song Gigi had loved. I decide to see it as a message.

US-82 with its billboards for fireworks and porn shops passes in a blur as I push eighty miles per hour the whole way, eager to reach my family now. Every so often throughout the drive to Perote, I catch a faint whiff of Willie's cigar smoke and find it weirdly comforting.

I'm off the highway when my bladder feels like it's about to burst. Gas stations are few and far between on these smaller, emptier roads that will take me the rest of the way. The scarier roads.

The last few years, whenever I've been on a stretch like this, all I can think about is Sandra Bland, and how easily a turn signal or a taillight could turn me into her. I glance in the rearview every few minutes, maintain the speed limit, careful and cautious, all the while resenting that I have to be so careful and cautious.

I slow when I finally see a couple of beat-up gas pumps. They look like relics from another era; they *are* relics from another era. An ancient sign rests against the tanks, announcing COCA-COLA SERVED HERE. Out front of the small store, two white guys sit on folding chairs. One has stringy blond hair that nearly grazes his shoulders, the other a newly shorn buzz cut, revealing a scarred bald scalp, lumpy in places.

I try to assess the situation, the potential for danger, but after six months in Philly my redneck radar is rusty — and with my bladder screaming like it is, I'm desperate. I'll have to take my chances. In the absence of any sort of parking lot, I pull over on the patchy red dirt, a few feet from where the men sit. The bald one squints at me hard, stands, and quickly closes the distance between him and my car.

"You need gas?" he asks through the closed window and makes a circle in the air with his closed fist to indicate that I should roll it down, which under other circumstances I'd probably find funny since I haven't seen a car with a crank window in about forever.

"Just the bathroom," I say through the crack as the window lowers. The gauge shows that I have half a tank. Daddy always told me to fill my gas tank before it dropped below half. "Because you never know when you'll get another chance," he said.

"Actually, yeah. Fill it up, regular, please."

"Bathroom's round back. Rooster's got the key."

If I went missing behind this gas station, would anyone ever know what happened to

303

me? I'm an easy target, a woman alone on a desolate road, a tragic headline in the making. My former colleagues a hundred miles down the way in Birmingham might even cover it.

Rooster spits a wad of tobacco on the ground before he hands over a metal spatula, the kind you use to flip hotcakes, a key tied to it with a dirty piece of twine.

"Bathroom's around the side. Sorry 'bout the toilet. It don't flush real well."

I swallow a gag as I squeeze myself into a bathroom the size of a closet. The toilet doesn't flush at all, and it's close to overflowing. I don't want to add to it, but what choice do I have?

As I come back around the shop, Rooster is standing right in my path to the car. My stomach quivers, then plunges.

This is it.

He takes a step toward me, blocking my way, and I don't even have time to think about where exactly I'll run, or remember whatever I learned in that one self-defense class I took in college, before he extends his hand.

"Can I get the key, please? I gotta piss," he mumbles. "Hope you don't mind, we went ahead and did the windows too."
Beyond Rooster's shoulder the bald guy

pulls a squeegee across my windshield.

"You okay?" he asks.

"Yeah, fine, fine." Relief quickly spirals into embarrassment.

"Where you headin'?"

"Perote."

"About a mile to the town line. Welcome." As promised, it's only a minute's drive before I see the sign PEROTE BULLOCK COUNTY. I snake through the desolate remnants of what was once probably a bustling main street, now deserted, lined with a general store, post office, the white church, the Black church, a diner, police station, library, and the city hall. The town is neither welcoming nor threatening, but it is depressing. Empty streets, boarded-up buildings, a stillness in the air, a reminder that entire towns, like people, can just wither and die. There's a certain inevitably to it, the understanding that heydays come and go and life marches on elsewhere while this husk of a place sits abandoned like a dusty artifact. Not even a quaint nostalgia lingers; there's only the sense of life, opportunity, and better days come and gone. There's no cell service, though I had the good sense to print out directions before leaving Philly. I had a feeling it'd be spotty. The little icon in the corner of my phone shows zero bars. Going off the grid like this makes me twitchy, imagining all the calls, emails, and news I'll miss in the next twenty-four hours. What if Scotty needs to reach me? Being completely unreachable almost feels like missing a limb. There's nothing I can do about it though, and there's a kind of exhilarating freedom in that.

The printed directions aren't much help since not all the roads are well marked. I'm stuck on what seems to be a narrow dead end, hemmed in on all sides by dense brush and knee-high red-ant hills. In my mind's eye, I see galloping horses and white robes, fiery crosses. I don't want to be out here after sundown, that's for sure.

Creeping along slowly, I search for the house, set back from the narrow road. When I finally see it, it feels like an accident, or like it decided to find me.

There are a few cars scattered randomly across the wide patchwork of weeds, dirt, and gravel that make up what can only loosely be called a yard. Uncle Rod's giant RV towers over all of them. It's bigger than the house.

I take in the modest brick ranch my great-grandfather Dash allegedly built with his own bare hands, which may explain why it leans slightly to one side. It's amazing to me that Gigi held on to this land for so long even though she never came back here except for Aunt Mabel's funeral. She used to rent it out to hunters during deer season and use the small income it generated as her "fun money," mostly paying the cable bill and buying scratchers. I guess she was also socking it away in that Hefty bag. The place has been empty for a few years though. It's four tiny rooms and one bath on a couple acres of land, but it was all hers, and Gigi was proud to have it. She said owning a piece of land made you someone, or at least it made you feel like you were someone. And no one could take it away from you . . . until they could. I have to shake the thought of my parents losing their house. One heartbreak is enough for now.

The railing shakes as I climb the uneven concrete stairs of the porch to the front door. It's propped open and everyone has gathered in the living room.

I haven't seen my uncle Rod since I was a kid. He and Momma have been estranged ever since they had a falling-out after Grandpa Leroy's funeral over something no one ever talks about. When he steps up to hug me, the smell of his pipe sends me hurtling right back to the second grade.

He's the only person I've ever seen smoke an honest-to-God pipe, like a Black Sherlock Holmes.

I give quick hugs to Aunt Rose and two of my cousins, twin girls in their early twenties who are essentially strangers to me and who immediately return to looking at their phones.

Shaun thrusts a glass of wine into my hand. "Here, saved this for you. That's the last of it, and we can't get more because of the dumbass blue laws down here. So better drink up."

The wine tastes like vinegar. That doesn't stop me from taking three fast sips.

"Where's Mom and Dad?"

"Dad went ahead to the cemetery to make sure everything's straight. The limos will be here to drive us over in twenty." Shaun looks me up and down. "Um, so you better start getting ready? Those sweats aren't going to cut it. You can guess where Mom is." He nods to the kitchen.

"Cleaning?" I already know the answer. Momma's cleaning habits are legendary. Growing up, Shaun and I had a weekend chore list a mile long. In my eighteen years living beneath her roof, the woman never went to bed with a dirty dish in the sink, and now I can't either. I tried once. I left an ice cream bowl because I'm a grown-ass woman who can leave a dirty bowl in the sink. The freedom! But I was so agitated an hour later, I got up and washed it at one in the morning.

I was eight when Momma first explained to me that white people often think Black people are dirty. I remember it vividly because it was the night of my very first sleepover (aside from those with Jen, who practically lived with us by that point) — Abigail from ballet was coming over. I had one of those intense little-girl crushes on her, with her long auburn pigtails and her dance bag with her name splashed across it in sparkly cursive crystals. To prepare, Momma and I spent the entire day cleaning. She was on her hands and knees, furiously attacking the linoleum under the kitchen cabinets, when she offered up that explanation. This didn't make one bit of sense to me, since our house always smelled like ammonia and lemon. I'd learned to vacuum before I could even really walk on my own. Not too long afterward, I was allowed to sleep over at Jen's house for the first and only time. I thought of what Momma had said as I took in the ring of grime around the tub, the crumbs trapped in the couch cushions.

"Germs are good for you," Lou said when she caught my jaw just about hanging on the floor. "Look at Jenny. Girl's never sick."

When it was time to take a bath, I couldn't find a washcloth. I asked Jen for one, and she told me they didn't use them. Momma had always made it clear that a washcloth was essential to keeping your private parts "spick-and-span."

It all left me confused as to who was clean and who was dirty and how these things were determined.

Here's Momma now in her best black dress, a tattered apron tied around her waist, her head stuck deep in a cabinet, furiously scrubbing.

"Ma?"

When she emerges from the far reaches of the cabinet, one of the curlers in her hair gets caught on the door. "Baby girl!" She drops the wet sponge and takes me up in a hug. "I didn't know you were here!"

"I just got here. Sorry I'm late."

"Oh, baby, you're right on time. Right on time. Here, hand me that roll of paper towels." She picks up the sponge without missing a beat, and for the first time I think about my mother's obsessive cleaning like my running, a way for her to feel a measure of control, or at least the alluring illusion of it.

"How are you, Momma?" I haven't seen her cry yet either.

"Oh, you know, I'm fine. I'm fine. I just want to get this nasty kitchen cleaned out. We may try to finally sell this place. Your father went ahead to the cemetery. I wanted him to buy some flowers. Heaven knows where he's going to get flowers around here, but he'll figure it out. That man is resourceful if nothing else."

"Okay, well, do you need help with anything?"

"No, no, you go get ready." Momma waves me away with a wet paper towel.

I leave her to her scrubbing and slip into the same black dress I wore for Justin's funeral. I've worn too many sad black dresses lately. I put on the pearls last, fastening the delicate strand around my neck, turning and turning it until the center pearl, the one that is slightly bigger than the others, sits exactly where it should, right above the hollow in my collarbone. I'm ready, and yet not ready at all.

In the back of a boxy Cadillac coupe from the seventies, thighs sticking to the cracked leather seat, my fingers return to the pearls. I stop when Momma looks at me, worried she'll scold me for fidgeting.

"They look nice on you," she says, and goes back to looking out the window, twisting her own wedding ring around her bony finger. If we had that type of relationship, I would reach for her hand now.

Finally, after snaking through a string of rural roads, we pull up to a small field. Crooked wrought iron gates frame a small sign announcing the "colored" cemetery, dating back to the 1800s. Daddy is standing in the middle of the clearing beside a minister from the local church. We don't know him personally. His people are from Perote for generations back, and they knew Gigi and her parents. My dad and the minister are backlit by the setting sun, standing tall, proud, and solemn with clasped hands. It reminds me of a Gordon Parks photograph. I want to run to Daddy like I did when I was a little girl, have him lift me into the air and spin me around. This was before cleaning thousands of toilets left him stooped with permanent back pain. Instead, he receives me with a tight hug.

We all stand around the casket. A bunch of flowers lie on top of it — wildflowers. My father must have picked them himself, probably right here in this field, and arranged them carefully over the shiny mahogany. His shoes are covered in flecks of red clay. My heart threatens to burst, picturing him bending over with his bad back to pull flower after flower from the dirt.

I've been trying to avoid looking at the coffin, same as I did at Justin's funeral. But there it is, not five feet away. It's closed, though I know my grandmother is in there, dressed to the nines just like she would have wanted: her favorite hat, a floral dress, her best white silk gloves. Picturing Gigi trapped in there sends pinpricks along my spine. But it's the hole, the giant hole in the ground, that makes my knees buckle. Shaun links his arm with mine. "I got you, sis. I got you."

Uncle Rod and his family stand on one side of the minister, Shaun, Daddy, Momma, and I on the other, forming a tight row. The pastor waits for the small nod from Momma indicating it's time to begin. Shaun holds me tighter. The minister starts to recite from Psalms. His voice, higher than Pastor Price's, is clear and strong and bounces off the ring of imposing cypress trees that surround us. Momma has asked me to read a poem. When the minister is finished, I slip the folded piece of paper, damp with sweat, from my dress pocket. My hands shake, and I'm reminded of Justin's cousin, Malik. The poem, "On a New Year's

Eve" by June Jordan, was a favorite of Gi-gi's.

"I don't really understand it altogether, but it stirs somethin' in you, don't it?" she'd said once.

It did. It does.

I'm suddenly self-conscious, shy, even though this is my family. I clear my throat and begin to read. " 'Infinity doesn't inter-est me, not altogether anymore. . . .' " I'm speaking in my newscaster voice; imagining a camera in front of me makes this easier. I purposely slow down on the last line. Maybe if I keep reading forever, we'll never get to the part where we have to put Gigi in that hole.

" 'All things are dear that disappear . . . all things are dear that disappear.' "

Not long enough. It's over.

Momma steps forward and hugs me. "That was beautiful, Leroya, beautiful."

Somehow the slip in my name feels exactly right.

I return to my place in the circle. The minister swats the flies away from his face and recites Genesis 3:19, " 'For dust you are and to dust you will return,' " before he calls for us to bow our heads.

After a moment of silence the pastor asks if anyone else would like to speak.

The only sound is a rustle in the trees until Shaun calls out, "Hey, pastor, what do you call a pony with a cough?"

The poor man looks so confused, but I've already broken into giggles. I holler out the answer: "A little hoarse."

God, Gigi loved these stupid little riddles. She had hundreds of them and would trot them out until they were as worn as old sheets.

Daddy jumps on the bandwagon. "But son, do you know why the octopus crossed the ocean?"

"Why no, Dad, I don't." Which is a lie; Shaun has only heard this one five hundred times. Gigi told it to us at the hospital just last week, when she found a reserve of energy.

"To get to the other tide."

All eyes turn to Momma, expectantly.

"Oh, y'all get out of here with this non-sense. This is not the time." Her eyes are glued to the casket. There's a long pause while we figure out what to do next, and then Momma's voice, still looking at the casket like she's talking to her mother.

"Why do seagulls fly over the sea?" She doesn't wait for an answer. "Because if they flew over the bay, they'd be bagels." And then she is laughing, laughing so hard tears stream down her face. "God, that woman's jokes were 'bout the corniest I've ever heard."

We're all laughing now. The pastor looks dismayed at first and then gives in to it, a substitute teacher who's lost control of the classroom.

I bring my hands to my face and find that my cheeks are wet. The tears have come. They stream down like rain; like Momma's, they're happy tears, or at least a mix of happy and heartbroken. I think of Gigi looking down on us right now, all of us together, laughing wildly on a small patch of land in rural Alabama on this warm December day, and I know it's just as she would have wanted it.

For the rest of the night we can't stop telling Gigi jokes. It even gives Momma and Uncle Rod something to bond over. But no one pushes their luck; not an hour after we return from the cemetery, my uncle and cousins retreat to the RV. They plan to get an early start back to Memphis in the morning, so now it's only us.

Daddy scrounged up enough wood in the backyard to start a small fire in the fireplace and puts an old Sam Cooke record on the ancient record player in the corner. Shaun found a dusty bottle of homemade whiskey in the cupboard. Even Momma drinks it. I make the mistake of sniffing it before I sip, and the scent alone burns my nostrils.

"Oh God, what is this?"

"Whatever they made down here when they couldn't find anything else." Shaun shrugs and slams back what's left in his glass.

"I don't know if we should be drinking this."

"Don't be a priss. Bottoms up."

I hold my nose and throw it back. The concoction tastes like it's made from two ingredients: gasoline and tree bark. Even after I chase it with the dregs of a nearby can of warm Coke, the noxious flavor clings to my tongue.

I'm still furiously swishing soda around my mouth when Momma gets up and returns to the table with a cardboard box filled with old photo albums. "Look what I found when I was cleaning out the hall closet earlier."

There's a tan leather one so old and dry it's broken into a web of cracks like a desert landscape. Newspaper clippings and recipes stick to the bottom of the box. I grab a tattered index card that features the ingredients and steps to make rhubarb pie in faded cursive.

"Can I have this?"

"Excuse me? Why? When was the last time you even turned on your stove?" Shaun jokes.

He has a point. I don't think I've ever made anything from scratch in my entire life, but suddenly, making this recipe is important to me. It doesn't matter that I've got no idea what rhubarb even looks like; I'm going to make this pie for Christmas. Why I'm suddenly seized by the urge to be some sort of Carla Hall wannabe is beyond me, but I'm desperate for any way to feel connected to Gigi. How many times had I watched her, her arms speckled with bright white flakes of flour, kneading dough or squinting over vats of hot grease she kept in a giant old tomato can that never moved from the back of the stove? How many times had I rolled my eyes as she joked — half joked — to me, "Get over here and learn to cook if you're ever gonna get a fine man?" How many times had she rolled her eyes at my pretentious lectures about the patriarchy. "Girl, there ain't nothin' wrong with wantin' a man."

"Putting a husband aside, cooking is history," she once told me as she made biscuits. "Me and my momma and my momma's momma before that have been making these 'zact same biscuits. That's a bond, ya hear. It's not much — some flour, some water, some salt — but it's what we had and it's a legacy, a connection."

She always said she felt the spirit of the ancestors, would have full-on conversations with them when she was in a tizzy about something or when she was in the kitchen. Kneading biscuits, dragging fat chicken thighs through flour, rolling out piecrust, it all made her feel close to them. So maybe it would do the same for me — connect me to them, to Gigi.

Speaking of legacy, Dad flips open the ancient album, its pages creaky and cracking at being disturbed. We spot Gigi in the first picture. She must be about five years old, in a white lace dress, head full of braids, spunky grin revealing two missing teeth.

A gangly teenager in crisp brown trousers and a white tank top revealing well-muscled arms stands beside her, his hands on her shoulders. They're in front of the house, and it looks exactly the same as it did when I came up the drive.

Momma turns it over and reads the handwriting on the back. " 'Marla and Jimmy, 1935.' " I grab hungrily at the picture. Jimmy's wearing a felt hat with a feather in the side. His nose is crooked like it was broken and never healed right. It doesn't make him any less handsome though, in fact just the opposite.

I rub my finger over the photo like I'm reaching through time.

"Who's Jimmy?" Shaun asks.

"Grandma's cousin," I start. "It's terrible. He was —"

And Momma holds up a hand to stop me, sighs into her drink. "Another time. Another time."

She's right. Tonight's a night to talk about Gigi, to reach for happy memories. So we do just that. Shaun launches into the time Gigi chased him through the house with a shoe for recording over an episode of *General Hospital* she hadn't watched yet, and we pick at the spread Momma managed to cobble together from the meager options at the tiny local store — a roast that's surprisingly tender, a big pot of turnip greens, a skillet of cornbread all brown around the edges.

"All we need is miracle bread," I say. "Who's making the miracle bread?"

The question makes me happy before it pains me. No one loved miracle bread like Jenny. I tug at the pearl bracelet circling my wrist. I've changed out of my dress, and the necklace is back in the box. I'm still wearing the bracelet.

"When are you going to give it to her?" Momma asks.

"This week, when we're back." I say it even though I don't know if it's true.

"What's going on with you two anyway?"

"Come on, Momma, you know what's going on."

"No, I don't, Riley, so you'll have to use your words." She says it exactly like she did when I was a toddler wordlessly begging for candy.

That's the problem. I don't have the words. It's hard to pinpoint, let alone describe exactly what's going on between us — this weird, unspoken rift. The longer we go without talking, the stranger it all feels, like we're in an invisible fight and neither of us understands the rules.

A loud snore comes from the threadbare couch where Daddy is stretched out.

"I'm gonna let y'all two talk *that* out," Shaun says, standing to kiss Momma, then me, before heading to the back bedroom. I'm exhausted from traveling and from the sadness of the day, though it's nice to sit here with my mother at this sticky linoleum table full of empty glasses and crumbs. Momma must be more than a little tipsy, because she makes no move to clean up the mess. My mind swims as I consider how best to explain what's going on with Jen, but Momma's moved on. Her eyes are a little glassy — could be heartache, or moonshine.

"You know, I bought Gigi a scarf for Christmas." Her voice is small. "I was hoping she'd hang on until then. I knew even if she did, she wouldn't last much past Christmas, and then I thought maybe we could bury her with the scarf, and then when I thought about that, I didn't want to give it to her at all." She tears a napkin into long white shreds. "I should've given her the scarf."

"Did you bring it down here?"

"Nah, I left it at home. It's in a box in the top of my closet. Maybe you'll wear it when we get back. It'd look nice on you. You and your grandmother have the same coloring, like a twice-toasted coconut. She always said that when you were a baby."

"I'll wear it. Put it under the tree for me and I'll pretend it's a big surprise."

Momma sighs. "The scarf isn't so much the point, honey. It's that we can't wait. You know, there's a lot I wish I'd said before your grandma passed. Now I'm wondering why we always wait to say things at all. It's mighty foolish of us to wait for anything. To wait to tell someone we love them or that we're mad as hell at them. Kevin did a terrible thing, it's true, and a young boy is dead and he has to live with that, with that heaviness in his soul. I'm not going to weigh in on how he should be punished. That's for God to decide. But Jenny is not Kevin, and that girl loves you, and sometimes we need to swallow our pride and reach out. Even when we don't know what to say and we're afraid of messing everything up by saying the wrong thing. It doesn't matter if you don't know how to talk about something. All that matters is that you try. The longer you let something go, the easier it is to stay silent, and the silence is where the resentment starts to fester and rot."

She stops to absently take another sip of the brown liquid in her glass. "I know, I'm a hypocrite over here telling you this. I'm not the best at reaching out. I didn't speak to my own brother all this time. And you know why?"

Momma releases a strange, high-pitched cackle. "I don't even know! That's the awful truth. That's something, right? I know we were both so mad and we said some terrible things to each other and then waited for the other to come to their senses and apologize while the years piled up. Now here we are, at our momma's grave, like strangers. I don't want that to happen to you and Jenny."

She stops again; then, instead of taking another drink, she gazes out the little kitchen window into the dark night. I wait, somewhat stunned by this turn the night's taken. Is it the grief of losing her mother? Is she that tipsy? Momma and I don't have heart-to-hearts. This was a woman who simply left a pamphlet about "your changing body" on my bed when I was twelve.

"I'll tell you something. I always wanted a friendship like what you have with Jenny. I was always a little jealous, truth be told. It's special to have someone like that. I mean, your dad can be a doggone fool sometimes, but God knows he's my best friend." She stops and looks over at Daddy, on the couch, with a rare display of tenderness and affection. "It's not the same as having a best girlfriend though. Side by side almost since you were knee-high. Y'all painting each other's toes, telling secrets, sneaking out of the house — don't think I don't know you did that too. I never really got to have that with anyone."

It was something, the topper to a surreal day, a surreal month, to have Momma opening herself up like this, confiding she was

324

jealous. Of me? I was never one of the girls who longed to have my mom as a best friend, chatting about clothes and boys, which she would have found laughable anyway. She always said, *I'm here to be your parent, not your girlfriend.* And anyway, I already had a best friend growing up. But having this moment with Momma, so sad about her own mom, unfurls something in me, a curiosity about her, a desire to know her more as a woman, a longing for a different kind of relationship. She's always been so distant, stern, hell-bent on properly molding us, like she couldn't allow any room for a softer side. But what if she had let her guard down more and I'd gotten to see this side of her, the side that admits to feelings? We might have had an entirely different relationship. Maybe that's possible now that I'm back home for the first time since I was eighteen; we could go out to lunch and talk, like a TV mother and daughter. It goes against everything I know about Sandra Wilson and thirty-plus years of history, but then I remember Gigi being lowered into the ground not five hours ago — a bittersweet reminder that Momma isn't going to be here forever — and my determination grows. I want to know, to really know, my mother as an adult, before it's too late.

"All I'm saying is, don't take your friendship for granted. You have something special, and a whole lotta history. That counts for something. I would hate for y'all to have to wait for something awful to happen to find each other again and then be sick to death at all the time you've wasted. And anyway, something awful already happened. Gigi died. And for anything that can be said about Jenny, that girl loved Gigi like her own grandma, and it's awful to think of her up there grieving all alone without a soul to talk to about her. And *you* need to talk too."

I do. I want to talk to Jenny. I want to call her up right now and say, "I don't know what to do with Gigi gone, Pony. I've never felt a loss like this. I don't know how to live in the world without her." I want her to say, "We'll figure it out, Puff. We'll never stop talking about her." I don't know why I keep pulling out our old nicknames now. Pony and Puff. It's like I'm clinging to the strands that connected Jenny and me so long ago in the hopes that they'll be enough. It's almost 1 a.m. though, I can't call her now.

I point this out to Momma.

"Darn, I didn't realize it was that late. We gotta get to bed. But you call her tomorrow, then. Call her when you wake up. Don't make excuses. You always keep everything so bottled up, Riley. I swear that's why you had so much constipation as a child. So much so Dr. Lexington told me you needed a therapist more than a laxative. I told him you needed Jesus, but heaven help me, you put up a wall with even Jesus. Always all up in your head trying to reason everything to death. Sometimes you can't think your way out of a thing. You have to feel it. And sometimes you just have to let it out. You can't just push it away and pretend it's not happening. Like with you and Jenny. Who knows what happens with you two from here? I'd like to think y'all find a way through this. I don't know how that happens. I'm struggling myself. When I think of Kevin pulling that trigger . . ." She stops and shakes her head. "But I also believe that he gets a chance to explain himself, Jenny too. Bad things have always happened in the world, especially to our folks, but we can't shut down every time they do. No choice but to keep pushing forward. It's the same for you and Jenny — you gotta talk and see where you go from here. See that she understands your pain and why. But one thing's for sure, just shutting down and shutting her out ain't going to accomplish one thing, 'cept leave you all stopped up."

Mortifying constipation references aside, I

know there's truth to what Momma says.

She yawns so wide I can see the pink flesh at the back of her throat.

"Get my night stuff, would you?"

I go to her small suitcase and retrieve the same floral silk scarf Momma's been wrapping her hair with since before I was alive and her giant jar of Noxzema. I stand behind her and wind the threadbare scarf around her soft curls, trying not to notice the thin patches. She opens the Noxzema jar, takes a big scoop, and rubs it all over her face. The smell of it, the way it burns the inside of my nose, will forever remind me of my mother.

"I miss her." It just comes out of me. I'm not sure if I mean Jenny or Gigi, but the ache is strong enough to cover them both.

Momma sighs and touches my cheek, the warmth of the fire in her hand.

"I do too, baby girl. She loved you something fierce, and I do too." She leans over and kisses the top of my head.

It's only when I can hear her slippers shuffling down the hall that I realize I didn't get to tell her about my visit to the memorial. I sit back in the chair and listen to the quiet hum around me, Daddy's snores, the crackle of the fire. There's a stillness and a peace inside me all of a sudden. If only I could bottle this feeling. That reminds me. The promise I made at the museum. The dirt, the tribute. Fueled by moonshine, sugar, and grief, I root around in the musty cabinets, searching for a jam jar.

A near full moon casts a glow across the yard, lighting my way as I walk barefoot to a spot near the tree line. The air smells different down here than in Philly — muskier, earthier, like burnt embers and riverbeds. I squat and dig into the earth, scooping the rocky dirt into the jar, letting it coat my palms and gather beneath my fingernails. A few specks dot the pearl bracelet, catch in its clasp. I dig and dig. I won't go back inside until the jar is full.

CHAPTER TEN

JEN

December 22 6:07 pm
From: jaybird2002@yahoo.com
To: rwilson@gmail.com

Riley:

This doesn't seem right for text. It's weird on email too, but I've been trying to call you all week and keep getting voice mail. It's like the only way I know about your life right now is by stalking Shaun's Instagram.

I'm sorry and so, so sad about Gigi. I still can't believe she's gone. I also can't believe I didn't get to say goodbye. I kept meaning to go to the hospital to see her, but then . . . everything. But I really don't understand why you didn't call me. It feels like you're pushing me away. Maybe you're not, but that's how it feels. And that hurts, because Gigi was a grandma to me too, you know. I mean, not like with the rest of you, I get there's a difference, but she was the closest thing I had to one, and you of all people know how much I loved that woman. I really wanted to be there for the service. I looked at plane tickets. I mean, even if you didn't want me there, I wanted to come and pay my respects, but they were too pricey. How was it? Please tell me you buried her in the purple hat. I remember her saying she was going to wear that hat one day when she shook hands with President Obama and then she did when he came to church that time. Talk about the tingles. God, I already miss her so much.

But you know who else I miss? You, Riley. I miss YOU. I'm sorry for all the reasons you're upset or anything I did to upset you.

xJ

PS: I made miracle bread. It wasn't as good as Gigi's. I can't believe we'll never have her miracle bread again.

December 23 7:13 am
From: rwilson@gmail.com
To: jaybird2002@yahoo.com

Jenny, I did call you about Gigi! I called you from the hospital that night, at least five times, and your phone must have been off. I wanted to talk to you, to hear your voice, and I didn't want to tell you in a message either. And then after that, it was just so hectic between the funeral and work and the holidays. It's not right, though. I'm sorry. I'm devastated about Gigi too. I keep accidentally turning to drive to the hospital . . . and then I remember she's gone. The funeral was nice, hard, beautiful, and terrible, all of the things funerals are. And yes, we buried her in the purple hat and her favorite dress, the one with the giant lilacs all over it. One of the last things she said to me was, *Make sure I look nice, ya hear. I want to look fine when I meet Jesus.* And she did. She looked . . . peaceful. I got to be right there when she passed on, holding her hand. I swear she had a smile on her face. Like she and Jesus already had an inside joke. It made it easier to know she was ready to go. She even said it a few times that last week, *I'm ready to get on outta here to the other side.* It's just that we weren't ready . . . we were never going to be ready.

Anyway, even though we haven't talked as much lately, I *have* been thinking and worrying about you, Jen. I swear. I'm sorry if that hasn't come across. Because I do realize how stressful it's been. For you, and for me too. It's hitting so close to home. I don't know how to explain it, because I didn't know Justin or the Dwyers, but his death hit me like the death of a family member. Because it could have been a member of my family, Jenny. It could have been Shaun.

This is all so hard . . . and weird. It's not easy for me to cover this story, to be objective when you're involved and to see the story from all sides, but I'm trying my best.

I have something for you . . . from Gigi. Let me know when we can meet up so I can give it to you.

December 24 12:48 pm
From: jaybird2002@yahoo.com
To: rwilson@gmail.com

I remember now, I had my phone turned off the night that Gigi died. I'd gone to my place (did I even tell you that Kevin and I moved in with Cookie and Frank since the media is hounding us?) and there was a bag of shit on my doorstep and someone had spray-painted MURDERER across our fence. So I was a wreck and just wanted to shut out the world. And that's just the tip of the iceberg. I wish you could see all the hate mail we've been getting. The awful trolls on social media. Have you seen what they say about us?? I mean, the first 400 or so times you're called a racist cunt, it hurts, and then it's like blah blah blah.

But anyway, Riley, what do you mean by sides? And if there are sides, shouldn't you be on mine?

I feel terrible for what happened. God, I feel so bad. I was at the funeral, you know. I know you know, because you saw me there. It was important for me to pay my respects, because I'm heartbroken too. For Justin's mom, that poor, poor woman. But also for Kevin. He didn't mean for this to happen — you know that, Riley. You know that.

This morning I was up before everyone and I found Cookie making Christmas bread. Before I knew what was happening she was all hugging me and crying and saying how we need to make sure this is the perfect Christmas because it could be Kevin's last holiday with us for a while. She was such a wreck, I felt like shit about every nasty thought I'd ever had about Cookie. I don't know who I'm more worried about actually, her or Kevin . . . or us?

December 25 12:12 am
From: rwilson@gmail.com
To: jaybird2002@yahoo.com

Don't worry about us, Jenny. We'll talk. Soon.

I'm sorry you're getting so many nasty notes online. It sucks. Believe me I know what it's like. Every single day I get comments on the news station website about my awful bangs, and how I shouldn't wear red or purple or blue. But worse is when they call me an ugly ape or say I should take my big lips back to Africa.

It's nothing new though. I was just going through some old yearbooks earlier. Momma thrust a box of stuff in my face and told me I might as well get started on going through whatever I still have here. They're preparing to put the house on the market, so I guess tomorrow will be our last Christmas there. It's strange to already feel nostalgic for something that isn't quite gone yet. But I am.

Anyway, I started reading all the things people wrote to me senior year. You took up the entire back cover! And then there was a note from Ryan DiNucci. Remember him? He had that stupid Backstreet Boys haircut. He wrote, "Good luck in college. You're gonna be famous someday." Which was crazy because back in seventh grade he left a note in my locker saying "you think you're so great you niger."

Which is my point: people are always going to say shit and you just have to deal with it. Hang in there. And try to have a happy Christmas, okay?

Actually, I just realized it's past midnight; it's already Christmas. Remember how we always used to say that at sleepovers? We stayed up until tomorrow. Merry Christmas, Jenny.

xR

December 25 3:02 pm
From: jaybird2002@yahoo.com
To: rwilson@gmail.com

I'm trying to have a happy Christmas over here, which means for right now hiding in the basement with the kids and just getting a moment to myself. There's too many people in this house. All the aunts and uncles and cousins down from Scranton. Kevin's family breeds like horny rabbits. Lou's here too and got so drunk last night on eggnog that she told Cookie her hair looked like a lampshade. Things were still chilly this morning as we opened presents, but then Lou gave Cookie a tea towel with Dolly Parton's face on it and then Cookie actually hugged her. I never thought I'd see the day. I felt so dumb giving Kevin the stupid scrapbook I made him since I couldn't afford a real gift, but I think he loved it. Then Matt gave him a real nice leather wallet with his initials on it and the words "we bleed blue" and Kevin shut down for the rest of the morning.

Why didn't you tell me about Ryan Di-Nucci when it happened? I would have punched him right in his fat face for you. And why didn't you tell me about getting called names online? I tell you absolutely everything about my life. I don't understand why you would keep stuff like that from me.

Getting together sounds great. Maybe next week, when it would have been my shower? Which is canceled, by the way. I think Cookie was going to call, but I guess that's obvious. It wouldn't be right. I'm disappointed, but I'm so excited to meet him soon, Riley. You have no idea.

December 25 4:12 pm
From: rwilson@gmail.com
To: jaybird2002@yahoo.com

Wait. HIM??? It's a boy?!

December 25 8:20 pm
From: jaybird2002@yahoo.com
To: rwilson@gmail.com

Oh shit — whoops! Yeah, it's a boy. I'm not telling anyone. Maybe it's stupid, but it's nice to have a secret. Something that's only mine. Even Kevin doesn't know. Don't say anything to anyone.

Things will be better soon. I have to believe that. They're going to complete the investigation and clear Kevin. It was a terrible tragedy, but he was strictly following his training and protocol. All our lives can go back to normal. You can come over to have dinner with Kevin and me and all this will be behind us.

December 26 11:20 pm
From: rwilson@gmail.com
To: jaybird2002@yahoo.com

Back to normal? Jesus, Jenny, an innocent boy is dead. And Kevin and Travis Cameron get to go on with their lives like nothing happened? I don't know how I can sit down with your husband and eat burgers and act like everything's a-okay. It's so not okay. And the fact that you don't get that . . .

CHAPTER ELEVEN

RILEY

That last email to Jen has sat, unsent, in my drafts folder for days. It's begging to be sent. So are the other ten emails I've drafted to her since then, some long rants, some heartfelt, one that was just a sentence: *What the hell, Jenny?*

But each time I go to press send, I stop myself. I tell myself it's because an email is a cop-out. I tell myself it's because I don't want to escalate things. I tell myself it's because I don't have time right now to deal with the fallout and it's easier just to tiptoe. I tell myself I'm being generous in giving *her* space right now. I tell myself I can just wait and bide my time and all this will go away, somehow things will go back to the way they were or some version of it. Of all these excuses, this last one is the biggest lie. Things can't go back to the way they were, because I'm too upset. That last message,

Jen's optimistic attitude, like she and Kevin can just put a dead kid behind them and move on, broke something in me. I mean, I get it, of course she doesn't want her husband to go to prison; she wants her life to return to normal. I want these things for her too. Or I should want them. I want to want them. There's a part of me though, deep and primal, that keeps returning to the fact that an innocent kid died. It may all be a tragic accident, but there need to be consequences. Wasn't that one of our earliest lessons at Sunshine Kids? Fairness. Or the blunter version that was drilled into me at Sunday school: an eye for an eye. Someone should pay. *Kevin should pay.* My breath catches on the betrayal.

But Kevin won't pay. Likely no one will pay. The facts are right there in front of me on my screen, when I close my email drafts folder. I've been working on background research for my story tonight, gathering statistics on cop indictments and convictions. They're startling and confirm a truth we've all seen borne out: cops are almost never charged or convicted for shootings on the job. There's always a defense, rationale, justification, wall of loyalty, or legal technicality to hide behind. There's always *something.* The stat I chose for my story tonight highlights this: Since 2005, 110 police officers have been charged with manslaughter or murder for an on-the-job shooting; only forty-two were convicted, often for lesser charges, the proverbial slap on the wrist. The coils in my stomach wind tighter as I shoot that text over to the graphics department to appear on-screen in my package for tonight's broadcast.

My work phone rings just as I'm trying to decide if I have time to escape my emails, my research, my feelings and run down to the vending machine before the afternoon news meeting. A bag of Cheetos I don't need is calling my name. No one ever calls my work phone, just my cell; only like three people even have the number. So somehow I know it's Gaby before I even pick up, and also that she's going to be annoyed with me.

"I figured I could finally catch you at work. I mean, damn. What's a girl gotta do to get a call back? I've been blowing up your phone."

"I know, sorry. It's just been crazy, Gabs."

There's something about just hearing her voice that makes me want to break down. I haven't spoken to her since right before Gigi's funeral. She was away on a family cruise for the holidays and I didn't want to bother her with my shit as she circled distant islands most people won't ever see.

"How are you? How were the holidays? You got my flowers?"

"Yeah, I did, thank you." They were literally the biggest bouquet of flowers I've ever seen.

"Are you hanging in there? What are you gonna do for New Year's?"

"Um, watch a marathon of old episodes of *Super Soul Sunday*?" The truth is, I volunteered to work tomorrow night, because what else do I have to do, but if I tell Gaby that, she'll give me another lecture about working too much.

"We can all use a little Oprah fo' sure, but that still sounds sad. *You* sound sad."

"I'm okay, just in my head."

"Who, *you*?" Gabrielle laughs.

But I'm in no mood for sarcasm.

"Okay, for real, what's going on, girl? You've been a mess. I'm worried about you."

I lower my voice, but the newsroom is buzzing along around me and no one is paying me any mind. "I know, Gabs. It's like . . . I don't know, I'm just pissed off at the whole world right now. It's been building and building . . . everything that happened to me in Birmingham, more Black men dying in the streets, a president whose dog whistle is so loud you can hear it from space. I'm just so raw and on edge. Like I'm so much more aware than I ever was before about all the ways the world is so unfair. It's getting harder and harder to let it go or to figure out how not to stay mad all the damn time. I'm even mad at Gigi for dying. Or maybe at God for taking her. I don't even know."

I can unload some of this anger on Gaby, like putting down a burden and shaking my arms out before I have to pick it back up again.

"Shit, Rye. I'm sorry. That's a lot. Of course, you're right to be mad — well, not at Gigi, that woman was a national treasure and lived a long life — but I hear you. But everything else? Yeah, I get it. I mean, maybe it's good that you're mad now, that you're letting it all out; maybe you haven't been mad enough?"

Maybe that was it. Maybe all the ways I've trained myself — even prided myself on being able — to let things slide, the snide comments at work, the teachers who accused me of cheating when my papers were too good, everything with Shaun, it was bound to take its toll. I'd always tried to take it in stride — a real Booker T. Washington. Work hard, excel, be respectable — that's what we were supposed to do. It was the only way to play a game where you didn't make the rules, a game set up to make you fail. But it wasn't a game at all — it was survival. And to survive, you couldn't get too mad, too upset, too defiant, because there would be consequences . . . a lost job, a lost mind . . . or worse, a lost life. It was a message that wormed its way deep inside of me, and stayed there like a clenched fist.

A memory comes: me turning to my dad after we watched a documentary together about Bloody Sunday, and I asked him, "How could you stand it?" He knew what I meant: the oppression of Jim Crow, all the slights and humiliations he'd experienced growing up in rural Georgia, drinking from segregated fountains, averting his eyes from any white person walking his way, being called "boy" — or worse. He was quiet for a moment, hands resting on his round belly, a sliver of skin showing above the waist of his pants.

"There are some things you can't change, baby girl. White folks are gonna do what white folks do, and the way I see it you can be resentful and angry all the time and let it eat away at you, which some people do, and how can you blame them? Or you can choose to control the one thing you can: your mind-set. You can decide, *Nope, I'm not going to let them get to me. I won't be bitter, I'm going to be better* — and better doesn't mean just working hard. It comes down to character, an ability to be defiant in your joy no matter what they do. That's what your mom and I tried to teach you kids."

But what's the point of the high road or of being the exception, the anomaly, of rising above, when your whole community is struggling, unable to catch a break, the thumbs of oppression on their necks?

Gaby takes a deep breath. I can tell she's gearing up to tell me something about myself, one of her favorite activities. "Look, you need to talk to Jen. You know, she's not necessarily my cup of tea, but I respect how close y'all are, and I'm sure if you guys talked it all out . . . You need to try to tell her how you feel. You've got to trust that on some level she'll understand, and if she doesn't, well, then she wasn't the friend you thought she was."

Maybe that's why I have a folder full of unsent drafts. At the end of the day, I'm afraid that Jen won't get it. Maybe I've always been afraid. That's why I didn't tell her about when Ryan left that note in my locker, or Birmingham, or even Shaun last year. She could listen, but she could never truly *get* it. I can't necessarily fault her for that, but it nags at me: Why don't we talk about race more? Gaby and I talk about it pretty much every single day, specifically some fucked-up thing in the news or our lives — like venting about ignorant BS like someone mistaking us for the sales clerk at the mall too many times. But I talk to Jen about things I rarely share with Gaby too, like my anxiety and depression and feelings of inadequacy. And besides, Jenny and I met when we were so young, during that brief, elusive period when kids are truly color-blind. We didn't talk about race when we were five, or ten, or fifteen, and now . . . it's a muscle we haven't used. So is it that I *can't* talk to Jenny or that I don't? Which leads me to an even more gut-wrenching question: What if, when it comes down to it, there will always be some essential part of me that is unknowable to her because of our different experiences? It's as if an unnoticeable crack between us has stretched into a chasm and our friendship risks falling right through it.

"What am I supposed to say, Gaby? 'I can't ever forgive your husband for what he did'? 'He's part of the chain of systemic racism that's killing men who look like my father and brother'? 'If you don't think race is the problem here, then you're completely clueless'?"

The fist in my stomach squeezes tighter at the fact that I even have to explain that.

"Um, hell yeah. That's a start. How can you have a friendship if you can't be honest with each other? I'm just gonna say it — you dance around things with her, from what I've seen over the years. I mean, I have about one white friend — you know, Kate, from work. She's like a half friend to grab lunch with, but whatever, I still tell her what's up all the time. And I call her out too. Like last week when she said our other coworker Lakeisha was being 'ghetto' in a meeting. Uh-uh, Katie, girl. We had to have a good, long talk. I mean, maybe I'm too much — don't answer that — but that's me. Bottom line: You should feel like you can say what you need to say to Jen. You need to get it all out there now."

"You're right, Gab. My mom said the same thing. I just have to find the time."

"Story of your life, girl."

"Speaking of, I'm late for a meeting. I gotta run."

I abandon my Cheeto dreams, grab my notebook, and dash into the conference room. I'm three minutes late and Scotty gives me a withering once-over, but he doesn't stop speaking. "Okay, who's on Mummers?"

Every year with the stupid Mummers — a century-old tradition where a bunch of xenophobic old white men dress in black-face, brown-face, redface, and women's clothes to parade through the city on New Year's Day. Shaun forwarded me a link this morning with an op-ed by Ernest Owens that ran in *Philly* mag a couple years ago with the headline WANT TO SOLVE THE MUMMERS' DIVERSITY PROBLEM? JUST CALL IT "THE WHITE HERITAGE PARADE."

I'm hardly going to raise my hand for this one, and Scotty has better sense than to even look my way. With everything happening this year you'd think they'd shut the parade down, but so far the mayor has simply issued a stern warning to the Mummers to be on their best behavior . . . or else.

My phone buzzes with a call. Because it's a newsroom, no one bats an eye. When I see who it is, I launch myself toward the door, pointing at the phone to indicate to Scotty that I have to take it. He'll be glad I did when he learns that it's Sabrina Cowell, who is hopefully calling to say she'll do the interview with me, especially since Scotty asks about it every other day. I haven't seen her since the fundraiser. I also don't recall giving her my number, but I'm not surprised that she managed to get it.

"Hello, this is Riley."

"Hi, Riley, it's Sabrina."

"Oh, hi, Sabrina. How are you —"

"Listen, the OIS has completed their investigation of the shooting and kicked it over to us. We're going for an indictment for Kevin Murphy and Travis Cameron." She pauses. "My plan is to bring the case to the grand jury next week. We're going for murder one. Now, I don't think a grand jury will go for that, but it sends a message."

The words hit me with such force I have to steady myself against the hallway wall. A part of me knew this was coming, and another thought Kevin would slip through the cracks of the justice system like so many others before him. Or at least he would face lesser charges, a slap on the wrist.

Then there's Jenny in my head.

I asked for this. I wanted it. I courted Sabrina so she'd give me a scoop, and now I hate that I have this information.

"Riley?"

"I'm here."

"We have some new information about Officer Murphy. . . ." Her pause seems to last a lifetime. "That he may be . . . less

350

culpable than Cameron."

Less culpable. My heart is racing. "What information?" I've been pressing my source at the district to get the police reports for weeks now, but given how high-profile and sensitive the case is, I've had no luck.

"I can't tell you that right now. What I can tell you is my singular goal here is justice, justice for Justin's family. I'd be satisfied punishing the officer who's most culpable, especially if we have evidence that justifies that and also sways public opinion. In fact, we would see it as a win for the Dwyers, especially if it saves Tamara Dwyer from a drawn-out trial reliving what happened to her son, and all the media attention that would come with it. But that would mean Officer Murphy testifying against his partner. I want every officer on the PPD to understand that they'll be held accountable for their actions, but that they are also accountable to the larger ethos and credibility of the whole department — no more cover-ups, no more turning the other cheek, no more blind loyalty. Every officer has to hold the others to the highest standard, and that means honesty and transparency, from the top down. It also means we send a message to officers who don't co-operate. In light of our talk and of your *tricky* position, I wanted to give you a heads-up on this."

Why, I wonder. Is it because of my connection to Jen? I haven't seen her for weeks though, and I don't have any influence over what Kevin will do. So if that's Sabrina's angle here, she's out of luck.

"Okay," I offer noncommittally.

"Part of the reason I wanted to loop you in is because I'm considering doing the interview you asked for when I announce the indictments. This isn't going to be an easy case, and shaping the story in the right way is going to be critical."

"What do you mean by 'shaping the story'?"

"You know as well as I do that the court of public opinion matters just as much as that of any court of law. I also don't have to tell you these cases are difficult to prosecute; the legal bar favors cops, which is something that we're going to have to change. I want a conviction here, I want some justice for the Dwyers, and I have a strategy for that. But I also want public pressure and attention. I want any potential jury pool and any Philadelphia citizen to understand what's at stake here, and how and why I'm — we're — trying to reform our city. That's where you come in."

In other words, I'm the stepping-stone for Sabrina's soapbox. Which is fine; she's not the first person to try to manipulate the media to her own ends and tilt her head toward the spotlight — she wouldn't be where she is if she hadn't. But still, the self-serving undertones and the means-to-an-end vibe make me wonder: Is Sabrina truly out for justice for Justin, or just out for Sabrina? But that line of thinking cuts too close to questioning my own motivations.

"In the meantime, this has to stay under wraps. If we can't get this indictment, I don't want the public to know we tried and failed. It wouldn't be good for the DA's office, the Dwyers, or the city of Philadelphia. There's too much at risk. It's a powder keg out there. I don't want to be the one who lights the match."

"Okay. I won't repeat any of this, Sabrina."

Whatever else this little disclosure is, it's a test of trust too.

Whose side are you on?

"Great, I'll be in touch," Sabrina says, then hangs up.

I'm still not sure what type of game she's playing, and I definitely don't know the rules. If staying quiet about this lands this interview, I'll play along, but I'm still stuck on two words. Murder. One.

The weight of the secret settles in my gut like a sinking stone, slowly, and then boom, it's lodged there, a part of me. Before I can even drop the phone from my ear, Scotty is bellowing my name. *What now?* Bart comes jogging over, eating a banana, because Bart always seems to be eating a banana. "Hey. Bad car accident on 676. Scotty wants us there stat."

Scotty's voice booms across the newsroom. "Riley, get there, *now*! I want you first on scene. Be ready to go live at the top of the show."

I dash around grabbing what I need, as efficient as a firefighter readying for a blaze. Coat, hat, heels, makeup bag in hand, and I'm climbing into the news van in under four minutes. Bart takes off before my door is even closed and then guns it like the NASCAR driver he once confessed he'd always wanted to be, racing through the neighborhoods, avoiding the clogged freeway until we're closer to the accident.

More than a decade in local news and I've seen my share of accident and crime scenes, blood and guts and dead bodies. It's easy to harden yourself to it all — sometimes it bothers me just how easy. As we pull up to the snarl of twisted metal, I take in the dark circles of bloodstained pavement, the one blue tennis shoe lying on the road, the acrid smell of burning oil and rubber. I try to focus on gathering the facts from the officers on-site. I'm happy to see Pete on the scene. He and I have crossed paths a few times on the job. At twenty-one, he seems more like a kid playing dress-up than an actual cop. The viewers in Joplin must have thought the same thing about me at that age, seeing me on their TV screens, a kid dressed up as a newscaster. It's amazing anyone can have a first job and be taken seriously; it's like we're all doing the career equivalent of walking around in our mothers' high heels.

I'm not a fan of most cops, but I like Pete, and the feeling seems to be mutual. He's always eager to help, unlike some of the other officers I've met on the job, who like to lord their information and access over me, make me work for every little scrap. He tells me there are two dead on scene and two going to the hospital. Paramedics work feverishly on an unconscious woman sprawled on the pavement, her shabby bra and fleshy belly completely exposed. Then I hear a sound I can't ignore, a hysterical shriek.

"Is that a baby?" I ask Pete.

His eyes dart over to the ambulance. "Yeah, three-year-old's about to head to the hospital. He's okay though. He was strapped into the car seat. It flipped but held him in. He's just scared. That's the mother." He nods at the woman on the ground. "She's touch-and-go. Other driver en route to the hospital may have been drunk. You can't report that until I get confirmation that I can release it."

"Will you have it by the time we go on air?"

"How long?"

"Maybe five minutes?"

"I'll do my best."

I race back to the van to touch up my makeup and get mic'ed, giving Scotty an update all the while.

"When it bleeds it leads, as they say, so we'll throw to you at 5:03, 5:04." He's already barking orders at someone else before he hangs up.

There's five minutes of downtime before I go on air, long enough to check my email. I then spend the next four minutes and fifty seconds regretting that decision.

"You have to be fucking kidding me." I don't realize I've said it out loud until Bart looks up, shocked.

"An f-bomb from Riley Wilson. Whoa.

What's up?"

"Nothing, nothing, it's fine." I tug at the scarf around my neck, which suddenly feels like it's choking me. I yank it off and open the passenger door to the van, toss the phone into the passenger seat like it's delivered an electric shock. Maybe by the time I pick it back up, the message won't be there anymore. It will be some trick my mind played on me. That name no longer at the top of my in-box.

Corey.

I accepted that he was never going to get in touch again, and why would he? Especially since I was pretty sure he'd moved on. I let myself look at his Facebook a couple of months ago. There was more than one picture of him and some girl, the exact kind of woman I'd imagined him with — an artsy bohemian type, judging from the peasant dresses and asymmetrical haircut; perky, white. All the things I'll never be.

So why now? Maybe they've broken up? Maybe he saw my interview with Tamara? Or maybe something's wrong with him? He has cancer, needs a kidney? I briefly allow myself to entertain a much more dangerous thought. Or maybe he never stopped loving me?

"Time to get the show on the road," Bart

says, and releases a long, low belch.

"You're a pig, Bart." I muster a wobbly laugh.

It's a blessing and a curse that live TV stops for no one. I slam the van door shut with my phone inside, the email away and out of mind for now. I attempt to smooth my bangs, pressing them close to my forehead, taking one last look in the side mirror to make sure my makeup is in place. It's a miracle: I look serene and composed; only my shaking knees would give me away.

As I get in place in front of the camera, Pete gives me a thumbs-up, letting me know I can report on the drunk driver in the broadcast.

It can be either invigorating or exhausting, switching to the on-air sparkle for the cameras. After all these years, it's become second nature to me to be able to turn everything else off and focus only on the three-inch camera lens ten feet away. It's taking a stage and the only thing that matters is delivering my lines, which happens now as I assume the position — mic held tight in gloved hand, eyes directly forward, back straight, warm gaze — and begin sharing the gruesome and tragic details of the car accident when Bart cues me in. Less than three minutes and the segment is over.

In my earpiece, Chip and Candace move on to a story about a house fire in Point Breeze. My work here is done.

I don't let myself look at my phone the entire ride back to the newsroom even though it takes twice as long with Bart following the speed limit. And I don't look when I'm back in the dressing room, wiping off my makeup. It remains tucked deep in the reaches of my tote bag as I walk home. It starts to rain on the way, a freezing drizzle, and I don't bother to cover my hair. Umbrellas, weather, my hair, it's all irrelevant.

In my apartment, I change into sweatpants as if it's a normal evening. My phone lies on the counter while I assemble the ingredients to make a vodka tonic, dragging the process out as long as possible, even cutting up a slice of a shriveled lemon that's been languishing on the counter. By this point my anticipation has become a sort of frenzy, almost euphoric. It's an exquisite torture to delay the inevitable, to speculate about what Corey might say, rather than to actually know.

I let the vodka do its job as our three-year relationship plays out in my mind like a short film. In fact, it started exactly like a movie, complete with the sudden rainstorm

I wasn't supposed to get caught in. I'd been in Chicago for an NABJ conference. During a break, I'd walked a few blocks from the hotel to grab a pastry at a bakery on Michigan Avenue that everyone had raved about, and the skies opened up out of nowhere and I was stuck without an umbrella, a true catastrophe, considering my freshly straightened hair and the panel I was supposed to attend in twenty minutes that would be filled with top network producers.

Like a fool, I tried to hail a taxi from underneath the bakery's awning. Then, when I finally spotted a yellow light, I dashed out into the street so fast I tripped and rolled my ankle on the curb and fell straight into the arms of a man with a sexy buzz cut and the longest eyelashes I'd ever seen. If it didn't happen to me, I would swear I'd made it up. Maybe it was the sheer romantic absurdity of it all that sucked me in at first, because this stranger wasn't my type. Shaun may have a taste for white girls, but I'd never even looked twice at a white guy.

He happened to be staying at the Hilton too, in town for a real estate conference. So we walked back, huddled together beneath his giant umbrella. He asked me to have dinner with him as soon as we made it through the revolving doors to the lobby.

"If I'm going to dinner with you, I'll need to know your name," I said, impressed with my attempt at flirting.

"I'm Corey, and you're Riley."

He met my confused and slightly panicked expression by pointing to the name tag pinned to my chest.

That night, we ate at a touristy diner in Greektown. There was something disarming and intimate about eating pancakes in one of those curved old booths, where you have to sit nearly side by side like you just ordered breakfast in bed. The whole time, I kept thinking that he must have slipped something in my drink. Otherwise, how could I account for how giddy I felt, bubbly even, drunk off the cheap sparkling wine, and why I kept telling him things, personal, embarrassing things — how I was jealous of Gabrielle's trust fund and big salary working at Nike; how I say I'm fluent in Spanish, when really I'm passable at best; or how I like to act all worldly when I don't even have a passport.

Corey had his own confessions, though they were more charming than embarrassing. He talked with a lisp until he was ten; he once failed miserably on an episode of college *Jeopardy!*; his first sex dream involved Maria from *Sesame Street.* His favorite movie was *The Lion King.*

"I cry every single time."

"Who doesn't?" I replied.

"Sociopaths," he said.

With each question he asked, I was more disarmed — and he was full of them, like he didn't want to waste time on small talk. After dinner, we walked through Grant Park, skipping straight to our romantic histories, six years with a college sweetheart for Corey, ended the year before; three underwhelming relationships for me, if you could even call them that: two lackluster flings in college with dudes who didn't worry too much about me not letting them in — it was enough just to be a pretty light-skinned girl with long hair — and then Alex, a fellow reporter in Joplin. That yearlong relationship was maybe the closest I'd ever come to love, but that was still eons away from the actual feeling. Sometimes I wondered if I was even capable of falling in love. I actually said that to him. Out loud. I had never vomited up so much personal information to a stranger before. It was an out-of-body experience for me, even more so when we headed back to his hotel room, which at some point in the evening became an unspoken inevitability.

When Corey slipped his hand in my pants before we'd even made it to his room, we were both shocked at how wet I was. It felt like my own body had betrayed me with this evidence of my desire. I would have been embarrassed by how primal it was, I would have been concerned about the cameras in the elevator and who might be watching, reminding myself, *Nice girls don't do this* — had I been capable of having any thoughts and feelings beyond *This, now.* Nothing else mattered. I didn't even care that after two hours of sex I'd sweated out my blowout. The entire night, I was a stranger to myself, free of any and all inhibitions.

Even thinking about it now brings a stirring between my legs. I press a throw pillow into my lap as if to muffle any lingering lust.

When I'd woken the next morning in Corey's suite, sore and spent, it had felt like waking from a fever dream, or what I imagine a heroin bender must feel like. I hobbled around, naked, to collect my clothes that had been scattered around the room, reaching under the bed for my bra, all while Corey watched me with this look, like he could see right through me. I didn't want him to look at me like that. I didn't want to feel the way I did. I didn't want to date a white guy. I didn't want a long-distance relationship. As I dressed, I explained that as best as I could (except for the white-guy part).

"Okay, Riley," Corey said, in a tone I couldn't read. Playful? Resigned? Annoyed? "It sounds like you know best. At least kiss me goodbye."

I leaned over the bed to give him a peck. Before I could pull away, he grabbed my face and drew me closer, his tongue probing mine, until I surrendered completely, too shaky and weak to resist. When I finally managed to tear myself away, I didn't trust myself to say goodbye; I just flew out of the room. Not an hour later, after I'd showered away all the last traces of sex and chalked it up as a once-in-a-lifetime blip that no one needed to know about, I received a text.

I'm booking a flight to Birmingham. You can't get rid of me that easily. We have to see where this goes.

I both loved and hated this about Core: his ability to proceed as if everything was going to fall into place for him, because it always had — the privilege of being a good-looking white guy from Connecticut. His confidence bordered on arrogance, and it was sexy as hell when it wasn't infuriating.

In any case, his Jedi mind tricks worked. Nine months later, I was introducing him to my family the weekend before Thanksgiving. God, how I had dreaded that visit. But then, there I was, watching Corey taking in our "Wall of Pride," the long hallway between the front door and the living room, every square inch covered in family portraits and the requisite photo of Martin Luther King Jr., along with framed mementos of Black excellence and history: the *New York Times* from the day Obama was elected president, two poems by Maya Angelou, a poster with a listing of Black inventions, etc. I explained the origins of the wall, parroting Momma.

"The world outside may try to tell you that you're less than, but as you come and go from this house, you're going to look at this wall and remember who you really are and who you can be." It was practically the family slogan.

Corey proclaimed the display "very cool." I was busy wondering if he'd ever even been inside a Black person's home before and why I'd never asked him this, when he leaned in for a closer look at the inventor poster.

"You know, it was a Black man who created the recipe for Jack Daniel's whiskey,"

Corey said. "Nathan Green, it was his creation."

By this point I was used to Corey being a fountain of random facts, but this one endeared him to my parents, who were watching from the hall. I let myself enjoy the tiniest bit of relief that this might go well.

I hadn't expected Corey to be so at ease at my family's table, though he was, completely, gamely submitting to piles of food and some friendly ribbing. ("I bet you never had grits before, have you, son?" Daddy asked. He hadn't.) I was the one on edge. I tried to calm myself by refilling glasses of iced tea and ferrying plates of food back and forth to the table. I couldn't shake the feeling that there was something wrong with this picture, that I was doing something illicit, like the first time I drank under my parents' roof or cursed or got my belly button pierced with Jen at that grimy shop on South Street.

Dating a white man — marrying one, if it came to that — felt disloyal. I always thought I should end up with a fine upstanding brother, build up the community, have two beautiful brown-skinned children who would be a credit as well, advance their race, the cause. Not with this white guy who played lacrosse in high school, went to Williams, and came from money to boot. Sometimes, as I lay beside him in bed, his pale body against mine, one word would float through my mind: "sellout." I swore I saw the same word floating like a cartoon bubble above Gigi's head when he visited that weekend. She was perfectly polite to Corey, but as soon as he was out of earshot, she couldn't help reminding me, "He's never going to get you, and you won't get him. Why add more heartache to your plate? The world is hard enough as it is. Find one of your own."

The entire time he was with my family, I was preoccupied, wondering what it would be like to meet Corey's parents, Steve and Catharine, an environmental lawyer and a landscape architect from Connecticut. All the energy it would take to make sure they understood that I was one of the good ones. All the condescending comments I might have to ignore, the fear that they'd be one way to my face and another behind my back. It was enough to make me want to avoid the whole thing altogether.

I brought it up once after we'd been dating a few months, after trying out the question in my mind for weeks. "What will your parents think of you dating someone . . .

like me?" In the versions I rehearsed, I'd said, "a Black girl."

"My dad is gonna be pissed." He paused for too long, long enough for me to get up off the couch. He grabbed my hand and pulled me back down, grinning. "I've never brought a Sixers fan home. Seriously, though, my parents are cool, Rye. They're gonna love you."

But what did "cool" mean exactly? Would his mom pull me into a hug and call me "girl"? Would they start talking about how they were die-hard Obama supporters, or gush about how "impressive" I was, or proudly tell me they'd just finished the new Ta-Nehisi Coates?

I'd never find out. I'd always have to wonder how "cool" Corey's parents were, because time ran out for us before I ever met them.

I finish the vodka, and force myself to remember the end of our story. The text:

We're not right for each other. I'm sorry.

If only I could call Jen so we could read his email together over the phone. She'd be able to come up with a plan, craft the best response. When Corey and I first started dating, she was my Cyrano de Bergerac, composing all my text messages so they hit the perfect tone, funny or witty or sexy. I

368

sometimes wonder if Corey actually fell in love with me or with her texts. She even convinced me to send a selfie once, insisting I wear an over-the-top bright-red push-up bra, even though the thought of my boobs traveling through cyberspace and landing on his phone had me nauseous with mortification.

Jen styled the cleavage shot, helped me find the right angle, scooping my left boob up a little, tightening my bra straps, even running a swipe of bronzer across my collarbone. After about twenty-three takes, the photo was ready to send. We both waited, equally nervous for the reply. Minutes later Corey wrote back:

Oh, shit. I forwarded that to my mom.

Seconds later, another text.

Kidding. You should be on a runway.

But I can't call Jen, because we're in this weird unspoken standoff and also because I have a secret about her husband and I can't talk to her as long as this stone is in my stomach.

I need to read this email and get it over with. My fingers quiver as I tap and swipe until it's right there. I skim the message, frantically scanning for terrifying words like "pregnant," "married," or "dying," and take in its length — which is short. I skip to the end to see how he signed it. Just "Corey." No "love." Then, finally, I return to the beginning and read each word, slowly this time, to make it last. He writes that he saw on my Facebook page that my grandmother passed away. So this is a condolence note. Nice, though disappointing. His tone is polite, like he's an old professor or colleague, not someone who's seen every inch of me naked. I read on, moderating my expectations. He writes how sorry he is. He writes that he knows I've moved back to Philadelphia and that he saw my interview with Tamara. "So powerful!" Corey doesn't use exclamation marks lightly, so I read that part twice. Then he says that he'll be in town next month, coming from New York for a work trip.

Finally, the last line, and when I get to it, a swarm of moths takes flight behind my rib cage. *It's been a long time. Can I see you when I'm in town?*

I'm about to go out on the balcony, as if fleeing from the question, but take a detour through the kitchen instead. I dig into the far recesses of the freezer, where I know there's an ancient pack of Parliaments hidden behind a stack of frozen pizzas. I found them in a box of lightbulbs and batteries when I moved in. I should have thrown the nasty things away. I hid them here in case of an emergency. I've never been a real smoker, but I learned on my first job in Joplin that most people in the news business are, and if I wanted one-on-one time with my producer, I'd better start. Gaby clowned me big-time when she first saw me with a cigarette. "Black girls don't smoke." Like it was a fact.

"Well, we also don't listen to Ani DiFranco or Taylor Swift, and I have whole albums on my phone," I said.

"Who the hell is Ani DiFranco?" Gaby said, grabbing my cigarette and taking a big inhale that ended in a spasm of violent coughs. "Girl, this is disgusting. I just killed a lung."

"You smoke weed, Gaby," I reminded her.

"That's different. I'm Jamaican, my genes are built for that."

And now I miss Gaby and want to call her, but she was always skeptical of Corey. She dated one white guy our freshman year, whose family had a house in Jamaica for forever and who'd once "joked" that it would be funny if his ancestors had owned her ancestors at some point. And she "joked" that it would be funny if she poured her red wine on him and then she did. Gaby had said it was "maybe for the best" when

I'd called to tell her it was over with Corey. So I'm not going to call her. Not yet. Not till I'm ready for her to tell me what a bad idea it would be to write him back.

When I step out on the balcony, my bare arms erupt in goose bumps in the cold.

Can I see you? Can I see you?

Why now? I agonize over the question as I flick the rusted wheel of a lighter I found in the junk drawer. The first inhale tastes like heaven. I regret the decision by the second, and I'm nauseous by the third.

My balcony is so tiny, if I spread my arms, I can touch both walls on either side. After I first moved in, I happened by a garage sale on one of my runs and found a cute little wicker chair and a matching side table that fit just right. I was so focused on the thrill of having a balcony with a view of Center City, giddy about my triumphant return, the chair felt like a victory. Now, when I look at it, the pathetic single chair, loneliness hits me with such force it's a minute before I remember to breathe. I smash the cigarette out on the iron railing and flee back inside, into the warm air. I go straight for my phone to reread Corey's email. Instead, my in-box opens to the last one from Jen, the one I never responded to.

All our lives can go back to normal.

That's not true, Jenny. It could be about to get a lot worse. The district attorney wants to convict your husband of murder.

I lunge for the glass on the coffee table and refill it, this time not even bothering with the tonic. I sip and sip, knowing I shouldn't be drinking alone right now, not with this stone in my stomach and Corey's email on my phone. But I'm not stopping. I sip until I can no longer picture the look on Jen's face when her husband and the father of her child is handcuffed and taken away to prison. I keep sipping until I'm tipsy enough to let myself do the thing I most want to do, the thing I'll later blame on the booze. I open my email and start to type.

CHAPTER TWELVE

JEN

Someone forgot to tell the manager at Target that it's time to change the music. Mariah Carey should not be telling you what she wants for Christmas two weeks into January. And yet here she is, belting it out of the too-loud speakers.

I had to get out this morning. I was like a feverish prisoner ready to make a break for it. If you asked me when I left the house before today, I couldn't tell you. I could tell you the last time I *almost* left. Last Thursday. I was supposed to meet Riley for a coffee. I was looking forward to it so bad. I was all dressed up, even blew out my hair, put on some lip gloss; then she canceled on me an hour before. Something came up at work. It was just an excuse. I wrote back, *No problem.* Even adding an emoji. And then I decided that I was officially done. I wasn't going to try again. The ball was in her court, and I wasn't holding my breath.

I was desperate for a change of scenery, and Target seemed as good a destination as any, especially since I have a $100 gift card, a Christmas present from Annie and Matt, burning a hole in my pocket. Since I'm not having a shower, I need to buy all the baby gear on my own, see how far I can stretch this $100, because I can't spend anything else.

A row of shiny wooden cribs announces the baby section. Frank's been spending a lot of time in his workroom in the garage, building "a surprise" for the baby that I suspect is probably a crib. Considering the prices I'm seeing here, a free crib sounds amazing to me, and it's given Frank something to do these last few weeks, an escape from Cookie and the broken son he has no idea how to fix.

I waddle slowly up and down the next aisle, leaning heavily on the cart handle. A baby swing catches my eye, and I lean over to the bottom shelf to look at the price. When I straighten, there's a familiar and distinct wetness between my legs. I probably peed myself again. It happens lately every time I sneeze, cough, or bend over. Just another one of those totally normal and gross symptoms of pregnancy that no one ever tells you about. I've started wearing these gigantic pads all the time, the same kind the kids in middle school used to leave on our seventh-grade teacher Mrs. Dobber's chair, sticky side up.

It feels more wet than usual this time though. It's gonna soak through my only pair of maternity jeans. My body is embarrassing enough without having to walk through Target with a dark splotch across my ass. I need a mirror to see how bad it looks.

Suddenly a searing pain rips through my midsection. I make it two more steps and there's another sharp stab, a hot blade slicing through me. I can't even catch my breath before there's another and another until I can't take it anymore. I collapse on the ground.

Worse even than the pain is the sudden and paralyzing certainty that something is wrong.

"Help me. Somebody help . . . me." I finally get out the words. The effort leaves me spent.

A pimply-faced teenager wearing a red polo shirt two sizes too big for him approaches but does nothing except stand there looking at me, useless. Finally a woman pushing a cart with three girls under the age of six shoves the store employee out of the way and places her hand on my back.

"Breathe, honey. Just breathe. It's gonna be okay."

"No, no, no. It's too soon."

The look on the woman's face says it all. She's had kids, those three little girls watching me now, silent and scared.

"Did your water break?"

"I don't know." The wet spot around my crotch is spreading, seeping down my thighs. The doctors and the websites all say it's unlikely that your water will break. It only happens 20 percent of the time. It's the smell that lets you know. But what's it supposed to smell like? All I can smell is my own fear, sour and metallic.

"Give me your phone. I'll call your husband."

"In my bag?"

The woman digs around in my purse, rooting through the loose change, crumpled receipts, the bruised banana I keep meaning to throw away, dirty tissues, the spare tampon that long ago lost its wrapper. As she continues to search the multiple pockets, I have a crystal-clear image of my phone sitting in the center console of the car.

The woman squats down, her kind eyes level to mine. "I can't find it. We can use mine. What's the number?"

I only knew three numbers by heart. Lou's home number, which is the same number I had growing up; Riley's cell, which has miraculously stayed the same all these years; and Kevin's cell, which I only know because he made me memorize it. Part of his training was making the family memorize important numbers. I squeak out Kevin's number and watch the woman punch it into her own phone.

"It went to voice mail."

Of course it did. He's not going to answer some random number and listen to someone scream at him again.

"Who else can I call?"

Before I can answer, a chain saw slices right through my stomach, cutting me in half. I roll over, an inhuman sound coming out of my mouth. I start bargaining with God, thinking of all the things I'll trade for Chase to be okay. It's a short-lived exercise, because the answer is everything, anything.

"Call 911!" the woman commands the pimply teenager, and he seems happy to be told what to do.

I think I'm nodding, though maybe my head isn't even moving. I'm squeezing my eyes shut against the agony. I sense the small crowd forming around us, staring at me with concern and pity, and a dash of excitement too, at being front row for an emergency, a story to tell later.

"Try my husband again," I manage.

The woman dutifully complies. "Still no answer, hon."

I could give her Riley's cell: 215-555-4810 . . . 215-555-4810. I've dialed it more than I've dialed Kevin's number, more than my own home phone. I've called it from pay phones and random guys' cell phones to let her know when our favorite song came on in some bar during a boring date. But no. I can't call Riley. Why? In the haze of pain it's hard to think straight. I'm done. But done with what? Done with Riley? I wasn't gonna call her again. Ever. The hard line had felt good, a sense of righteous satisfaction. Now that reasoning doesn't make sense. Riley's my best friend? The thought forms itself into a question.

"Anyone else, honey?" The woman asks, a frantic pitch to her voice. One of her little girls whimpers.

"My best friend . . . Call Riley," I manage. From a distance, over the sound of my own labored panting, I can faintly hear Riley say hello to Judy through the phone. I'm not sure how I know the woman's name is Judy. She must have told me.

"I think your friend has gone into labor," Judy explains. I need Judy to take those words back. Hearing them out loud makes it real. When I'm seized by another crippling contraction, I focus on Judy's three girls, all of them with white-blond hair and wide eyes like baby deer. The little one who was whimpering has stopped. She's now staring at me, along with her sisters, as if I'm an animal in a zoo as she slurps loudly out of a Little Mermaid cup. Judy holds the phone down, and Riley's voice is closer now, right in my ear.

"Jenny, it's going to be okay. I'm going to find Kevin and we'll meet you at the hospital. Okay, Jenny? You're going to be fine. He's going to be fine." I'm so happy to hear Riley's voice, even if she's lying to me again. I'm not going to be fine. But there's a chance Chase could be. He has to be. There's no other outcome that I can bear.

The small crowd that's gathered gives way to the paramedics, who lift me into an ambulance.

The paramedics tell me we're headed to St. Mary, and this is the first thing that's brought me peace in what feels like hours. *Annie's hospital.* If I can't deliver downtown, as I planned, this is the next best option. I have no idea if she's working, but at least my sister-in-law can put in a good word with the staff, make sure we receive the best care.

My relief is so short-lived it's barely enough time to remember the feeling. Another wave of staggering pain washes over me, like a riptide pulling me under. There's no point in fighting. How is it possible that my body is capable of so much agony? As soon as I can breathe again, I ask what's happening, if the baby is okay. The two paramedics respond in a soothing, even tone that makes me want to kick them in the teeth. How dare they be so calm at a time like this? They're not gonna tell me what's really happening anyway. They won't tell me that Chase is in trouble, but I know. Riley's not the only one with the tingles.

Minutes, seconds, or hours after we arrive at the hospital, Kevin bursts through the flimsy curtain surrounding my bed in the ER. The paramedics gave me a shot of something. It's dulled the sensations, or maybe I've grown used to them.

"Babe, are you okay?" Kevin asks, panic pulsing off him. He practically slams into the bed and pats me frantically with both hands, as if checking for injuries. He looks like he does right before he's going to be sick, pale and shaky.

I'm hit hard with a surge of love for him right then, and relief, and sympathy; it's all there swirling around, making me dizzy. I want to spare him the truth, so I don't say anything at all. I simply grab his hand. When we touch, something unspoken passes between us, a solidarity that gives me strength.

We turn, still holding on to each other, as a stocky man in a crisp white coat comes through the curtain. "I'm Dr. Atunde, the ob-gyn resident on duty tonight."

My stomach sinks, taking in the doctor, his dark skin. Kevin stiffens like he's having the same thought. What if this doctor recognizes my husband from the news? Will it impact how hard he works to save our baby? No, that's impossible. Doctors don't do that. They took oaths not to do that. They save terrorists and serial killers.

"You're going to be a father today," the doctor says to Kevin, with measured joy. Kevin lets go of my hand so he can take the doctor's, who shakes it vigorously. The hand that Kevin released finds its way to my belly.

I'm going to be a mother today. It's a prayer, more than a statement. I focus every fiber of my being on Chase, willing him to be okay with a fervor that borders on unhinged. I have never needed and will never need or want anything more desperately than this, and the simple clarity of that is overwhelming. *If I get this, I will never ask for another thing as long as I live.* It's the purest promise I will ever make.

Even though Dr. Atunde calmly explains what's going to happen next, there's an unmistakable urgency in his voice too. "Jennifer, we're concerned about the fetal heart rate. It's too fast; your blood pressure is rising, and the labor isn't progressing. We have to do an emergency C-section. We need to get this baby out of you as quickly as possible. I'm going to get washed up and I'll see you up there. The anesthesiologist is ready for you. Any questions?"

Kevin shivers as he strokes my hair, murmuring over and over, "Jenny, it's gonna be okay." His breath, with the faintest trace of beer, is warm on my face. But then it's Riley's voice I think I hear calling my name. It comes again, louder, my full name. And then Riley is there, bursting through the curtain, standing right at my feet.

"You came." I don't entirely believe it.

"Oh Jenny, of course I came." She rushes over and kisses me on my clammy forehead.

Kevin and Riley are in the same room. It's a struggle to arrange this fact in my mind. Not even the same room, in the same claustrophobic space. I glance at the heart-rate monitor, worried it'll spike and give away how tense this makes me.

Riley nods hello at Kevin and moves to the opposite side of my bed. He responds with an unmistakable hint of anger that's quickly replaced with relief. He no longer has to deal with this alone.

"Are you okay?" Riley glances at the beeping monitor, where the squiggly lines build to a pointy mountain every seven minutes or so. "Is Chase okay?"

"Chase?" Kevin looks confused. He takes a step backward, as if he's been physically pushed. "Wait. It's a boy? She knew?" He seems to be trying to process these facts as Riley stands there completely stricken. This has the makings of a hilarious setup in some wacky sitcom, except that exactly nothing about our life is hilarious right now.

"It was an accident, Kevin. I found out by accident," Riley explains, desperately looking to me for guidance.

I don't have enough energy for this moment. I grab Kevin's hand and hope that does what it's supposed to do, says all the things I can't summon, mainly that I'm sorry.

A balloon of tension grows until a slow grin starts to take over his face, deflating it just like that. "It's a boy." He says the words with a reverential joy, and even though I had nothing to do with this, it was all biology and fate and genes, I still feel like I'm giving him a gift.

"I thought it was a girl. I don't know . . . but a boy. I wanted a boy," Kevin says, positively giddy now, like he's revealing his own secret, even though I knew perfectly well how badly he wanted a son.

Riley's wide brown eyes blaze with concern when I turn to look at her.

"They have to cut him out of me, Rye." My voice cracks. "It's too early."

She leans over so her face is inches from mine. She smells faintly of sweat and cocoa butter.

"It's okay. It's going to be okay. You're strong. Chase is strong. You've got this." She straightens up to look at Kevin. "You've both got this. Gigi would say, 'Women been making babies since the beginning of babies. Our bodies know what to do. You know what to do.' "

"No, I don't know what to do. My body isn't doing the right thing."

"It is." Riley places both of my hands between hers. Hers are bigger than mine. They always have been. We'd compare them when we were little, placing our palms against each other's, checking to see how much longer Riley's fingers stretched than mine. Then I'd flip Riley's palm up to the sky and pretend I knew how to read her future in the fine lines etched into the skin. "Your life line is long. Look at this love line. You're going to have three great loves in your life and four babies and a mansion in Miami on the beach." Now, Riley's long fingers wrap around mine, a lifeline.

"Do you think he's scared? Chase?" The question is ridiculous, but it's what I want to know.

Both Kevin and Riley speak at the same time. "No. No. He isn't scared. He doesn't know what's happening."

I stare straight up at the ceiling. "I'm scared, you guys."

"You'll be fine. You're going to do great," Riley reassures me again.

"Hi, Momma, how about we get this baby out?" another nurse asks as she comes in and starts to unplug and unhook with ruthless efficiency.

"It's a boy," I blurt. "It's a boy, and his name is Chase. Can we please use his name?" In case the worst happens, I need everyone to call him by his name, like he's a real person in the world. He exists.

The nurse stops moving long enough to look right at me. "Got it, are you ready to meet Chase?"

Riley grabs my hand, runs her finger across my palm. It's an old code we used to have when we were at the dinner table or church and couldn't even whisper without someone hearing. A scratch on the palm means, *Are you good?* Two squeezes means yes. One means no. I squeeze Riley's hand two times.

"She's ready," Riley tells the nurse, still looking at me.

"You've got this. You can do this, Jaybird," Kevin adds, leaning over to kiss my damp forehead.

Riley and Kevin step away from the bed as the nurses prepare to move me. Without either of them touching me I feel suddenly untethered, lost.

"Will you be here?" I ask Riley. Of course Kevin will stay, but I'm terrified that she'll leave, walk out the door, and we'll go back to strained emails, unanswered text messages, and broken plans. The thought that I might have to text Riley the first picture of Chase makes me unspeakably sad. I'd always imagined her being in the hospital to see my baby when he was brand-new to the world, to touch him and hold him and kiss his head and help me count his fingers and toes. I need Riley to be one of the first people Chase ever knows.

"I'll be here." Riley smiles her big TV smile, no trace of fear, at least to someone who doesn't know her. But I see it there. I can see through the mask.

"While you're doing your thing up there, I'm going to buy a bottle of champagne. So we can celebrate after."

Soon, I'm in motion through the hospital halls, being wheeled into an OR. It's all a blur.

And then I hear it. The best sound I've ever heard — my baby's wail. Dr. Atunde lifts Chase Anderson Murphy, triumphantly, high into the air.

"His lungs are working," Dr. Atunde says, the relief in his voice revealing that he was prepared for a different outcome. I feel a rush of love for this stranger, for getting Chase out in time.

I watch Kevin walk from where he's been stationed at the top of the bed to the other side of the coarse blue curtain at my waist. He's not prepared for the sight of my belly sliced open from side to side — all of my guts exposed. I see his face flit from fear to disgust to confusion in a matter of seconds before his eyes land on Chase, and then there is only awe.

"Oh God, Jenny, he's so small." He sounds

terrified and happy and overwhelmed.

The nurse holds up a pair of scissors. "We're going to have to get this little guy over to the NICU. Do you want to cut the cord, Daddy?"

Kevin murmurs something that sounds like "uh-huh" and the nurse lowers the sheet enough so that I can see Kevin's hands shake as he cuts through the ropy string of tissue connecting me to Chase. It doesn't look like a cord at all, rather some kind of lumpy, spongy tube with a pulse, a life all its own.

As soon as he's finished, Dr. Atunde holds Chase up for me to see. He looks impossibly fragile, with arms like tiny twigs. His hair is thick and black like Kevin's, his skin almost translucent, and I can make out blue veins furiously pumping blood into his little heart that thumps so hard in his chest I worry it might burst out of his skin.

When I first see him, gooey and gorgeous, I think I might die for the second time that day. It doesn't seem possible that you could live with this staggering amount of love. It's almost daunting to feel so much at once. All of the women who said, "Oh, you just wait until you hold your baby the first time and the love you experience," like it was a mystical passage that you couldn't comprehend until you were on the other side — I get it now; they were right.

When I think of how much we went through to get here, the miscarriages, the needles, and all the times I nearly forced myself to give up, until some small seed inside me said, *No, you can't.* I know the road was supposed to lead me here. Right here. And whatever happens from this point forward, I have this; I have my baby.

A champagne bottle, an expensive-looking one with a French name that I can't pronounce, is the first thing I see when my eyes flutter open later, my head foggy with drugs and exhaustion. I'm in a proper room now. It's not private though, our insurance wouldn't cover that, but no one is in the bed next to mine. I turn and there's Riley asleep on a hard chair in the corner.

Riley is here.

Another realization breaks through, the sun burning off the fog. *I am a mother.* My heart stutters with a stunned relief as I remember this miraculous fact. The rest I piece together more slowly, my mind still sluggish. Kevin went home to get the hospital bag I never packed and plans to return later with Cookie. I need to stay in the hospital three more nights. Chase will have to stay in the hospital a few more weeks. He'll need the help of a respirator as his lungs continue to grow, and he can't regulate his temperature yet, but he's okay. *He's okay. He's okay.*

I'm working up the energy to get Riley's attention when a nurse wheels a cart into the room. As if I had conjured him, there he is. My baby.

The nurse maneuvers the cart next to the bed.

Riley jerks awake and leaps out of her chair over to the cart, gazes down at Chase like she's unwrapped a present. "He's adorable, Jenny."

The nurse picks him up. He's bundled tightly in a cotton swaddle, which gives him more bulk. An IV and monitors are bolted to his rolling crib, and wires crisscross his little body. "He can only be out of the NICU for a few minutes. I figured you'd want some time with him. Skin-to-skin contact helps these little guys, if you want to lie with him for a little while, Mommy." She starts to unfurl Chase from the blanket, and I shimmy my gown to expose my skin and swollen boobs. I'm ravenous for him, desperate to touch him by the time the nurse negotiates all of the cords and settles him into my arms.

Riley reaches over and touches his foot as if it's made of glass. "Look at these tiny toes."

Seeing the way she looks at him brings me just as much joy as I thought it would. More actually, much more.

"Toes that I made in my stomach!" I look up at Riley, watch her watch Chase. "You made this happen, Riley . . . without you, we wouldn't have tried again and we wouldn't . . ."

I can't even finish the sentence. It will never be possible for Riley to understand how much her part in this miracle has meant to me.

"I was happy to help. But you did this, Jenny. You made a baby!" She moves closer and rubs her finger along Chase's veiny scalp.

"I didn't know how much I would love him. It's like . . ." I don't know how to explain this to Riley, the sheer force of this love. It's something that she won't understand until she becomes a mother, like all those women who'd told me, "Just wait."

"He looks so much like Kevin," Riley observes. I know Cookie will say the same thing as soon as she arrives, likely with a stack of Kevin's baby pictures in hand as proof.

"How's Kevin doing . . . with everything?" Riley asks tentatively.

What should I say? What can I say? That I had to hide the sleeping pills and lock up the knives at Cookie's? That I watch him through the bedroom window pacing the backyard in the middle of the night?

"Today was a good day. You should have seen him in the delivery room. He cried, Rye. I don't think I've ever seen him cry before."

"I'm so happy for you . . . for you both."

I can tell she means it. It's a bone-deep truth and it chases away the bad feelings of the last few weeks. Almost.

"Thank you for being here, Riley. It means a lot."

"Oh, Jenny, of course I would be here."

"I didn't know. . . ." I wish Riley would acknowledge this, the feeling that we are slipping away from each other. That I'm not imagining it. That's it's real, and if it's real, then we can fix it.

Riley shakes her head. "Shhhh. Not now. Not right now. It's not the time. We don't have anything to talk about except for you and this little man. Can I get you anything? Does anything hurt? What do you need?"

I reach out for Riley's hand and squeeze.

"I'm okay, I don't need anything."

What more could I need? For one single moment, I have everything.

CHAPTER THIRTEEN

RILEY

A news story is like a fire. It has to be fed, nurtured in order to stay alive. It can be stoked with meager bits, pieces of kindling, small developments that turn a puff of smoke into a spark. Or sometimes it's doused with an entire bottle of lighter fluid and surges into an inferno. That's what happens when the video of Justin Dwyer's shooting is released to the public. A fresh wave of visceral outrage.

This is becoming a grim ritual — the video release of a racist encounter or worse, a murder. Granted, I understand why they go viral, why the media plays them on a constant loop. There's a prurient, click-bait quality that people can't turn away from. But sometimes it gets to be too much. You're buying a pair of shoes online and, boom, you're seeing someone get brutally Tasered at a traffic stop while his toddler waits in the car, all because he didn't signal properly. You're catching up on your friend's wedding photos on Facebook and, with one click, there's cops savagely slamming a teenage girl in a swimsuit to the ground and punching her while she cries for someone to please call her mom. It's all a relentless reminder that there will always be people who see you, and people who look like you, as dangerous, or unwelcome, or inferior. The hurt that comes with watching these videos accumulates, a scab breaking open again and again. Then comes the paranoia: after all, these are only the incidents caught on camera; you have to wonder what people are doing or saying beyond the reach of the lens — a lot worse, probably. So it's hard, harder every day, harder with every video, to stuff down the humiliation and anger to simply get on with breakfast, bedtime . . . life. But still, however painful, I recognize the power these videos have to say, *Look, this happens, this is real, please do not turn away.* It's the same reason I do my job: *People need to see this.*

I could only bring myself to watch the video of Justin dying a few times, and it already felt like too many. It's vivid in its shock even if it's grainy and soundless. In the first frame a figure runs through the alley in a flash and then it's gone. When Justin appears on the screen seconds later, he's sauntering along, minding his own business, head bopping up and down as if he's listening to a song he really likes. He's nearly at the end of the alleyway, about to turn right, about to walk two blocks east, back to his house. He's nearly there, and for a split second, I think it could end differently. He might keep walking, turn that corner and continue on home, grab himself a Coke out of the fridge, and sit down to play some video games.

That's not what happens.

Justin stops in his tracks. What unfolds next occurs so quickly that many of the news outlets, including KYX, have shown a slow-motion version, which is somehow more disturbing, drawing the scene out even longer. Justin stops walking, reaches into his right coat pocket. He pulls out a dark object, about the size of his hand. He takes an earbud from his ear as he turns. The footage is too grainy to make out his expression. I see it in my mind anyway, the curiosity morphing into shock as he jerks one way, then the other, and then falls to the ground. How quickly he collapses, like something in a cartoon.

But what stands out about the video

beyond Justin's tragic death are two things. Justin doesn't match the description of the guy they were looking for — Rick Sargent. Even in the black-and-white video it's clear that Justin is wearing a bright green North Face jacket, not the black coat Rick was reported as wearing. He's also a good six inches shorter. I know all this from the incident report I finally got from my police source. It underscores that Cameron shouldn't have shot. And that's the other thing about the video. You can see Cameron charge around the corner a split second before Kevin. This is why I watched the video the second and third time, in slow motion. Kevin didn't shoot first. In the video Kevin follows Cameron, sees his partner shooting, raises his gun, and fires. Then, while Cameron just stands there, Kevin runs over, drops down to his knees like he's whispering something to Justin.

"What the hell did that cop say to the kid after he shot him?" a pundit shouts on WHYY. As I drive, morning talk radio is on fire dissecting the shooting. Everyone and their cousin has an opinion.

"You saw him reach into his pocket. He could have been reaching for a gun. Those officers had a reason to shoot. These young-sters need to listen."

"That's what he was trying to do — taking out his headphones. He was dead before he got a chance to listen!"

"That guy who ran across the shot. I bet that's who they was really after, but we all look alike, right?"

"You shouldn't be a police officer if you're that afraid."

"No one goes to work saying, 'I'm going to kill someone today.' "

"Police officers have a split second to act. Blink your eyes. Can you make a decision that fast?"

"If you keep attacking cops, and claim they're racist, they'll stop policing."

I switch to another station. There's a man talking about racism against white people, the author of yet another book about why white men are so righteously angry. He's arguing that anti-white rhetoric is reaching "dangerous levels" and that there's nothing wrong with having pride in your nationality.

"I know I'm supposed to be ashamed to be a white man in America right now. Well, let me tell you I am not," he says.

I slam my hand against the control and switch the station again. Beyoncé has never been a more welcome presence in my life.

Rush hour traffic is a beast. I shouldn't have tried to drive all the way out to St.

Mary's hospital before work, but I just wanted to bring Jen's shower gift — the Mama Bird T-shirt — so she knew I was thinking of her, especially today, before Sabrina announces the indictment. Sabrina called the press conference last night, right after she leaked the video footage to MSNBC. At least, I suspect it was her, to drum fervor in time for her announcement. She wants as big a stage as possible. And she got one, fifteen full minutes with Joy Reid and an Anderson Cooper appearance, which means she doesn't need me anymore. I don't begrudge her this, though I am annoyed that she reneged on an exclusive interview with me and she hasn't returned my calls the last two days. Her office has been dodging me. The best I can hope for is a few minutes after the press conference today.

The press conference that will change my friend's life.

I've called and texted Jen at least once every day since Chase was born and haven't received a single response. I tell myself it's because she's busy with the baby, especially since he's probably still in the NICU. I don't want to stress her out or force myself on her, so I'm just going to drop off the gift at the front desk and hope they'll get it to her. I'm still waiting for some magical moment when Jen and I can reset, pick up where we left off. *Where did we leave off?*

The visitor lot is full so I pull into the patient lot, hoping it won't matter if I take a space for five minutes to run this to the nurse's station. I haven't even opened my door when I spot Jen's beat-up Camry in the row in front of mine. The engine is running, I can tell by the plume of exhaust fanning into the cold, and even through the fogged-up windows I can see Jen's blond hair, her head slumped down on the steering wheel.

My first instinct is to drive away. We've got to talk, yes, but I don't have the time right now without being late to work, and I hadn't planned on actually seeing Jenny at all, but I can't leave her like this.

"Jenny?" I rap on the passenger-side window. Her head jerks up and I see that tears are streaming down her face. I open the door and slide into the front seat. The last time I saw Jen cry was in first grade when Lou shaved her head during a lice outbreak because it was cheaper than buying the expensive shampoo. I rush over to the passenger side and let myself in. *Did something happen with Chase?*

"I can't take it, Riley. I can't take it

anymore!" She launches in as if she expected me all along. "It's just too much. I'm so fucking tired of all these people treating my husband like a villain and a scapegoat."

These people?

"Kevin's not a racist, or a bad apple, or a 'symptom of the systemic ills plaguing the police forces across America.'" She jabs her finger at the radio. She was clearly listening to the same morning shows I was. "This is such bullshit. And now in a few hours that stupid DA is going to stand in front of a zillion TV cameras and announce she wants Kevin's head on a platter. Can you believe that, Riley? And on top of everything, I feel like you've abandoned me and that's making all of this even worse." Her tears escalate to full-blown sobs. "I don't care, I had to say that. I'm mad, Riley. Really mad."

I haven't gotten a word in edgewise, but I stare out the window at the swirling red lights of an idling ambulance and try to figure out how to respond to this tirade.

"Well, Jen, to say I haven't been there for you . . . that's not really fair. I told you, I've been trying to cover the story and I've been busy —"

"Yeah, yeah, Riley, you're always busy. I mean, when are you not busy? So whatever."

Her tone is bruising . . . and annoying, frankly. Maybe Jen can't relate to eighty-hour work weeks as a receptionist, but she shouldn't judge me. I don't have a chance to defend myself, as she's already moved on. She turns to face me, shoulders squared, confrontation in her eyes.

"Tell me this, Riley. Do you think Kevin should go to jail? I just need to know."

So we're doing this?

"I don't know, Jen, that's not really for me to decide."

"I know that, Riley. I'm just asking what you *think*. If you think Kevin's some sort of racist monster, like everyone else seems to. Is that why you're angry at him? At us? Because that's not fair."

"Not fair? First of all, you can't say my feelings, whatever they are, aren't fair. Also, if you want to talk about unfair, let's talk about how unarmed Black men are being shot over and over and over. It's endless, Jen. Endless! Do you think *that's* fair? And most of these killers never face any legal consequences. I have pages of stats for you on that if you're interested. So yeah, maybe it sucks that Kevin is being put out there as an example when so many police officers have gotten off for doing the exact same thing. But the world isn't fair, Jenny."

She's biting down hard on her bottom lip so at first her words are a little slurry. "But I just don't think you understand how hard this has all been. I kept trying to explain on email. I'm all alone and people are making all these judgments and they're treating Kevin like he's some sort of 'issue' to be dealt with. Like we have to be punished on behalf of all white people or something. Which is ridiculous, when Kevin risks his life every day to make sure people — Black people too! — are safe. All the attacks, they're so personal. This is destroying me and I don't deserve it. I just don't."

A flash of fury jolts my entire body. This was classic Jenny, always self-absorbed, always the victim. Maybe I've indulged these tendencies too much. Part of our friendship, of any relationship really, is the tacit agreement to allow a generous latitude for flaws and grievances. A trade-off that goes both ways, glass houses and whatnot — and besides, if you start holding your friends accountable for all their flaws, if you let the annoyances add up on a mental spreadsheet, the whole thing could come toppling down. I think back to our time at the bar the night of the shooting, how comfortable it was, both of us settled in our ways, how much I appreciated it then that one could truly know, and accept, someone the way she and I know and accept each other. It's a paradox, loving someone precisely because you know them so well, inside and out, and at the same time nursing a tiny fantasy that they can be different in the specific ways you want them to be. Maybe it isn't fair to expect Jen to change after all these years. But it's eating at me, her inclination to be aggrieved, to always be so quick to think life has been unfair, that it should be easier for her.

"Are you kidding me, Jen? Destroying *you*? First of all, this isn't about you. And second, talk about hitting close to home? Or it being personal? Every time a Black person dies an unwarranted or unnecessary death, it's personal to me, Jen! It cuts close to home. All of it does. All the times I've been followed, questioned, second-guessed, judged, scrutinized, deemed inferior. All the vile comments I have to deal with — for the last ten years of my career, for a lifetime, not just for a few weeks. Everything that happened with Shaun! I mean, just weeks ago I learned that someone in my family was lynched, Jen. Strung up from a tree and riddled with bullets! So don't talk to me about fair or how life is hard for you, okay? I'm not diminishing what you're going

405

through, and I want to be there for you, I do, but you've got to realize that you're not the only one struggling."

We both sit in a sort of stunned silence at all I've unleashed.

"I'm sorry, Rye. Okay. I'm sorry I haven't been a better *ally*. That's all they've been talking about this morning — ally this and ally that." Her condescending tone irks the hell out of me.

"But there you go again, Jen. Yes, you could actually be a better ally! They're using *that* word because it means something. That's exactly what I'm talking about. And that starts with looking at your behavior and your biases. It's like when you slammed the door in that reporter's face and screamed that your best friend is Black and that's why you can't possibly be racist. Come on! And I debated calling you out on it, but I didn't, and maybe I should have just said something right away instead of letting it fester."

Jen looks confused. "But you are my best friend and you are Black. So what?"

"It felt like you were using me as a shield. And by the way, you don't get points for having one Black friend. I mean, you're not hiding any others anywhere, are you?" My sarcasm is a low blow, but Jen isn't the only one who's "really mad" now.

"Jesus, Riley. Ouch."

"I'm sorry, Jen, but it's the truth. It's weird to me that all of your friends these days are white."

"Well, what am I supposed to do? Go out and introduce myself to every Black woman I see on the street and say, 'Heya, want to come over and watch *The Bachelorette* with me?' "

I can see Jenny's knuckles turning white on the steering wheel. She looks like she's trying to focus on her breathing, to calm herself down. She glances at the clock. I know she probably has to get up to Chase and maybe this is enough for now. I'm at the end of my rope.

"Maybe I should just shut up, then. I'm never going to say the right thing."

"That's not what I want either. The last thing I want is for you to be silent and pretend none of this is happening."

"Well, it's not me that doesn't want to talk about things, Riley. You're the one that's always so closed off. You've never said anything like this to me before, and yeah, it totally sucks to hear it, but it sucks even more that we've been friends for almost thirty years and suddenly you're unleashing on me like I'm your enemy. Like you've been thinking all this shit and keeping it inside forever."

She's not wrong. "Look, Jen, I'm sorry if you feel this is coming out of nowhere. But put yourself in my shoes. I didn't want to be the Black girl always talking about race. That's no fun. And I don't know what your reaction would be if I told you about all the shit I have to deal with because I'm a Black woman. What if you didn't have the right reaction?"

"What's the right reaction?" She seems genuinely curious and confused, like she truly has no idea.

"Like showing me you get it, Jen. Or at least that you're trying to." I want to reach over and grab her by her ratty sweatshirt and shake her.

"Well, maybe you need to give me the benefit of the doubt. You never give anyone the benefit of the doubt. Maybe I haven't been all politically correct and perfect, but maybe I'm scared too. Maybe I'm scared of saying the wrong thing or something stupid and everyone pouncing on me and calling me a racist because I use the wrong words. Even you."

I feel a pressure to explain myself, but I also have to get to work and Jen needs to get to Chase; we don't have enough time. I wonder if we'll ever have enough time. "I don't know, Jen — *do* you really get it? Do you get that my life and experiences as a Black woman have been completely different than yours as a white woman? Do you understand why people are destroyed right now, Jen, destroyed by Justin's death? And not just the Dwyers. It's what it signifies — all the ways that Black people, people who look like me, aren't safe. Everything you're saying about the shooting makes me question whether you understand any of this. And maybe it's not fair, but it just brought up a lot of stuff that we never talk about or acknowledge. Like I talk to Gaby about race all the time and I never do with you. And we're supposed to be best friends — that's a problem."

"I never said I didn't want to talk about race with you. I just don't even think of it most of the time; I don't even think about you being Black."

"That's exactly my point, Jen!" I yell so loud a woman walking by looks over her shoulder. I watch her for a minute and try to summon some perspective and calm. "I need you to think about it, especially with what's going on. You're so blindly focused on Kevin, which I get, that you're not seeing the larger implications or issues. It's a privilege to never think about race. I don't have that privilege. I love you, Jenny, but I just need you to, I don't know, wake up a little more."

What I really need is an out. I need out, period. I'm exhausted and I'm going to be so late to work.

"Look, the reason I stopped by was to bring this for you, and let you know I *was* thinking of you." I thrust the bag at her.

"Thank you," she says sincerely, but tosses the bag in the back seat without looking inside.

"How's Chase?"

"He's okay. I've gotta get upstairs. The pulmonary team is coming at nine to test his breathing and then more doctors will be there to try to take out his feeding tubes, and then a CAT scan. It's a busy morning. It's a terrible day. But I don't know if I'm allowed to say that."

"Of course you can say that, Jenny."

Neither of us moves though; neither of us knows how this conversation ends. Or even if it is an end. Maybe, just maybe, as hard as it is, it's a beginning. Who knows.

I'm so hopped-up on adrenaline from my conversation with Jen that my finger can barely connect with the elevator button as I jab it over and over.

"Girl, pushing that button isn't gonna make the elevator come one bit faster."

In the corner of the lobby, the octogenarian janitor teeters on a stepladder unwrapping the lights from the towering Christmas tree. I adore Sid; he reminds me of my dad. Both are tall, with thinning salt-and-pepper Afros, the kind of men who exude dignity while doing a job a rung or two below what they would have aspired to had the world been a different place.

"You need help up there, Sid?" I don't have time to help, but I have to ask because I was raised right. Besides, I know full well he won't accept the offer.

"You think I can't handle taking some lights off a tree? Get on up to work now." Sid waves me away playfully.

I know what he's going to say next before he opens his mouth.

"You're doing such a good job, sweetheart, darn good. It sure is something to see you on TV. Representin'! I tell you."

Sid says the same thing every time he sees me. It should get old, though it never does. It's a reminder that my success is not only mine, but that of everyone who came before and sacrificed so that I could have this unimaginable opportunity. So I pause to say a sincere thank-you, even if I'm not fully

411

here in this moment, but stuck somewhere across time in the parking lot at St. Mary's.

No sooner do the elevator doors open into the newsroom than I hear Scotty's voice thundering. "There you are, Wilson! My office, now!"

He turns to walk down the hall. I don't even bother to stop and drop my coat and purse off at my desk before I hurry to catch up with him. He slams his office door behind me and then leans against his desk, glaring, arms crossed.

"How do you know Jennifer Murphy?"

A screaming static fills my head. It takes every ounce of strength to remain calm and collected. This was bound to happen. If Sabrina found out, it was only a matter of time before Scotty did too. I was reckless to think it wouldn't. But today of all days. I need to do damage control; I'm just not sure how, until I know what exactly Scotty knows.

"We grew up together." It's a Herculean effort to keep my voice even.

"And you were close? Friends?" His tone matches mine, which doesn't give me a lot to work with — it's more unsettling than if he were shouting.

"Yes," I answer, forcing myself to not look away. *At least we were.* "But that hasn't stopped me from being completely professional in my coverage."

He makes a noise somewhere between a grunt and a snort and sits in the chair on the other side of his desk. It creaks under the crush of his weight.

"What did I tell you when I hired you, Riley? What's the one thing I can't stand?"

"Drama and bullshit." I'd even written it in my notebook that day. *No drama. No bullshit.* Which is technically two things, but I obviously didn't point that out.

He stares hard at me across his absurdly messy desk, takeout wrappers everywhere, like he's trying to decide what to do with me. Once again, I'm on the brink of losing something I desperately want. If Scotty pulls me from the story, there's no way I'll get the anchor chair. I may never get back in his good graces again. My career in Philly could be over before it's begun, my miracle second chance squandered.

After what feels like an hour, he speaks. "You should have told me, Riley. I expected better from you."

"I'm sorry, Scotty. I am. But I knew that I could be objective. I knew I was the best person for this story, and I didn't want to give you any reason to doubt me." I can hear the waver in my voice. I hope he doesn't. "This is my job, and that's my personal life. I can keep them separate. I haven't compromised this story."

"Yeah, yeah. Not so far you haven't. But Jennifer Murphy had a baby ten days ago. A preemie. I assume you knew that."

"I did." I'm not about to lie now. "But it's not part of this story, Scotty. The baby isn't. We're not TMZ."

That's not true. The baby *is* a part of the story. Anything related to the Murphys is part of the story. It's surprising that no one has discovered it until now. Would I have reported it if Jen wasn't Jen? Probably. I would never do that to her though. There are lines I won't cross. Which is what I tell Scotty now.

"I'm covering this case, Scotty. Not Kevin Murphy's personal life."

He drums his fingers on the desk.

"First of all, you should have told me about the baby. Also, you cover what I tell you to cover." His voice is cold.

We're back to the brink. I wait, steel myself for what happens next, dizzy from anticipation and adrenaline. Am I off the story? Will Scotty send Quinn to cover the press conference to punish me? The thought makes me want to vomit right into my lap.

"You don't have much time to get to city hall," he says, traces of frustration lingering.

He nods at the door to dismiss me.

I'm light-headed with relief and have to fight the sudden desire to walk around the desk and hug him. "I'm ready," I say.

I'm in the hall when Scotty calls out to me. "Don't make me regret this, Wilson. I'm not giving you another chance."

I walk back into the newsroom and look for Bart. There he is perched on Quinn's desk eating a banana. "We gotta head out," I tell him.

As soon as we're in the van, I sink into the passenger seat and feel the full weight of my fear, relief, and embarrassment. *Remember, what's done in the dark always comes to light.* Another one of Gigi's favorite mantras. I probably deserved to be pulled from the story. At this point though, I've become the face of it for KYX. Scotty had little choice, or he'd risk curious viewers asking questions. It kills me that I put him in such a position, that he may always doubt if he can trust me. For now, I picture my conversations with Jen and Scotty as words I can put in a box, and then I lock that box away.

We hear the crowds at city hall before we see them. Bart angles the news van in line with a dozen others in the designated press area. Through the smudgy windows, I see that the swarm of protesters has divided into two groups facing off like regiment soldiers on a battlefield; rather than muskets, they carry signs proclaiming whose lives matter — Black or blue. The burden of keeping these two groups apart so their passions aren't stoked into violence falls on a grim-faced line of Philadelphia police officers. I spot a young Black mother with her son perched on her shoulders carrying a sign that reads, IS MY BABY NEXT? Across the imaginary dividing line, a group of women stretch a blue vinyl banner between them — BLESS OUR HUSBANDS, THE PEACEMAKERS. BLUE LIVES MATTER.

Bart, in the driver's seat, whistles. "This shit is intense."

It is. If it wasn't for my job, I would be out there too, sign in hand. I might even be screaming through a bullhorn at those women with the banner. "Tell your husbands to stop fucking killing us." But that's not my part in this.

As we leave the van and push through the masses, the energy is fervent, almost suffocating. A dangerous charge hovers in the frigid air, a sense of barely contained chaos, water seconds before a boil. I walk past the bronze statue of Frank Rizzo facing city hall and see that someone has defaced the likeness of the former mayor; a shock of red paint covers his pumpkin-shaped head, drips like blood down over the shoulders, onto a pile of old snow. There are still some people in this city who consider Rizzo a hometown hero, a scrappy cop who rose through the ranks of the PPD before serving his two terms as mayor. Others remember him as the guy who famously told Philadelphians to "vote white," or who was captured in a photo showing up to a race riot in Gray's Ferry in 1969 wearing a tuxedo with a nightstick tucked in his cummerbund. He looked like all he needed was a water hose or snarling dog. Pastor Price has been leading a charge to have this statue ripped down. The city finally seems to be listening.

The hush inside the stately marble lobby is jarring after the chaos outside. Bart and I pass through security and head down the hall to a conference room where other reporters are already milling around. A small dais has been set up at the front of the room, positioned carefully against the backdrop of the city seal. Bart and I edge in, find a place along the press line in the back. He busies himself setting up the camera, while I try to get a handle on the scene and who is already there.

It's ten past two, and Sabrina is nowhere in sight. I wonder if something went wrong with the indictment. That it's happening at all is unprecedented and speaks to Sabrina's single-minded determination, if not public opinion.

Will this bring Tamara peace? Joy? Relief? I tried to call her and Wes at least three times this week, to keep the lines open, to see if I'd be able to get a comment after the press conference. I don't know why I took it personally that I never heard back from Wes other than to direct me to their new media consultant. I let it hurt my feelings when I knew better. I'm sure they've been advised to close down all communications by their new spokesperson and lawyer, Jerome Gardner, who also happens, ironically, to be the partner at Sabrina's old firm. He's also tried at least a dozen different cases against the PPD. That's the incestuous legal world of Philly for you. Sources tell me they're starting to pull together a wrongful-death lawsuit against the city. Upward of forty million dollars — is that the value of a teenage boy's life? The money would definitely change things for Tamara — with millions of dollars to spend, she can live anywhere, do anything, buy whatever luxuries her heart desires — but all of it blood money she would no doubt trade in a heartbeat to wrap her arms around her son one more time.

The press corps grows increasingly restless as we wait. Bart starts playing Candy Crush. I take a peek at the calendar on my phone to obsessively check that the conference was supposed to be at 2 p.m. and not two thirty, and another date stands out. February seventh. When I agreed to see Corey. Our date is marked right there, the one we made after three rounds of hyperformal emails. I should cancel. Opening, reopening, this can of worms on top of everything else? It's too much. I just need to make it through this day first. I close my eyes and take a deep breath, employ a trick I read on some mental health blog. Breathe in a positive mantra and out a negative thought. Inhale: *You are strong, Riley.* Exhale: *Everything is broken.* When I open my eyes Sabrina is emerging from a discreet wood-paneled door, all six feet of her, shoulders back, head held high. She ascends the two steps to the elevated platform. Tamara, Wes, Jerome, and a woman I don't recognize enter right behind her, and take their places solemnly as if it's been rehearsed, which of course it has been. The woman must be their media consultant, Jackie Snyder, who made a name for herself

419

in a Stand Your Ground shooting in Florida. Now she's developed quite the niche flying around the country advising people who've lost children to gun violence. What a world we live in that that has become a full-time job. There's some shuffling and settling in the crowd and on the platform. I see Wes reach in his pocket and quickly fiddle with his phone.

Sabrina waits a beat, against the soundtrack of clicking cameras. The buzz of my phone is jarring in the quiet. I peek down to discover Wes had just been texting me. *It's good to see a friendly face here. I know it's your job, but nice all the same.* I try to catch his eye, but he's focused now on Sabrina, as I am too. Her expansive crown of curls aligns with the arc of the city seal behind her, forming a bronze halo around her hair. Sabrina usually wears a tight French braid for court or media appearances. The fact that she sports a voluminous Afro today feels intentional, bold, defiant, the same tone she uses when she begins to speak.

"By now, I'm sure you have all seen the video of Justin Dwyer murdered a couple of blocks from his home."

No doubt images from the video are now flickering through everyone's minds, priming us all for her announcement, exactly as she intended.

"This is a tragic event that could have been avoided. Justin was only fourteen years old when he was killed by police officers Kevin Murphy and Travis Cameron. After a thorough investigation and evaluation of the law, my office presented a case to the grand jury, which returned an indictment for first-degree murder against officers Murphy and Cameron."

Sabrina lets her words simmer, just like she did at the fundraiser. I think about Jenny, what she's doing right now as the whole city learns her husband's fate. Is there a TV in the NICU? Is she watching?

Tamara stares above all of our heads into the middle distance. This poor woman has seen a video of her son being shot, crumpling into a heap in a dark alley. What must it be like for her to have this be one of the last images she has of her only child?

I turn my attention back to Sabrina as she concludes.

"This office has the utmost respect for the police force of Philadelphia and all efforts to protect our citizens and enforce the law. At the same time, no officer is above the law and we cannot allow this kind of state-sanctioned anti-Black violence to continue here in Philadelphia. We have an obligation as citizens and I have an obligation as the chief legal authority in this city to uphold justice. And to my mind justice means that every single person in this city and in this country lives in social conditions and under a social contract that allows them freedom, safety, and fair treatment under the law. We too often violate that contract when it comes to our Black citizens. And the time has beyond passed for that to change — not lip service — real change. And real change comes when people understand there will be consequences for violating that contract; real change comes when everyone pushes back against the status quo. In the past few weeks thousands of people have marched through our streets, all of them demanding an end to that status quo and demanding that I and other leaders relentlessly battle the insidious forces of corruption and racism that poison our police department. That's just what I intend to do, now and in the future. Our city will not be able to heal until justice is served for the Dwyer family. And, mark my words, justice will be served here." She pauses again and ends with a curt, "That will be all."

Reporters immediately rush the platform shouting questions. I elbow my way to the front of the scrum. My height always helps in these situations, as I shoot my mic over a petite woman slightly in front of me. Tamara and her entourage are whisked out of the wood-paneled door before anyone can successfully thrust a microphone in their faces. But Sabrina holds back.

"Will Murphy and Cameron be arrested today?" The question is less surreal when it's drowned out by a dozen other equally zealous reporters shouting similar inquiries.

Sabrina turns to look directly at me and at the camera perched on Bart's shoulder.

"We are working with Officers Cameron and Murphy to arrange for them to turn themselves in by the end of the week. This isn't a witch hunt. My office has no interest in causing any further disruption. As I said, we're only here to make sure that justice is served for Justin Dwyer and that there is oversight in law enforcement."

Sabrina scans the press pool, ready for another question. It comes from the CNN legal affairs reporter, whom I've always admired.

"Are you aware that Officer Murphy's wife recently gave birth?"

I stop jostling the others for a better position and freeze in place.

"I wish Officer Murphy and his wife the

best when it comes to raising a happy and healthy child." Sabrina looks directly into Bart's camera. "That's what every parent deserves. That's exactly why we're here today."

CHAPTER FOURTEEN

JEN

By this time tomorrow we'll know where we stand.

"I've never been so humiliated, Jen," Kevin says, staring at the ceiling, still in his clothes.

Moments ago, I'd stripped off my sweats and T-shirt that smell like hospital and crawled into bed next to him in my bra and underwear. I've been at the NICU for ten hours and my eyelids are dry as sandpaper, but I've got to keep them open because he needs someone to listen to every single excruciating detail of turning himself in this afternoon — the fingerprinting, the mug shot, the paperwork, the shame of being on the other side, all the sympathetic *I'm only doing my job* shrugs from his fellow officers, who wouldn't even look him in the eye. He'd thought Cameron would be there too, that they could have gone through the hell together, but Cameron isn't surrendering until next week. His lawyer asked for more time. Kevin wanted to get it over with — and at least he didn't have to spend a night in jail, thanks to the $50,000 bond Cookie and Frank scrounged together. I'd heard them talking in the kitchen a few days ago, about how they'd have to give up their dream of a little house not far from the beach in South Carolina. There goes their easy retirement filled only with the drama of grandkids and hurricane warnings. Even so, Cookie never hesitated, never even complained. She never will.

I can hardly focus on what Kevin's saying since I know I've got to get up in a few hours to get back to the hospital. I just want to drift off picturing Chase's little eyelashes, counting each individual strand framing his deep blue eyes, but Kevin needs me.

"I'm a failure. I feel like I've already ruined his life, Jen," he says, his voice flat. "It hasn't even really begun yet, and I've ruined Chase's life."

I won't let that happen.

He drops his arm across my tender boobs. "I'm sorry. I'm so sorry, Jaybird."

I blink at him, my face so close to his that I could kiss him. I don't. I can't remember the last time I kissed him. "I know, I know,"

I murmur, patting him on the shoulder. Kevin is sorry. He's always sorry. He's been nothing but sorry for weeks now. His apologies are like background music.

"What did Brice say?"

"He's all over the place. Says we have a good shot at trial as long as Cameron and I keep our stories straight, stick together, and then five minutes later he was all, 'They might offer you a deal if you'd be willing to testify against Cameron,' since the video footage shows him shooting before I even turned the corner. He didn't properly identify the suspect or confirm the weapon."

The idea of a deal has been vague, always floating in the air in the Murphy house, with no one willing to let it seem real. It isn't real to any of them because of the simple fact that cops don't snitch. I know enough to know that. A cop who snitches isn't a real cop. He's a pariah, a pussy, a traitor. But he would also be safe. He'd still be my husband and Chase's father, and I'll take pariah and pussy if I can have my fucking family.

Besides, Kevin can't go to prison. It would break him. He would never survive. The fact of being a cop in prison would mean his life was at risk every day. I wouldn't survive the fear.

Last night I heard the nurses gossiping about me as I rocked Chase in the NICU nursery.

"That woman would last about two seconds visiting her baby daddy up in prison. Can you imagine?" They both got a big kick out of this.

Yeah, I was "that woman." I didn't even have it in me to be pissed, because it was true. I should have walked over and told them that they're right. I can't imagine sitting across from Kevin, holding our baby up to a filmy plate of glass to show off his first smile, first words, first steps, first everything.

When we decided that Kevin was going to turn himself in today, all my attempts at positive thoughts and promises to stand by my man were immediately replaced by one screaming question: *How can I stay with him?* I don't just mean in the moral sense, I mean in the actual sense of how will I manage as a single mother with a husband locked away? I can't let him get locked away.

For a full minute, I lay there wishing I had fought against Kevin's decision to become a police officer all those years ago and that he was back selling ads, as soul crushing as that might have been for him. Why didn't I fight harder? Well, I have to now. "Kev, if they offer you a deal, you have to take it."

"But, Jen, I'd have to throw Cameron under the bus. I'd have to get up there and say that he made the wrong decision. That his judgment was bad."

"But it *was* bad. You shot because Cameron shot, but your life was never in danger from that kid and you knew it the second you actually saw him. I watched the video. I saw your face. In the split second after the gun went off, you knew you shouldn't have shot."

Kevin releases a low moan. "They'll all crucify me. If I betray my brothers. I mean, remember when I talked to Ramirez a while back and I was so upset? You know what he said to me, Jen? He said he would never be able to look me in the eye ever again if I testified against Cameron. Said he would never be able to forgive me. My best friend said that, the guy I want to be Chase's godparent. He asked me how I could live with myself. How could I, Jen? How could I lose my best friend?"

"Easy for Ramirez to say: he's not facing decades in prison. You can't go to prison, Kevin. If there's a way out, you have to take it. For me, for Chase." I look over at Kevin when I say this, imploring him, and it's like he's disintegrating before my eyes. We're running out of time and options.

"And you should have heard Matt laying into me. I mean, Jesus. 'Imagine if that were me, you'd turn on me like that?' " He does a dead-on imitation of his brother. "I don't know, Jen, would I? It was a bad call. Cameron made a bad call. He should pay for that. But I should too, you know. But, like, how much? Matt asked me if Cameron deserved to lose everything for doing his job. It's not that simple though, right? I mean, a kid is dead."

"No, it isn't that simple. You both fucked up. But maybe, just maybe, Cameron fucked up worse, and there need to be real consequences for that."

Kevin lets that sink in and turns to me. "I know I said it, but today wasn't the worst day of my life. The day I pulled the trigger was the worst day of my life." There's nothing to say in the wake of that truth, so I finally do kiss him, but only because it feels like a way to end this conversation. Both of us surrender to our sweaty sheets and our private thoughts about how tomorrow will play out.

I'm at the hospital before dawn, to get a few minutes with my son before today gets out of hand. Chase feels heavier in my arms today than he did yesterday — at this morning's weigh-in, he'd gained a full ounce. He's nearly six pounds now and fits perfectly in the crook below my chin. He squeaks and snuffles against my neck as I push myself back and forth in the rocker in the NICU just as the sun creeps over the horizon.

"He's a fighter. A little Rocky," Eva, my favorite NICU nurse, says now in her heavy South Philly accent. Eva says this a lot, and I love her for it. She plays "Eye of the Tiger" at least once a day on her phone and always treats Chase like a baby, not like some fragile doll — and she doesn't gossip about me, at least not within earshot.

"He is, isn't he?" I say. It's ridiculous how proud I am of my son already, just for thriving.

"I'm gonna miss this little guy." It's hard to believe this will be Chase's last night here. We can bring him home tomorrow, provided his last breathing test today looks good. Frank gave us the crib he made, which is the most beautiful piece of furniture I've ever seen — he carved all of our initials into the wood, so Chase "would be surrounded by everyone who loves him while he sleeps." It's all set up at home, with sheets I've washed five times.

"You look nice," Eva tells me. She's trying to make me feel better. She knows why I'm dressed up today and not in my usual dirty sweats and no makeup. My eyeliner is crooked. I couldn't hold my hand steady enough to draw a straight line this morning — and this frilly blue dress isn't exactly right for going to court, but it's the only maternity dress I own, the one I was going to wear for my shower. None of my pre-pregnancy clothes fit me yet. I didn't realize my stomach would still look six months pregnant weeks after giving birth. I can barely shove my still-swollen feet into kitten heels. I've already kicked them off. Apparently, when your husband goes in front of a judge to find out whether he'll be locked up for the rest of his life, you're supposed to look "classy." That's how Julia described it when she came over a few nights ago to prep us. She prepared a short statement for Kevin to read after the hearing but said he could also let Brice read it for him. I don't know what he'll do. Julia said I should be prepared for photos and that I should hold Kevin's hand as much as possible. "And don't get caught laughing or smiling." As if either of those things are something I am capable of these days.

"Here, let me take him." Eva leans down, and I have the irrational urge to turn away so she can't take my baby. Sensing my resistance, she steps back.

I move Chase to my lap, nestle him in the small crevice between my thighs. "I'm sorry I have to go, baby boy. But I'll be back soon. I won't be long."

Chase's eyes flicker open at the sound of my voice. This is happening more and more; each time, it's no less magical. He focuses his eyes right on me. *It's you,* they say. Then he opens his little mouth, his pillow lips, and I think he's about to yawn. Instead, he lets out a wail, high and shrill. His pink skin turns purple from the effort and I reflexively start to bounce and rock to soothe him. His breathless sobs make me feel desperate, useless, especially since I can't stay. How can I leave him like this? Why do I have to leave him like this? I curse the fact that I'm being forced to spend the day away from my baby.

Eva doesn't ask this time, she just leans down and lifts Chase from my arms, and I want to snatch him right back. I can't, though. It's time. I push against the arms of the chair and slowly stand — any sudden movement sends a crackle of pain through my still-raw incision. I move around like a turtle. I try to steady myself on the kitten heels and then kick the dumb things off again. I'll carry them to the car.

"Good luck today, Jen." The look in Eva's eyes, the tone of her voice, her kindness. It's so genuine I have to turn away.

It's not luck we need. I don't know what we need.

I kiss the fuzz on top of Chase's head one last time, then each of his feet, then his little hand, the size of an acorn. "I'm sorry I have to go, baby boy. But I'll be back soon. I won't be long."

When I step outside, I stand facing skyward, blinking into the too-bright glare. After weeks of leaving the hospital well after dark and returning before sunrise, I barely recognize the sun, and I want to suck down the light as if it can make me strong for the day.

The one great thing about my rusty old car is that it still has a six-disc CD changer in the trunk with a rotation that hasn't changed much since high school. I have a plan for the ride to the courthouse. As soon as I start the engine, I cue up Guns N' Roses' *Greatest Hits.* The first notes come on — the guitar revving faster and faster into a startling crescendo. The electric intensity matches my mood and I turn the volume way up, as loud as it will go. And then I sing — no, I scream, lungs burning — the whole ride from the hospital to City Center. "Welcome to the Jungle," "Paradise City," and finally "Patience." At a red light, a man in the blue Chevy beside me stares at me like I've lost my mind. I look directly at him and belt out the lyrics even louder.

It's a madhouse when I arrive; what looks like a million people and cameras surround the courthouse, and I toy with an exhilarating thought. *What if I keep driving, get as far away as possible?*

By the time I do another slow loop around the block, I'm back to reality and searching for the rear parking lot and entrance that Brice told us would be private, protected by security. There's also no media allowed inside the courtroom today, a blessing; it means I don't have to face Riley. Yet, anyway. We have to talk; I just have to get through all of *this,* this part first. And get Chase home, and maybe get six full hours of sleep, and then Riley and I will talk again.

As soon as I pull into the gated lot, I see the Murphys, gathered in a cluster near the back door, looking beat down, like they're waiting for a funeral to begin. I park as far away as possible and walk slowly toward them, taking in Cookie, her hands clasped tightly around Frank's arm, hip to hip, in

435

solidarity and also to help him stand, which he has trouble doing for long periods. Next to her, Matt talks to Brice. I feel queasy at the sight of the lawyer with his thinning hair slicked back with so much gel it gleams in the sun, just like his Crest Whitestripped teeth.

I've really turned on Brice these last few weeks. I can't shake the feeling that he's out of his depth here. He's a suburban lawyer who specializes in DUIs and slip-and-falls and then happened to stumble on a high-profile, headline-making case because his mom joined a book club. You can practically see him salivating at the publicity. He's become so puffed up, I don't know how he buttons his too-shiny suits.

I'm almost there when Kevin turns around as if he senses me. He looks so pathetic when he sees me, I worry I can't give him all the strength he so desperately needs.

He's lost so much weight that his one good suit is now at least two sizes too big.

"Well, finally," Cookie says, thrilled to be exasperated at something. But then she leans over to button my coat. "You're going to catch a cold." No matter that we're a couple yards from the door.

"You guys didn't have to wait out here."

"Mom thought we should all go in together," Kevin says, taking my hand.

It seems silly, as if a few Murphys walking together down a largely empty hallway is going to make one bit of a difference, but as we make our way through the dingy alcove, it does feel safer in our little pack, a united front.

Cookie asks me about Chase and I tell her that he gained an ounce overnight. I don't think I've ever loved her more than right then as her face lights up and she says, "That's our boy."

Brice lets Cookie and Frank lead the way as we file through the maze of the old building. Once they're out of earshot, he whispers to Kevin. "You'll plead not guilty, just like we talked about. I thought the DA might put a deal on the table before it came to this, but she wants to go through with all the theatrics, draw it out." Cookie and Frank are too far ahead to hear this conversation, but Matt can.

"My brother ain't a snitch, man." He spits the words in Brice's direction. He looks like he's about to say more, to make a scene, but Annie grabs him by the elbow and pushes him toward his mother.

"Don't listen to him," I say.

Kevin stops short in the entrance — filling three rows of benches on one side are his buddies from the Twenty-Second. I can tell he didn't know they would be here. It's a bizarre kind of surprise party. Instead of screaming, "Surprise!" they all turn to look at him, communicate their solidarity through solemn nods and serious expressions. They know it could have been any one of them in Kevin's shoes. Some of them stare at me. Some look shyly away. They're standing by him now, but what happens if Kevin testifies against Cameron? Will they all abandon my husband? I know the answer and so does he.

There's another case being heard. Brice told us to expect to wait, so we find an empty bench and sit watching, waiting as it finishes. The judge is delivering a stern lecture to a sullen teenager about getting his life together and how he needs to support all of his "baby mamas" because that isn't the taxpayers' job. It's impossible to focus. I can't stop thinking about Chase in the NICU, wondering what he's doing, whether he's awake, whether he misses me. My arms are so empty without him in them. A dark laugh threatens to escape as it hits me that I'd rather be back in the NICU, that terrible place of purgatory and sick babies, than here in this courtroom. But at least something is finally happening. Of all the difficult parts of the last few months, the not knowing has been the hardest. I can't be a proper mother to my little boy in this constant state of limbo. Maybe it'll all be over soon, whatever the end looks like. I've prepared myself to deal with any outcome. I just need clarity. I need to know what comes next.

I've never been in a courtroom before, and I'm surprised to find it's so dark and dingy: faded paint peels off the walls, abandoned cans of Coke and a stack of brown accordion folders crowd the judge's desk. The ancient radiators clang and grunt. The judge herself looks bored. I can't believe our fate will be decided in this depressing room, or one exactly like it if Kevin goes to trial.

The judge strikes her gavel, startling both of us. There's a sudden churn in the courtroom as the cases turn over — actors taking their places, including me. I scoot back on the bench and sit up straighter, readying myself. Kevin stands when the bailiff calls his name. All eyes turn as he and Brice make their way to the table before the judge. I want to offer some final words of encouragement, but Kevin is out of his seat, trudging forward like a zombie before I have the chance.

That horrible district attorney appears

from out of nowhere and stands at a table in front of the judge. I want to stick a big wad of gum in her hair. I shoot daggers at Sabrina Cowell and hope she can feel my rage. When she starts to speak, I want to cover my ears against her self-righteousness, her smug tone.

"Kevin Murphy . . .

"Second-degree murder . . .

"Manslaughter . . .

It's all so fast, a jumble, a blur of legalese and formalities and jargon that's too hard to follow. Only one moment breaks through, like everything else in the room has stopped, when Kevin speaks. Two words, his voice so hoarse the judge has to ask him to repeat himself.

"Not guilty."

And just like that, it's over. It hardly seems worth all the bother of leaving Chase, but when Kevin returns to the bench and collapses in my arms as if he's run a marathon, I'm glad I came. *For better or worse.*

We all file back out into the hall, unsure how to behave, what to do now.

"I've gotta pee." I've been holding it for hours now and rush off to find a bathroom. In the stall I take my time, thumb through pictures of Chase on my phone for a minute to soothe my nerves. I'm still bleeding and I need another pad, but that would involve going to ask Cookie if she has a quarter and then she'll ask why and it will be mortifying. Someone comes in. Maybe I can borrow some change.

I walk out and nearly turn back into the stall. It's her, Tamara Dwyer, so close I can smell her perfume. My knees buckle. I didn't see her in the courtroom, but of course she would be here. I've seen her on television and from a distance at Justin's funeral, but here, under the flickering fluorescent lights that are mandatory in every sorry municipal building in this city, she looks like a ghost. She locks eyes with me right away. We're alone with three feet of space between us.

"Congratulations," she says quietly, looking at my swollen stomach.

"Thank you." A whisper as I take a small step back to the toilet stall.

"You had a boy, right?"

"Yes." I can't allow the guilt brought on by that simple fact to drown me. She doesn't need my guilt. "Mrs. Dwyer, I'm so sorry. My husband is so sorry."

"I don't want your apologies."

"I understand."

"No, you don't. What would you do if someone killed your baby?"

I don't even hesitate, because I've thought about this every single day since Chase was born. "I'd kill them with my bare hands."

"Exactly." The hard look in Tamara's eyes tells me that she's imagined it too.

"But it wouldn't do anything, would it?" I stutter a little. "Would it make it better?"

She glares at me in the mirror. "Sometimes I think so. A life for a life. But that's not what I want. I want my son back. I want my baby back. I want to wrap my arms around him and kiss his sweaty head and never let him go back outside into a world where a man like your husband will shoot him in the chest for walking home from school."

This is what we deserve. My son is alive.

Both her hands grip the edges of the sink, and we're talking through her reflection in the mirror. I can leave right now, walk away from this woman and her anguish. But I have to face her, face up to her. I risk reaching out to touch her and she jumps away from my hand so violently I pull back like I've been burned.

"Don't touch me."

"I'm sorry —"

"And don't say you're sorry. I don't want your sorrys." Her eyes meet mine again, cold pools of anger and grief.

"Chase — my baby, his name is Chase — he came early. I thought I'd lose him. I knew I'd die if that happened."

"But you wouldn't die. You'd have to keep going, and that is so much worse."

She turns and grabs at the door handle, pulling so hard the door flies open and slams into the wall hard enough to startle us both.

"Tell your husband to do the right thing." She spits the words and then she's gone. I wait another minute because I'll crumple if I see her again in the hallway. And I need to try to collect myself anyway.

My wobbly legs barely get me back to the Murphys, to their tight semicircle. Brice is talking, animated, rocking back and forth, heel to toe, explaining this and that to everyone and no one.

"If it gets to it, I like our chances at trial. I like them. That video. That kid is clearly pulling something out of his pocket. The jury only needs to find him a reasonable threat. Everyone wants to believe they wouldn't shoot," Brice says. "But no one really knows what they would do in that situation. No juror truly knows."

Cookie glances at me. "Are you okay? You're trembling."

I grab one hand in the other to hold it

still. "I'm fine." She doesn't look convinced, but we're all distracted by something else: Sabrina Cowell striding toward us from down the long hall, the enemy approaching, a hyena circling the hippos.

Cookie pinches her lips together so tightly I worry she might swallow her tongue.

"Can I speak to you, Brice?" Sabrina asks. He nods eagerly, like the coach just called him off the bench in the last ten minutes of the game.

As she and Brice walk away, Matt announces he's going for a smoke. Cookie wants to go to the ladies' room, and Frank needs to find a place to sit. Kevin and I are alone.

The stone silence is killing me, so I start whistling the first few bars of "Patience." " 'You and I got what it takes to make it,' " I sing softly into Kevin's ear.

When Brice returns some ten minutes later, we hear his heavy footsteps echoing on the marble floors before we see him. Kevin rushes over to close the distance between them. I waddle behind him as fast as I can. "Well?"

"Finally. She wants to offer you a deal."

"So what is it?" Kevin asks.

Brice pauses for dramatic effect. "Reckless homicide. Ten years' probation. And it's a felony conviction. But no prison time. It's a good deal overall. It's an unbelievable deal."

No prison time. Hearing this is such a relief my entire body goes slack, my bones turned to jelly. I won't have to take my baby to see his father behind a grimy plate-glass window. This is way better than we could have hoped for. Kevin doesn't seem happy or relieved though. I can see him turning it over in his mind.

"Well, the catch is you have to testify against Cameron, of course." Brice adds this like it's a tiny hiccup. "It's him she's gunning for. In a trial he still has a strong defense. He can say he thought the kid was pulling out a gun, say that he truly believed he was shooting the other guy. You'll need to say that the second you laid eyes on the kid, you knew he was the wrong guy, that you believe Cameron made a bad call. You're the only other person who was there. Your testimony would probably sway a jury and she knows it. Without you, she might not get the conviction she wants. But if you both go to trial, you could both end up serving time. She wants an answer by the end of the week. I suspect she wants to know where you stand before Cameron turns himself in and is arraigned. She extended the deadline from forty-eight hours. Well, I got her to give us more time." Brice quickly revises his statement to place himself at the center of the achievement. "It's a big decision."

Kevin turns to lean his forehead against the puke-green walls.

"Oh, and you can't be a cop anymore, anywhere in PA. You resign effective immediately," Brice adds.

"I can't be a cop anymore?" Kevin sounds like a child who's been told he can never see his mother again.

He looks at me. I just nod. *Tell your husband to do the right thing.*

Brice goes on. "If you want my advice — and that's why you pay me the big bucks — I say take it. If it's you or the other guy, might as well be the other guy, you know?"

Thank God Matt and Frank aren't here. "All those guys," Kevin chokes. "They came here to support me. If I turn on Cameron, I'm turning on all of them."

Frustration seeps from Brice's long sigh. Kevin is ruining his big moment. "Look, you have a week to think about it. But it's a good deal."

We've been dangling from a cliff for so long, and someone has finally thrown us a rope, only Kevin isn't reaching for it. Why isn't he reaching for it?

"We'll make the right decision," I tell Brice and grab my husband's hand. "Come on, let's go to the hospital."

Back to Chase.

Chapter Fifteen

RILEY

"It looks nice on you."

I look down at the silk blouse, unsure.

My mom reaches up and firmly tucks the silk into the back of my jeans and then stands behind me in the closet-size dressing room, appraising me. I haven't been shopping with her since my last back to school shopping trip to JCPenney in the summer before seventh grade.

"I don't know, it's expensive." The price tag makes me wince and I want to hide it from my mom like it's a shameful secret, but then, it was her idea to duck into this tiny boutique on Sansom Street in the first place. This whole outing today — lunch and shopping — was her idea, an invite she shocked me with this morning. I look up in the mirror at our chummy reflections — we're just like the TV mother and daughter I'd imagined. At least, we have been for the last few hours. We even ordered aperol spritzes and gossiped, though I'm not sure she knew that aperol was alcohol and I decided not to tell her until she took a sip and pronounced it, "So refreshing!" I even told her I was meeting Corey today, in thirty minutes actually. I hadn't intended to, but there we were, talking about Shaun and Staci's latest spat and how my cousin was getting married in the summer and Momma would like us all to go to Memphis for the wedding, having made strides to make peace with Uncle Rod. So it just seemed natural to tell her about my love life, even if it's terrain I avoided with a ten-foot pole all my life. New leaves and all that. That's how we ended up here in this overpriced store — she insisted I should get a new blouse for our date. The tan sweater I was wearing was apparently underwhelming. "I've seen people wear sexier outfits to Bible study, Riley." That must have been the second aperol talking for her to use "Bible study" and "sexy" in the same sentence, let alone drag me by the hand into a store that sells $400 cashmere sweaters.

"I always wondered what happened to him, that Corey," she says now.

"You didn't hate him, then?" I just assumed she did. I assume everyone starts out on Sandra's bad side and has to work mighty hard to get anywhere from there.

"Child, I barely knew the boy. You brought him around all of once. He seemed nice enough and you liked him. That I could tell. You got this look in your eye. Damned if it wasn't a sparkle. That's why I was confused when he was up and gone."

So was I, Momma. Sometimes I confuse my own self. I turn and angle myself to get a side view of the shirt. It's blue, which is a plus; Corey loves blue.

"You look pretty." She reaches up to smooth the collar. This compliment is also a surprise. Momma always said being pretty was a curse. "And especially with that long straight hair of yours, girls gonna hate you just for that," she told me in middle school, and then said that I shouldn't ever look in a mirror in front of other girls because they'll think I'm conceited, that I am admiring myself. To this day I feel self-conscious seeing my reflection. Which probably means I've been walking around with food in my teeth most of the time.

"You also look nervous," she says to me. She can always read me. I'm laid bare in front of her no matter how much I like to think I'm my own person with my own private thoughts and smoke screen of serenity.

"I guess I am. A little. Is it that obvious?"

"Oh, please. I know you. You were me, before you were you. Don't forget that."

I don't know exactly what she means, but I get it. For all the ways I want to be different from my mother, there are many more we're alike. It's an idea I could learn to embrace.

"I wish we'd gotten to know him better, Corey. Why'd you fall so hard for him? Your nose was wide open!"

"I don't know, Mom, he made me feel seen. It's hard to explain. Like I could just be my real self. I didn't overthink with him, I just was. When he looked at me, I felt like both the person I am and wanted to be. He made me feel, I don't know . . . special, confident . . . as dumb as that sounds."

"Riley Wilson, you're the most confident, exceptional human being I know. I raised you to know that. To know your worth."

"Well, it's not that easy sometimes." I don't add that she raised me to constantly be a better version of myself and that that was exhausting and that Corey loved the version of me that already existed, flawed as she may be. But we're having such a nice moment, I'm determined not to ruin it by mining my childhood for grievances.

"But I know, Momma, I know. I appreciate you."

"Get the blouse. You deserve it. You've been working so hard. Treat yo'self. Ain't that what the kids say?"

She reaches over and digs into her pocketbook and hands me a $20. "Here, let me put something toward it. I want you to have it."

"No, no, I got it." I'm still getting used to the idea, and the guilt, of making more money than anyone in my family.

"Well, keep that money and use it to pay your way tonight. Girls let men pay for them and these men expect something, you know."

There's only one thing Corey expects from me: an explanation.

I start to take off the blouse and then remember I'm going to wear it tonight. I hand my drab sweater to my mom. It won't fit in my tiny clutch. "Could you take this home with you?"

"Home? I'm going to take it right over there to the Salvation Army!"

We walk to the register and my mother leans in and lowers her voice like she's prepared to divulge another secret. Is this the day I learn about her secret love child?

"So, you think Kevin's going to take the deal?" she asks in a stage whisper that people from a mile around could hear.

Over lunch, I told my mom in confidence how Sabrina had called me to tell me about the offer. It was now clear that using Kevin as leverage had been Sabrina's strategy all along. It was Cameron whose head she wanted on a platter — his was the more solid legal case to make. Cameron shot first and he shot someone who didn't match the description of the suspect they were chasing. Sabrina was confident that she could get a guilty verdict and a long prison sentence. "Ten years, at least," she told me. "That's some justice." So Kevin now had a lifeline, and it would be crazy for him not to take it. Except we're already three days in and he hasn't decided.

"I don't know, Mom. He'd be crazy not to, though."

"Yeah, but those cops rather go to jail than rat on each other. Even the Black ones get all caught up in that. But I guess we'll see. You're seeing Jenny next week, right? That's good, that's good."

I'd told Momma at lunch about my talk with Jenny, how hard and infuriating it was. But how it was also a relief, to finally get out everything I've been thinking, even if it changes everything between us.

"But at least you're talking," she'd said. "Just keep going on. You can't expect everyone to get everything. Sometimes you've gotta meet people where they are and bring them along. It's not always worth it, but you love Jen through and through and vice versa and y'all will get through this."

"We're meeting up the week after, actually."

The only thing I'd heard from Jenny was a cryptic text the day after Kevin's arraignment saying she was going out of town but could we see each other when she's back. It's funny that I have the same feeling thinking about meeting up with Jenny after our last conversation as I do about Corey, an excited dread, like I'm preparing for something, but what?

I hand the tag to the sales clerk. "Could you ring me up with this? I'm just going to wear the blouse now."

"It looks great on you," she says.

"I appreciate y'all didn't hover over us and follow us around like we were going to steal something," Mom says to the sales clerk, nodding her head in vigorous agreement with her own thoughts.

The young blond woman has no idea what to do with this strange "compliment."

We walk out into the dusk, the sun casting a labyrinth of shadows on the sidewalk. I strangely have the urge to keep our mother-daughter date going — drinks at Parc or pedis, but Corey awaits. And besides, we may not want to push our luck.

"I'll see you and your brother at five p.m. sharp on Saturday, right?"

Both Shaun and I are dreading this, but we agreed to go look at apartments in Bensalem with our parents this weekend. Momma puts on a chipper facade whenever she talks about downsizing and claims to be looking forward to having so many fewer rooms to clean. She's working hard to hide her despair. I learned from the best.

"At least we'll get a discount on moving, with your brother's gig." Her laughter feels genuine enough for me to allow myself the hope that this move and losing the house won't break her — maybe it's a fresh start.

"Well, wish me luck," I say.

"You don't need luck, you have God. And you don't need any man."

"I don't need a man . . . but maybe I want one." I hug her as we laugh and say good-bye.

It's only a ten-minute walk to the diner but I already know Corey is going to be there when I arrive, because he always said it was better to be an hour early than a minute late. No CP time for Corey.

Sure enough, when I go through the doors and the quaint bell jingles above my head, I spot him right away, even in the crowded restaurant.

It's like I'm at the peak of a roller coaster, right at that split second before it goes into free fall. Corey sees me and breaks into a wide grin. The coaster plummets. As I walk over, I take him in greedily. He looks exactly the same, which is to say, as attractive as ever — same tall, lean frame, olive skin, that dimple in his left cheek.

When I reach the table, he gets up to greet me, leaning in to kiss me on the cheek. I count the seconds his warm lips graze the space near my mouth. It's not long enough.

"Breakfast for dinner. You remembered."

I knew Corey would dig this West Philly diner because he loves a place that serves breakfast for dinner, which is why I chose it, and also as a stupid nod to our first date, pancakes in Chicago. The downside is they don't serve alcohol, and my need is bordering on desperate, but he looks so touched, the sacrifice is almost worth it.

"Yeah, I figured you'd like this place."

I've said exactly one sentence to Corey, and I'm already second-guessing it as my mind races ahead, trying to think of the right thing to say next. Then it registers that it's not my turn to speak again, as if I've lost grasp of the basic rules of conversation.

"You look great," he says, settling into the vinyl booth.

"You too. We sort of match." We both look down at our blue shirts.

There's a beat, long enough for me to worry that we're on the verge of an awkward moment, when he looks up at me, his expression more serious. Another split second is enough for me to panic that he's going to dive right in and tell me about his STD . . . or his engagement.

He tilts toward me. "I'm really sorry about your grandma, Rye. She was a great lady."

"Thank you, I miss her." I hadn't steeled myself for this, his concern, for him looking at me like he's hugging me with his eyes.

"I don't think she liked me that much. I know she called me White Corey. Which always made me wonder, was there ever a Black Corey?"

This makes me laugh. "There wasn't."

"Are you doing okay though? I know how close you two were." His fingers stroke the back of my hand. I'm not prepared for the current that shoots down from the top of my head and lodges between my legs.

I turn to the neighboring table when I sense someone staring, an older white woman eating alone. There's a twinge of self-consciousness as Corey's hand lingers on mine. I fix my face to say, *This is none of your business.*

This is familiar, all the stares and double takes Corey and I experienced when we were together, especially when he came to visit me in Alabama. Stares that I took to mean, *Why's he with her?* even though Corey was somehow completely oblivious to them. Whenever I'd point these things out, he'd say I was imagining it.

"You're being paranoid. People are staring at you because you're gorgeous, and they're staring at me because they're wondering how a bum like me ended up with a girl like you." It would have been easier to let myself believe he was right.

I turn back and Corey's hand is no longer touching mine. I try to work out when that happened and how I could possibly already miss it so much.

"I'm sure she's one of your adoring fans," he whispers, having also noticed the woman staring. When he leans over the table, I catch a strong whiff of his absurdly expensive minty aftershave from one of those stores dedicated to the so-called art of shaving. I wonder if it's the same bottle I bought him for his birthday two years ago. "It was crazy to see you on my TV in New York. I looked up, and there you were, Riley Wilson on CNN. They only showed a short clip of the interview with that kid's mom —"

Justin, I want to say. *His name is Justin.*

"But then I went to YouTube and watched the whole thing. So powerful. You're such a force on camera, Rye. You were born for it."

"Thanks. That means a lot." And it did. There it was, the praise from Corey that never failed to validate me in some essential way. I used to hate that — hate the way he made me feel, like it gave him some power over me. But then I realized why I valued his admiration so much — I never had to work for it. With everyone else in my life, I was always tap dancing, always on a stage, always trying to be "impressive" — with teachers, bosses, mentors, even my parents, even with Alex in Joplin. I was always trying to live up to some glossy magazine version of the Black media power couple he wanted us to one day be — I knew we had to break up the fifth time he referenced me as the Michelle to his Barack. Corey was the first person who I didn't try to impress. In fact, the opposite. If anything, I was going to make it clear to him and myself that I wasn't going to go out of my way trying to prove anything to him — this random white guy I literally stumbled into — and it turns out, I didn't have to. Because I also stumbled into the miraculous discovery of being loved without having to put so much effort into striving to feel worthy of it.

Here he is now looking at me like *that* again. Like he sees me, sees right *through* me. This is what I was trying to describe to Momma, the feeling I had with Corey, like I had no choice but to let him see the real me. Maybe it's what we all want from the people we love: to be seen for exactly who we are. It was a simple realization, so why did it feel like such a miracle? But the surprise is how fast the feelings return, like the first drops of blood from a deep cut. The shock of raw white tissue, then the rush of red. All I can do is swallow it all down. It's as good a plan as I've got in the moment.

Corey holds up the giant glossy menu covered in pictures of greasy eggs. "So, first things first, the pressing matter of what to order. What do you want?" Corey asks.

I want you. I want to have sex with you. The thought is unwelcome and impractical, and also clear as the sun is bright. I can feel it — my body betraying me again, the dampness gathering in my underwear as I remember the way Corey used to make me feel, electric with desire, the way I lost all inhibition, saying, thinking, doing, wanting, letting him do things I never could have imagined.

Except touch my hair, at least at first. It's funny now to think of how it took me at least four sleepovers to get used to that. He liked to grab it as he pushed himself inside of me. It took three more before I was willing to wear my headscarf to bed in front of him.

"What's that?" he asked the first time, and though I'd known he would, I still cringed and considered all the things I would have to explain to him.

I must be smiling now. "What's so funny?" Corey grins at me, eager to be in on the joke.

"Nothing," I mumble into my glass as I take a sip of water to cool off and push my thoughts to safer ground: menu choices.

It's like old times when we agree to two dishes, steak and eggs and French toast, and share everything. It's so comfortable it hurts.

"So, how's Sullivan Rose?" I ask once the waiter disappears.

Corey has been working for the developer

since we met; we'd even made a bet — a trip to Puerto Rico — about who would reach their coveted milestone first, Corey to VP or me to anchor.

"Same old, same old. I'm pretty excited about our project here in Philly. We're looking to invest in one of the opportunity zones on North Broad, build a big mixed-use housing complex, and I had to come check out the site. If the deal goes through, I'll be down about once a month."

Corey will be here once a month. Corey will be here once a month. This fact echoes over and over.

Somehow, as we ease into our conversation, I manage to eat, which I didn't think would be possible. Our plates are still half-full, and I'm stuffed, picking at what's left. If I stop, then this, whatever this is, will be over — and I'm not ready for this night to be a memory. I have no clue what's supposed to happen next. It's clear that neither of us has any idea what we're doing here.

Corey pushes away his plate and rubs his tight, flat stomach. *This is it. We say goodbye and then that's that.* It feels like the last stretch of the race. I only have seconds to close the distance. And yet, I can't. I don't know what to do.

The relief is almost physical when he says,

462

"Hey, how about we go somewhere else? Can I buy you a real drink? So we can talk?"

I know just the spot, a dark, intimate lounge near my house. Whenever I walk by after work, I ogle the sleek couples cuddled on velvet lounge chairs in front of the steamed-up windows, like they're mannequins arranged just so. I'm about to suggest it, it's on the tip of my tongue, when I suddenly say something else entirely.

"How about my place? I have a bottle of Maker's." This wasn't an accident. I'd gone to buy Corey's favorite bourbon, just in case. He answers right away, yet it's enough of a pause to send my heart skipping.

"Sure, that sounds good."

The whole Uber ride to my apartment, I'm hyperconscious of his body next to mine. Am I sitting too close? Too far? I imagine him walking through my place, looking at the photos I've finally hung, touching my things. I hope he'll be impressed.

As soon as we get in the door, I busy myself making drinks and try not to feel self-conscious and exposed as Corey wanders around, exploring every corner.

"What's this?" he calls out, standing at the fireplace mantel.

I peek around the kitchen island to see

that he's holding the jar of dirt from Alabama. "Uh, long story." I don't want the outside world, or the past, to intrude on this moment.

He sets it down, picks up the photo Jen gave me of the two of us when I moved in. Two little girls in matching bikinis. "You guys were so cute." And then he makes his way to the balcony, taking in the city views through the floor-to-ceiling windows. He does seem impressed, at least with the view. When I'm done making the drinks, I turn, icy glass in each hand, and there he is, settled right on my couch like it's the most normal thing in the world, like he belongs there. I walk over and take a seat right by his side, like I belong there too. It's too quiet in the apartment, only the clinking of ice in our glasses. It's too quiet, so I flip on the TV. The Flyers game fills the screen.

"Remember when I took you to that game in Chicago?"

"How could I forget? It's the only hockey game I've been to in my entire life," I say, and allow myself to enjoy the memory. We decided to meet in Chicago, where we first met, to celebrate our one-year anniversary. Corey surprised me with Blackhawks/Flyers tickets that weekend — the playoffs. I could tell he was disappointed that I wasn't more excited, since they were incredibly hard seats to come by, but hockey is like NAS-CAR, not too many brown faces in the stands.

Turns out, the game was a lot of fun, but then we were in that giddy phase where a waterless trek through the desert would have been a good time.

After the game, Corey gave me a piece of paper, not the gift I was expecting. He'd stuttered as he handed it to me. "It's, it's lame . . ." On the paper, Corey had listed "12 Reasons I Love You."

"It's one for each month we've been together," he piped in as I read, still clearly worried this might be a dumb idea. It wasn't dumb or lame, it was perfect. If he walked into my bedroom right now, he'd find the list tucked away in a box under my bed, with my birth certificate and diploma, a flash drive with a recording of my first broadcast and my resignation letter from Birmingham. I pull the paper out sometimes — just to touch it, because I have the list memorized. *Reason #3: The way you always wear socks because you hate your long toes (for the record, even your toes are beautiful). Reason #6: How you worry so much about everyone you love and how you work so hard to make everything better and easier for them.*

Reason #11: You give the best advice and you always make it seem like it was my idea in the first place. Reason #4: The way you're always reorganizing my wallet and figuring out the best strategies to get more airline points. Reason #8: You have an adorable snore like a newborn puppy.

That night was the first time I was brave enough to tell Corey that I loved him, to say the words aloud, even though it had been months since I'd realized the depth of my feelings, growing wild, out of control, until they had become a central fact of my life. And the truth was, I hated being out of control, the nights I spent thinking about him, missing him instead of focusing on my work, hated that I'd let myself become someone who could get their heart broken. I hated it all, and what I wouldn't trade for it now.

"You know why they're called the Flyers?" Corey asks.

"Absolutely no idea."

"No reason at all! The first owner's wife just liked the word. Isn't that ridiculous?"

There it is, Corey's love for random facts. Another thing that always made me crazy about him. The small talk and the way his foot is bobbing up and down tells me that he's nervous too. Sitting here on my couch with drinks, the catching up part of the evening has run its course, a fog of anticipation hovers around us. It's clear something is going to happen, but what?

"So . . ." He looks at me with a sort of confused smile.

"So," I repeat. It's all I've got.

"So, this last year has been hard, since you . . . disappeared on me. No explanation, no nothing. I keep asking myself, *What did I do wrong? What went wrong?* I just need to know what happened, Riley. I thought things were great between us. Weren't they? Did I imagine that? I just don't get it."

I can see how much this is costing him; his hands are trembling enough that the ice clinks around in his glass.

He's right, I do owe him. An explanation, if not so much more. I'd known this was the night I was going to tell him everything, explain what happened. Now that the moment is finally here, my mouth is too dry. I down the rest of my drink. It doesn't help. He speaks again before I have the chance. He doesn't realize I'm not dodging, only preparing myself.

"You were coming to see me in New York. And then, nothing. What happened?"

I so clearly remember packing for that

trip. I'd bought a silk kimono dress after Corey told me he'd made us reservations at Nobu. I'd also dropped two hundred bucks I couldn't afford on a lingerie set at a store in downtown Birmingham called the Diva's Den. I folded the delicate lace bra and underwear so carefully in my bag. Corey had recently moved into a new two-bedroom apartment that I was going to see for the first time.

"I was just about to leave my apartment to go to the airport and my mom called. She was hysterical. She told me they got Shaun."

"Who got him?"

"The cops. He was driving home from a boxing gym in Fishtown with three guys he knew from high school. The driver, Lamar Chambers, who my mother always called 'plain trouble,' got pulled over on North Fifth. He'd given the cop some lip about stopping him, said it was because they were 'driving while Black,' and that it was 'bullshit.' The cops ordered everyone out of the car, told them to get down on their knees in a row on the sidewalk while they searched it. Turns out Lamar had an unlicensed gun in his glove compartment, and a dime bag of marijuana. The cops arrested all four of them."

Looking at Corey's face as I say this is impossible. I'm sure he's only ever seen people arrested on television.

"It was a probation violation. It wasn't Shaun's first arrest. He got in a fight his sophomore year at Temple. With this white kid. They were playing a pickup basketball game and it got heated. Kid called Shaun a stupid nigger."

Corey flinches at the word.

"Shaun punched him and broke his nose. The guy pressed charges, and just like that Shaun had a felony conviction. He lost his full ride soccer scholarship and couldn't afford Temple anymore. He owed thousands of dollars for the guy's medical bills and legal fees, which my family and I are still paying off. All that promise, gone. Just like that. But at least he didn't have to go to jail. He got ten years' probation."

Even without looking at him, I know he's giving me the look, the Corey look — direct, focused, impossible to hide from.

"When he was arrested in the car, he could have been sent to prison for ten years for the violation. So that weekend, I had to be with my family and support Shaun in court. Thankfully, the judge showed leniency — Shaun was lucky."

I question my choice of words; nothing

about Shaun's life recently has been lucky. It's been unfair and stressful and cruel and yet somehow my brother carries on, cracking jokes, keeping his nose down and head up, when he could so easily sink into resentment. I don't tell him enough how much I admire him for that.

"It was too late to change my flight from LaGuardia. So I got a cab from there to Penn Station."

"I could have picked you up at the airport. I would have driven you to Philly, Rye. But I didn't know any of this was happening."

"And then what? You would come to the jail with me and talk to Shaun in a grimy windowless room?"

"That's exactly what I would have done."

Hearing that, his quick steadfast assurances, my heart seizes. A part of me *had* wanted him to come to Philly, wrap his arms around me and promise me that everything would be all right. Maybe I even wanted his help talking to the lawyers, figuring out the best strategy to ensure Shaun stayed out of prison. But it was my burden, and to bring my boyfriend into it, my white boyfriend, a man whose closest contact with the courts was defending overdue parking tickets, I couldn't bring myself to do it. And if I couldn't share this with him? If I couldn't ask for his help at such a difficult time, how could we build a life together? How could I ever move into his nice two-bedroom apartment in a doorman high-rise off Columbus Circle? Something I had been secretly contemplating. I couldn't. Not if I couldn't be honest with him. And so I made up my mind that Corey and I were not meant to go the distance after all. Like a prosecutor, I mined the evidence of why it would never work: The time we went to Proud Papa's barbecue in a Black neighborhood in Birmingham and he'd asked me if it was "safe." Or when we were talking about oppression and he volleyed with a point about how the Jews were able to bounce back after the horrors of the Holocaust to build a strong economic foundation, and he didn't understand why Black people hadn't been able to do the same after slavery. This was typical of Corey, who always treated any discussion of race and oppression as an intellectual exercise, with the passion and objectivity of a high school debate team champion and not *lived* experience. I convinced myself that these were deal breakers, trip wires we could never get past, and on top of that there were Gigi's words: *Find one of your own.*

And so I made up my mind and trusted

my heart would follow. Sitting alone on a hard bench, in a dank hallway of the court-house, where Shaun would soon be called for his appearance before the judge, I pulled out my phone. As I searched for the right words, I looked up to see two Black teen-agers, hands and feet in chains, shuffling down the hall, escorted by a grim-faced white guard. One of them had his head hung so low it was almost at ninety degrees; the other held his head high, though his eyes were a void. If I had been waffling before, something about the scene, this boy's dead eyes, cemented my decision. My fingers flew across the screen before I could stop myself.

Something came up today and I'm not go-ing to make it this weekend. And I don't think I can do this, Corey. We're not right for each other. I'm sorry.

It's hard to read Corey's expression now. Partly because I avoided looking directly at him as I unspooled this story.

I finally turn toward him, and his face is contorted with confusion. "So I still don't understand. Why couldn't you tell me all of this then? Why did you just ghost me?"

This is the part that's hard to explain, why I didn't want to tell Corey the truth, how I was overwhelmed with shame and embarrassment and I let it control me. I didn't want to become some sort of stereotype in his eyes, to give him any reason to look down on me or my family. I thought of Corey telling his own parents — with their matching Range Rovers, their annual ski trips to Sun Valley — that my brother was in jail, the judgments and assumptions they would make. How they might even be proud of me for "rising above her circumstances." For "getting out of the hood."

The fact that the two of us would never truly be on equal playing fields or share the same experiences had seemed insurmountable. Maybe I was afraid to give the benefit of the doubt, to give someone the leeway to do the right thing. Exactly as Jenny called me out in the car at the hospital. It *was* easier not to give Corey the benefit of the doubt, not to trust that he would be able to understand, not to give him the chance to create an irreparable breech by saying the wrong thing if we tackled tricky subjects. That fear of being disappointed, or dismissed, was real — and crippling. As with Jenny, there was the worry that talking would be futile and somehow make things worse instead of better. But Jen, or Corey for that matter, had never given me reason to believe they wouldn't understand, or at least try to understand.

"It's just hard, Corey . . . to talk about some of this stuff, like how to explain my experience in the world in a way you'd understand. It scared me that you would be capable because we're so different. And also, I didn't want you to think badly of my family," I mutter. All of my muscles clench with the effort of keeping my emotions, my tears, reined in.

"I would never do that, Rye. Honestly, it kills me that you didn't think you could tell me any of this. And I would hate to think it was something I said or did to make you feel that way. Because I want you to be able to talk to me about anything . . . about everything. That's the only way any relationship works. But especially between us . . . we'd have to be able and willing to lay it out, even if it's uncomfortable. That includes me. I admit, I probably shied away from stuff too, but . . ." He trails off as if he's trying to summon more words and then changes his mind and decides to let his body say the rest. First his hand is around my shoulders, then he's pulling me closer. His arm is heavy on my back, a satisfying weight pressing me hard against him, holding me there. I have no choice in the matter; my body relaxes despite itself, though I don't cry. There's another kind of release. A year's worth of regret and anguish and guilt falling away. And in its place a revelation about how wrong I was, how hasty and even cruel it was to disappear. I tried to hide from my feelings. I tried to pretend I was in control, which was laughable, only it wasn't funny at all. *When you know better, you do better.* Gigi had a pillow on her lounger with that saying.

"I'm so, so sorry, Corey. I should have called you and told you. I should have trusted you. You deserved better than that. Our relationship deserved more than that." I say it all into the fabric of his shirt. It's easier than looking him in the eye.

"It's okay . . . well, it's not. I did deserve better than a text message, after three years."

"I know, I really am sorry." I say it again, as if repeating the words will make them any more true.

"Hey, look at me," he says.

I lay a hand on his chest and push myself up so I can look at him. His face is close to mine. I can see the slight chip in his bottom front tooth. "I loved you, Rye."

Loved. Loved. The past tense makes me feel like I've been turned inside out. I'm raw to the world and it's my own fault. I'd done an excellent job of convincing myself that Corey would never be right for me, not for the long term. Because our relationship *doesn't* make sense, on paper at least. On paper, I don't end up with the white guy, especially considering how consumed I've been these last few months (or a lifetime, really) with all the ways race oozes its sticky tentacles into every relationship, every interaction, every intention. It's damn near blown up my relationship with my best friend. But here I am, my cheek on this pale chest, realizing that Corey may well be a white man, but he's no more "wrong" or "wrong for me" as a best friend or a life partner than Jen is. I'd talked myself out of loving him because I had an expectation of what my life should look like, who I *should* be with had clouded my vision of who I *wanted* to be with. There are no easy choices, no safe choices, you can't plan your way to happiness. So even though it goes against everything I've ever told myself about how my life should look, and it won't be easy or uncomplicated, I know it's what I want, who I want. So there's only one thing to do.

I close the two inches between Corey's face and mine. I kiss him. It's not enough. I'm not close enough. I climb on top of him and arrange myself so that as many parts of me are touching as many parts of him as possible.

We're not going to make it to the bedroom, to the fresh sheets I put on the bed this morning, just in case. Within seconds, Corey is shimmying out of his dark jeans and I have the familiar shock of his pale penis and blond pubic hair. Before Corey, I somehow thought all of them were the same color, so his bright pink dick took me by surprise. Right now, it may be the most beautiful thing I've ever seen. And while I used to love our drawn-out foreplay, I don't want or need any of that. I'm desperate for him to be inside me as quickly as possible. I want to give myself over to him completely, until we both can't take it anymore, and that's exactly what happens. It's been too long since I've had this feeling, a euphoric release and total surrender that I only ever experience during sex or at certain points in running, consumed not by thoughts or worries or anything at all, except the purest of pleasure. It's bliss.

Corey looks up at me, flushed with pleasure when we're done. "So yeah, wow." He traces a lazy finger around the edge of the black lace bra I carefully selected — again, just in case.

"Like old times." I smile down at him, wipe the beads of sweat from his forehead.

We take a minute to rearrange ourselves on the couch so that I am lying on top of him. Our breathing slows, starts to match breath for breath. I wait for Corey to say something and sense he's waiting for the same. *Now what?*

There's a lot of things I want in this moment: Corey to stay over (I don't even care that his hideously loud snoring will keep me up all night); for him to wake me by burying his face between my legs like he used to; or for him to wear my pink bathrobe in the morning while I make us eggs. All the fears, the doubts — they're still there, and I could let myself give in to them and convince myself all over again that it's too much, that it would be too hard, it's too late. Or, or, or. It's funny that I'm acting like I have a choice at all. This, whatever it is, is happening.

Through the panel of windows, I watch fluffy white flakes flutter through the ink-black air. As I work up the nerve to say what needs to be said, I hear the most beautiful sound.

Do it, baby girl. Show him your heart. Gigi is back.

CHAPTER SIXTEEN

JEN

Dear Tamara,

I don't know if you'll read this letter, and maybe it's selfish or wrong for me to reach out to you, but I had to try.

There's nothing I can do to take away your pain, but I want you to know how badly I feel for your loss, how I think about your son every single day, how I will regret what I did for the rest of my life.

I have a son now too. His name is Chase and he's six weeks old today. Becoming a father has changed me, made me a better man. I think about this little person all the time. I'll do anything I can to keep him safe, to protect him. I'd die for him. And I don't know what I would do if anyone ever took him away from me.

I can't make excuses for what happened in those five seconds, but I want to own up to what I did. You deserve that. You deserve your son back; I wish I could give that to you, but I can't. One day I will have to tell my own boy what I did. I'll have to tell him so that he understands the power we all have to harm other people even when we don't mean to.

I'll tell him because I want him to be better than me, to do better than me.

I became a cop so I could help people, not hurt them, and I fell short. And even though I'll never work as a police officer again, I hope I can still find a way to help people, to do some good.

I don't know if you want to hear this. My wife says as a mother this is what she would want to know. I held Justin's hand while we waited for the ambulance. He told me his name and I told him to hang on. He asked for you and I said you were on your way.

I don't want you to think that I believe there's anything I can say or do to make this right. There's not, I know that. I don't expect you to forgive me. I only want you to know that I will carry your son's memory and do the best I can with my own life to honor his.

Kevin Murphy

The letter lies there on the kitchen table, tucked beneath a vase of fresh deli daisies. The words slant across the page in Kevin's best penmanship, the cursive the nuns taught him at St. Francis. He had debated typing it.

"No. That's too formal. Typing it wouldn't be right," he said, to himself more than to me.

Each time he messed up he started over with a fresh piece of paper, the discarded attempts crumbled and scattered like little rocks across the floor. Until finally, he had a version he was happy with — then it sat right here on the table for two days, while Kevin decided what, if anything, to do with it. Neither of us has touched it, by some sort of unspoken agreement.

I don't want it to be the first thing Riley sees when she gets here. *It's just Riley,* I remind myself.

My kitchen's a wreck and I regret I didn't clean up more. There are half-packed boxes everywhere, adding to the chaos. I make a half-hearted attempt to wipe up spilled breast milk from the table with my bare hand, throw some odds and ends cluttering

481

the counter into a box, along with the letter, laid carefully on top before I close the flaps.

The bread sizzles in the frying pan on the stove. I add more butter, brown sugar, and the bacon bits. I had to go to three different stores to find them. I flip each slice one last time, then turn the heat to low and cover the pan.

When the doorbell rings, I start to holler to come on in, then look down at Chase, strapped to me in the BabyBjörn, and think better of it. He's not asleep, but he's not exactly awake either. I cross through the living room and fling open the door. There's a burst of air that carries the faintest hint of an early spring.

Fred makes a mad dash to greet our visitor. I can barely see Riley over the giant baby stroller she's struggling to push around the dog and up the one step of our porch. With its dual cup holders and cozy detachable bassinet, it's the opposite of the stained and rickety hand-me-down of Annie and Matt's that we've been using since Chase came home from the hospital.

I stand there a little dumbstruck.

"It was on your registry." Riley says it so casually, like it's a rattle and not a $500 stroller, the nicest item on the list. "I bought it months ago. When you first posted it."

We manage to wrestle it into the tiny foyer. "It's incredible. Thank you."

I want to hug Riley hello, except the stroller stands between us, a barrier, and by the time she maneuvers around it in the narrow hallway, the moment has passed. Instead of reaching for me, she peeks at Chase in the carrier. "Is he asleep?"

"Sort of. I need to feed him pretty soon. I should also feed Fred. I just remembered that. Nothing makes you forget that you have a dog like having a baby."

Riley trails behind me to the kitchen and I see her take in the mess — all the boxes.

"What's all this?"

"Surprise?" That was stupid, but I'm nervous to see Riley and tell her my news. "We're . . . we're moving. I wanted to tell you in person."

Riley looks around for a place to sit and I rush over. "Here, here, let me get that." All of the kitchen chairs are filled with various junk, a string of Christmas lights, piles of old tax returns. I grab everything and push it into a pile on top of the table. "Sit, sit." I gesture to the chair as if it's a throne.

"Where are you going?" She sags into the wooden chair.

"Jacksonville."

"Jacksonville! As in Florida?"

"Yeah, birthplace of Burger King!"

"Jen . . . this is serious. I can't believe it. You're leaving? Just like that?"

"I know, I know. It all happened so fast. We went to visit last week. Kevin's got a cousin who bought us two tickets with his airline miles. At first we just left so Kevin could have some space to think about the deal, but while we were there the cousin offered him a job — at his landscaping business. And it just . . . it makes sense. To get out of here."

"Wow, okay. It's a lot. I'm trying to process."

"I know, me too." Moving almost a thousand miles away from the only place we've ever lived is not what I imagined for our future, but nothing has been what I imagined.

We were walking on the beach when Kevin finally made his decision about the deal.

"I'm going to do it, Jen," he said. "I'm not going to put you and Chase through any more hell."

"You're sure?" I said.

"I'm sure. You don't deserve it and, besides, it wouldn't be right. I can't get on that stand and say that I feared for my life."

He wrung his hands, working his knuckles into loud cracks. "Maybe I did in the moment. Maybe I want to believe that I did. But it's still no excuse. I . . . reacted. And I can't look that boy's mother in the eye and say that I feared for my life. This is what I deserve — worse, probably — but at least this."

We both stared at the foamy waves that lapped our toes. I could only hope something good comes of this, not for our family, but for the system, as Riley called it. The DA said she wanted to make Kevin an example. Well, now he is one, an example of someone who accepts consequences, who breaks the silence. More people need to. I get that now. Maybe it'll make a difference. Maybe it's some small silver lining.

Kevin called Brice to tell him his decision, and then he passed out for twenty-four hours straight. I hovered by the bed, watching him, worried out of my mind that we'd entered another terrible phase, that Kevin's plan was to sleep (or drink) his way through the rest of his life and that I'd regret my decision to stand by him no matter what. But then he woke up, and the color was back in his face; he stood up straighter, as if a weight had been lifted. Our second night in Florida, we laid with our limbs twisted together like we used to do when we were first dating, only this time Chase was nestled between us. Kevin held on to our son's tiny fist with his own meaty hands. "We made a person, Jaybird. I can't believe it." He smiled then, a barely there smile. Any trace of happiness still feels like an indulgence, something we shouldn't get to have after everything that's happened. How much is he entitled to after what he did? The guilt follows us everywhere like a shadow. And sometimes, when we're happy, when we dare to smile, or delight in our child, or feel optimistic about the future, that shadow reminds us to be humble. And grateful for mercy.

"I want him to respect me," Kevin said. "To look up to me, but I'll never be able to change what happened."

"No, no, you won't," I replied simply. I could only offer my husband the truth, my unconditional love, and the fact that I had stayed.

He paused before he said what we had both been thinking. "What if we lived here?"

We both knew staying in Philly would be impossible now that he's testifying at Cameron's trial in a few months. We're already pariahs among people we thought were family, and members of our actual family too.

Ramirez won't speak to Kevin. No one on the force will either. And despite Cookie's best efforts, Frank and Matt are a cold wall of silence. And then there's the fact that no one in Philly will hire the guy who shot the kid. Down in Florida, Kevin has the chance to work. Our financial situation has gone from bad to bleak to impossible, and we still don't know if we're going to be personally sued; it's like waiting for the results of a test to see if you have a horrible disease. There's nothing we can do except hope for the best. But in the meantime, we have food, and Chase has clothes, even if they're almost all Archie's hand-me-downs, and with the security deposit on this place and Kevin's last paycheck, we'll be able to cover our first month's rent in Jacksonville, and that's what I focus on: our immediate needs are met. It made it easy to decide what to do with that $10,000 check from the Order of Kings: that money was never mine or Kevin's to keep. When I cashed it, I did it at one of those dodgy check-cash places where they take 10 percent and don't need to know your name. I got a $5,000 money order and sent it anonymously to Strawberry Mansion High School with instructions to start a scholarship fund in Justin's name. I made out a check to Riley with the rest, right there in my wallet.

"Let me get you something to drink. How about a Coke?" I open the fridge hoping we actually have Coke.

"Whoa, is all that breast milk?" Riley looks stunned at the rows and rows of plastic bottles piled on the top shelf.

"It is. I told the doctor this was the first time in my life that I've ever been over-productive at anything. I'm not so great at getting pregnant, but man, I sure can make milk."

"Have you tasted it?" It's such a Riley thing to ask, like she's interviewing me for a segment on new motherhood.

"Omigod, I did!" I haven't even admitted this to Kevin, worried he would be too grossed out. "It's sweet, kinda sour, a little grassy too."

"Hey, look what I made us!" I grab the warm pan from the stove and carry it over to the table. That's how Gigi always served miracle bread, right out of the pan. I take off the lid with a flourish like I'm present-ing a prize. "Miracle bread!"

It works, a layer of tension melts between us.

Riley grabs greedily at the fork I hand her. "Jenny — I can't believe you made this, with everything else you have to do." She tears at a piece of bread and lifts it to her lips. When she swallows, her joy consumes her entire face. I don't want to make a big deal out of how happy this makes me, so I just move a pile of baby clothes and sit down, place the entire skillet in front of her.

The quiet is comfortable — nice even — as we chew thick sweet bites of the mushy bread. Riley actually moans. "It's so good, Jen. Gigi would be proud."

I swallow the lump in my throat with another bite.

"So, Jacksonville, huh?" Riley is still processing, and it makes me a little happy that she seems sad. She's sad for me to go.

"Yep, I got a job there, too. Or almost." I go on to explain that Dr. Kudlick came by with the sweater and sneakers I'd left at the office and a cute little outfit for the baby, and mentioned that he had a friend from dental school, with a large practice with offices in Jacksonville and Orlando, looking for an experienced office manager.

"Kevin's friend can't afford to pay benefits at the landscaping gig, so one of us has to have health insurance. Chase still needs to see the doctor once a week."

"Well, Kevin was really lucky to get a good job, and so fast. It's hard with a record," Riley says. "Shaun just got let go from the

489

moving company. Said they were downsizing, but he thinks it's because some speakers went missing and it was easy to pin it on him and get rid of him. He's sent out twenty résumés in the past two weeks. Hasn't heard back from anyone."

It couldn't have been easy for Riley to help her family deal with all of that, and maybe I'd underestimated the stakes and consequences when it happened. Maybe I hadn't given her enough credit or support back then. The maybes continue to pile up, a Jenga tower of maybes.

I've been replaying our conversation at the hospital, the kind of obsessive reenactments where I say different things, where I'm less defensive and less scared. I go into a spiral where I think I'm a horrible person, a terrible friend. The distance between Riley and me these past couple of months has felt like losing a limb, and I'll do anything to try to make it right.

"About what we talked about in the car —"

"Jenny, we were both so worked up that morning."

"No. Stop. You said you want us to talk. I want that too." I don't want to pick at our scabs, now that it feels like they're healing, but there's no other way. "I get what you

490

were saying, it is real easy for me not to think about race. And I don't even think about it when I look at you because when I look at you I see this person I've loved for like my whole life, my sister. All I can say is I'm here for you. I'm here for all of it. And I might say stupid things when we talk, but I want to talk, keep talking."

I don't even know if the words coming out of my mouth make any sense, but I hope Riley can feel what it is I'm trying to get across.

"Thank you," Riley says quietly. "It's good to hear you say that. I don't want us to walk on eggshells around each other. I know I probably haven't opened up enough about my challenges as a Black woman. Or I don't know, maybe you haven't probed enough either?"

There *are* questions I want to ask Riley, like about her family member who she said was lynched or all the comments on her stories, or all those other things I don't know about. "I can probe. I'm good at probing. I love to probe."

Riley laughs. There's nothing better than making Riley laugh.

This is it, a start, a knot loosening. Given that Riley is the most contained person I've ever known, these delicate conversations —

calm and kind — are how we can start to rebuild. It might not be such a bad thing after all; maybe we don't need to rehash every miscommunication or slight in painful detail, or go backward to move forward. We can trust that we will eventually return to normal, that the strength of our shared history is enough to fall back on, to carry us through. I allow myself to feel hopeful that this is exactly what's happening right now. And that after all of this, we could become even closer.

Chase, who'd fallen asleep, wakes with an angry howl that seems far too fierce for such a tiny person. He brings his right fist up to his face, always the right, and presses it tightly to his earlobe. It's one of the peculiarities about my baby that I'm loving to discover — like how he smacks his lips so hard when he's ready to nurse that you can practically hear him in the next room. Or the way he can already turn his head from side to side, even as a six-week-old preemie, which Kevin takes as proof of his early athletic potential. Each day it's a different Chase; there is something completely new to discover about him, to fall in love with. There have been so many surprises the last few months, most of them terrible, but the one good one is that I love motherhood even more than I thought I would, even more than I would have thought possible.

I pull Chase away from me so I can look down at his scrunched-up little face. His crazy-long lashes are collecting teardrops. "He'll calm down in a sec. Do you want to hold him?"

"Of course. It's all I've been thinking about. Do I need to wash my hands? I'll go wash my hands."

Riley furiously scrubs every inch of her hands like she's going into surgery. Then she comes and lifts Chase out of my arms, gently, careful to support his wobbly little head. As soon as he's nestled in the crook of Riley's elbow he stops crying. She looks down at his chest and cracks up.

I'm confused about why Riley is laughing at my baby until I remember that I'd dressed him in the onesie Lou bought him, in case my mom decided to drop by this afternoon like she said she would. It's bright Eagles green with "DALLAS SUCKS" written across the chest.

"Let me guess, Lou?"

"Who else? She doesn't bother to come meet her grandson for almost a month and then she shows up with these obnoxious onesies and a bottle of whiskey, which she says is to help my breastfeeding. I told her that it's beer that's supposed to help with breast milk and that it's an old wives' tale anyway, so she opened it up and made herself a cocktail."

Lou didn't visit Chase once in the hospital, a fact I didn't bother to confront her with because I knew all she would say was, "You know I don't do hospitals." I was too distracted and exhausted to be enraged about it anyway, until the day we finally brought Chase home and I worked out the math. He had been alive for three full weeks and had yet to meet his grandmother, who lived not ten miles away. The anger was all-consuming. Maybe it was a lifetime's worth. I railed and raged for days, and then I was out for a walk with Chase, taking advantage of the fact that the temperatures had climbed into the fifties, and I almost let him fall out of his stroller. He was so small. I didn't have him buckled in right, and when I hit a bump, he flopped loose and almost slid to the ground. I frantically swiveled my head around to see if anyone had witnessed what a terrible, inept mother I was. It felt like hours before my heart stopped hammering. It occurred to me right there on the sidewalk that being a mother meant I would fail a little every day, and this was the first of many mistakes I would make even as I vowed to do my best, to keep him safe and protect him. Hopefully, I wouldn't fail as spectacularly as Lou did, but for the first time in my life I was willing to sympathize. As soon as I got home, before I could change my mind, I texted her a picture of Chase and told her we were both excited to see her, that we wanted her to come to the house to visit.

Since then Lou's been better, coming over every few days, even spending the night once, making me a frozen Stouffer's pizza while I breastfed Chase at two in the morning. She ate frosting with her fingers out of a tub of Betty Crocker and ranted about the new bar she worked at.

"The drinks are fourteen dollars and the damn snobs still only tip a dollar for two drinks, even though each cocktail is like a meal with the cut up cilantro and the egg whites and the smashed up fruit."

Chase clamped down on my raw nipple and I yelped.

"This is impossible."

Lou came over and stuffed a pillow under my elbow so I could reposition the baby's mouth.

"You think this is hard. Try having one of these when you're seventeen and living alone over a garage. And you had the colic, so you screamed and screamed nonstop. I didn't sleep for a year. And look what you did to my boobs?" Lou cupped her sagging breasts and then took a swig from her whiskey.

"I didn't know you breastfed," I said.

"I sure as hell did. You sapped me dry. Now I've got a couple of sun-dried tomatoes. I did a lot of things you don't give me credit for."

I never think about seventeen-year-old Lou with a tiny, crying baby, both of us helpless. She probably made the same promises to newborn me that I make to Chase, intense vows I offer up in the dark. Lou loved me as much as she could, as fiercely as I love my own son. It seemed easier to forgive my mother than to hold on to the anger that's lived inside me like blood and bone since I was a little girl.

"You did your best, Lou. It's all good, Lou," I said to my mother . . . and meant it.

Then I rubbed my hand around the pink edge of Chase's tiny ear and added a silent wish that he would one day forgive me for all the ways I'll inevitably screw him up.

Now Chase tries to focus on Riley, then he loses interest and intently works his mouth into strange shapes as if he's trying to figure out what a person possibly does with a mouth. Riley is a natural with him. *She should be a mother. She should know this joy.* It's my greatest wish for my friend.

"Does it make you want one?" I ask.

"A whiskey?" Riley jokes, before she seriously considers my question. "You mean a baby? I don't know. Maybe someday, when I'm not so busy."

I don't want to tell Riley that such a day will never come. Riley will never not be busy. A baby is something you have to make time for. I can sense it — our lives going in different directions. We've shared so much, I wanted us to share this too, as childish as that is. Since we were little, I had a stupid fantasy that Riley and I would have babies at the same time, and those little girls would grow up to be best friends, like something out of *The Sisterhood of the Traveling Pants*. Now I worry it may never happen for her and that my friend is too busy, closed off, and might always be alone. The pity that sweeps through me then borders on mean.

But also a fear too, that this is the most important thing in my life and Riley won't understand what I'm going through. All the things she won't care about and will have to pretend to be interested in — sleep training, Chase's first teeth, the specific agony of breastfeeding, how I hate it but never want to give it up.

But I see the way she looks at Chase now and I know it will be okay. She loves my baby, I can tell, and that's all that matters. No, what really matters is this baby wouldn't even be here without her. I can give her her money back, but it will still be a debt I can never repay.

I get up to get the check, in my wallet on the counter. When I turnaround, Riley has a look on her face, that *I have to tell you something* look, and my stomach plummets.

CHAPTER SEVENTEEN

RILEY

Jen slips back into her chair, a slip of paper in her hand. "What?"

"What do you mean, what?"

"You have a look on your face like you're about to tell me something awful. Is something wrong with Shaun? Your mom?"

"No. It's nothing bad. It's just news." It's strange recounting my life to Jenny like this, in person, sitting at a table, when she used to just know things about me because I would text her everything as it happened. And even though she's still the first person I want to tell when something good or happy happens, that's not where we are right now. I'm still not sure whether we'll ever get back to that exact place.

"Did you hear about the anchor job?"

"Actually, I did." Jen isn't the only one who has big news.

"Annnnndd? Come on, don't keep me

499

waiting. I saw they announced Candace's retirement."

"I got it!" I can feel my mouth form itself into a grin big enough for the billboard I'll be on soon.

Jenny squeals and hugs me before I can get the rest out — the catch.

"Well, it's not permanent though. Quinn and I are going to trade off. Scotty's testing us out . . . or pitting us against each other. We'll see." I rein in my big cheese and my excitement. It's still too early to celebrate. But I'm closer, closer than ever. And I know exactly why; so does Jen. It sits there between us, the reason for my rather swift promotion: covering the shooting was my big break. It put me on the national stage, just as I hoped it would. I've heard from a few network and cable news execs, feelers to keep in touch, invites to lunch or coffee the next time I'm in New York or Atlanta.

"That wasn't what I was going to tell you though . . . it's something else." In my pause, I see Jen brace herself. I hurry up and blurt it out lest she think this is another big scary talk we need to have.

"I saw Corey! I may still be in love with Corey." Now I brace myself for her reaction. Part of me doesn't know how I feel about something until I know how Jenny feels —

it's always been like that. She doesn't squeal and hug me this time. She looks confused, maybe even a little worried.

"Whoa? That's huge. Tell me everything."

I do, I tell her everything. Starting with finally explaining why we broke up in the first place, how he wasn't the one who broke up with me, how it was me, all me. I ignore that she has the same hurt look on her face as Corey did; otherwise I wouldn't be able to get it all out.

"I don't understand. Why didn't you tell me?" The pain is in her voice, too.

"Well . . . you've had your own stuff going on the last few weeks. I didn't want to bother you with the fact that my ex-boyfriend wanted to meet up. And we've been in a bad place and —"

"No, I mean back then. Last year. When you broke up with him, when Shaun got arrested. Jesus. If I had known, I could have been with you."

"You'd just found out that the IVF didn't work again. You were a mess. I didn't want to burden you. And also, honestly, I really didn't want to talk about it. I was trying to shut everyone and everything out. I guess that doesn't work so well."

"No, it doesn't work. It hasn't been working. Riley . . . you have to tell me things."

"I know I do, Jenny." And I mean that. I really do. I also know that I can no longer be gentle with her. I will have to call her out sometimes. I'll have to push her to think harder, to get outside her little bubble, a bubble I worry will grow smaller in the Florida suburbs.

"So what now, I mean with Corey?"

I start nervously folding a pile of onesies sitting haphazardly on the table, turning them into neat little squares. "We'll see. He's going to come down next month again and we'll have dinner."

"That's great. It's good you're open to this. I have a good feeling."

It *is* great. Hearing Jen say it confirms it. This is good. I let myself be excited. Even though I'm scared of so many things, that long distance won't work, that I will always feel judged for dating a white dude, that if we do decide to have children, he won't understand what it's like to raise a Black man in our fucked-up world. I worry about keeping this anchor chair, about being at the top of my game and having to choose between being a big fish in Philadelphia or giving it up to be a little fish in New York and live with Corey. Could I ever ask him to move here to be closer to me? But I'm learning that feelings are okay, or at least unavoidable, even having more than one at once. And right now we're still in the fun stage, the dirty-texting stage, the weekend visits. But this isn't something new. We have history, and we will be right back in that serious make-or-break place before we know it. But I want to be optimistic. I want to feel good about something in my life after these months, this year of dread. I deserve it. I'm starting to believe that.

"I might have a white bestie on one side and a white boyfriend on the other. Talk about Oreo. Ugh."

There's a split-second pause where Jen looks at me to see if she's allowed to laugh, and then she does. "Well, the ones with chocolate crème always were my favorite." We crack up again. And we might as well be tucked into sleeping bags in my parents' wood-paneled basement for how much it feels — blissfully — like old times.

"What's that?" I nod at the paper in her hand, distracting us before we can get too deep into Corey, and the future. As excited as I am, it's all still too fragile to bear the weight of too much scrutiny of what the future will bring. Baby steps.

Jenny unfolds the rectangle of paper. It's a check, with my name on it in Jenny's neat block letters.

"Jenny, you don't have to . . ." I stop her hand as it slides along the table. I never expected that she would repay me. I don't need the money, and she needs it now so much more than I do. I'd rather we just forget about it altogether.

"Riley, let me do this. I owe you — this and so much more."

"Where did you get —" There's no way Jenny had five grand lying around. Especially with Kevin's legal bills, and the lawsuits that may be coming, and now the move.

"Don't ask. Just take the money, Rye. Please. If you love me, you'll take it. I don't want to owe you anything. I want a clean slate."

And I do too, so I take the check and tuck it into the back pocket of my jeans. I told her I would take it, but I don't promise to cash it.

And now it's my turn. I didn't know if it would feel like the right time to do this, but it is. It has to be. Especially now that Jenny is leaving. It sinks in now. She'll be gone in a couple of weeks. It's a punch in the gut, but also maybe a relief. I love her. I'll always love her, but maybe distance is what we both need. It's what we're used to. Maybe the miles between us haven't been a barrier but a way to maintain our connection despite how different our lives have become. I can picture us sitting on a beach in Florida, side by side, a giant pitcher of frozen margaritas on a rickety table between our beach chairs — the mandatory best-friend getaway. How had we gone our whole lives without a real beach trip? The time Lou took us to Atlantic City and then left us on a dirty strip of sand while she gambled at Harrah's and made me swear I wouldn't tell my mother doesn't count. This trip will count. I'm determined to carve out three days for this. Soon.

"Well, I have something else for you too, actually. Hang on, it's in my bag."

"You already got me the Lexus of strollers. You have to stop!" Jenny calls out as I run into the foyer, return with the dark vinyl jewelry box.

"Are you proposing? If so, the answer is yes. I'll be your sister wife. Can I get on your health insurance?"

But Jenny's laughter catches in her throat as she opens the box. Inside is the delicate bracelet of pearls and the note from Gigi.

Jenny's lips move as she reads Gigi's last words to her, words I have already read dozens of times. She slides the string of iridescent beads over her still-swollen fingers and onto her wrist.

"I never want to take it off."

"I have a necklace too. It's a set." My hand floats to the milky strand peeking from beneath my purple cowl-neck sweater.

"Now we don't have to get those half-heart friendship necklaces. This is much classier." Tears are streaming down Jen's cheeks. We stare at each other, appreciating this moment, the fragile peace. It makes me think of the little bean seeds we planted in Dixie cups in fourth grade — when the minuscule bright green sprout peeked out from the dark soil, fragile but promising, striving for the light.

"Can I show you something?" Jen asks me.

"Of course."

Jen goes over to a box and pulls out another piece of paper and hands it to me. It's not Jenny's block letters, but a crisp perfect cursive.

I read silently, lips moving, and when I finish I start at the top and read it again. Then I look out the window to the back-yard. I can see, just barely, the shadows on the fence, three letters hidden behind white paint — M-U-R. I can fill in the rest. Jen is staring at me, waiting, biting her lip.

"It's . . . nice." Kevin clearly spent time with this letter; it's the most emotion I've ever seen from him. But it's also completely inadequate and maybe even a little selfish. He wants to unload his burden, but that's impossible. When I imagine Tamara reading this letter — But who am I to judge? How do I know what she needs or doesn't need?

"Do you really think so?"

"Well, nothing will make it better, but sometimes you want to know that the other person sees you and your pain." This is all I can offer.

"Can you . . ." Jen starts, but I know what she's going to ask before she even finishes.

"Yes, I can get it to her." I tuck the letter carefully into my bag. I check on Tamara once a week. Sometimes she's up for talking, sometimes it's just a text back. I will keep checking on her. In time, maybe she'll be up for lunch or coffee. In time, maybe we can be friends. I think of all the stories I've covered and the people I never hear from or speak to again — the man who single-handedly brought his daughter's rapist to justice, the woman who lost all three of her kids in an apartment fire, the couple who adopted triplets with severe special needs. They touched my lives and vice versa, and then, after a few weeks of interviews and minutes of airtime, they were gone. It's the nature of the beast. But Tamara is different; this story was different. This story changed everything, including me — especially me.

We sit quietly again, the only sounds Chase's soft little snuffles.

"Puff?" Jenny whispers so softly I almost don't hear her.

"Yeah?"

"What about us?"

"Us?"

"Are we going to be okay?"

Instead of answering, I reach for her hand across the table — the pearl bracelet glistens in the sunlight through the window — and when my hand is in hers, I squeeze hard. Twice for yes.

EPILOGUE

Tamara digs in the drawer, patting around among all the extra batteries and rubber bands and a faded pack of fossilized Trident, until she finds it — the battered envelope with the letter inside.

She hadn't even wanted to touch it when the journalist Riley Wilson had pushed the paper across the table slowly at the little café, like she wasn't sure she was doing the right thing. It was exactly four months and three days after her son died (she was and is still counting the days), and Riley reached out to see if she could take her for coffee, to see if she was okay, which was sweet. Since then, through the summer, they still meet up sometimes, for coffees, once for a drink, a fledging but distant friendship, like people who sing in the same choir or have kids on the same football team, even though their connection is much stranger. She has nothing in common really with the reporter, but she appreciates that Riley checks on her and asks her questions about Justin when everyone else is too scared to talk about him. It was Riley she ended up telling things to — like how Justin's toothbrush is still in a cup on the sink. Its bristles are frayed and worn, and every morning she thinks about how it's time to throw this one out and buy him a new one. Or how she lives in fear that Justin's fish will die and she won't know what to do with herself when that happens.

When she talks about Justin it's like he's still alive, like she can imagine he's just sleeping over at his grandma's for a couple of nights. Which is still, even after all this time, a common phenomenon. The forgetting. Like she'll wonder what Justin was doing right now, studying for a chem test or playing *Madden* at Ty's house. One time, she even drove all the way to school to pick him up before she remembered: Justin wasn't at school, or at a friend's. Justin was nowhere. But he was still everywhere too — his gap-toothed smile on that mural on Diamond Street. Just last week, she saw someone wearing a T-shirt at Kroger with her son's face on it, a vivid photograph on black cotton, and she reached out and touched this stranger's chest before he violently batted her hand away. "What the hell, back off, lady!" The man didn't know this was her son — she was only reaching for her son.

She pulls the letter from the drawer now with shaking hands. When Riley had given it to her she couldn't read it right away. Part of her didn't care what this man had to say to her. It wouldn't change anything. The only thing that gave her even an ounce of satisfaction at all was thinking of Travis Cameron sitting in a jail cell for ten years, Cameron, who wasn't sorry at all — who didn't even look at her when she bawled through her victim impact statement, who claimed over and over that he was just "doing his job." Sometimes she indulges in long daydreams about what his life is like in prison and they give her a rush of pleasure, and then she feels a little guilty for that. But not too much.

It was Wes who read the letter first and then told her, "It's worth reading, Sis." And she did and she felt nothing. Just like she'd told Kevin Murphy's wife, who had the nerve to look so broken when she saw her in the courtroom bathroom that time: she didn't want apologies. But she kept the letter, tucked away in this drawer, and she rereads it now because today another boy was murdered — a nineteen-year-old, with a head full of twists and knobby arms that reminded her of Justin's. This teen was shot in the back twelve times in West Baltimore for allegedly breaking into a car. The fervor and outrage is familiar, a well-oiled machine by now. She's part of the inner circle, a club no one wants to be a member of, the moms bonded by grief. Her phone blew up this morning with dozens of texts and calls, she'll get out her Mothers of the Movement hat, drive to Baltimore, go to the marches. All of the steps of this heartbreaking and seemingly endless ritual. In a few minutes, she'll call the boy's mom and they will just sit on the phone, not having to say a word. Their silence will form a communion stronger than words. After all, what can words do?

She drops the letter, grips the kitchen counter, grits her teeth and waits for the despair to pass. It comes in waves, moments like these, a sense of hopelessness so strong it steals her breath. The sense that no one will understand and nothing will ever change. That white folks will just go about their lives and pity Black folks, and wonder why they can't get ahead, get a break, just behave already, listen to the police. Those white folks will send their children off to school and know they're safe. They'll do all the things white folks have done for years and somehow be able to tune out the cries: *Good Lord, please, is it so hard to stop killing our children? Can you stop justifying their murders?*

It's the one thing she appreciates about this letter. He doesn't try to justify himself. Some things can't be justified. Still, the letter won't bring peace or closure. Nothing will. But on a good day, when the sun is shining and when her memories of her son are the strongest, when she feels him in the room with her, on those days, she lets herself believe that maybe, just maybe, there's a world in which another mother won't have to go through this pain. She lets herself believe that people will do the right thing, that things will change. She lets herself believe that Justin didn't die for nothing. And then she'll grab his still-unwashed pillow and hold it to her face and feel as close to hopeful as possible.

Today, though, as another mother grieves, is not one of those days.

ACKNOWLEDGMENTS

It truly takes a village to make a book. We're so thankful for ours. It might be a little unorthodox for us to start off by thanking each other, but we're just going to do it. Writing this book together has deepened our friendship and our professional relationship in so many ways. It wasn't always easy — nothing worthwhile ever is — but our goal was always to create something that neither of us could have done alone, and it's gratifying to believe we achieved that. Having a partner makes the process of writing, usually such a solitary endeavor, so much less lonely. Thanks for teaching me how to make an em-dash, Jo, and being patient when I forgot over and over . . . thankfully you made me a mug to remind me. And, Christine, thank you for getting so dressed up for all of our Google Hangouts. I'll never forget your bathrobe.

We're indebted to the early readers of this

book, and those people who were generous enough to let us interview them — every one of whom offered invaluable feedback and information. So thank you to: Kelly Robbins, Darrell Jordan, Shauna Robinson, Kate Kennedy, Brenda Copeland, Melissa Danaczko, Kara Logan Berlin, Chelley Talbert, Matthew Horace, Julie Kauffunger, Karyn Marcus, Laura Lewis, Molly Goodson, Glynnis MacNicol, Amy Benzinger, Dave Williams, Cyndi Doyle, Dawn Turner, Lashanda Anakwah, and Jo's Lit Club — Emily Foote, Leslie Mariotti, Alison Goldblum, Sarah Pierce, Dana Duffy, Gabrielle Canno, Johanna Dunleavy, and Nydia Han. Massive thanks to Dan Wakeford for being such a wonderful (and handsome) cheerleader.

Bringing this book into the world was quite a journey. It's hard to even find words to describe how blessed we feel that this book landed with Atria and HQ and two incredible editors.

Thank you to Lindsay Sagnette and Manpreet Grewal for your care with and passion for this story and for treating Riley and Jen like close friends. And to the entire teams at Atria and HQ: we see you, we appreciate you, we couldn't have done any of this without you. Also a special shout-out to

Laywan Kwan for designing a jacket that was love at first sight.

Our agents, Pilar Queen and Byrd Leavell, believed in this book from the first day they read it. In the midst of the unpredictable twists and turns in the journey of this book, not to mention one of the craziest years of modern human history, they were ports in the storm and gave us the confidence to keep pushing forward. We will forever be grateful for your kindness, enthusiasm, and tenacity and for generally being two of the best people in publishing.

That's tough competition, because as two people who have been involved in this industry in various capacities for almost two decades, it's our great fortune that we've gotten to count some of the sharpest, most curious, generous, and supportive people as colleagues, creative guides, mentors, and friends. The list is too numerous to name, but you know who you are, and we appreciate you.

And now for some individual thank-yous . . .

Jo:

I always worried that being a mom would put an end to my writing career. How could I possibly find the time to do something as self-indulgent as disappearing into fictional worlds while trying to keep small humans alive? I'm happy to report that my kids, Charlie and Bea, have made me a better, happier, and more prolific writer in so many ways, but mostly by cracking my heart wide open to new parts of the human experience. Thank you to my mom, Tracey Piazza, for taking the two little monsters away on plenty of overnights so I could have time to write and sleep and breathe. Thank you also for being my biggest fan. And to Tshiamo Monnakgotla for loving my kids like your own family and letting me be a working mom. My long-suffering husband, Nick Aster, is the only person on the planet besides my mother who has read everything I've ever written, and he read and critiqued this book over and over again, even after I promised him it was finished. Of course, it was never truly finished. Thank you, my dear. Ten thousand years of love.

Christine:

In the immortal words of the very wise Mindy Kaling, *a best friend isn't a person, it's a tier,* and I'm so fortunate to have so many people in that tier it threatens to topple. It's a good problem to have that I can't name everyone here without taking up too much space, but you know who you are and you know I would be lost without you.

What you can't know is how grateful I am for you, and how much I love you, because it's nearly beyond comprehension. But it is the most important truth of my life. Another truth: this book wouldn't exist without you.

Not only do I have the best friends, I lucked out in the family department too. Sitting at the poker table with the Prides, or around a dinner table piled high with John Pride's famous ribs, or in the back of the family van heading toward Alabama with Sam Cooke on the 8-track are but a few of a zillion experiences and memories that, stitched together, constituted the happiest childhood a good girl could ask for. That's largely thanks to my parents, the two best people I know. They taught me by word and example that it doesn't matter how smart or successful or popular you are, the one thing you should work really hard at above all else is being a good person. I've tried to live by that philosophy and it's served me well. I'm happy to have written a book if only to have a public forum to memorialize these words in print: *Thank you to John and Sallie for being you and helping me to become me. I can never repay you for all the unwavering support, wise advice, grounding calm, cheerful optimism, and endless generosity (and, of course, the jokes. So many jokes.). But know this: To make you proud is the point of every-thing.*

■ ■ ■ ■

Reader's Guide: We Are Not Like Them

CHRISTINE PRIDE
AND JO PIAZZA

■ ■ ■ ■

This reading group guide for *We Are Not Like Them* includes an introduction, discussion questions, and ideas for enhancing your book club. The suggested questions are intended to help your reading group find new and interesting angles and topics for your discussion. We hope that these ideas will enrich your conversation and increase your enjoyment of the book.

INTRODUCTION

Jen and Riley have been best friends since childhood. But one event severely tests the deep bond they share: Jen's husband, a city police officer, is involved in the shooting of an unarmed Black teenager. Six months pregnant, Jen is in free fall as her future, her husband's freedom, and her friendship with Riley are thrown into uncertainty. Covering this career-making story, Riley wrestles with the implications of this tragic incident for her community, her ambitions, and her relationship with her lifelong friend. Told from alternating perspectives, this novel is a powerful and poignant exploration of race in America today and its devastating impact on ordinary lives.

TOPICS & QUESTIONS
FOR DISCUSSION

1. What emotions did you experience while reading the prologue? Why do you think the authors chose to open with this scene?

2. How did you interpret Kevin's behaviors after the incident? Did you feel any sympathy for him, and do you think he deserved everything that happened after? Who do you blame for what happened?

3. Did you find yourself torn over how to feel about any of the characters' reactions or decisions in the novel? What moments were particularly controversial to you, and how did they challenge your perceptions?

4. Discuss how this novel exhibits instances of prejudice based on privilege, class, and race. What about instances of unconscious bias?

5. Riley says to Jen: "I didn't want to be the Black girl always talking about race. That's no fun. And I don't know what your reaction would be if I told you about all the shit I have to deal with because I'm a Black woman. What if you didn't have the right reaction?" (page 408). How might we be able to more openly discuss our feelings about these sensitive issues? Do you think there's ever a reason these things should be left undiscussed? Have you ever struggled to express a feeling or observation about race out of fear of being dismissed or misunderstood?

6. Did Jen and Riley's alternating voices highlight any important similarities or differences about their experiences during the novel? Did you relate to one character in particular?

7. Riley and Jen are pulled between their friendship and their commitments to their careers, families, and communities. Do you think they made the right choices? Have you ever felt caught between your obligations to others and yourself?

8. Jen struggles with supporting her husband and her complicated feelings about his ac-

tions and innocence. Do you think she's too afraid of his family to question him more? How does family influence your decisions?

9. How did you interpret the reactions from the media and social platforms throughout the novel? How are these mediums helpful or harmful to the people at the center of the story?

10. The tragedy that sparks the divide in Riley and Jen's relationship exposes some fault lines in their shared history. When is a friendship worth hanging on to, and when is it time to let go? How did their bond change by the end of the novel, for better or worse?

11. Were there parts of the novel that made you uncomfortable, and why?

12. What do you think of the book's title? What does it encapsulate about this story? Who are "We" and "Them" in the title?

ENHANCE YOUR BOOK CLUB

1. "What we didn't understand is that adulthood would be a relentless series of beginnings" (page 28). Discuss how you invisioned adult life as a kid. What is something that you were not expecting to experience — a new city, new job prospects, or a different lifestyle?

2. Riley tells Jen, "It's a privilege to never think about race" (page 409). How has privilege affected your life? How has the absence of privilege affected your life? Discuss an event where you recognized that privilege affected the outcome.

3. A 2014 study found that three out of four white people have no nonwhite friends. Are you surprised by this statistic? How does where you grew up affect the friends you make into adulthood?

A CONVERSATION WITH CHRISTINE PRIDE AND JO PIAZZA

We Are Not Like Them opens with the police shooting of an unarmed Black teenage boy. Why did you choose this event as the catalyst, and how did you work to get it right?

From the very beginning we knew we wanted to tell the story of a lifelong friendship between two women, a white woman and a Black woman, and explore how race impacts that relationship in unexpected ways. The issue of shootings of unarmed Black men was very much at the forefront of a national conversation when we started the book (and, sadly, remains so), capturing headlines across the country and sparking a movement — not to mention a lot of inflamed feelings and divisiveness. We were attracted to the idea of humanizing this hot-button issue and to the opportunity to foster a conversation about race through the lens of one powerful (and wholly relatable) friendship. Also, one of Christine's close (white) friends from childhood is married to a (white) cop, and this premise was loosely inspired by wondering what would happen if Christine found herself in a similar scenario as Riley.

Jo brought the point of view of a longtime journalist to the project and we tried to interview as many people as possible, not just to make sure our portrayal was accurate, but to make sure we captured the different emotions of everyone involved. We spoke to police officers (and their spouses), district attorneys, community activists, and the mothers of shooting victims, and read and researched firsthand accounts and statistics.

How did your own friendship inspire you to write this book?

We became incredibly close while working together on Jo's last novel, *Charlotte Walsh Likes to Win,* which Christine published at Simon & Schuster. As our friendship evolved so did our conversations about race. We knew we were lucky and privileged to even be able to have them. Statistics show that fewer than 10 percent of people have a close friend of another race. We were energized by the idea of working together in a unique way, as both friends and collaborators, and leveraging our relationship to tell a story that would help readers have their own conversations about race and think more deeply about their own friendships.

Your novel shows how stereotyping and racism can seep into even the closest of relationships. Why did you choose to show two characters experiencing this dynamic within a treasured friendship?

It's hard to have a friend of another race in America. The hard truth is that in our country, race permeates almost all aspects of our lives in one way or another, even our intimate relationships, and this story attempts to pull the curtain back to show how that happens in ways we don't always realize or can't avoid. It was important to us that both Black women and white women be able to relate to our characters. We chose to write in the first person so that we could dig deep into their minds and give voice to some of the difficult thoughts (spoken and unspoken) and pitfalls about race and racism from both perspectives. Our goal was to show the very real and relatable challenges people might have in trying to understand another's experience and mindset. It's the greatest goal of the novel to spark empathy and that was what we hope to do here, to offer a bridge over what can sometimes feel like a yawning gap in understanding and awareness, and help readers recognize and reckon with some of their own blind spots and beliefs.

Two different voices and experiences are captured in *We Are Not Like Them*, but you avoid creating a sense of false balance around the shooting. How did you approach the dual perspectives?

Our world is so polarized right now, and the issue that animates our plot — a police shooting — invites a lot of impassioned opinions and feelings. We were aware it risked lending itself to a good guy/bad guy dichotomy pretty quickly, and we wanted to avoid that at all costs. Readers may come in with preconceived notions, so we had to be careful that our audience didn't "side" with any one woman over the other, but the richness of the read comes from the seesaw back-and-forth between identifying with both. It was vital that we be clear that we didn't have an agenda and were committed to showing the many nuances and complexities.

We wanted our characters to be real and not just representative, so we also spent a long time talking about who they were, what motivated them, what scared them, what they loved, what they hated. We came up with lists about their likes and dislikes, their passions and fears, etc., much of which never even made it into the book in the literal sense, but colors all of their experiences and reactions. We loved this idea that a somewhat random twist of fate brought these two young girls together who may not have become close friends had they met in another way, or had they met at any other time (when their differences would have been more pronounced). In many ways, Riley and Jen are a somewhat odd match, even aside from their race, and it was fun to explore the intangible bonds that pull and hold us to each other even when a relationship is unlikely, and even when it's tested.

It was important to us that each character earned and deserved both sympathy and frustration in equal measure. Our hope is that the reader will say, *"I can see why she did/thought that"* when it comes to both Riley and Jen, even if there are moments when you want to scream at them too. All the while, all through the ups and downs, we wanted the reader to be able to root for not just the two characters, but, most important, the friendship itself.

Can you tell us about your shared writing process?

Thank the Lord for Google Docs. We've tried everything in terms of collaboration and it took a long time, but we finally came up with a process that works. We discuss the big ideas and broad strokes in a comprehensive outline first. And then, chapter by chapter, one of us takes a pass at the blank page. This is often the hardest part . . . especially the first chapter. (We can't tell you how many drafts we went through there.) And then we trade it back and forth, working in the suggestion and commenting modes. Then we'll get on the phone, or video chat or meet in person, to go over the things that can't easily be resolved on the page.

What challenges did you face in writing this book?

Writing a book is hard. Writing a book with someone else is hard. All that vulnerability and fear and self-doubt that's so much a baked-in part of the process is on full display. It's like letting someone watch you sing badly in the shower after eating a sheet cake. And then add difficult talks about race to the mix? *Woo-wee* is the only term that captures this particular perfect storm. There were times when we were truly tested and worried our friendship might not recover. There were weeks when our emotions were rubbed raw and we often joked about going to couples' counseling. We've also thought about writing an essay called "How Writing a Book About Race Almost Destroyed Our Interracial Friendship." But it was also one of the most meaningful things that either of us have ever done. In a single day of writing, we could start out laughing, butt heads, cry alone in our bathrooms, send a shy apology text, nail an incredible paragraph/page/chapter, laugh together, and push each other harder. And the result, at the end of a string of a million days like those, is a book we're proud of and a friendship and professional relationship that's stronger and better because of this journey together.

Were there any other novels or works that inspired you during this writing process?

The most excruciating part of the writing process is feeling like everyone else is doing it better and having an easier time of it. When you read someone else's perfect sentence, or ending, or a scene that brings tears to your eyes and you think, *Wow, I want to be able to do that.* That said, it's incredibly motivating too. And we're both such voracious readers — during the period we wrote this book, we probably read well over one hundred books between us — so it wasn't so much any one book that inspired us, but all of them, collectively. All of these fellow writers who inspired us with their characters and stories and craft and sparkling prose. Reading widely while we were working really pushed us and educated us, and often helped us troubleshoot when we were wrestling with something thorny. The way to become a better writer is to be a better reader, after all. We're constantly awed and adoring and deeply admiring when it comes to people who put their hearts on the page and create these beautiful words, and it's a privilege to be in this company.

Christine, this is your first novel. What was your journey to becoming a writer and how did you know this was the right book?

Being an editor for the last fifteen years has truly been a gift; some people have jobs, but I've really felt lucky to have found a calling and to have gotten to work with wildly talented writers and publish books that have touched readers. But throughout my career, I've also witnessed how the industry has been woefully underrepresentative in the types of stories and characters that are championed. As a kid, I craved more books (and TV shows, for that matter) that featured people who looked like me, that reflected my reality and my community, and as an adult, despite lots of great strides, I still notice that gap. There's a thirst and moral imperative for even more offerings that reflect more diverse experiences and stories and voices. I realized I could offer that; I could write that book — a novel that featured a character and a friendship and realities about being a Black woman in America that were familiar to me. And furthermore, that could tackle a topic that feels urgent and important to boot. My greatest goal as an editor — and now as a writer — is to give readers a vehicle to reflect on their lives and experiences in a meaningful way, and to feel emotionally stirred in a way that leaves an imprint long after the last page of the story.

From a practical standpoint, it's a little surreal to be on the other side. The thing about working in publishing for so long, "behind the scenes" so to speak, is that I know firsthand the overwhelming passion and commitment my colleagues bring to the table, working tirelessly on behalf of books they love in a business that's not always easy. It's a special experience now to have that support and community and vision from a different vantage point. Getting to see things from another perspective has also made me empathize with my authors more. For example, all the times I've reminded someone over the years that they shouldn't constantly check their Amazon ranking or read too much into it, I now understand how futile that was, and how difficult it will be to not give into the irrational inclination to hit that refresh button.

Jo, you've written many novels before, most recently *Charlotte Walsh Likes to Win*. How was writing *We Are Not Like Them* different for you?

My past novels have been told from one point of view. For *We Are Not Like Them*, we needed to get into the heads of two completely different women and see a single event from their very divergent and emotional points of view.

It can be exhausting to try to be two people at once. Each character really was a collaboration with Christine, so we each had to inhabit Jen and Riley at different times. I'd go for weeks only working on Riley chapters because it was the only way I could nail down her feelings and intentions without Jen getting in the way. I often did the same thing while reading through the book. I would read Jen's chapters all the way through and then Riley's chapters all the way through as if each of them were their own book.

Are you planning to write more books together?

Yes! We've already started the next one.

What do you hope readers will take away from _We Are Not Like Them?_

Our running joke about _We Are Not Like Them_ is: Come for the friendship, stay for the social justice. We hope we give readers a starting point for difficult conversations about race. We know that a lot of women don't have close friends of another race, and we're hoping that the friendship between Riley and Jen can give them some perspective on what it is like and an entryway into the conversations Riley and Jen are forced to have with themselves and with each other.

We also hope that the book can help readers initiate hard conversations about race when they're confronted with a shocking headline about a racially motivated shooting, hate speech, bias, and racism. We want to provide readers with new language and stories to approach these really difficult stories and events.

But above all that, even, we hope that readers will relish this book as a celebration of friendship and be inspired to take stock and appreciate their own close friends. If readers turn the last page and want to call their bestie, it means we've done our job.

ABOUT THE AUTHORS

Christine Pride is a writer, editor, and longtime publishing veteran. She's held editorial posts at many different trade imprints, including Doubleday, Broadway, Crown, Hyperion, and Simon & Schuster. As an editor, Christine has published a range of books, with a special emphasis on inspirational stories and memoirs, including numerous *New York Times* bestsellers. As a freelance editorial consultant, she does select editing and proposal/content development, as well as teaching and coaching, and pens a regular column — Race Matters — for *A Cup of Jo.* She lives in New York City.

Jo Piazza is an award-winning journalist, editor, and podcast host. Her work has appeared in the *New York Times,* the *Wall Street Journal,* CNN, *Marie Claire, Glamour,* and other notable publications. She is also the author of *Charlotte Walsh Likes to Win,*

How to Be Married, The Knockoff, Fitness Junkie, and *If Nuns Ruled the World.* She lives in Philadelphia with her husband and two small children.

BEYOND NEGATIVE THINKING

BREAKING THE CYCLE OF DEPRESSING AND ANXIOUS THOUGHTS

BEYOND NEGATIVE THINKING

BREAKING THE CYCLE OF DEPRESSING AND ANXIOUS THOUGHTS

JOSEPH T. MARTORANO, M.D.
AND
JOHN P. KILDAHL, PH.D.

INSIGHT BOOKS
PLENUM PRESS • NEW YORK AND LONDON

Library of Congress Cataloging in Publication Data

Martorano, Joseph T.
  Beyond negative thinking: breaking the cycle of depressing and anxious
thoughts / Joseph T. Martorano and John P. Kildahl.
     p.   cm.
  Includes bibliographical references and index.
  ISBN 0-306-43196-3
  1. Negativism. 2. Self-talk. 3. Cognitive therapy. I. Kildahl, John P. II. Title.
BF698.35.N44M37   1989   89-7583
153.4′2—dc20   CIP

10 9 8 7 6 5

Names, places, and other identifying facts contained
herein have been fictionalized, and no similarity to
any persons, living or dead, is intended.

© 1989 Joseph T. Martorano and John P. Kildahl
Plenum Press is a Division of Plenum Publishing Corporation
233 Spring Street, New York, N.Y. 10013
An *Insight Book*

Printed in the United States of America

PREFACE

Why does traditional psychotherapy take so long?

In a world where everything is moving faster, can't we find a way to effect psychological change that doesn't run into years and cost a fortune?

This was the prime question we asked ourselves during our combined half-century of clinical experience in psychiatry and clinical psychology.

First of all, we began to synthesize our knowledge about various schools of psychotherapy with the emerging data from the new science of thinking, or cognition. We devoted particularly close study to the process by which individuals achieve personal change. The bottom line seemed to be this:

Ask someone how his life has changed for the better and one thing you will be sure to hear is *"my thinking has changed."*

This synopsis led us to experiment with a therapeutic design that would help people *change their thinking* from the very outset of their psychotherapy. Research on thinking was discovering that *thoughts pre-*

ceded feelings. Many traditional therapies had focused on the *by-products* of thinking—that is, the feelings and behavior of the patient. What seemed a direct approach—after all, what is more immediate than what we feel or how we act?—turns out to be an oblique one. Probably nobody ever claimed that feelings and behavior are the royal road to insight—but, in fact, traditional psychotherapy was going by way of Troy!

Naturally, then, meaningful change took long to accomplish. Habitual, but often unnoticed thought patterns were given too little weight. People forty years old were making the same mistakes they made at fourteen. Their lives may have seen a dramatic run of events—career successes and setbacks, marriage, family, divorce; but the basic pattern of their lives—withdrawal, negativism, depression—persisted due to the same thought patterns that produced their feelings.

The key to changing feelings and behavior is to change how and what one thinks. Nearly all our patients asserted that they could think anything they wanted to think. After all, we're all capable of thinking for ourselves, aren't we? Nobody's brainwashing us, nobody's playing with our minds. Theoretically, at least, then, our patients should be able to feel however they chose to feel—since their feelings were the end product of the very thoughts they chose to think, and over which they took mastery for granted.

In this logical sequence, obviously, there seemed to be many a slip. But further research and psychotherapy experience showed us that thought processes could be accessed directly: for thinking is made up of words, *is* "inner speech." We were able to demonstrate that people *could* control their inner speech, their word-thoughts. Their problem was that they generally pushed all the wrong buttons. And the choice of thoughts—often a wrong choice—determined what feelings would follow. People needed help in choosing the thoughts that were in their own best interests. At this they balked. Thoughts must be *"true."* And the truth must be against them. Truth is negative. How else can you tell it's true? Thus ran the consensus of "thinking on thinking."

We had our work cut out for us. Early results with patients led to some successes. We formed the basis for a system that people could understand, take home with them, and practice by themselves to produce clear-cut results. This was only the beginning. We kept fine-tuning the system until we had structured five distinct progressive steps in individual thinking that in turn produced sustained transformation in feeling. We related these thinking changes to more effective behavior and, in time, to an overall happier life for the individual.

Joseph T. Martorano
John P. Kildahl

Acknowledgments

We wish to express our appreciation for the kindness, professional expertise, and help of Maureen Martorano and Joyce Kildahl.

Our happy association with Dr. Sheldon Roen, former president of Human Sciences Press, opened the doors and resources which made this volume an actuality. Ms. Norma Fox, Executive Editor, has done more for us than any other person to bring our work to completion. Ms. Fox's skills during countless meetings, conversations, letters, and editing sessions have been invaluable.

The guidance of Mr. Nick Beilenson motivated us early on to continue our efforts to produce a helpful book. We appreciated the ear for dialogue that Mike DeBeck brought to us. Ms. Geraldine Richelson's writing skills added much when we called on her for help. The apt, perceptive editing by Ms. May Dikeman significantly bettered our work. We are grateful that Ms. Ann Gerlock and Ms. Gladys Chantelau typed our manuscript so handsomely for us.

We are fortunate to have worked in psychotherapy with an extraordinarily wide range of patients—from the severely disturbed in psychiatric hospitals to the outstandingly mature persons who chose therapy as a way to enhance their creative capacities. We are grateful to these patients. In many thousands of hours of therapy, they have taught us, and we have learned. This volume owes much to them.

Finally, we authors want to express our appreciation to each other. As friends and colleagues we have completed a task which we would have not done alone. It has been good.

J.T.M.
J.P.K.

CONTENTS

HOW YOU CAN BENEFIT FROM INNER SPEECH TRAINING

The growth of the human mind is still high adventure, in many ways, the highest adventure on earth.
Norman Cousins

Everyone knows a story of someone's therapy that didn't quite work. Maybe it wasn't totally ineffective but it cost too much for what the person got out of it. Perhaps the patient found it comforting to have someone to talk to week after week, but nothing much changed. Or, it could have been the type of treatment where the patient lay on the couch and free-associated for five 50-minute sessions per week, and heard hardly anything from the analyst at all.

What went wrong? The old therapies were seductive, but just telling someone how you feel is not enough. Psychoanalytic theories are fascinating. Free association is intriguing. But as treatments for helping people in need, many of the old therapies are inefficient, not cost-effective.

3

Dramatic advances in research have led to new therapies which much more rapidly get at the underlying causes of emotional problems, and then offer direct solutions. These new studies have led to a new understanding of thinking, feelings, and behavior, and how to change and improve them. In every science, each decade brings breakthroughs that build on past advances. That has happened in the field of psychotherapy.

Cognitive therapy (literally, "thinking therapy") is a result of this research.

This new cognitive therapy is accessible to everyone. You do not need to be a student of psychology to understand how to change your life. You can use the five specific, practical, and jargon-free techniques described in this book to make significant changes in your thinking, and therefore, in your life.

How can this be?

First, thinking is now *a measurable process*. The brain is more active than formerly believed and new computerized instruments can review and record precise information about what happens in the brain when someone is thinking.

Second, *thinking precedes feeling*. This is a fundamental finding from brain research. What does it mean for you? It means that if you want to feel better, and have a better life, the crucial question is not "How are you feeling?" but "What are you thinking? What were you thinking that *caused* your feeling?" For your thoughts precede and therefore produce your feelings.

If you are in psychotherapy treatment, or have ever been in therapy, review in your mind a session you remember. How much time did you spend talking about your feelings? Then ask yourself how much time you spent talking about your thoughts behind your feelings.

You need to identify the thought behind the feeling if you want to stop repeating the same old errors over and over again. You do not have to be passive about your therapy or your life. You have the best access to your own thoughts, and you can actively study your thoughts and thereby improve your feelings and your life. The Inner Speech System gives you the guidelines to do this.

Third, your thinking is not automatic. You can change your thoughts. You can improve your thoughts on a permanent basis. Someone once said, "The brain is only as strong as its weakest think."

It will be helpful for you to follow a system to help you step outside your mind, and see exactly how to change your thinking. This is the system the authors have designed as a result of their combined half-century of practical, clinical experience with people.

This system starts with the cause of people's problems—their thinking. When your thinking is changed to become more effective, the symptom of weak thinking, namely your feelings, will change. As you probably already know, it is virtually impossible to correct the feeling through just working on the feelings. But when you reconstruct the underlying *thought*, change takes place.

Power Thinking has the advantage of standing on the shoulders of many scholars, researchers, practitioners, and authors. We have studied the best of them, and have tried to fine-tune the factors that make all therapies effective. Contributions from psychoanalysis, neo-Freudianism, existential and humanistic psychologies, behavior therapy, ego psychology, object relations, and others can be seen as forming the foundations of our theories in this volume. Of special relevance to us is the "Voice Therapy" developed by Robert W. Firestone.

In the field of cognitive psychotherapy, Donald Meichenbaum, Albert Ellis, Aaron Beck, Wayne Dyer, and David Burns are among the many psychologists and psychiatrists who have led the way with their research and writing. Their work is now the foundation of many projects, ranging from brief magazine articles to major governmental studies. Cognitive therapy has entered the mainstream of American culture.

Yet cognitive therapy is by no means the only effective therapy. Tastes in therapy, as in everything, vary, and satisfaction comes in different forms for differing people. We do not exclude other theories and therapies in our own approach. But we do know from decades of practice that cognitive therapy provides powerful forces for change and growth in every branch of the therapeutic spectrum.

If you listen to the description of any successful therapeutic experience, of whatever form of therapy, you can be sure that the patient has somehow learned to think differently. When patients *think* differently, they *feel* differently—and they *act* differently.

You can control what you think about, once you learn how to do it.

John Milton wrote, "The mind is its own place, and in itself can make a heaven of hell, a hell of heaven."

The choice is yours.

CHAPTER 1

INNER SPEECH TRAINING
FIVE TECHNIQUES THAT CAN
CHANGE YOUR THINKING

How often have you had a thought like—

> "With *my* kind of *luck*—"
> "*All my life, nothing's* panned out."
> "Nothing *ever* goes like I planned."
> "Where does it leave me *if*—?"
> "I'll *never* meet the right person."
> "I *always* screw up."

How do such *thoughts* make you *feel*?

Do they contribute to your fulfillment, your happiness, satisfaction, health, success, or to helping people around you feel hopeful?

After all, if your own mind isn't on your side, who's going to come out *for* you?

Can you learn to make your thoughts work *for*, rather than against you? If thoughts can make you feel defeated and bitter, can you alter your thoughts so that you feel confident, pleased at things you've accomplished, and at new possibilities ahead? Certainly, if your thoughts can turn your feelings one way, they can lead them in a different direction. To *feel* better, you should *think* better.

By applying five simple, practical thinking techniques, you can learn to become the master instead of the victim of your thoughts and feelings. These techniques are:

1. *Listening In.* Training to hear yourself thinking.
2. *Underlining.* Selecting the specific words in your internal dialogue that are detrimental to you and your own best interests.
3. *Stopping.* Shutting off the negative words in your internal thought speech.
4. *Switching.* Interrupting harmful inner speech and substituting positive internal voices.
5. *Reorienting.* Changing the thrust of your thinking to an active, problem-solving mode.

WHAT IS THINKING?

Your thinking, your feelings—in fact, your entire consciousness—is based upon the words and the combinations of words you have learned to use. You form your thoughts by choosing words. That is Inner Speech.

A word is the *smallest* possible unit of *communication.* Try to achieve anything beyond the simplest communication without words. It is very difficult. We may be able to experience non-word, complex visual or abstract thoughts, but in order to *communicate* our thoughts—even to *ourselves*—words are all we've got.

Indeed, even when we are just communicating to ourselves, our words form a *dialogue*, as if *we are talking to ourselves.*

Thinking is inner speech. To think is to speak silently, *internally* — an inner voice is repeating the words on this page as you read them.

As you read, you have the opportunity to analyze your thinking. Listen In to your inner speech as you make your way across a page. The words in print are transcribed into inner speech. The sentences are repeated in your mind. Inner speech is the experience of thinking. Your brain also develops its own thoughts as you read. You hear an internalization of your own voice talking to yourself as you produce your inner response to the page before your eyes. ("Right, right — I've done that." — "Maybe not *that*, but what *I* do is worse.")

A revealing experiment is to take a quiet few minutes alone, sit down comfortably, and tune in to your mind. Do you hear a stream of words, phrases, whole sentences, jangling, jibing, warning, rehashing, nagging, often beleaguering you? With thoughts like these, who needs enemies? Like all Inner Voices, yours has been piling up negative messages for years. "You know you're absentminded." — that's your mother. "The trouble with you is you think there are forty-eight hours in every day, fourteen days..." — your father. "It's funny that all the rest of the class heard me!" — Ms. Gaffney, your fifth-grade teacher. Your Inner Voice absorbed them all, and now it plays them back to you like a nonstop tape. The theme is that *only you* forget, fudge, fail, and that is all you can be counted on for. Your Inner Voice harps on regrets and recriminations, worries, and fears. And it transfers them all to you, speaking to you and for you. "I should have spoken up, but I'm so chicken." "It was crazy of me to get enraged at Alison." "I know I'll blow that test." "Ron's been so *considerate* lately. Has he got something going with that new lady in Material Control?"

Do these sound anything like some thoughts you think? If they do, this is not some aberration on your part; it's a quite standard state of affairs. Our minds are at work 24 hours a day, asleep or awake, and like it or not, we're profoundly affected by whatever thoughts fill our minds. If those messages spell gloom and doom, that's where we're headed. More literally than we have ever imagined, we travel through life with our thoughts as navigator, and we veer in whichever direction they guide us.

WHAT IS HEALTHY THINKING?

All of this obtaining and processing of information by your brain into thoughts and feelings seem to go on quite automatically or unconsciously. Unfortunately, sometimes your mind is programmed like the voice of an antagonistic commentator or parents. The kind of parents who believed it was their job to create a perfect specimen—morally, mentally, and physically—and not of the person we are, but of one *they* may have wished to be—perhaps one who never was. Then the language of your inner speech, instead of coming out for you, as it always should, may undermine or actually sabotage your desire to be confident, secure, and happy. Insidious inner speech damages everything you do.

Inner Speech Training is the method by which you control the words in your head that are used in the formation of your thoughts, and direct these words, and therefore your thoughts, in a positive and profitable direction.

HOW DO YOU BECOME A WELL-TRAINED THINKER?

The five techniques that have been set forth—*Listening In, Underlining, Stopping, Switching,* and *Reorienting*—can be mastered one by one. This system of Inner Speech Training can help you to become a thinker who finds his thoughts his best resource, not one who wants to run from them.

This method is an alternative to feeling as though your inner speech is beyond your control. Through Inner Speech Training you can identify particular problem areas in your thinking. Once you've learned where the problem areas are, you'll learn specific techniques to stop these unwanted voices. When you've mastered stopping your unwanted thought patterns, you can learn to tune the voices inside your head until you control them so that they speak only at your command. And when they do speak, they will be *yours*, not the voices of your detractors, or the voices of the past.

As you become aware of your internal voice or voices, you will realize that Internal Speech shapes your life more than any other single force. This may well sound familiar; the Book of Proverbs says: "As a man thinketh in his heart, so is he."

Inner Speech Training is a new technique similar to what therapists call "cognitive restructuring." These therapies, including I.S.T., work by changing the basic way your mind perceives and shapes events. They are user-friendly, and can supplement whatever form of therapy and self-help that works well for you.

LISTENING IN TO YOUR INTERNAL VOICES

Is your thinking a meeting of committees? Are your thoughts dominated by dissenting factions that all have to have their say and keep you from getting on to more pleasurable living and productive activities? The *Grievance Committee* is one that tends to convene often and run late; just to remind you how you're pushed around:

"I don't have to take
this garbage."

"It would be one thing
if I was getting paid
what I'm worth."

"I'm through covering
for her after the way
she bad-mouthed me."

Then there's the *Committee for Self-Criticism*, that aims to keep you on your toes:

"If I could just keep
my big mouth shut."

"I get too upset."

"I'm not into other
people enough."

"I get on people's
nerves. I rub them the
wrong way."

Or the *Committee of Regrets*:

"If I could just go back
and do it over."

"I wish I hadn't said
anything."

"I didn't know when I
was well off."

"I could have handled
it differently."

Is your mind filled with unending dialogues?

Are there voices in your head right now anxiously preparing future discussions with your friends, your spouse, your boss, a parent, or teacher?

Are you forever listening in to these discussions so that you can't concentrate on the real things going on around you?

Is your mind overpreparing each coming event by endlessly mulling over all the possibilities for what might occur?

"What will I do if he
says he wants to cool
it?"

"What will I do if she
says it isn't working
out?"

"What if Davis quits?
He's my real backer in
the office."

Or is your mind a battlefield, constantly filled with explosions?

"I should have
punched him out."

"Why didn't I tell him
to shove it?"

Some inner voices tear us down, other voices keep
saying, in various ways, "What's the use?" And we consider that this is dealing with "reality," "*facing* it." Some
inner voices are not even our own, but are other people's thoughts and feelings taking over our thoughts.
Learning *how you think* could be the most important thing you can do to prepare yourself for the rest of
your life.

HOW DOES YOUR THINKING WORK?

All productive thinking is done in the form of Internal Speech—either monologues or dialogues that
you experience as *voices* in the middle of your head
(your Internal Speech Center). Most of your thinking
takes the form of a dialogue. Word-thoughts make up
most of your thinking.

Example:
Do you ever think...?

What will I do
if...   ...when I get there
                                         Mrs. Howard says,
                                         "Oh, we meant *next*
                                         Thursday!"?

                                         ...the elevator gets
                                         stuck?

These word-thoughts are linked together to form dialogues.
The dialogue is experienced as *Inner Speech* to yourself
or a dialogue between yourself and someone else.

"Should I keep going out with him? He's *nice,...* but he doesn't turn me on." (your voice)

"Yes, you go into the woods looking for a straight stick and you come out with a crooked one!" (Mother's voice)

INNER SPEECH TRAINING

Inner Speech Training—I.S.T.—is a system to help you learn to improve how you think. I.S.T.

Enables you to repattern the entire set of your mind;

Identifies the *cause*, not the symptom (feelings and behavior are resulting symptoms);

Provides a guide to *permanent change* by attacking the problems *at their point of origin* in your mind;

Unlocks the *secrets* of *how* you think and gives you effective techniques to deal with problem areas;

Allows you to achieve mastery over your feelings and your behavior by attacking the source of the difficulties in your mind;

Gives you control over the *tyrannical voices* you may hear in your head, voices that have prevented your becoming an independent person.

The Inner Speech Training system builds on the facts that

you think in words;

your thinking produces

   your feelings

   and

   your actions; and

the words and phrases of your mind select the building blocks of

   your thinking,

   your feeling,

   and

   your actions.

If you tend to use the same words in your thoughts, you will tend to feel always the same way, and act the same way.

If you think in clichés, your actions will also be stereotypic.

If you think in tired old words, you will feel and act in tired old ways.

If you select different, unusual words, you create the possibility that you will feel and act in a new way. If you use upbeat words, you increase your chances of feeling and acting optimistically. If you choose power words with vitality in them, you will be more apt to feel and act enthusiastically and purposefully.

Here is how to feel *worse*:

A patient called. She said,

     "I got some bad news."

     "What happened?"

     "The doctor said the x-rays didn't look good."

"What exactly did your doctor say?"

"He said, 'The x-rays don't look too bad.'
See? Something's wrong."

Or visualize two people in their fifties:

A. "I really feel old."
B. "I feel like I finally grew up. I really feel
    mature."

Try repeating each of the last two comments. Both
of them acknowledge the passage of time. Neither one
"quarrels with the rules of the game." B doesn't say,
"Life begins at fifty-seven." But the statements feel different by the shading of the words. "Old" means "I've
had it." "Mature" means "I can cope."

That's how much difference your choice of words in
your internal speech can make to you.

The following chapters describe the five steps by
which you can train yourself to think more powerfully.

CHAPTER 2

THE CASE OF AMY
HER FIRST EXPERIENCE WITH INNER SPEECH TRAINING

The first thing Amy said when she came in the office and sat down was, "I know you can't do anything for me, Doctor. I don't want you to feel bad about it." Amy's second remark was, "I'm a total mess. I've screwed up everything in my life. I've tried everything. Nothing helped."

Her new therapist asked her to tell more about herself.

"Things are going down the tubes at work. I keep lousing up, and I'm sure I'm going to be canned. My personal life is more of the same. Don—the guy I've been seeing—hasn't called for three days. He must be seeing someone else."

Amy put herself down ten consecutive times in the first ten sentences she spoke. Gradually, her story moved past the putdowns. Amy was twenty-eight. She had received her MBA two years ago, and was already making $40,000 a year. That didn't seem like a total screw-up. What had gone wrong with Don?

She really didn't know, she said. They had been seeing each other with increasing frequency for the better part of a year. They hadn't had a fight or any kind of "discussion." In fact, everything had seemed great. He kissed her good night like always. And yet, it hadn't occurred to Amy to call Don to check if he was okay. Instead, she jumped to the conclusion that in three days' time he had met and gotten hooked on another woman.

Amy said, "Some of my classmates are making much more than I am. And just yesterday my boss told me I was being transferred to another brand. He called it a promotion. But if I were doing a good job on the brand I have now, why would he take me off it? I don't even know if I can handle the new assignment. I'll probably fall on my face. In fact, they could be setting me up." "Have you tried to listen to your thoughts about yourself?" she was asked. "Do you know that your thoughts are doing destructive things to you?"

"Well, I can't help the way I *think*," was her immediate reaction. Her doctor assured her that someday she *could* be able to help the way she thought.

Amy was asked how she would feel if someone at work told her she was going to make a fool of herself. "Insulted!" she said.

"And what would you do if your best friend told you Don probably has someone else?" Without a moment's hesitation, Amy said, "I'd tell her just to cool it. What was she trying to do, making me feel worse?" "Exactly," the therapist responded. "And now you can get into the habit of 'cooling it' yourself."

This was a totally new concept to Amy. She had never compared her own voice to the voices of others.

The idea that she had been insulting herself, trying to make herself feel worse, was staggering to her. It was explained to her that her Inner Voice was in reality an amalgam of outside voices, many of them critical and pessimistic, many of them dating from early childhood. Without realizing it, she had assimilated them and was now playing them back in a steady stream to the detriment of her well-being. The actual repetition of those critical thoughts was the immediate cause of her depression.

At the end of her first visit, Amy was told to monitor her thoughts. She was asked to listen throughout the day—and particularly at night, if she was having trouble falling asleep. It would be even more helpful for her to jot down what she heard. Amy was skeptical at first that this would have any effect on the despair she was experiencing. But at her next appointment she confessed to being shocked by the relentless beating she was giving herself. She admitted, "In one day alone, I wrote down 26 negative thoughts. And I'm sure there were plenty I missed. No wonder I'm always tired and depressed." Her list included:

"I'm not really smart. I got ahead by a bunch of flukes."

"I'll never get that report done by the deadline."

"That meeting tomorrow will be a disaster. I never chaired a meeting before. Basically I'm a very shy person."

"Why is Don rejecting me? It's like I can have a relationship for seven months, and he gets the seven-month itch!"

"Nancy looks terrific today. I never look so put together."

"I wish that memo I wrote yesterday had been more tactful. Interpersonal stuff just is not my bag."

"My boss looked furious this morning. I wonder what I did."

"Uh-oh, Kathy wants to see me. What's bugging her now?"

"What will I do if Don never calls again?"

Her therapist then asked her to imagine someone close to her saying to her: "Amy, you're not smart." "Amy, you will never get that report done." "Amy, that meeting you're chairing tomorrow will be a disaster." "Amy, face it, you never do look as good as Nancy." "Amy, that was not a tactful memo you wrote. You just can't make it with people."

Amy began to grin in recognition. At the same time she was appalled at what she was doing to herself. Right there in the doctor's office she had become depressed about the terrible things being said to her. But then she began to get angry and stopped her therapist from going on and on down the list about how awful she was.

And then she realized that all these attacks on her were of her own making. She had never realized before that *that hurts just as much as if someone else put her down.* And she had the sense and the willpower to say "Stop" to her own thoughts.

That was Amy's introduction to Inner Speech Training.

Hearing that list read out loud, hearing her fears, doubts, and forebodings piled up like that—26 in one day, with more falling between the cracks—made her realize how much energy she was squandering on imagined catastrophes.

GETTING STARTED

Of course, Amy didn't turn her life around after two visits. She had a lot of work to do before she could conquer her self-critical, depressive thoughts and direct her Inner Voice into more powerful channels. What was important about those early visits is that she was able to see, for the first time, what her own thoughts were doing to *her*. She was putting the whammy on herself. That insight was the pivot on which her transformation turned.

Awareness is the crucial ingredient in any changes you want to make in yourself. And since your thoughts produce your feelings, it behooves you to be aware of your thoughts. Say you inexplicably felt anxious and uncomfortable all week. Nothing of consequence went wrong, yet the uneasiness is persistent. Since you can't shed the feeling, you console yourself by thinking, "It's something I can't control. Maybe it's all this rain we've been having. Dark days get everybody down." And so the gloomy feelings continue, slowing you down and taking the edge off life's small enjoyments.

But let's write another scenario. Suppose you sat down and probed systematically and got back to Tuesday morning when you overheard your boss say something about getting rid of the "dead wood." Immediately you thought, "That's me." *That thought* triggered your anxiety, and blocked further thought. If you had chosen to think further, you would have remembered that two staff members are due to retire and one keeps remarking, "This company is headed for Chapter Eleven, but it's no skin off my teeth."

Also, the new receptionist, a civic leader on his own time and on much of the office's, is on the phone to his state assemblyman more than he's taking incoming company calls.

There's dead wood to burn! You could have figured that out and saved yourself a week out of your life.

Can you change the way you think? With some practice you can, and that means you can also change your life. By focusing on your thinking, which is the cornerstone of your personality, you can achieve real personal growth. Again, Listen In to your thoughts as you read. Do you hear an internal voice repeating the words? That's what thinking is: silent, internal speaking. Do you also hear other words? Is your Inner Voice talking back as it absorbs the text, agreeing or disagreeing on some points, and elaborating on others with anecdotes of its own ("Like, what I tend to fall into...")?

This sort of thing goes on continually, and it influences both your moods and your responses to your environment. If you think of your mind in computer terms, you'll realize why data processors have the expression, "Garbage in, garbage out." What this means, simply, is that the result can't be better than the input. And the same principle applies to your mind.

To continue the analogy: *negative in, negative out.* Sometimes your mind seems programmed with put-down words as if your worst enemy were talking. (If

you're that dangerous, you're actually pretty powerful.)
When that occurs, the language of your inner speech
will sabotage your confidence and satisfaction instead
of offering support and encouragement.

As we'll see in the next chapter, your Inner Voice
draws on many sources in the development of its incessant monologue. Since infancy, it has heard many
voices saying many different things; yet it selects only
certain of these to store in its memory. *All persons develop a particular style of thinking*, which in turn *determines their feelings and behavior*. Not everyone's inner
speech is the same. Amy's was depressive; yours may
be something quite different. But you can diagnose
your own thinking and make it more effective. Once
you're in control of your thoughts, you'll be able to
eliminate many false moves.

You can remember when someone you admired
said something very positive to you. Perhaps an upper-
classman remarked that you had terrific energy. *"Energy?"* you thought, electrified. "You mean I'm not the
lazy slob I always assumed?" That admired friend used
cognitive restructuring on you. He or she said something that made you see yourself differently. And you
became more secure and confident because that is the
way that you then thought about yourself.

The shortcoming of many of those treasured acco-
lades is that the inner speech that was implanted in
your mind did not control your thinking for very long.
All too soon, the habits of the years took over in your
mind, and you were your old self—which meant that
you hadn't restructured your thoughts permanently.

But for at least a brief time you had experienced
that something transforming could happen to you by

having a psychological "implant" in your brain—that is, the implant of some thoughts about you that were wonderfully positive. The person who complimented you gave you a new truth about yourself. The next chapter begins with the first technique that will help you implant some new truths about yourself—permanently.

When Amy came for therapy she would say: "I feel like I haven't really gotten anywhere. I feel like I missed the boat somehow." Amy began to make lasting progress in therapy when she learned the difference between her symptoms and her problem. Her symptoms were her discouraged feelings. She did not know what her problems were. She began to catch on when it was explained this way:

When you have a 103-degree fever, the fever is not the illness. A high fever is only a symptom of the illness—which may be, for example, an infection or a virus. The 103-degree fever is the effect. The infection is the cause. Amy's feelings were about as oppressive and disabling as a 103-degree fever; but they were not the cause. Those 103-degree feelings were the result of her problem.

She felt depressed, but that symptom was caused by her underlying problem which was: she thought she was a failure, she thought tomorrow would be a disaster, she thought she did not "have what it takes," that she had gotten by by faking it. Sometimes she thought she was going crazy.

After Amy understood that her recurrent thoughts were the real cause of her misery, she had a handle on her life, something that she could go to work on. It gave her a lift to know that she needed to work on her thoughts. She knew that here was something she could do.

The one basic precept to keep in mind is: You are what you think. Remember also that you have the right and the wherewithal to direct your thinking into channels that work for you.

It's *your* mind.

CHAPTER 3

COGNITIVE RESTRUCTURING
CHANGING YOUR THINKING

Psychotherapy has come a long way since the days of endlessly probing into one's past and one's feelings. Not that either is to be discounted. Both our past and our feelings affect our actions. But people are thinking beings, and our thoughts exert a greater influence over our behavior. In the past decade, helping techniques have undergone a quiet but dramatic revolution. Treatment has become more effective and less time-consuming, with patients taking an active, rather than a passive, role in their own transformations.

Techniques come and go, but rarely does one produce results, in conjunction with more traditional therapies, as effectively as Cognitive Restructuring. The reason it seems to work is that it addresses the thinking human being we all know ourselves to be, and pride ourselves on being.

As important as it is to be in touch with our feelings, it is even more important to be *in touch with our thoughts*. Thoughts are often so entrenched we're not even conscious of their impact on us. Until we become aware of that Inner Voice, we may not know where our troubles come from: the weather, the family, the boss, our co-workers, our neighbors, any and all outside forces, whatever or whoever is handy. If these were the culprits, however, our lives would be hopeless because there isn't too much we can do about outside forces. Fortunately, though, we *can* change ourselves, and the truth is that at least 90 percent of our problems are self-generated by the thoughts we think. "The fault, dear Brutus, is not in our stars, but in ourselves—"

People who have Listened In on their minds at every opportunity have usually been aghast at what they've heard. Those who genuinely thought of themselves as victims of circumstance were suddenly introduced to an inner negative side of themselves they had never suspected was there.

They were the captive audience of inner speeches to themselves—inner speeches about themselves—that often predicted ruin and warned of danger. The result of those thoughts was that their thinkers felt frightened and helpless.

Cognitive restructuring—or "thought-changing" —teaches that you can be assertive in dealing with your own thoughts. It's *your* mind. So far, your mind may have had free rein. It's time to see what *you* can do— time to step in as director and take over. Since it *is* your mind, you have the right and the responsibility to decide what messages you want to receive. If the words you have been hearing attack you, demean you, or forecast failure and grief, they are saboteurs—in fact vandals—trashing your life, and you have the obligation to rout them. The mind is the domain of reason, but of *your* reason.

Once, years ago, we trained our minds so that

when we thought "nine times seven," we then thought 63. For a while we may have thought seven times eight was 63. As for the spelling of "weird," it's not "after *c*," and it's not "sounded like *a*," so who expects "*ei*"? Nevertheless we made the adjustment. Nine times seven being 63 and "weird" with *i after e* became second nature.

Most of us have some thinking patterns that make trouble for us—they may even program us to be anxious, frustrated, or to fail. Eventually, though, we can have habits of thinking that raise our spirits. We all know people who do it now. Few if any. Somehow they learned how to do it. You can learn to do it, too. If you change some of your thoughts, you can be more productive, and more fulfilled.

You can learn to instill habits of thinking which lift your spirits, and reduce depressing and anxious thoughts and feelings. You did it with arithmetic and spelling, and you can do it with your emotions—which are more important, and which you can't verify with a calculator or a dictionary.

The term Inner Speech Training is directly pictorial. "Inner" refers to your mental life. "Speech" means expressed in words. "Training" refers to a technique that can be learned. Nearly everyone has taken some form of training that worked. Relatively few people have been in therapy, and sometimes with uneven results. Since I.S.T. is available to all, the word "training" rather than therapy is used, although it is, of course, a form of therapy.

What is known about its effectiveness?

The National Institute of Mental Health, which is funded by the federal government, completed a $10 million study which was conducted over 6 years. The purpose of the study was, among others, to see if cognitive therapy for depression was as effective as drug treatment. The answer was a strong affirmative, and the results were publicized nationwide in the media.

It is on the principles of cognitive therapy that Inner Speech Training builds. Many of those methods have been refined in ways calculated to make them more quickly learned, more easily used, and better remembered. The next chapter describes how to begin to work at changing the distorted and destructive views of yourself that cause anxiety and depression. *Thinking that leads to depression is illogical*. Logic can be applied to such thinking in a way that lifts the depression.

The art of thinking is now being taught even in kindergartens. Many schools require courses in *how to think*, that is, how to find out how to solve problems and what causes what effect. Rather than just for memorizing facts, these new courses in thinking help students reflect upon whether or not an argument is logical, and whether the conclusions are supported by the facts.

Inner Speech Training builds on the research on thinking that is increasingly widespread in our general education system. Some psychology is mainly about thinking effectively about history or politics or literature. Here, the newest techniques of thinking are applied to your emotions and to your behavior. The research indicates that the more *actively* you process new learning, the better you retain it. If you will actively process your own thinking as you read, according to the methods set forth, you will be launched on the way to improving your mental health and well-being.

You can make your life miserable with what you

think, or you can change your thoughts and free yourself to make the most of life's experiences. Some people feel depressed when it rains. It is not the rain that causes their depression, but their *thoughts about* the rain. Others find a rainy day "nice and peaceful," or that "it makes the house so cozy." Any art student can tell you that it is an overcast landscape, not a sunny one, that shows its colors most intensely. It's on a "gray day" that the grass is actually *greenest*.

You can dwell on all the things that are "getting worse": the traffic, the mails, the neighborhood, and, of course, "the *service*." Your thoughts won't get the bank to hire more tellers, won't erase graffiti, or alter other drivers' manners. But you can decide to stop your inner emotional irritation by changing what you are thinking about. You can monitor what is called your "useless worry" and use your 13 billion brain cells for subjects far more diverting.

Inner Speech Training will not make you a mindless Pollyanna, which is not the idea. But a number of studies have discovered that choosing to think optimistically will actually bring about a more successful outcome.

Self-fulfilling prophecies do tend to produce the results they predict. The research shows that if you can prophesy in your inner speech that you will do well in a test, or prophesy as you prepare for a dinner party that your guests will have a good time, you will be in much better form for the test and for the dinner party. You can give your thoughts the power to improve your behavior. Pessimistic thinking, on the other hand, saps your mental energy and slows down your responses.

You may have grown up in a home where you were taught to expect the worst. That is a set of thoughts that *has been proved to produce depression.* Since that style of thinking was *learned, it can be unlearned.*

You probably want to change at least some of your self-talk. Here is how to get started.

CHAPTER 4

INNER SPEECH TECHNIQUE #1: LISTENING IN
LOCATING YOUR INNER VOICE

The first basic step in Inner Speech Training is

POWER THINKING TECHNIQUE #1: LISTENING IN
Listening In is training to hear yourself thinking.

Thinking is *Inner Speech*.

Thoughts require words which unite to form dialogues internally as inner speech *to ourselves*—or *between* ourselves and *someone else*.

To "Listen In" to the dialogues in your head, train yourself to become more aware of exactly what your thoughts are telling you at any given moment.

The first basic idea of Cognitive Therapy is that the thinking we do—the very thoughts we think—influences our feelings and behavior. The second is that by monitoring our thinking, we can change it. Once we do that, we will automatically have gained *power over our feelings and behavior*, and as soon as we start to use that power, our lives take on a new brightness.

How do you train yourself to hear the voices of your inner speech?

This is a *real* voice we're talking about, not an imaginary one. It rules you with its choice of words. The unhealthy voices have a tendency to use the same words again and again. They specialize in imperatives, put-downs, doubts, and regrets. Over and over, you're getting messages like, "You've got to..." "You'll never..." "I wish..." "See what you went and did?," and these messages undermine you. Once you're tuned into your Inner Voice, you're on your way to taking charge. You'll be able to make your thoughts do your bidding, rather than the other way around. And once that happens, your feelings and actions will change, too.

1. Identify *who* is doing the speaking.
2. Identify *what* actual words are used.
3. Identify the *tone* of voice. Is it critical carping, judgmental?
4. What *feelings* are triggered by the word-thoughts in your head? Do your feelings show the words to be guilt-producing—and outdated, inappropriate ones?

Why don't you?	Why can't you?
When I was your age...	Why haven't you?
	You'd better be!
You should do that.	You must be punctual
You should be!	to be successful.

These are examples of how our Inner Voices interfere with our conscious intentions. Multiply them a thousandfold, and you'll see to what extent you're being diverted from your positive goals. Unless you listen carefully to your thoughts, they control you and cause you to *act against yourself*. By not answering that insidious Inner Voice, you allow it to continue dominating your mind.

A CASE OF SIMPLE CONFUSION

Consider the case of the well-meaning young married woman who kept confusing herself. In her head, she thought she heard: "I love my husband, Steve, so much." Yet she felt anger and even resentment at her husband constantly for his staying out late at night.

When she worked at it and learned to Listen In accurately she could hear the actual voice in her head, which turned out to be: "I'm being taken advantage of. I *hate* it." No wonder she was confused without being able to be aware and listen in to her thinking.

Remember that it is important *actually* to hear the "exact" words so that you can then account for the distortion in your feelings.

Listening In can be used in a variety of circumstances. For example, consider the thoughts connected with feelings such as

Regret. "What should I have done?"

Mind racing (anticipation). "What will I do if..."

Performance anxiety. "How will I ever get done on time?"

Depression (universalizations and generalizations). "Nothing ever goes right for me."

Obsession. "Did I remember to turn off the gas?"

WHERE DO YOU THINK?

You have an Inner Speech Center where your thinking actually occurs. Practice locating your inner voice center.

Place your index finger as far into your mouth as you can reach and touch the top part of your mouth (your upper palate). Your inner voice is *usually centered* just above and a little behind this point. If you close your eyes and listen carefully, it probably feels as if it is almost behind your eyes and midway between your ears. Some people locate it a bit differently, at the base of the skull.

Listen In carefully as you read and think the words in front of your eyes. Can you vividly feel the spot in your head where your inner speech is located? You are hearing an *Internalization* of your own voice. Say the words "inner voice" to yourself. Did you feel and hear where you said it?

Right now, you are experiencing the words before you. This very moment you are having the sense of the words being repeated in your mind as you read: This is what thinking is.

Train yourself to experience the sensation of thinking as you think about some other thoughts.

Picture yourself at an intersection.

"Which road shall I take?"

Listen In. Could you hear the inner dialogue and word-thoughts that come as a response to that question located by the same control part of your head?

Thinking is to speak silently, internally, with an inner

voice. Your inner voices are not permanent. If you teach yourself to Listen In to your thoughts, you can train yourself, and in time, change yourself.

In fact, *all psychotherapy is training yourself to think better*. It provides a system to approach one's own mind. You can use your brain to work on your brain. Unmonitored and unexamined inner speech can lead you to become your own worst enemy. Fortunately, human beings are unique in their capacity for self-improvement and change.

Have you ever —

Caught yourself thinking about something else while you are making love so that you couldn't really enjoy lovemaking?

Worried so much about an examination that you couldn't study?

Experienced mind-racing which occurs when thoughts are going so fast that you can't fall asleep because your mind is too busy — trying to undo your past — or planning your future, trying to resolve yet unborn problems?

If you have done these things, you need to practice *Listening In* as the first step, the first building block in your new thinking system.

We all know people like Fran S., the woman whose critical internal voice said,

"I'm only a secretary."

If she had Listened In to her own inner speech, she would have heard the weakening of her personality and self-confidence conveyed in the use of the word "only."

THE STORY OF LINDA

To illustrate why tuning in to your thoughts is so important, there is the extreme case of an intelligent young woman who had cut herself off from her Inner Voice until it was nearly too late. Rather than getting in touch with the source of her problem, Linda had been distracting herself with food. As soon as she felt tense, she'd eat something, and that would help her relax. Once she bought herself a cheesecake and a spoon, and ate it, undefrosted, in her parked car. She felt she should lose 10 or 15 pounds, but had not been able to do it, even though she had tried three expensive diet programs—one, costing $200, limiting her menu to three vitamin beverages a day.

When Linda began Inner Speech Training to work on her weight and her depression, she was asked what was troubling her. She replied that she was lonely and frightened. Frightened of what? She wasn't sure—just a general feeling of fear that seemed to be with her all the time. Therapy began with the detective work of uncovering the causes of her fears.

Linda was given an assignment to work on between sessions: "Jot down the thought that comes to mind each time you think of having something to eat. Your thought may not always be complete, but even a word or two will help. Also, jot down any thought you had just before your mood dropped."

During the next few sessions, Linda made progress in sketching her background. Her father had always been a drinker, given to the classic behavior patterns of the alcoholic. His moods were unpredictable and extreme, alternating between angry outbursts and tenderness and sentimentality. In his wilder moments, he would swear at his three children and frighten them with threats of beating. At other times, he would reverse himself, accuse them of avoiding him, and lavish caresses on them.

It made for an insecure, tense environment. Linda was a good student, popular with girlfriends, but she avoided boys. As soon as she had her high school diploma in hand, she left home for New York City. She started college part-time and got a good job as a hostess in a high-class restaurant. She was tall, slim, attractive, and had a pleasant smile. She looked sophisticated and handled both the job and her college schedule well.

Men seemed to like Linda. They often complimented her, and in the restaurant, she was conscious of their eyes on her. From time to time, customers asked her out, and occasionally she went, but she never dated anyone more than once or twice. "Between school and work, I was too busy for a social life," she said.

After a few months, Linda had found herself struggling to get ready to go to work every evening. She had no idea why. She felt a vague uneasiness when she was at the restaurant. A sense of discomfort accompanied her every time she walked across the room to seat a guest, and it seemed even more oppressive when she walked back to her station alone. But, somehow she found no link between her disquiet and the admiring stares.

She began staying behind the little reservation desk as much as possible, as if hiding. She began to perspire when she had to go into the bar. She soon found she could breathe more easily out in the kitchen, and she began to make excuses to go there. She'd nibble on something and immediately feel more relaxed.

"Oh," she thought, "I'll take a bowl of peanuts from the bar and keep it handy at the reservation stand." The peanuts led to bread sticks and rolls; the bread, to desserts; the desserts, to chocolate bars in her purse. Soon she couldn't leave for work without having a bite to eat, in spite of the fact that her job included dinner. Naturally enough, she gained weight.

As Linda told her story, she was asked occasionally about what she was thinking, and to check on whether she was listening to herself as she talked. Little by little, she learned the habit of hearing what she was saying. Finally, she made a breakthrough. She was talking about her father, saying that he wasn't really so bad — "He really loved us" — when she started to cry. She said, "He was a shit. He was Dad, so we loved him, but he was a shit." Here at last was her honest Inner Speech about her father (and men).

She had started to overeat when her job required her to be in contact with men, and what was worse for her, when she was required to be pleasant and friendly to them. Food worked for Linda like a tranquilizer. She could smother her thoughts with food. When she discovered that her problems were based on her disgust and fear of men, she learned to Listen In to those thoughts and deal with them directly. She soon was able to catch the thought that disturbed her, before she turned to thoughts of food. The dieting was still not easy, and her depression hung on for some time, but now she knew *where to attack* her misery. Her time was better spent working on her thoughts and fears of men, rather than trying to avoid calories.

Like Linda, most people are not always aware of what their inner voice is saying. Linda found that Inner Speech Training helped her to "think out" her problems rather than "act out." When she could face the thought about her mistrust of men, she did not need to resort to food in order to tranquilize her fearful, but largely sub-conscious, thought. Linda had begun to have trouble with her weight at the same time that she began to be seriously attracted to men. Her inner speech problem was that she had contradictory voices trying to occupy her mind at the same time. She liked men and she distrusted them, and she began to overeat to stop the inner tension she felt.

Do you ever feel divided in your thinking? Is there a sense that your thoughts are dominated by dissenting factions? The pros and cons are filibustering in your head.

"This new job has a future."	"But fifteen years with a company, you just don't walk away from."
"If I accept this date, we might hit it off and have a great time."	"If he gets pushy because he thinks he's supposed to, it'll just be so embarrassing."

With debates like these spinning their wheels, of course you're never going to get anywhere.

LEARNING HOW YOU THINK

Before you can fix something, you need to know how it works, which is why *Listening In* is Step 1 of the I.S.T. program. It starts when you make a conscious effort to hear the words that are churning inside your head. Repeat them out loud if that will help you capture them, even tape them. Jot them down if you have a chance. But whatever you do, be as *precise* as you can. The most helpful clues are the actual words themselves.

Whenever you have just had a change in your mood, *a thought preceded* and *caused* that mood change. If your mood lightened so that you felt more upbeat, you had an optimistic, pleasant or (for you) a rewarding thought. The new thought may have been something as simple as *Listening In* to a one-liner in a show you watched, or overheard in a store.

If you find that your mood dropped and you became gloomy, it was caused by your thought of being overwhelmed by something—anything from breaking your shoelace when you were in a rush, to thinking about how you were going to pay for your children's college.

You will learn better how to influence your feelings, and ultimately your whole life, when you become a master at *connecting* your *mood* changes *with the thought* that caused the dip or upswing. When you know the cause of your feelings, you can change them.

After you've had some practice, *Listening In* will become increasingly automatic. As you're walking along the street or driving in your car or sitting in someone's waiting room, you can actually be intrigued by your inner speech. You can tune in to your silent broadcast. Think of it as an educational program sponsored by yourself for yourself.

You will find it instructive to identify the substance of what you're hearing. Is it critical? Contradictory? Discouraging? Take a few minutes to analyze your messages, and then see how they make you feel. Are they guilt-producing? Do you hear your parents so often that you feel like a child again—in which case, how can you possibly lead an adult's life, even a very simple one? Do you feel harassed by "don'ts" and "shoulds" and endless streams of commands? "Don't interrupt." "Don't get in over your head." "You should always listen." "Don't be foolhardy." "Make the most of any opportunity." "Being a maverick will get you nowhere." "Staying with the herd you'll never get ahead." "Get a haircut." "Remember, the first thing people see is your fingernails."

Too many of us tolerate critical and demeaning voices in our minds, to prove that we "can take criticism." These self-critical thoughts can lead to a disabling loss of self-esteem. *Listen In, and you can change*!

SUMMING UP

Listening In is Technique #1 of I.S.T. It involves getting in touch with your Inner Voice, a process that will lead to astonishing disclosures. *Listening In* will intensify your awareness of what is going on in your head, and it will start you off on the program that can make the rest of your life easier and more gratifying.

CHAPTER 5

INNER SPEECH TECHNIQUE #2: UNDERLINING
LOCATING YOUR DESTRUCTIVE VOICE

Underlining, the second major technique for under-standing and changing your thinking, builds on Tech-nique #1—*Listening In*.

POWER THINKING TECHNIQUE #2: UNDERLINING

Underlining means selecting the specific words in your internal dialogue that are destructive to you. As you *Listen In* to your word thoughts, some words will soon stand out as culprits. *Underline* them so that they become obvious to you. Once you have Underlined the words, you can act to change them constructively.

Have you ever tried to break a bad habit? Cutting down on coffee, for example. You may get through the first day without too much effort, but the minute the stress piles up, you reach for a cup. That is, unless you're very alert.

It's the same with your thoughts. They are habits

and they are persistent. You will need a *plan*, so that your habitual thoughts don't prevail. Now that you have heard what's going on in your head and realize that at times your Inner Voice is more negative than is doing you any good, recall the words of Thomas Mann: "Self-Examination, if it is thorough enough, is nearly always the first step toward change."

Perhaps you noticed a kind of sameness when you practiced *Listening In*. Perhaps certain words and phrases cropped up more often than you had expected. Think back. Did some thoughts have a familiar ring, like an old song—not necessarily a goldie—that gets stuck in your head and haunts you all day long? If they did, those are the thoughts to be on the lookout for. They're the ones that probably are sabotaging you. They have to be watched. Many of us tend to be careless with our thinking, allowing it to "just happen." It usually "just happens" to fall into repetitive patterns.

Think of all the people you know whose speech is peppered with verbal tics, who can't get through a sentence without "I mean," "Know what I'm saying?" "Right?" or some other jab-in-the-ribs phrase. And the ones who preface every anecdote with "Listen to this" or "You'll never believe..."?

Much the same is true of our Inner Voices. Over the years, they have developed a particular style, and more often than not, those stock phrases are damaging. Like Fran S.'s Inner Voice that kept telling her that she was "only a secretary," Mark's kept telling him that he was "just a salesman." With the seemingly unimportant word "only," or "just," both of them were not only downgrading their job, but by extension, themselves. Fran S. and Mark were both victims of their own Inner Voice.

For Mark, *Listening In* was a revelation, and when he moved on to *Underlining*, he began to make progress. *Underlining* helped him highlight his Inner Speech errors. For the first time, he caught vivid glimpses of what his Inner Voice was doing to him.

Underlining builds very closely on *Listening In.* When you practiced listening, you became aware of what your Inner Speech was like. Now, with *Underlining*, you'll be highlighting the deadly words and phrases that poison your thoughts. The positive parts of your thinking, the thoughts that bolster you, don't need any attention. They're doing their job. What you need to concentrate on are the messages you don't need to hear.

WHEN TO USE UNDERLINING

Underlining can be particularly effective if you have a tendency to make *premature judgments* either *about yourself* or other people.

"I always feel dumb at parties."

"I'll never pick up an instrument, I don't have an ear."

Or if you are troubled by *painful recurring* thoughts...

"Why can't he feel about me like I do about him?"

Or if you can't handle relationships and they get out of control. First your thoughts *set you up* and then *put you down*.

"I don't have any trouble *getting* someone—
it's hanging *onto* them. It shows something's
lacking in me."

By *Underlining* the negative word or phrase, you can
easily see the damage you do to yourself.

The following dialogues show how to Underline
the culprit. Watch for the anxiety-creating and
depression-producing words.

Listen In and Underline the damaging thoughts in
this inner dialogue.

INNER DIALOGUE #1

"I'm a *lousy* swimmer (tennis player, golfer,
lover, cook, carpenter, conversationalist,
etc.)."

Comment: The "damaging" word to Underline
here is "lousy." All this statement does is make you feel
hopeless. It is *useless self-criticism*. Why is it necessary
to judge yourself that way? Is it possible that you enjoy
splashing around in the water even though you can't
swim well?

Your thoughts may be stimulated by what is happening in the *present* but their destructive powers *origi-
nate* out of *habits* built in the most impressionable years,
the period of early life. In emotionally charged situations, the tendency is very strong to draw on and repeat
the old automatic thoughts without stopping to examine and explore more effective alternatives. These old
destructive word-thoughts will continue automatically
unless they are underlined.

For instance, do you hear:

External (Someone remarks to you):	*Your translation* (As heard in your voice thoughts):
"What are you doing here?"	"He's not happy to see me."
"I was going to call you."	"But you thought better of it."
"How are you holding up in this heat?"	"I look pretty scuzzy."

These are defects in the way that you perceive and relate to your world. If your own thinking is set up to discredit you, you are speaking internally to yourself in ways that produce the two major factors in neurosis: anxiety and depression.

This is a critical area. You may be misinterpreting how others see you. You may be using an inner language, or system of inner dialogues, that leads to feeling weak or immature, because your inner thoughts distort what others mean by what they say.

Ask yourself if your internal language is a positive one. Do you cause things to go well for you? Or is your language a negative one? Are the negative voices limited to certain areas like sex or relationships with peers or authority persons? Are you distorting the same things over and over in your mind? Hardly anyone uses enough power in his or her thinking.

The choice of the words in your inner speech makes the difference between success or failure, between mental health and neurosis.

The boss said, "You're looking good." You heard in your mind, "I don't look as fat."

Is your inner speech a wrong interpretation that leads to disturbing feelings?

You can *disconnect* the external remark from the faulty translation. You can do this by hearing the *exact words* of the other person. "You're looking good." *Do not add any other words.*

Inner Dialogue #2

Listen In and Underline the weak word.

"I'll never get out of sex what people are supposed to. I'm just not any good at making love."

Comment: Underline *Never*. "Never" is used here to deny responsibility for your sexuality, and promote failure. What about enjoying *love*? Keep score of your self-criticisms. Count the number of times you criticize yourself in an hour. Who gets punished beside yourself?

Inner Dialogue #3

Weak Thinking:

"Why did I pig out on that birthday cake? I'll always be a blimp."

Comment: Underline *"always be a blimp."* Don't weaken yourself further by thinking in *self-critical* terms that prevent you from reaching your goal.

INNER DIALOGUE #4

Weak Thinking:

"*Nothing* I do *ever* seems to come out *right*."

Comment: Underline 2½ damaging words. "Nothing" and "ever" definitely serve to deplete the thinker. Also, the word "right" often defeats a person. This is a perfect example of *depressogenic* thinking—which actually generates depression. It can make you depressed because it overgeneralizes, and sabotages your basic good feelings about yourself.

INNER DIALOGUE #5

Weak Thinking: How many times have you heard in your own mind, or in someone else's speech:

"*If only* I would meet the right person, then *nothing else would really matter*."

Comment: Underline the two weak phrases "*if only*" and "*nothing else would really matter*." That kind of thinking condemns you to procrastination and lack of action. If you keep waiting for a magical solution that is going to take care of everything, your thoughts will grind your life to a halt.

You can practice by *Listening In*, and listing the most common ways you criticize yourself.

1. "I always have problems with figures..." (The use of "*always*" condemns you.)

(Try filling in the next two examples.)
2. I...
3. I...

While you are *Listening In*, try to isolate and Underline the weakening words or phrases.

Finally, try to notice *who* is doing the criticism in your internal voices. Is it your own voice, or is someone else controlling your thinking? What is the tone of voice used?

It is important at this point to decide whether the invading voices are supportive and friendly, or contemptuous, harsh, and hostile. Once you determine these characteristics, and to whom the voice belongs, you can more easily decide whether the voice is saying anything real or whether it should be blotted out.

INNER DIALOGUE #6

Weak Thinking:

"Nothing I do makes any sense."

Combine the first two power thinking techniques now:

Listen In: "Nothing I do makes any sense."

Underline: "*Nothing* I do makes *any* sense." Say it slowly. Brake it: Nothing—I—do—makes—any—sense. Can you hear the damaging words you are saying to yourself?

Braking here slows down the speed of your thoughts and allows you to have a better sense of where the word-thoughts are leading. It is a helpful part of *Listening In* and *Underlining*. You can consciously put the brake on your speeding thoughts.

Slow — down — the — words — in — each — sentence — in — your — head. Listen in to each word and replay it at low speed. Take—it—easy. Train yourself to relax by applying the brakes to your internal dialogue.

Psychotherapy sessions often include *Underlining* and *Braking* in order to help a patient hear the self-defeating statement he or she just made. When the words are slowed down enough so they can be heard more clearly, the patient can stop the "mindless" repetitive self-putdowns.

These techniques are vital to gaining control over unwanted thoughts and fears. There is a real "inner self" in a person which can evaluate the absurdity of obsessional and phobic thoughts—once those thoughts are pinpointed through *Listening In* and *Underlining*.

When you Underline a damaging word, you don't actually have to write the words down and draw a line underneath them. But if you can, it helps. The more you stress the destructive words and bring them into the open, the more power you have over them. Once they're written down, you can confront them in black-and-white. They cease to be fleeting, hit-and-run type missiles that wing you and take off. You can look at them several times during the day and memorize them.

Saying them out loud is also effective, especially if you repeat them a few times. If you're in a situation where you don't want to be seen talking to yourself, repeat them silently.

Those seemingly innocuous, but actually harmful words have gone unnoticed too long. What has made them so powerful until now was their ability to escape exposure, to strike when you weren't paying attention, or your resistance was low. Once you have isolated them and brought them out of hiding, the odds change in your favor. You'll be able to change those hurtful words to more constructive ones.

For Fran S. and Mark, the culprit was "only," or "just." Once that negative word is eliminated from the message, there's nothing weakening about thinking or saying "I'm a salesman," or "I'm a secretary." On the contrary, both statements hold possibilities. They open the door to many positive follow-ups, such as "I make a bundle, when you figure fringes," or "I'm on my way up the ladder."

Most of us have too many words like "only" in our thoughts. "Never" is one of the most common culprits.

The Experience of Nora

Nora came to therapy in a state of shock that her boyfriend had called her "basically cold." "Our sex life's the greatest," she insisted. "If anything, I'm more horny than he is, but I know not to make a bunch of demands."

In fact, it turned out Nora "knew not to" show much of any feelings at all. It was a family code. "Never show blood to the enemy," her father had told her. Her mother said, "Never let on to a man he means anything to you. Right then he loses interest."

Nora had lived with her boyfriend for three years, they had joint bank accounts and discussed marriage and children, but true to the principle of "Never show weakness," she had never told him she loved him. Yet it seemed that the omission itself handed him a weapon. When they broke up he said, "You never said you loved me." "You see?" said her father. "Men never know what they want." "He should know," said her mother. "You did right. You never put yourself on the line." Nora's "never" family was vindicated indeed. Asked if she *did* love her boyfriend, Nora said, "I never really thought about it." In a reserved voice, as if queried on a sexual technicality, she explained, "I never really deal in terms of that."

Our first relationships were formed with our parents. To at least some extent, what happened between us and them serves as a model for all our subsequent relationships. It's not our purpose here to delve into those interactions, nor to turn parents as a group into scapegoats. To be pointed out, however, is that parents have the singular job of civilizing us—of teaching to discriminate right from wrong, of passing along social skills, of protecting us from danger. And some parents, however well-meaning they were, left us with fears and guilts that do not help us at all as adults. "Never cross against the lights" won't protect us from the turning cars, and "Never let anybody be too sure of you" is no protection against loss.

If your parents were overzealous about their responsibilities, or if they were weighted down with more than their share of their own fears and inhibitions, you may have been overwhelmed with injunctions.

Few of us have to think long to recall some of those "shoulds," "shouldn'ts," "oughts," and "musts." "You should have tried harder." "You shouldn't have stayed out so late." "You ought to be glad you have a new brother." "You either clean up your mess or I'm throwing it all out." All those precepts live on inside of us. We can overhaul and streamline lives by discarding the ones that do not apply to us now. If your *Underlining* technique is always handy, you will learn to pick up on the words and phrases that hurt you now.

Your most tenacious habits were formed in your most impressionable years—the years of early life. As you were learning to speak, your Inner Voice was learning right along with you. It has had many years to build up a stockpile of messages that condition you and cause you to do their bidding. Under emotionally charged situations, the tendency is even stronger to draw on these old accustomed responses without stopping to examine and explore more effective and appropriate alternatives. Unless your word-thoughts are interrupted, they're virtually automatic.

Underlining will put you into touch with your own weak thoughts. Suppose you're *Listening In* and you hear your Inner Voice state, "I'm hopeless at math." Immediately underline "hopeless." That term (the inner words in your mind) makes you feel exactly that. It certainly serves no positive purpose. To whom are you comparing yourself, Goedel?

Your thinking has just discredited you. You have been victimized by your own putdown. A damaging area, this. In the putdown, your Inner Voice sent you subtle, failure-provoking messages that caused you to feel weak or immature. Be on the lookout for them. Underline them. Just the existence of that thought in your mind, "hopeless," causes you to feel less of a person. It may seem too simple a technique to you right now; but if you *do not think that thought*, you will feel more effectual. Here is a challenge:

You can become a winner in the contest with your thoughts. You have now two valuable techniques that build on each other to help you. As you train yourself to use them, they'll become increasingly effective, and you'll find yourself gaining confidence in situations that used to throw you. Follow these Inner Speech Training pointers:

1. Review the procedures for *Listening In*.
2. Add *Underlining*.
3. Identify the weakening words you hear in your thoughts.
4. Repeat them. Write them down or say them out loud if you can. If not, say them silently.
5. Disconnect other people's words from the words your Inner Voice is saying.
6. Brake your damaging thoughts. Slow — them — down — so — you — can — really — hear — them. Those "never" sentences often have one plus; they're good for a laugh, and not on you.

Chapter 6

Inner Speech Technique #3: Stopping
Ending Negative Thinking

TECHNIQUE #3: STOPPING

Stopping occurs after you become aware of a particular thought by *Listening In* and using *Underlining* to decide that the thought is undesirable and needs to be stopped. The technique itself involves producing a word—"STOP"—in your internal thinking. Whenever the undesirable thought or thoughts occur you give the command, STOP!

Stopping is a definite technique in which you extinguish the weakening thought. Each time, Stop.

"What will I do if...?" STOP

"What will I do...?" STOP

Interrupt each time at an earlier and earlier point. Train yourself to interrupt your inner speech earlier.

"What will I...?" STOP

"What will...?" STOP

"What...?" STOP

STOP

That makes sense...But...But what do I do when I'm panicked?

The first thing you do is to STOP the inner voice...the speech that ignited and triggered the panic.

To demonstrate the importance of *Stopping*, we'd like to tell you about two men—Paul and Harvey—whose harmful thinking followed a remarkably similar course. Both of them were in their thirties, had good jobs, devoted wives, and adorable children. In both cases, the trouble started when their jobs required them to fly out of state once a week. Both Paul and Harvey were afraid of flying. Neither of them could get on a plane without hearing the alarm go off: "What if we crash?"

Both men were logical and well-informed. On a rational level, they knew that flying was safer than driving a car. But their Inner Voices were insistent. As each trip approached, the same message began banging away, "Suppose we crash.."

Paul and Harvey (who didn't know each other) both saw this phobia ruining their lives. They both decided to try therapy. Paul went into conventional psychotherapy. In the course of his treatment he came to understand that his fear was due to an early separation anxiety. He learned a lot about himself and his fears. He and his therapist were sure that in due time, he would work out his anxieties, including the phobia about flying. But by then, he might have been shoved aside in favor of an employee who always had his under-the-seater packed for Rio, Tokyo, and you name it.

Harvey, on the other hand, had heard about Inner Speech Therapy from a friend. His first appointment happened to be on the day following a trip. As he told his story, he broke out into a sweat. The mere mention of a plane was enough to set him off. But he began to work immediately on his phobia. Painstakingly he concentrated on identifying those "what ifs" and "supposes." He isolated his tendency to catastrophize. He went through I.S.T. step by step. Before many days had passed, Harvey learned to confront that Inner Voice of his and deal with it directly. He traced the source of his messages to a particularly fear-ridden housekeeper who had had charge of him when he was a child. He paid close attention to the weakening words—those fear-filled thoughts he had been taught to think when he was small. And he heard a variation of those thoughts when he boarded a plane.

As he moved on to the technique of *Stopping*, and mastered it, he had increasing success. To his amazement, he found himself able to *cut off* the voices that petrified him; slowly at first, but more rapidly as he practiced. From *Stopping*, he went on to the next step, *Switching*, where he learned to substitute more positive, fortifying thoughts, coupled with relaxation techniques—more about which in the next chapters. For now, it's important to know that it took Harvey only a small fraction of the time (and money) that Paul spent before he was able to fly without a panic attack.

When time is of the essence, I.S.T. gets to the heart of the matter—namely, a defect in your thinking—with dispatch. And it allows you to act against what is causing you to be afraid.

"What will I do if the plane crashes?" This is a worthless thought. It leads to phobias; it touches off a ridiculous type of worry about a situation over which you have no control. This thought has served to wreck more vacations than rain. You want to STOP such thinking. How to do it is to *STOP!*

In theory, *Stopping* is a very simple technique. In practice, it's not as easy as it sounds. All it requires is to produce one short word—STOP—every time you hear a weakening word in your head: that's all. To be effective at *Stopping*, you want to be forceful, assertive, tenacious. This is no time for a dialogue. Those damaging thoughts must be crushed as soon as they begin. *Stopping* takes determination—and a lot of practice.

Vera, who had been suffering from a chronic depression for years, was enthusiastic about Inner Speech Therapy and couldn't understand why it wasn't working for her. She was a musician and inclined to be introverted. Very diligent and sensitive, as a child she had been subjected to the strictest discipline: hours of practice on the cello; high standards for school work; punishment for the slightest infraction; no excuses allowed; no talking back.

When she demonstrated to her therapist how she practiced *Stopping*, it became clear why Vera wasn't getting any results. Her "Stop" came out in a whisper. It was so halting and almost pleading that her thoughts went sailing over it without the least hesitation. It took time, but eventually Vera learned to assert herself— even to bark "Stop" like a drill sergeant to help her release her inhibitions and to learn that it was permissible to be tough.

"Tough" is the operative word here. If, like Vera, you've never been tough before, train yourself. Raise your voice. And when you give a command, make it a monologue. Don't let those weakening words have a chance. It's your show. Picture yourself drowning out

the inner voice of fear. It's your own mind. You are entitled to quash and rout invaders.

Here we come to a paradox. At the same time that
you're being relentless with your negative thoughts,
you want to be kind to yourself. Always keep in mind
whose side you're on. *You* are not the enemy. The enemy is the negative thoughts. You don't want to add to
your distress. Remember: You're on *your* side. Although
you have to be harsh with the unpleasant *thought*, to
Stop it, you don't extend the harshness to *yourself*. Here
are some "Don'ts" to keep in mind:

> Don't say things to yourself like, "Stop it, stupid."
> Name-calling is no way to treat the person who
> means the most to you.
> Don't harp on your lapses (no "There you go
> again" or "Why can't you learn?")
> Don't be judgmental.

No one who has ever waked up with the kind of
thoughts that come before it gets light will say that it is
easy to Stop and Switch. Those thoughts of people you
won't be seeing again, of unfulfilled ambitions, of a raft
of unfinished and seemingly impossible chores, and a
twinge in an infected hangnail bound to be gangrenous
by morning are sometimes called the 4 a.m. "crazies."
Crazy, because everyone is "crazy" when asleep, and
therefore perhaps half-crazy when half-asleep. At 4
a.m. the body is at its lowest ebb, blood sugar and energy down, not having been fed since dinner the night
before. Depression is partly physical and partly
mental.

At these rock-bottom hours, *kindness toward yourself* is your best strategy. In those darkest periods, you

most need the Stop and Switch techniques, but that is when they seem most impossible to use. Practicing without demanding perfection of yourself at 4 a.m. will eventually help you gain better control of your thoughts. No one is perfect. Mistakes are a fact of life, and that's the way it is. But you can hold the hope that your use of I.S.T. will make you much stronger in your thinking than before you began to use it. You'll get far more desirable results by being sympathetic to yourself and lenient toward your efforts.

A good way to follow up your STOP command is to say something like, "You're dwelling on old regrets." "Your thoughts are filled with useless recriminations." "Your Inner Voice is making you feel depressed." "The kind of thinking you're doing is panicking you."

Another good idea is to ask yourself, "*Why* am I doing this to myself?" "Is it helpful?" "Is it making me feel better?" "Is it cost-effective?" "Do these thoughts solve any of my problems—past, present, or future?" If the answer is "no," STOP. STOP. STOP. Don't victimize yourself.

HOW TO APPLY STOPPING

In its straightforward way, *Stopping* is a high-powered technique for extinguishing your weakening thoughts. Whenever an undesirable message comes through, give the command, STOP. Try to block the thought as *early* as you can. Nip it in the bud. The forceful manner we described above will help. If possible, keep the thought from finishing itself. This will take some practice, but don't get discouraged. As you persevere, you'll become more adept at the technique, just as runners or swimmers or violinists do at the techniques they're trying to perfect.

Some thoughts will yield themselves to the technique of Stopping more readily than others. You may have an instant triumph with a chance thought like, "Jerk that I am, I forgot to turn off the radio." If that kind of thought is not part of your habitual thinking, it will respond at once to your STOP command. And it should be stopped. There are better ways to talk to yourself about an oversight.

Where you'll have more difficulty is with the thoughts that *are* habitual: the ones your Inner Voice sends forth with regularity. The put-downs that make you feel worthless. The constant harping on a particular subject: "I'll never win any popularity contest. I could count my friends on one hand and include slight acquaintances." Comparisons with others! "I'm two years older than Pete, and he's rich." "I'm not a barrel of laughs like Beth—I'm a heavy." Wish fantasies: "If Dreamboat Brad from back in school would call me up and say, 'All these years I've never been able to get you out of my mind.' "

We all have some category of thinking that is our own private patented brand of negativity. These thoughts are the persistent ones. As you probably learned when you practiced Listening In, they recur interminably. They'll do their best to defeat you, to slip past your STOP commands, to reappear when you're off guard. You may have to turn them off 20 or 30 times a day. But keep at it. *These* are the *really* destructive thoughts, the ones that sap your energy, deprive you of good feelings, throw you into a panic, and destroy your self-confidence. Those habitual painful thoughts are probably criticisms or teasings that you heard a thousand times as a child. "Call her anything but late for dinner." "Foot in your mouth." "Two left feet." What do you still hear from your childhood?

For these persistent messages, *Stopping* is more effective when it's done out loud. Whenever you can, let yourself *hear* that word, STOP. It reinforces the process and makes you stronger next time. Another helpful device is keeping track of how many times a day you're confronted by a particular thought. You'll get a lot of encouragement from seeing the number of repetitions dwindle as you become more skilled at *Stopping*.

WORRYING

Worry seems to be a basic fact of life. No one escapes it entirely, but some of us make a career of it. For the really accomplished worrier, who worries day and night about things that may or may not happen, everything is grist for the mill. Burglars. Accidents. Failures. What other people will think. What the weather will be tomorrow. We even know someone who worries because he read that the sun has only 2 billion years of life left.

There's no sense in worrying about things you can't help: That the Polar ice cap is melting and its flood is heading for New York, particularly East 20th Street. But we all have worries that are equally fruitless. A divorced mother has let four-year-old Garth visit his father, counting on her ex's girlfriend to look after Garth. Suddenly she is tormented by worry. What if the girlfriend is some seventeen-year-old bimbo stoned on coke who will have Garth snorting with them? There are some practical steps this mother can take to check out the situation—but worry will do nothing but rob her of her week till she gets Garth back.

A thousand times a day, thoughts like that mother's cross our minds. They don't settle anything or change the course of events, but they do waste our time. They do divert us from more positive thoughts. Worrying is one of the most common thinking errors. Fortunately, it responds well to the technique of *Stopping*. Order each worrisome thought to STOP, and gradually you'll break your Inner Voice of the habit. As the worries disappear, your life will become unbelievably more pleasant.

Vincent, a hard-working bachelor in his late twenties, was a middle-management executive in a large company. His mother had died when he was young, and his father had raised him. They had gotten along famously, more or less taking care of each other, the only drawback—a slight one—being that the father had tended to be overprotective, filling Vincent's head with many thoughts of all the things he should worry about.

Without realizing it, Vincent had carried these with him into his adult life. His Inner Voice had successfully taken over his father's role. Vincent was a worrier.

Although he was strongly attracted to a young woman in his department, he never got around to asking her for a date. His worries took over. "It's not a good idea to date someone you work with." "If she says no, it'll be embarrassing." "I saw her chatting with Dick at the water cooler this morning. Maybe she's dating him."

Don't let futile worries immobilize you. Train yourself to differentiate between legitimate concerns and futile self-torment. If your worry is something you can do something about, fine: Do it. For example, if you find yourself wondering whether you're handling a job correctly, analyze the situation, get advice if you can, and take some action. That's productive. If you're worried about a cosmic eventuality, STOP.

As for Vincent, he came for I.S.T. about another matter entirely, and in the course of it, he got an unexpected bonus. When he Listened In, he heard the useless pile-up of worries that were restricting him. He Underlined the weakening thoughts. And he Stopped his Inner Voice. When he had sufficiently dammed that stream of worries, he asked the young woman in his office out. Not only did she accept, she asked her own question: "Vincent, what took you so long?"

Now practice the *Stopping* technique with some of your thoughts: Which of the following give you difficulty with persistent thoughts that you want to *Stop*?

		Practice Stopping
Do you hear?	1. "I can't do it...."	STOP
	2. "I'm lousy at...."	STOP
	or	
You fill in	3. "I'm _____...."	STOP
	4. "I _____...."	STOP

Pick one of your undesirable thoughts and practice stopping it several times a day. Keep track of your successes and failures. Try *Listening In* to other types of thoughts—ones that depress or inhibit you. List the three recurring things you keep thinking *about* but believe you can't *stop*:

1. I _____
2. I _____
3. I _____

Now, after each time the thought occurs, train yourself to *overpower the thought* with a more intriguing and attractive one.

Why does *Stopping* work? The answer is incredibly simple. YOU CAN THINK OF ONLY ONE THING AT A TIME. If you can lock the word STOP in your thinking space (your Inner Speech Center), there is *no room* for the negative thought.

SUMMING UP

The biggest advantage I.S.T. gives you is that it's *always at hand*. You don't have to go to a gym or rehearsal hall to practice. Wherever *you* are, your thoughts are. You can Listen In and Underline all through the day. And now that you know how, you can put *Stopping* to work.

Although you learned these three techniques separately, the second advantage of the system is that they combine naturally and well. As you become more accustomed to *Stopping*, you'll be able to intervene more quickly and merge the three steps until they become practically simultaneous. In the meantime, continue to review each step individually and keep these points in mind about *Stopping*:

1. When a negative message starts, Stop it as *soon* as you can.
2. Use the one-word command, STOP.
3. Be forceful. Take charge. Don't allow the bad news to continue.
4. Say the word STOP out loud when you can. It strengthens your position.

5. Practice until you can Stop the thought earlier each time you try.
6. Be on the alert for the most persistent messages.
7. Brake—the—thought. Slow—it—down—so—you—hear—it—clearly.

Integrate what you have learned so far, and proceed to Technique #4: What do you do after you Stop?

CHAPTER 7

INNER SPEECH TECHNIQUE #4: SWITCHING

CHANGING THE CONTENT OF YOUR INNER SPEECH

Do not just Stop your damaging inner speech and leave yourself with an empty head! Move on immediately to master:

POWER THINKING TECHNIQUE #4: SWITCHING

Switching is deliberately to interrupt damaging inner speech and replace it with *positive* internal voices.

So far we've discussed the first three techniques of Inner Speech Therapy. You've learned to hear what's going on in your head (*Listening In*); to isolate the damaging messages (*Underlining*); and to stop them as soon as they begin (*Stopping*). But what happens after you exorcise the demons? Minds don't stay empty. They fill up of their own accord, and that's precisely what you don't want yours to do. And unless you replace the damaging thought, it will return. That is a key point to remember.

WHAT IS SWITCHING?

One person described *Switching* this way: "Every night, I lie in bed, frantic to fall asleep, but kept awake by a whirlpool of thoughts that keep spinning, spinning, spinning around in my head. It's as if my mind is out of control, and I'm being carried along with it. These are never constructive thoughts. They rehash yesterday. Could I have done something better? Was I too harsh with the children? I forgot to return the client's call.

"From yesterday I go to tomorrow and an equally senseless bombardment. I hear my thoughts fighting with each other over the way to handle matters that in all likelihood will never arise. I'm completely wrung out from all this activity. And then—finally, when I'm just about at my wits' end—something happens. I hear my own voice break in, saying, Stop! Cut it out! What are you doing to yourself? Haven't you had enough? Think about the wonderful day you had with Jenny at the zoo. Remember how she laughed at those chimps?

"Soon my head is filled with pleasant memories, my thoughts slow down, and I'm able to fall asleep. Sometimes it takes quite a few Stops and Switches, but it works if I keep working it."

That's *Switching*: replacing bad thoughts with good ones. It can happen spontaneously, as in the case just described, or it can be an intentional act on your part. Be sure to keep in mind that *Switching* can be intentional, that it can be learned. With a little diligence, you can train yourself to be good at it. Here are some tips on going about it.

First, remember that *Stopping* and *Switching* go

hand in hand. As soon as you hear an undesirable thought, break in with the *Stopping* technique. Cut off the thought as early as you can and as many times as you have to. Some thoughts are doggedly persistent, but you can be more so.

Think of yourself in the position of the telephone operator who breaks in to tell you, "Your time is up. Deposit another quarter, please." If you continue talking, she breaks in a second time. The third time, the line goes dead. You have to persevere with *Stopping* in the same way, not harshly, but firmly. If you do, the negative thought will fade. You'll be able to replace it with something more helpful.

The more quickly that *Switching* fills the void left by Stopping, the more effective it will be. Empty periods of mind time breed trouble. Try to be ready to fill any gaps with a *Switching* sentence you've prepared in advance. Think of something now and memorize it, so it will be available when you need it. Here are some examples of the kind of thing that works: "I'll switch to thinking about the promotion I got. I said, 'This means a lot to me,' and he said, 'You mean a lot to us.'" "I'll switch to thinking about that day in the mountains. Next time I'm going to take the other trail, clear to the top."

Be sure your *Switching* sentence is something that gives you pleasure or fortifies you in some way. The importance of what we think about has been understood since ancient times. In the words of the Bible, "Whatever is honorable... whatever is lovely... whatever is gracious... think about these things."

In one true story, the *Switching* was crucial. The patient, Joanna, was a capable woman with a history of recurrent, severe depressions which even included occasional thoughts of suicide. Her Inner Speech was filled with depressing thoughts:

"Nothing has ever gone right for me."
"I have nothing to show for my life."

Then it happened that she went to see James Stewart in the movie *It's a Wonderful Life*. Joanna was no James Stewart, and she hadn't done nearly as many wonderful things for her community as he had done in the movie. But from that time, she and her therapist began to Switch to thinking to what she *had* done, and *planned* to do in her life. When she made a list of the contributions she had made in life, it was not spectacular, no awards nor special honors. But there were the accomplishments of a basically good person who had performed the services that came her way, volunteering for some, pressed into service by necessity in others. Like many "good" people, she judged herself far too harshly, never feeling she measured up to her own standards.

The Stewart movie helped her decide that she could Switch her usual thoughts about herself. In therapy she had been exposed to the idea that whenever she was depressed, it was because she was allowing herself to have a pessimistic thought about herself, and her life. The movie gave her a scenario to follow. Her Switch was to James Stewart, and then to herself. It lifted her spirits because she could count events in her life that were not failures. She thought about those things.

She Switched her thoughts. Eventually, using therapy, she retrained her thinking so that she could Switch her depressing thoughts almost as soon as they began. She remembered happy occasions. When she wasn't burdened throughout her days and nights with thoughts of failure she had more energy to do things that were productive.

If your mind is obsessed with *negative thoughts*, you can interrupt your thinking and control its flow (*Listening In, Underlining, Stopping*). You will then move in a positive direction (*Switching*).

If your mind is filled with self-assured thoughts, you can control the thinking and *not allow negative Switching to happen*. The secret is in observing how you think; learning how your thoughts flow and change, and training yourself to Switch thoughts in mid-flow. You can improve your mental life and you can avoid Pitfalls.

A Pitfall occurs when you hear your own inner speech interrupted *by an undesirable voice that belongs to someone else*. That voice takes over your thinking.

You are anticipating a first-time visit from a congenial pen-pal from the Coast. Your plans are interrupted by a voice suggesting:

"How do you know he's not married?"

Or you hear your parents:

"What are the neighbors going to think?"

Are your neighbors thinking? Have you ever known what they think? When you really get down to it—what is more important? *Your* thinking, or your neighbors'? You will feel better if you Switch whenever you find yourself the victim of such pitfalls.

The pitfalls to watch for most carefully are the inner monologues that put you down and damage your self-respect. This kind of thinking usually features Over-personalizing, a troublemaker which accomplishes nothing. It only makes you feel insecure. And it is insecure people make the most errors in their thinking and in their relationships.

Over-personalizing is blaming *yourself* for everything that happens in a relationship; feeling that if anything goes wrong, it must be *your* fault. To recognize Over-personalizing, look for Voice Thoughts like these: "Why didn't he call? There must be something the matter with me—I don't wear well on people." Have you noticed which words to Underline? *Must. The matter with me.* Those words don't do you a bit of good. Stop them. Then Switch to a more purposeful thought. "I'll wash my hair, so I'll look good tomorrow. Or "I'll call Betsy. She's always full of news and bright ideas."

Another way we Over-personalize is with thoughts like this one: "She can't do this to me." Can't she? Well, don't bet on it. She just did. The harmful part of that thought is the "to me." Did she do whatever she did because you're you? Probably not. More likely, she did it because that's the kind of thing she does, and you happened to be there. If you were to investigate, you'd be apt to find she "does it" to everyone. So stop Over-personalizing. That kind of thinking often leads to a vicious cycle that needs to be interrupted.

Brooding is another danger area, composed of thoughts that cause pain and go on too long. "How could he have treated me that way after all we went through together?" "Why did I get passed over for a raise with all the overtime I put in?" These are unanswerable, debilitating thoughts that sap your strength. Break in on them. Stop them. Talk back to them. Intervene with your own *Switching* question.

Ask your Inner Voice, "What are you doing to me? I have better thoughts to think." Then go ahead and think them.

Speculation is another way we torture ourselves. "What will I do if the company's lease expires and they move out of town?" Switch immediately to, "It's silly to worry about that now. There's a good program on." Not that it has to be TV, of course. That's only an example of something that will occupy your mind in a less punishing way. The secret is not to remain passive, but to take some sort of active stance. Give your mind new scenarios to follow so the old thoughts can't crowd back in.

SWITCHING EFFECTIVELY

Distracting yourself is helpful while you're practicing the *Switching* technique. But *Switching* is most effective when you can be instructive in your replacement thoughts. For instance, if you hear, "I'll never be able to do that," it isn't enough just to intervene with, "Stop. I can do that." That's too vague, too easy a generalization. Merely saying you can cope won't necessarily cause it to happen. You'll make much more progress if you break your statements down into specific suggestions. "I'm patient. I can figure this out. I'll see if there's a book in the library that will help me." Or, "I've done harder things in my life. Maybe I'll have to work it out by trial and error, but I'll give it my best shot." Thoughts like those take longer, but they constitute healthy thinking. They allow you to break a problem down into workable parts.

Perhaps you're having money problems. Your Inner

Voice takes you to task. You hear it saying, "I spend money as fast as I earn it." Look behind that. Do you hear something else? Is an echo of a parent's critical voice coming through asking, "Do you have to spend it just because you've got it?" Tell that critical voice to Stop. Switch your own voice to, "I want to figure out how to budget."

That's positive *Switching*, the kind that leads to solutions. Once you've gotten that far, you can break your problem down into more manageable parts. "I've had trouble dealing with money in the past. I don't put enough aside for future needs." Get even more specific. "If I calculate how much my vacation is going to cost, and save a percentage of it each week, I'll enjoy it more when the time comes."

BENEVOLENT VOICES

We want to stress the importance of sorting out the voices in your head. Often, the spontaneous *Switching* you do is in the useful voice of a Benevolent Friend. This can be any one of a number of people: a current buddy, a friend from the past, a mentor at work, a teacher, a kindly uncle or aunt, a grandparent, an understanding sibling, a therapist. It can be one of your parents. Whoever it is, it's a voice you want to keep. It's usually helpful, interested, often more experienced than you are, and a patient guide through a difficult time.

The Benevolent Friend treats you as you would treat a person of whom you were very fond. It's someone who helps you interrupt the negative flow in your mind by substituting a more positive voice. Eventually

you yourself should be your Benevolent Friend, ready
to intercede in your own behalf. The goal of I.S.T. is to
train your own Inner Voice for this role. Let's say, for
instance, you hear that old negative voice at work:
"Why does everyone take advantage of me?" Stop. Now
substitute a benevolent voice with a *Switching* thought:
"Not everyone takes advantage. You have good friends
who do come through for you. Think this one through
again."

A change in your thinking automatically changes
your feelings. Your life is controlled by your thinking,
which is why *Switching* is so significant. When you are
at your best, and feeling good, you know you can think
anything you want to think. Once you've mastered the
Switching technique, you have a tool that is always at
your disposal that helps you take charge of your thinking directly.

TAKEOVERS

These days, we're all familiar with Takeovers, especially if we read the business pages of our daily newspaper. Dozens of companies have been appropriated by
other firms, some in friendly transactions, others in
moves that are termed "hostile." Our minds are subject
to hostile Takeovers, too, and we can spare ourselves
much suffering by being on the alert for them.

Takeovers are instances of negative *Switching*,
times when your own Inner Speech is interrupted by
an undesirable voice that belongs to somebody else, an
alien voice that takes over your thinking. You might be
feeling great, contemplating an exciting sexual experience when all of a sudden that critical voice erupts

with, "What if my timing is off?" The rapture fades, and you're left with the dark cloud of a thought that you'll fail your partner.

If your mind is filled with self-assured thoughts, you'll be able to prevent Takeovers. The secret is in observing how you think, learning how your thoughts flow and change, and training yourself to Switch to helpful thoughts in mid-flow. Rid yourself of Takeovers.

Here is an exercise for you. You think the thought:

"I've never been so happy with anybody."

Then your next thought suddenly appears:

"What if the relationship doesn't last?"

Now, using Inner Speech Training, how would you help yourself at that moment?

SUMMING UP

Of the four steps we've discussed so far, *Switching* is by far the most powerful. It bolsters you by reducing the painful pressures your Inner Voice has been putting on you. *Switching* can be learned, but it requires vigilance. You'll want to keep the following pointers in mind as you practice it.

1. Make a habit of *Listening In* and *Underlining.* They keep you aware.
2. As soon as you hear an unwanted thought, Stop it. If the thought persists, Stop it as many times

as you need to, always trying to intervene as early as possible.

3. Talk to yourself in a sympathetic voice. You can Stop unwanted dialogues more easily if you're not judgmental.

4. Have a *Switching* thought ready to substitute for the thought you've just stopped.

5. Break your thoughts down into achievable parts. Be as specific as you can.

6. Be on the lookout for unfriendly, critical voices. They have no right to invade your thoughts. Don't be one of those people who automatically Switches your thinking to something grim when you are feeling good.

7. Make the most of any help you get from a benevolent friend.

8. Don't be discouraged if you have a failure or two. You're learning a new way of thinking and that takes time.

CHAPTER 8

INNER SPEECH TECHNIQUE #5: REORIENTING
DIRECTING YOUR THINKING TO A DIFFERENT GOAL

Have you ever been tired and down late in the day, and someone said, "Let's go out"?

Your spirits picked up, and you began thinking about washing your face, putting on some fresh clothes, and hearing music in your head.

That is the experience of *Reorienting*. You reoriented the direction of your thinking. Your mood changed as you began to focus on a different target. The thing that produced your new enthusiasm was a reoriented *thought*. This is the power of Technique #5: *Reorienting*.

POWER THINKING TECHNIQUE #5: REORIENTING

Reorienting is to change the direction of your thinking. Your thinking deliberately focuses on a different target. If you are preparing for a takeoff when flying, you can Reorient your thinking from whether the engines will fail to what you are going to do when you are in Boston.

Change the direction of your thinking and you will change the direction you move today—and every day from now on. When you are in trouble, find a *directing circumstance that positively demands your attention.*

Sylvia R. had a severe fear of going outside and being alone (agoraphobia). Despite therapy, she had barely improved. She needed some practical techniques to combine with the insights she had already learned.

We suggested that Sylvia Reorient her thoughts when she went out marketing. She agreed that each time she went, she would make a complete list of what she had to do. Then when she finally got outside (although she still felt anxious), she refocused and Reoriented her attention to a recording of precisely what she had to do. Using all the willpower she could muster, she kept her thoughts on what she was doing that very moment: ("Salad dressing, in Aisle 5; now Produce, for broccoli—on sale—and a cantaloupe, if ripe"). By retraining her thought patterns, she eventually was able to go outside by herself with enough thinking power to overcome her anxiety.

Reorient yourself right now. You are tense because you have a deadline and must finish a huge project by Friday. Now Reorient: On Saturday you plan to have fun by going shopping with your friends. Your project will be completed and you will have the day off.

Reorient from "Friday workload" to "Saturday fun." Your feelings will follow your new Reoriented thoughts if you practice seeking out different, more attractive goals. It takes training to Reorient from preoccupation with an ordeal to prospects that are pleasurable.

Also practice this technique to Reorient away from painful anxiety to *an active, problem-solving framework.*

For example, the next time your plane is landing, get yourself interested in the pattern of lights and roads near the airport, and the structures on the ground. Think about some activity on the ground that absorbs you and pulls your thinking to that subject.

If you concentrate on your *fear*—of elevators, crowds, or being rejected by a friend—you could panic.

If you choose to concentrate on some *attractive goal* and actively *change the focus* of your attention, you will feel much more in command, calmer, and more competent.

Visualize yourself doing a job well. Once people learned that they could do better by watching successful rehearsals in their minds, they were able to hit a golf ball better, improve their skiing, and almost immediately cope with all sorts of physical activity that had previously frustrated them. They Reoriented from a clumsy, inept image of themselves to a smooth, professional one.

Reorienting means to *see yourself managing successfully* in a stressful situation. It is *a rehearsal in your mind* in which you vividly picture yourself handling a difficult issue with methods well chosen to see you through. For example, you see yourself riding to the eighth floor in an elevator, and practicing healthy thinking techniques when the elevator doors close. You can visualize yourself making love with your partner. You hold and stroke each other and find each other's mouths, kissing deeply.

Reorient yourself by visualizing that you are handling with aplomb some of the encounters in your life that make you anxious or depressed. Important: Don't be simplistic—visualize the detailed techniques by which you meet every phase of the occasion.

Reorienting worked very well for Suzanne B. She was a severely depressed executive secretary who was suffering from what is termed a depressing triad—she gathered evidence from the past, present, and future that nothing had gone right, was going right, or would ever go right. By using her patterns of repetitive cognitions, she locked herself into a severely depressed state and intensified it by her misperception of what was going on around her.

She viewed everything in a negative light. The most trivial event was always interpreted by her depressive style to portend something ominous.

In therapy, Suzanne B. was asked to make a list of what made her feel *good*—not an easy task for her. It had to be emphasized that she could include anything, no matter how insignificant. The list was initially a short one. It included hiking, watching certain television shows, and hand-painting her own greeting cards. She was asked to spend more time doing these small things that gave her pleasure and to record how she felt afterwards. When she started to note relaxed or cheerful feelings, she was able to keep focusing on the things that she enjoyed and to stop using her former approach of examining every event pessimistically. Thus, in small but positive steps, her depression dwindled away.

Reorienting helped Suzanne B. see herself as less helpless than before, and with visual rehearsal she soon had more confidence to go out and mix successfully with her fellow hikers. Her "helpless" self-concept changed to the point where she realized that she was not helpless, and with that change in outlook, she became less depressed.

Switching and *Reorienting* have much in common. But there is an important difference. You will find it useful when you are either anxious or depressed to follow all the way to this fifth I.S.T. step of *Reorienting*.

Switching is an immediate thinking technique which should follow immediately after *Stopping*. *Stopping* alone is not enough, because your mind abhors a vacuum, and some thought will arrive momentarily and fill that vacuum if you do not deliberately choose what thought you want to occupy your mind. Your conscious choice of a useful thought will be far more helpful than letting an old automatic thought take over. Chapter 7 described how the best *Switching* is toward an idea that begins to solve the immediate problem at hand. If that is not possible at the moment, then it is valuable for you to have some pleasant and successful thoughts memorized in advance to Switch into place. Eventually, those affirming thoughts about yourself and your world can become your automatic thoughts. Many people, of course, do not believe that comforting thoughts can ever become automatic. You were not born with your thought patterns. You learned them. And if some of those habitual thoughts are not doing you much good, you can learn a different and more serviceable pattern of inner speech.

Bill is a man who is no wiser nor dumber than the average person. He makes his share of mistakes. He once remarked to his therapist that he probably does 10,000 different things in a week. Those include things like tying his shoes, taking a milk carton out of the refrigerator, driving to work, writing a letter, trying to settle an argument between his two children, making love, balancing his checkbook, trying to make some sense out of the conflicts in Northern Ireland, and so on. So he is like most people.

Bill has never tried to figure out how many mistakes he makes in a week, but he knows that the number adds up. He has learned to do something constructive for himself when he makes a mistake. He pays attention to the mistake, gives it some thought, and then thinks something like this: "That isn't like you, Bill. You don't want to do that. Next time I will_____." And then Bill thinks of a better way to do the thing at which he just made a mistake. He coaches himself gently. His I.S.T. has paid off for him. He accepts that mistakes are a part of life. *Switching* has helped him acknowledge his mistakes in a way that corrects them and keeps him from belittling himself.

Reorienting, in contrast to *Switching*, is a much broader technique. You can Reorient to a grander view of your life. You can learn to see yourself differently. You can learn to see the world around you differently, in big and little ways.

Pete was a lineman for a college football team that was playing for the national championship on a November Saturday afternoon. The game was close, the stakes were especially enormous for Bill, because he was the team captain. He broke his leg during a play in the third quarter of the game. He continued to play the rest of the game and never felt any pain until the game was over.

How could this be? The answer is that Bill was so oriented toward winning the game, and playing his part in it, that he literally paid no conscious attention to his broken leg and felt no pain. When he returned to the locker room after the game, the pain became so great that he writhed on the floor crying. Did the pain not exist until the game was over? You may answer that for yourself in any way that makes sense to you. The fact is that Bill felt no pain. His focus on the game completely blocked it.

That is a true story, and it has been duplicated countless times in the lives of people who were oriented toward goals that totally dominated their thinking so that no other thought or sensation could make its way into their consciousness.

In an episode parallel to that of Bill's, a ballerina finished dancing *Coppelia* with a broken ankle. Granted, there are physiologic factors that also could be adduced for delayed reaction to trauma. But our point here is that if you set your thoughts on a goal that is worthy of your best self, you will be so drawn to do your best that you will block out some of the crippling thoughts that have held you back.

Reorienting is akin to Imaging. We prefer the term *Reorienting* because it implies a larger vision of yourself, and a wider view of your possibilities. It is important to Image your goals. It is even more helpful to Reorient and see yourself as a person who can control more and more of your life by controlling your thinking.

You can Reorient around an optimistic frame of reference. If you think you can do anything, you increase your chances of doing it. A Reorientation toward optimism gets you moving. In contrast, depressing thoughts bog you down and stymie you, because you are thinking "What's the use?"

Optimists keep trying, because they believe they can reach their goal. This is not mindless daydreaming. An optimist tries. A daydreamer just daydreams.

You can make it a habit of remembering your best self, your best inner speech, your best images of the you that you want to be. Reorient yourself toward the best (and honest) compliments that you have received in your life. Remember particularly those things about which you have consistently been complimented.

That's the real you. Make that the frame of reference for your life. Now you are creating a new orientation, a new image of yourself. This is who you want to be. If you think it, you can make more and more of it come true for yourself. You know you have often made yourself feel miserable because of what you thought. It works the same the other way. A picture of your best self, of you at your best, of you the way you have always wanted to be—will pull you along in that direction.

Reorienting works like a magnet. Picture yourself reaching your goals, and you will feel the tug of the magnet pulling you.

Here are three ways to Reorient your thinking—and your life—thoughts that build you up, not put you down:

1. Think of a truly helpful compliment that you once received. You then Reorient toward *your assets*.
2. Think of what is genuinely important to you. You then Reorient toward *satisfying feelings*.
3. Think of something to be excited about. You then Reorient toward *stimulating goal-directed* ideas.

Write down the three right now. Then you will have them ready the next time that you need to Reorient.

Think of_____
Think of_____
Think of_____

Now you have the five basics of Power Thinking, ready to put to use.

TEN POWERFUL THINGS
YOU CAN DO RIGHT NOW

You've learned the five crucial steps of the Inner Speech system. What are you going to do with them?

The most natural tendency is already in your mind. A small but overbearing voice. "Okay. Now I can take a break."

On the contrary, it's now time to start, if you want to change your life, so change that thought. Let the corrective power of Inner Speech Training go to work for you by immediately instituting a simple series of steps in your everyday life.

The first thing to do is to start keeping a continuous updated record of your erroneous thinking.

Most people usually get the best results with the use of a small diary to record their weakening repetitive thoughts. Buy a small 3×5 notebook that you can carry with you. Then circle the most damaging negative parts of these thoughts. Use your new knowledge to ascertain exactly which part is most damaging.

Example: The thought, "Is that all there is in my

life?" Try changing it to "What else can I put in my life?"

Here now are the ten powerful things you can do—right now.

1. STOP ALL-OR-NOTHING THINKING

Quiz yourself. Do you tend to think in extremes or absolutes? "I have to be first." "I'm nothing but a slob." "I have to have the most." "Nothing works for me." Those thoughts will make you suffer. Underline those extremes and Stop.

2. AVOID OVERGENERALIZING

This can best be done by underlining all the universalizing (the everythings and forevers) you hear in your mind. Then work on *Stopping* them. The cliché "Never say never" is good advice.

3. LISTEN IN ACCURATELY TO THE FEEDBACK FROM YOUR BODY

Signals from your body need to be listened to, and then accurately interpreted. Let your body feed your mind, but with good stuff. When your body is tired, it is telling you something. What are the thoughts that accompany the tiredness? Listen. The thought may be saying "Do something nice for yourself." Other times, your body will be giving you a pleasure message. Go with it. Think of the pleasure your body has given you throughout your life. Yes, sometimes your body has ached, too, but you will do something wonderful for your mood if you think about the wonderful feelings your body has brought you.

4. THINK IN MICROSTEPS

Solve a problem by breaking it down into the smallest possible steps—steps so small that anyone could take them, like putting one foot in front of the other. Then as you work on the little picture with microsteps, you can eventually Switch to the big picture, put together with many microsteps. One hundred quantitative steps (that is, one hundred changes in your thoughts) will bring a qualitative change in your feeling about yourself and about your life.

5. MINIMIZE YOUR MAGNIFICATIONS

Do not exaggerate your thinking. "It was the worst thing I ever heard." "I was totally crushed." "I nearly died." "I was destroyed." "I thought I'd explode." No such things happened. Those are thoughts that produce helpless feelings about yourself. You deserve to think better of yourself.

6. MONITOR THE WAR BETWEEN YOUR THOUGHTS

Some quarreling between your thoughts is an important part of thinking. It develops judgment. But if your mind is a constant battlefield, Listen In and identify the different voices and thoughts so you can decide whose to Stop. If your thoughts go round and round, you are only repeating yourself, and not moving on to finding the solution to the problem. When you're caught up in circular thinking, that is a signal to Stop and come at things from a different angle.

7. KEEP YOUR THOUGHTS IN YOUR OWN VOICE

When you have conflicts, Underline your own internal voice. Then Stop the unwanted voice of someone else. We have spoken of the reservoir of common sense deep inside you. Abide by its voice. We do not mean that every impulse you have should be acted on. We are referring to your "measured judgment." You have relied on it countless times. You know the tone of voice of your inner common sense. Those are the thoughts to act on.

8. AVOID OVERLOOKING

Do you perceive all that you are capable of perceiving? Choose not to think the stressful thoughts because they block you from seeing things from a deep and wide perspective. Take a laugh break. Change a losing pattern. Get outside yourself. Imagine that you are Bertrand Russell. How would he perceive your situation?

9. THINK "MAINTENANCE OR MISSION?"

Some people usually think "maintenance" thoughts; that is like straightening up your sock drawer. Others usually think "mission thoughts"; those are thoughts that move you ahead, such as planning a project that will bring you a satisfying new experience. Maintenance is about cleaning up the past. Mission is moving ahead. When you find yourself thinking about a maintenance task, nudge yourself over into a mission task.

10. KEEP YOUR THINKING GOAL DIRECTED

Most systems work less well than our expectations. Don't waste your time with the critical voices holding you back. Monitor your inner speech to keep your goals clear. Direct yourself in your own strong voice: "This is where I want to go."

CHAPTER 9

POWER SHIFTING
STRENGTHENING YOUR INNER SPEECH

And Lucy said:

> "You, Charlie Brown, are a foul ball in the line drive of life. You're in the shadow of your own goal posts... You are a miscue... You are three putts on the eighteenth green... You are a seven-ten split in the tenth frame... A love set. You have dropped a rod and reel in the lake of life... You are a missed free throw, a shanked nine iron, and a called third strike."

Have you mastered enough Power Thinking techniques to see what the trouble is, and how to change it, for poor Charlie Brown? If Charlie's thinking about himself contains Lucy's words, he is in big trouble!

If you are getting some help already from the five basic techniques, you are ready to go on to your own more powerful thinking. Here are ways to strengthen your mind by alerting yourself to the content and character of your inner speech—and then shifting to Power.

1. IS YOUR INTERNAL SPEECH MERELY A REPEAT OF YOUR CHILDHOOD THINKING?

You wouldn't want Lucy's voice talking in your head. Too many times, your mind may be filled with other people's voices talking to you as if you were a six-year-old, saying nasty things about you.

Can you remember hearing, earlier in your life, the voice of a mother who apparently believed you didn't have the sense to come in out of the rain:

"Could you please try and take care of your-self? You know how you tend to catch cold."

Or,

"You never had any sense of time. I under-stand that that's the way you are, but it makes such a bad impression because it looks so rude and inconsiderate."

You may need to shift the character of your inner speech and start listening to your *own* voice.

We should be doing the speaking for ourselves—especially *internally*, where it counts the most.

Practice listing the voices that you hear in your head. When you are thinking, does your inner speech sound like a recording of someone else's words? Here is an exercise to help you Listen In, so you can hear whether your inner voices are your voice, or someone else's, and whether the voices are helpful or harmful.

Review your memories of each of the persons listed. The way to do this is to remember the words and the tone of voice of these people. Pay close attention also to the feeling you get when you think of one of these people saying something to you. Let's begin with two easy examples:

What does the voice of a best friend sound like in your mind?

What does the voice of a worst enemy sound like in your mind?

Now you are ready to go on to the others. What is the image of each of these people in your mind? Do the words of each of these people do something for you or against you?

	Positive influence	Negative influence
Mother	_____	_____
Father	_____	_____
Husband/wife	_____	_____
Boy/girlfriend	_____	_____
Child	_____	_____
Teacher	_____	_____
Boss	_____	_____
Clergy	_____	_____
Best friend	_____	_____
Worst enemy	_____	_____
Childhood rival	_____	_____
Coach	_____	_____
Special linger-ing voice	_____	_____

The key to being your own person is to monitor your own inner voice. Be sure that the words and thoughts are your *own* thoughts. You will when you are at your best. The more familiar you are with your mature inner voice, the quicker you will be able to recognize unwanted voices when they are disguised as your own.

Find the missing voice in the following case:

Cathy B. came into therapy because of a "depression." She had just broken up for the third time with her boyfriend. He said he couldn't marry her because she was still too dependent on her mother and helping with her invalid father. Her mind was a ménage à trois. Endless conversations occurred between Frank, her boyfriend, her mother, and occasionally even her own small voice—dialogues that reflected the conflicts between the two polarizing forces in her life.

Boyfriend's voice	Mother's voice
"I've got to go to Palm Springs for this conference. Why don't you come along? I won't be working the whole time, and it would be a change for you—you could use a dose of sun."	"He's so manipulative. He's always putting pressure on you..."
"I'm getting heavy into Chinese cooking. Why don't you come over tonight and check out my moo goo gai pan."	"He's not very honest about saying what he's really got in mind..."

Cathy's voice
"I can't decide..."

Cathy B. felt so depressed that she couldn't concentrate on her job. She had taken a mild tranquilizer to help her with her anxieties, but she still felt terribly upset most of the time.

The real problem in this case was the *Missing Voice*—and it was Cathy's *own voice*. Two contrasting voices were making opposing demands on her, and she was in constant conflict as to which one to obey. Her boyfriend's and her mother's voices were in her head almost constantly, trying to control her mind. This led to a neurotic conflict between two different voices, and Cathy B. was unable to make up her mind.

In therapy, Cathy B. was able to listen in to their voices, work on *Stopping* them, and then switch to listening to her own healthy thinking.

Every time she heard her mother's voice inside her head, she would recognize it and say "Stop." Then she carefully thought her own thoughts about Frank. She would ask herself, "What do *I* really think? What is best for *me*? What do *I* want? What is in *my* best interests? Knowing Frank as I do, what are my honest thoughts about him?"

The answers to these questions helped her to do her own thinking. Sometimes her thoughts were the same as her mother's thoughts. Sometimes her thoughts were the same as Frank's. She didn't have to reject their thoughts just for the sake of being contrary. But when she did find her own thoughts, she knew they were her thoughts, and she didn't feel manipulated by anyone else. It was the emergence, finally, of an independent voice.

Do your parents dominate your inner speech? Start with your childhood. Can you remember a voice that said, "Don't stand under a tree in a thunderstorm."

"Don't go anywhere with anyone, even if they say I've been in an accident and they're supposed to get you." Without such a voice, you probably couldn't have survived in a complex world.

In adolescence, the voices started to change. There were more dialogues and often angry exchanges. The adolescent fought back the attempts of parents to guide via mind control.

Can you recall discussions in your head like: "What do you know about what's okay for kids? It's Saturday night and all the other kids are staying out late—" And the inevitable inner voice when the hands of the clock got near midnight—"It's time to go home—I'm late—I've got to find a phone." Or even more controlling were the early forays of sexuality—"Are you sure you feel you're ready to handle this?" Your mother's voice, cautioning you through your sexual experience, and often lingering when you perhaps didn't want her presence in your mind. "I don't care how much things change, people always judge the *girl*!"

Finally, as we mature, the voices become more complex and intricate. Witness the surgical resident about to perform a difficult operation. In her head she can hear the voice of her mentors guiding her through each tedious, necessary step:

> "Make sure you tie off *all* the bleeders before going into the peritoneum."

These voices are necessary for our continued education and growth. We get them from our teachers, our parents, the people around us, and even worthy books. The sounder the teaching, the better the voices guide us through the complexities of human, sexual, and professional life.

2. DO GUILT-RIDDEN VOICES DOMINATE YOUR INNER SPEECH?

You may be controlled by the neurotic thinking of others in more immediate ways. Consider going to the movies with an obsessive personality, and you are required to share his worry about whether or not he parked the car in a legal space and won't be towed away. "I'm not sure, but I *think* I parked the car in a no-parking zone. I'll probably get a ticket. For what that'll cost, we could have done a Broadway play."

"Step on a crack, break your grandmother's back." "Tattle-Tale Tit/Your tongue shall be slit/And all the dogs in our town/Shall have a little bit." One reason such rhymes stick in our minds is that they dramatize childhood guilt. Guilt is on children's minds most of the time, although they do a pretty good job of concealing that fact from their parents. Most children at the age of nine would like to change their first names, because they heard their first names used most often in a way that put guilt, shame, or fear into their minds. "Jimmy, you get in here right now." "Billy, you're filthy." "Melissa, look at you!" "Matthew, you're a disgrace." "Ellen, you should be ashamed."

Guilt is built in during the ordinary traditional experiences of childhood. This is why the critical voices haunt one's conscious thought. Those guilt-producing voices are most apt to sound like your parents' voices. But many of you will say, "My parents weren't really grim. I had a pretty good childhood. And I was always a pretty good girl." And when asked, "Did your parents expect you to be a good girl?"

"Oh boy, did they ever! But I didn't think I lived up to their expectations."

"How do you know that?"

"The voice in my head never lets me rest."

That is the inner voice that now needs to be examined in the light of your adult mind.

Many groups think they have a corner on guilt. There is Catholic guilt. There is Jewish guilt. There is the Protestant work ethic guilt. The fact is that no one escapes it, and many conventional patterns of thinking foster it. "Poor Mom! She never got to buy a new stick of furniture in her life, and she loved to try to make the place look cute." "Poor Pop. He never got to work in a field he loved." Actually, if Mom did wonders with Early Salvation Army, that was a triumph. Ernest Becker, in his last interview, said that a man who just supports his family is a hero. But, even if Mom and Pop did have it rough, we do not amend their deprivations by guilt-tripping ourselves. Their gallantry we can admire. Their self-pity we can sympathize with. Our admiration and our sympathy are worthier of them and of us than greeting-card guilt. The present-day task is to recognize guilt-tripping, and stop it when it is a useless mental tic.

The useful way to handle guilt is to *learn* from it. If you yourself were in error, if you were wrong, if you did make a mistake, then note it, think about how you can change it the next time you are faced with a similar situation. Then do not *harbor* it in your mind. Move on!

Your reservoir of common sense, to which we have referred, you know is there, because it has often led you to make effective decisions, and overrule destructive guilt. Hear your *own* voice. You can let the *best* part of you win the battle of the inner voices.

3. Does Your Thinking Set You Up?

Do you hear yourself thinking, "I don't know what to do about invitations to Marcia and Phoebe, since they don't speak—" If you do this type of thinking, you set up defeating circumstances. A more productive stance is... *"While I still don't know what to do about inviting them, I am considering the possibilities. I will work it out by the time I have to mail the invitations."*

Self-fulfilling prophecies are as real as two plus two equals four. You can live out a failure prophecy, or a success prophecy. If you imagine that you will do well, superstition to the contrary, it will increase your chances of doing well. If you will increase the sense of *hope* in your thinking about a forthcoming performance, this will improve your behavior just as tangibly as taking a class in how to do the performance. Of course, it is important to do both: be hopeful for a happy outcome, and prepare wisely for it. But part of *wisdom* is to *hope* and *expect* to do well. Your behavior will imitate what you think about.

If you are trying to stop smoking, you can think about the next time someone offers you a cigarette. You can think to yourself: "That will be a rough moment. I probably will not be able to say no." That will set you up to increase your chances of failure. You also have the choice of preparing a better response in advance for the time someone offers you a cigarette: "No thank you. I am a nonsmoker." That script, when readied in your mind in advance of the test situation, will dramatically increase your chances of being the nonsmoker you want to be.

Your inner speech can be successfully combined with imaging yourself succeeding at whatever you plan to do. Our Olympic athletes use mental rehearsal to increase their agility. Tennis players have proven over and over again that it is not helpful for them to say to themselves before they serve, "I won't make an error," because that puts the word "error" in their minds. They will be more apt to succeed if they think before they serve, "The ball will go in."

4. DOES YOUR INNER SPEECH STAY IN THE PRESENT?

Examine your Inner Speech from the following time perspectives:
Inner statements about the past...

"Nothing ever went right for me."

Inner statements about the future...

"I'll never meet the right person."
"I'll never get the right job."

"How am I ever going to live when I retire if inflation keeps going on?" This was the thinking of a 27-year-old law school senior. He hadn't even *started* to earn a living and had already started to *worry* about the *distant* future.

Living in the present is a key to fulfillment and happiness. Your thinking exerts its greatest power when it deals in the present. For instance, let's look at "worry."

Worry is to think about what *might* possibly *happen*

in the *future*. Worry is a useless expenditure of your thought and time, because you cannot do anything useful by wondering, for example, if your husband will have a car accident while you are sitting at home.

Worry is not the same as constructive planning, which leads to constructive action. Worry focuses mental energy on situations that your mind cannot resolve; thus it is useless.

You are in control of this very moment. You cannot do anything to change yesterday. Tomorrow is not here, so you cannot live it now. But you have complete control over what you want to think at this very moment. You also have exciting freedom to do something right now. You can have the freedom to do many things that are satisfying, interesting, productive, relaxing, fun. You also have the freedom to do something or think something to make yourself miserable right now.

Take tiny steps in changing your thoughts right now and you will find that you will change how you feel. Take tiny steps that you know will succeed and you will accomplish something. Passive procrastination has no payoff that is worth having.

5. IS YOUR INNER SPEECH APPROPRIATE TO THE SITUATION?

Do you chronically overreact? Is your head filled with thoughts like:

"I'd like to kill him."

or

"If I can't have a new outfit, I rather skip the reception."

"Either they give me the raise or I walk off the job."

Are you hurting yourself by thinking inappropriate *angry* thoughts when the situation calls for *assertive* ones?

Check your Inner Speech to see if you *personalize* situations. A police car cruises up the block and you hear in your mind:

"Are they coming to notify me of an accident?"

Your husband is staring at a blond on television and you hear in your mind:

"Why aren't I always glamorous and irresistible?"

Your children are overtired and teasing each other, and you hear in your mind:

"Why aren't I the kind of mother who always makes the home peaceful and happy?"

The elevator man doesn't smile and you hear in your mind:

"Wasn't my Christmas tip enough?"

In each of these situations, there are probably several reasons why things are going wrong. Yet your mind has learned to behave inappropriately by taking every issue *personally*. Something *you* have done is not usually the cause of the problem in other people.

That kind of pessimism about oneself is a major factor in causing emotional depression. Current research in psychotherapy has proven that chronic pessimistic thinking can be changed with study and practice. Just as pessimism is a learned style of thinking, optimistic thinking can be learned. Take for example a worried thought like, "I guess I have no future." When *Listening In* to that thought, most people will immediately recognize that it is not useful nor helpful. The pessimism will persist, however, until the worrier catches on that he is hurting himself with that thought. Then he can substitute something of some value to him, which may either be a quick Switch to his vacation planning, or to a long-range Reorienting in which he sets some life goals that will create a future for him.

Inappropriate Inner Speech weakens your thinking and your ability to direct your life. To achieve control of your own mind and life, keep your internal voices in key with the actual situation; think in appropriate terms. Keep a perspective on each situation. Listen In: If you will take a moment to think *about* what you are thinking, you almost certainly will be able to tell yourself when you are overreacting.

Here is a reminder to encourage you to do your own Power Shifting: Every conscious act has an inner dialogue that accompanies it. You are thinking all of the time. You can Power Shift your life if you will concentrate on what you think and how you think.

Again, there is solid research evidence that to think constructively and to visualize a productive outcome will greatly enhance your success in whatever you do.

Remember the Five Power Shifts that have been developed in this chapter to train your Inner Speech to make your thinking more powerful:

1. Your internal speech should be in *your own adult voice.*
2. Your internal speech should not echo *childhood guilt.*
3. Your internal speech should not *set you up.*
4. Your internal speech should be *in the present.*
5. Your internal speech should be *appropriate to the given situation.*

CHAPTER 10

WHAT TYPE OF THINKER (PERSON) ARE YOU?
IDENTIFYING THE PERSONALITY PATTERNS IN YOUR INNER SPEECH

Where are you in your life? All of us reach our own turning points over and over in our lives; in fact, turning points may occur every time we choose what to think.

Critical choices occur daily, but you may simply fail to notice them. Therefore, you need to maintain an alert sense of your own thinking—to step aside and observe your Inner Speech, especially during these daily turning points.

This is the basis of I.S.T.: Your style of thinking (indeed, the very thoughts you think) influences your feelings and behavior which form the turning points in your life. The second point is that you *can* change your style of thinking.

This chapter offers you a checklist to discover persistent patterns in your thinking and to guide you in how to change your thinking—and yourself.

You have the choice to think what you want.

Each person develops a special "style" of thinking. This "style" is what we call *personality*. Generally, personality is identified by what is seen on the surface—

the characteristic patterns of feelings and behavior that differentiate one individual from another. However, the *reverse* is actually true: these characteristic personality traits develop from one's style of thinking when a particular voice dominates the inner speech.

This chapter and those that follow offer an opportunity to examine your patterns of thinking. We will describe six unproductive, perhaps even neurotic, styles of thinking: Anxious/Phobic, Obsessive, Depressive, Narcissistic, Masochistic, and Defensive/Detached. By the final chapter, you will also have learned about a seventh thinking style—a healthy one. You can learn how, with practice, to convert your negative patterns into effective ones that bring happiness to yourself and to those around you. You will see changes in your personality and outlook, and will be able to develop new ways to solve many of your problems. Keep in mind that one of the key words is "Switch." To Switch your thoughts is not as easy as to switch a light from off to on; but it is worth the effort to learn to do it with your thinking. *Switching* puts circumstances in a brighter, truer light. It is enlightening. People are constantly doing it by *Switching* thoughts.

The following checklist is designed to help you diagnose your thinking and personality patterns. There is no grade scale, not even a pass/fail. Its purpose is to enable you to get to know your thinking and yourself a bit better.

THE CHECKLIST

1. a. Is your panic button almost always on "Alert"?

yes

b. Does your mind scream "disaster" as you buckle the plane's seat belt? *yes*

c. Do you tend to think your headaches are a sign of a brain tumor? *yes*

d. Do you have trouble breathing in crowded or enclosed spaces? *no*

e. Do people say you overreact to things? *no*

f. Do frightening voices in your head freak you out? *no*

2. a. Is your life largely blah? *yes*

b. Do many things seem impossibly hard to do? *yes no*

c. Does your mind seem empty? *no*

d. Do you often wonder if you have a future? *yes*

e. Is sex more trouble than it is worth? *no*

f. "The worst is yet to come." Could that be your motto? *yes*

3. a. Are you a prisoner of your thoughts? *yes*

b. Is it tough for you to take a stand? *no*

c. Do repetitive concerns plague you? *yes*

d. Are you too controlled? *no*

e. Are you quite stingy about showing your own feelings? *no*

f. Does a lingering anger occupy your thoughts? *no*

4. a. Is it safer to be alone? *yes*

b. Do you tend to regard an inquiry as an attack?

c. Does your mind work overtime to one-up people?

d. Do you feel it necessary to defend every decision you make?

    e. Do you think self-sufficiency is of major importance?

    f. Do you treasure being special and unique?

5. a. Do you feel sorry for yourself?

    b. Is it hard for you to see yourself first in line?

    c. Do things go wrong just when you are about to succeed?

    d. Do you keep your anger bottled up?

    e. Do you feel good when you feel bad?

    f. Do you feel more noble than those who are just having fun in life?

6. a. Are your preoccupied with yourself?

    b. Is your appearance the constant companion of your mind?

    c. Do you find that you switch the conversation to yourself?

    d. Do you feel diminished when someone else has the center of attention?

    e. Do your mind games have only one voice—yours?

    f. "Make my day. Tell me I'm wonderful." Does that sound like you?

7. Do you think:

    a. What if, what if, what if?

    b. I'll probably lose my job.

    c. My date will probably reject me.

    d. Sure, I got an "A" this time, but what will happen next time?

    e. I could faint in the supermarket.

    f. "Caution. Danger ahead." Could that be your motto?

8. a. Does nothing ever seem to go right?

b. Do you always seem to love someone who doesn't love you?

c. Is it easiest to make conversation when you are complaining?

d. Does it seem that there is no sense in going on?

e. Do you think you won't ever be happy?

f. Is your motto, "What a life!"?

9. a. Do your problems become permanent residents in your mind?

b. Are you irritated that others don't respect your careful planning?

c. "How can she have done that to me?" That was 6 months ago, and it still bugs you.

d. Should I or shouldn't I? Does it take terribly long to decide?

e. Do you long to be more perfect and have everything under control?

f. "To be or not to be?" Is that your question?

10. a. Do you spend a lot of time justifying yourself?

b. Do people tell you that you didn't answer the question?

c. Do you have a private inner life that no one should know about?

d. Are you considered a maverick, or a loner?

e. Do you prepare your excuses in advance?

f. "Keep your hands off me." Could that be your motto?

11. a. Do you often feel exploited?

b. Do you think you are a born loser?

c. Do you think you work harder than most everyone else?

      d. Do you rescue failure from the jaws of success?

      e. Do you do nothing when someone behind you talks throughout the movie?

      f. Does your sexual partner use you?

12. a. Do you think more about being loved than loving someone?

      b. Does your day center around getting compliments?

      c. Do people complain that you are self-centered?

      d. Do you become enraged when your faults are pointed out?

      e. Do you continue your single ways in a marriage?

      f. "Just mention my name." Is that a motto of yours?

After finishing the checklist, add the "trues" in each group. If you found that your "trues" are widely scattered, it probably indicates that your thinking is not rigid, and consequently, the more flexible is your personality. Your negativity is probably mild, and you have a large potential for growth.

If you had a large number of "trues" be careful not to catch "psychology student's disease," which is the belief that you have every problem and symptom in the book. Most beginning psychology students get this disease, but it is curable by further study.

If you found most of your answers concentrated in a few categories, you have learned the value of *Listening In*. You probably discovered some of your most common inner speeches. Those are the ones to watch for, think about, and probably Stop and Switch. In one way or other, all the thoughts in the checklist could be hurtful to you, and you will both think and feel better if you know your voice thoughts so intimately that you can change them the moment they pop up in your mind. *Knowing* your thoughts is the first step in *improving* them.

As we identify for you how we have grouped the various thoughts in the checklist, remember that this is not a test. Your answers will *not* "diagnose" your personality. It is simply a guide to help you Listen In.

CHECKLIST CATEGORIES

1 and 7 are Anxious/Phobic
2 and 8 are Depressive
3 and 9 are Obsessive
4 and 10 are Defensive/Detached
5 and 11 are Masochistic
6 and 12 are Narcissistic
The next chapters discuss them one at a time.

CHAPTER 11

THE ANXIOUS/PHOBIC THINKER
IT'S PANIC TIME

When a small child calls out to us at night that there's a monster in his room, we remain calm, turn on the light, and reassure him, because we know the monster is only in his imagination. We help him think differently, and that reassures him. Our fears change as we grow older, but they do not disappear. Sometimes those fears run wild and become an irrational and persistent dread. Then the fear is called a phobia.

If you're a phobic thinker, your mind is a welter of unreasonable fears, which deplete your energies and deprive you of enjoyment. Instead of thinking, "I'm really looking forward to the theater tonight," and setting yourself for a good time, you think, "What will we do if we forget our tickets?" "What if there's no parking space?" "What if there's a fire and people all crowd for the exits?"

"What if somebody I had a fight with is at the party?"

"What if a cute guy comes on to me and I can't think of a thing to say?"

"What if the elevator gets stuck?"

More desperate scenarios may come to mind: "*What will I do if there's a gunman in the bank—*" This can lead to the ultimate *What ifs*. "What will happen to me if I go outside?" "What will happen if I get out of bed?" Focusing on fears (which is to think about fears) increases fear, and fears may build to phobias.

We can fill our minds around the clock with fears of muggings, collisions, dangerous storms, and hijackings that never materialize. Even if something does go wrong, it won't be made any better by our having agonized about it for hours in advance. Those were simply ineffectual thoughts with no value whatsoever. Those fears neither prevented nor solved the problem.

What they have done was hurt us in many ways. They deprived us of space for more productive thinking, caused us unnecessary suffering, and destroyed our enjoyment of life. Worst of all, they threaten to turn into full-fledged phobias which can contract and restrict our lives. We all know people who never leave their houses, or never fly, or can't be in a room with a dog, a cat, a bird, or a bug. How impoverished they are!

Has this scene ever happened to you? Has your thinking been *so weak* that you were unable to write a positive script? Or you were so consumed by an unremitting worry that you couldn't enjoy anything? Have you been so frightened by an imaginary fear that you were not able to prevent your own mind from racing ahead with scene after scene of every possible type of disaster?

The most common frightening mind script is, What Will I Do If—? What will I do if—

I can't think of anything to say?

the boat sinks?

the cable breaks?

I can't find a bathroom?

I lose my mind?

Underline the weakening word... *IF*.

Note that all these experiences follow a *programmed "if" script*—they occur in the mind of the scriptwriter. The internal speech creates elaborate enactments of disasters that are *painful*. The "if" is followed by a disaster. The pain is being created by the thinker who finishes his sentence with a catastrophe.

Since it is not helpful for you to produce sentences in your head that begin with an "if" and end with a tragedy, now is a time to think of a different ending for your "if" sentences.

"If I call Bill and ask him to have lunch with me, it could be fun catching up on the news."

"If I take a trip, I will see a lot of fascinating places."

"If I take the elevator, that will be faster and easier than climbing the stairs."

You can choose to end your sentences any way you wish. It just takes practice. Reorient your thinking away from your fears even *before* the fearful thought gets a chance to get started.

If you are afraid of elevators, choose not to think about the elevator when you are in it.

If you are afraid of crowds, or going out, try to

think of what you are going to do when you reach your destination. Concentrate on each minute detail.

When you are anxious, you are thinking that there is something dangerous that you are unable to manage successfully. When you are thinking at your best, you know that there are *few* things in life that are so dangerous that you won't be able to handle them safely. But if your thoughts of danger seem to be overwhelming you, Switch off that thought of danger.

Even if it is only an immediate Switch to reading a grocery list in your mind, if you can fill your Inner Speech with a less frightening subject, you will drive out the fear and eventually move to a more pleasant subject.

NANCY'S PHOBIA

Nancy was a professor at a university in New York. She was a high achiever, worked very hard, and probably worried more than was good for her. Yet, she was the last person that you would expect to have a phobia. She was successful at her work, had a wide circle of friends, and basically enjoyed her life. One winter weekend she was in the northern part of New Hampshire skiing with a friend, and driving back to New York on a Sunday night they were caught in a terrible blizzard called a white-out, because visibility is reduced to nearly zero. The road became impassable, and the highway patrol advised all cars to pull off the road. Nancy was able to get off the highway and about ten feet up into the driveway of an abandoned farmhouse. As the snow and the wind raged, Nancy and her friend did not dare to leave the car. They kept running the engine for brief periods so they could use the car's heater. But they did not leave the engine on for too long for fear that they would run out of gas and freeze.

About an hour after the sun came up, the storm quieted, and a snowplow came through and made the highway passable.

When Nancy returned to New York, she felt very shaken by the experience of being trapped in a dark, enclosed space, not knowing for sure where she was, and not knowing when, or even if, she would ever get out safely.

The following day when she was taking her usual subway ride to the university, she broke out in a cold sweat, her vision blurred, her heart beat so frantically she felt as if it would burst through her chest wall, she felt she was going to faint, she was dizzy, and she wondered if she was dying.

It was a full-blown panic attack, a severe attack of claustrophobia. Nancy had ridden that subway hundreds of times, and never felt anything like this before in her life—either in or out of a subway. She made her way out of the subway at the next stop, and got a taxi to the college. But it was about 100 blocks from her apartment, and she knew she could not afford that twice a day. At the same time, she did not dare risk getting into the subway alone again. She did manage it when she was with a friend, but that was not a practical solution for her phobia.

She tried psychotherapy, and found a therapist who could help her quiet her panic by direct attack on her phobic symptoms. Nancy was quick to see the relationship between being trapped in a car on a dark night, and being in a subway car in a dark subterranean tunnel. But knowing that did not dissolve the fear.

The method that helped her calm her fears, and ride the subway successfully was to understand what was going on in her Inner Speech. Her phobia began when she was thinking neither about being trapped in her car nor about the dark subway tunnel. But unwittingly, something had caused her to trigger the fears that she had felt during that long night of the blizzard.

It would have been *interesting* for Nancy and her therapist to know exactly what the thought or memory was that started the phobia; but it was not *necessary* to do so in order for her to overcome her fears. She needed prompt results, because her fears were upsetting, they were beginning to affect other areas of her life, and the phobia was expensive—two hundred blocks a day in a taxi.

In her therapist's office she made a list of all the things that she probably could think about in the subway which would frighten her: being alone in the midst of strangers; all the doors were closed; when the train stopped between stations, would it start again; the tunnel was dark; what would happen if there was a blackout and all power was shut off, and they were led across the third rail.

These were the thoughts she learned to Stop. She practiced *Stopping* over and over again. Before long she could Stop the thought by the time she had thought *the first word* of any of her fears.

Then she practiced *Switching*. She prepared 10 pleasant, exciting, successful thoughts. She brought reading material that would hold her attention. She discovered that reading a technical work in her professional field, biochemistry, did not divert her attention from her fears. A suspenseful novel helped her Switch.

Then she Reoriented. She remembered her goals

and ambitions. She made a wish list, and kept adding to it as new ideas occurred to her. As she *reinforced her basic identity*, she strengthened her resolve to be rid of anything so sabotaging as a phobia.

With a mind filled with useful thoughts and Inner Speech Training techniques, she engaged a friend to ride the subway with her—but to sit across the aisle from her so she would be left alone to do her I.S.T. Then she had her friend sit at the other end of the car from her, and eventually in the next car. Then eventually she soloed, without a companion on the subway train with her. She was somewhat anxious. But she succeeded in riding all the way to the university, even though she had promised herself she could get off at any stop if the stress got too great for her.

The optimum therapy for Nancy was to help her develop her own set of thoughts and to be able to block out the thoughts that led to fears and phobias. One of the successful aspects of Inner Speech Training is that it enables a person to become his own therapist in a relatively short time. That in itself is a boost to one's self-confidence, and it provides another happy thought to Switch to, when overcoming an old fear.

Fears are in everyone. We start life about 20 inches long, 7 pounds of urges and appetites demanding satisfaction. We are helpless, and the rest of the world looms awesomely large. And so our fears begin.

The fears of infancy and childhood have been catalogued. The earliest fear is the loss of safety, especially the fear that arises from a sense of being dropped. A second fear at birth is of sudden loud noises. At eight months, the fear of strangers begins, followed swiftly by panic when separated from parents. By the time a child is a year old, the fear of physical injury is added to the list, and by age two, a child is thoughtful enough to have added fears of the dark, of large objects, and of changes in his familiar surroundings. The fear of animals arises at about age three, and threatening, mysterious, or supernatural creatures fearfully invade one's thoughts during the years six through eight. Growing intelligence after age nine allows one to become frightened of catastrophic events in the news, including one's own death. In preadolescence and adolescence, performance factors become fearsome, including fears of not being popular, of not succeeding in school, and the fear of sexual feelings and involvement.

Do those fears sound familiar to you? Well they may, because the same fears continue throughout life, staying basically the same while taking a somewhat more sophisticated shape. A loud truck in the street may not be frightening to an adult, but a sudden sonic boom will provoke thoughts of danger which will bring on that feeling of anxious dread.

The fear of abandonment, the fear of loss of love, and the fear of physical hurt are three fundamental fears that are thought to encompass all the specific fears that habitually, automatically, arise in our minds day after day.

The fears of childhood never are fully overcome; that is a fact of life. A goal of Inner Speech Training is to *recognize* fear, and not *deny* it. This is *Listening In*. It is important to *reflect* on the fear; this is *Underlining*. Processing what is going on in your mind will help you *evaluate* your fear.

Is it an accurate fear—exaggerated—childish—useful? Does the fear make sense? Will your fear lead you to better living? Slow it down. Does it do you any good?

JULIAN'S FEAR OF ABANDONMENT

Julian had a basic fear, one of those which has been there since infancy, and will show up in your mind all through your life. He had the fear of being alone, the fear of abandonment. He had these sentences occurring in his Inner Speech center: "I am alone. I am lonely. There is no one here for me. I don't know what I am going to do. Will it always be like this? I will probably spend my whole life alone. I am getting older. No one will want me."

What to do? Listen In. Identify the problem. The problem is that Julian thinks he is and will be alone. So far that is useful thinking because the problem has been pinpointed. What should be Underlined? Words like "no one," "always," "my whole life alone." Julian has now spent enough time dwelling on these thoughts. If he has begun to train his Inner Speech he will understand that it is not useful to keep those thoughts active in his mind. It is time to Switch. He knows the problem, and he knows he will depress himself if he dwells on the thought of being lonely, especially the thought that he will "always" be alone. Even the hardiest of personalities would become depressed if he were repetitiously to think that thought.

The task for Julian is to Switch immediately to any other thought. It is best to Switch to a thought that is pleasant, interesting, humorous, productive—anything to get off that abandonment theme as soon as possible.

Julian Switched to thinking about sports. If it was winter, he thought about basketball or boxing. If it was summer he Switched to baseball thoughts. That sounds like a superficial thing to do. But a pleasant, even though trivial thought, will be far more *helpful* to Julian than thinking that he will be alone all his life. Whenever his abandonment fears entered his head, Julian had a list of Switch thoughts.

Reorienting came next, and that meant solving the problem of his loneliness by thinking, imaging, and visualizing himself as a person with friends, companions, and eventually, someone to love. This was a longer-range project. He visualized a perfect day for himself now, a year from now, 5 years from now. That gave him a picture of his idealized self. He had a goal. He imagined what he would like a biographer to write about him. This gave him an idea about his basic values in life, the kind of man he was, what he stood for. Then he learned how to use a common time management technique. Several times a day he would ask himself how he could use the next few minutes to reach his goal of not being lonely. This motivated him to pick up the phone and chat for a few minutes. Other times he would read a book on how to make conversation, or photocopy diagrams of his family tree and send them to all his cousins, or follow through on his plans to take a course in assertiveness training. His Reorienting was successful because he daydreamed what he wanted to do, and then took sequential small practical steps to become who he wanted to be, and go where he wanted to go.

Julian had come by his fears of abandonment honestly. There were good reasons in his life history for him to have those fears, and they did not disappear from his mind entirely. Late at night, or when he woke up too early in the morning, or when he was very tired and under great stress, those old familiar thoughts of being alone would return. But a five-step I.S.T. program gave him the tools to overcome his fears, and he felt very much better about himself when he found that he was not helpless in the face of those fears.

Fears can gain control of vital areas of your life. If your fears prevent you from carrying on your normal everyday activities, or if, in the opinion of the average person, you are living an inhibited life—then you need to give your fears special attention so they will not stay with you, or encroach on you even further for the rest of your life. How can you tell if your fears are serious enough to require special, perhaps professional attention? Here is how to answer that question. The serious fears are the ones that sabotage your productive work, that block you from receiving and giving love, and that interfere with having fun. You are seriously hurting yourself if you let those fears go without treatment.

The goal of Inner Speech Training is to help you make your fears manageable; to change self-defeating thoughts into useful ones; and give you better control of your life. With this kind of training, fears can be mastered.

CHAPTER 12

THE OBSESSIVE THINKER
HE LOVES ME, HE LOVES ME NOT

"Should I go?
—What if I don't?"

Do you hear your Inner Speech saying, "Should I or shouldn't I?" Double-talk—both sides of every question—verbal juggling.

The minds of obsessive thinkers are very busy places. Thoughts are always feverishly at work inside them but, unfortunately, they're the kind of thoughts that never get anywhere. They just keep going round and round, exhausting their thinker and accomplishing nothing. They're the embodiment of Henry David Thoreau's observation that "It is not enough to be busy— the question is: What are we busy *about*?"

THE CURIOUS CASE OF CATHY

Cathy had gone on a cruise two years before and had become involved with a member of the crew. He was French, charming, and Cathy had really fallen for him.

Unfortunately, he was also married, which Cathy knew, but which didn't have much reality for her since she never saw him in a domestic situation. As Cathy put it, "Totally, unexpectedly, I fell in love. I realized what was happening one night on board ship when I spent a totally sleepless night. I knew then it was love. I couldn't get my mind off him. I couldn't bear for him to be out of my sight. Amazing things happened. It was very good for me. I began to exercise every day. I lost five pounds. I stood erect, and I felt beautiful. I day-dreamed beautiful thoughts for hours at a time. I wanted to dance instead of walk. It was just good being alive. At the same time, I wondered what was happening to me. I felt I must be crazy. Was this the real Cathy? But I didn't care. I was ecstatic when I was with him. When I wasn't with him, he was on my mind constantly, and even my thoughts were infatuating."

After the cruise was over, the affair continued. Jacques' ship docked in New York on Tuesdays, and he and Cathy would meet at her apartment and spend the afternoon making love. She had told her boss a story about prolonged dental work and needing to take off Tuesday afternoons.

Cathy worried about the limitations of the affair. But she had a skilled lover and she daydreamed of the time when they would be together more. At least she was sure she would keep seeing him Tuesday afternoons. But one day Jacques' ship was assigned to a new route, and the New York stops ended. Some painful thoughts began to creep into Cathy's mind.

A couple of weeks went by without any word from him, and she began to think about Jacques even more. There must have been some mistake. Did the mail get lost? Could he have mislaid her phone number?

The longer Cathy didn't hear from Jacques, the more strongly she heard her obsessive voices. "He'll call. I know he misses me." "He's got to call. I won't be able to stand it if he doesn't." Cathy's obsession nearly took over her life. It was a torment, with that voice at her every moment. "Suppose he calls and you are not here." Cathy knew she was contributing to her own suffering, but she seemed powerless to let go of her obsession. She clung to it because it was her *only link* with Jacques.

Gradually, as she talked about Jacques in her therapy sessions, she recognized that her hidden thoughts about him were filled with rage at him for what he had done to her. Cathy finally heard her own angry voice. She was furious at Jacques. She imagined a confrontation. She wrote a scenario in her head in which the telephone rang—in her head, of course. It was Jacques calling her back after the 6 months that had gone by since the cruise. Cathy took a deep breath and said to him, "Shove it. I don't care if your ship sank. Get lost, low life."

That was the voice that broke the spell. After she practiced that inner speech about fifty times, usually out loud, with plenty of feeling, she emerged from her obsessive thinking. She began to reclaim her mind, and herself. The power she had *given to Jacques* at last had returned to the place it belonged—inside her own head in her own inner speech center.

BEING STUCK

Every day, millions of people wake up in a jail— prisoners of their own thoughts. If you're one of these people, you wake up each morning to the same dialogue you woke up to yesterday morning—and the day before. Your thoughts are repetitive, inconclusive, and usually useless. Obsessive thoughts don't move you forward, and you know it; yet you can't seem to stop.

No matter how many times you ask yourself, "Why doesn't he call? He *said* he'd call," the phone is unlikely to ring. The answer to your question and the power to pick up the phone are in *his* head, not yours, and you can't put yourself into somebody else's head. What you need to do instead is redirect your thinking to its proper province: your *own* head.

Once you do that, you're on your way to freedom. You'll be able to get to the root of your obsessions by sorting out and expressing your true emotions.

Not all obsessions are without value. Many of the great moments of mankind have been due to a particular obsession, ranging from great scientific discoveries like radium to the building of castles and cathedrals that took centuries to complete. Much of our great literature is concerned with obsessiveness, ranging from *Madame Bovary*'s erotic preoccupations to the pursuit of the White Whale *Moby-Dick*. Many of the major characters in the fictional landscapes are governed and ruled by passions or obsessions, whether they be the immortal *Don Quixote* on his endless quest or the simple lusting of more modern Candides.

Almost all professional people are highly obsessive in their thinking. They have to be—to survive in working their way through professional training and, later, to retain good work habits which are often, by necessity, meticulous, repetitive, and dogged: what Freud ironically called—lining out the scientific method—"our poor patchy attempts."

Who would want to go to a doctor who did not make a *complete* inquiry about all the related symptoms, or to an attorney who neglected to incorporate *all* the relevant facts in preparing a case? Obsessive style serves us well in developing good school and work habits. The well-prepared homemaker should be a bit obsessive if she or he is going to do all of the necessary work effectively. The hidden clue here is, "What is all of the *necessary* work?" The obsessive thinker often can't decide.

Unfortunately, the obsessive style may also lead to constant undesirable thoughts that intrude painfully and control the inner speech. Obsessive thoughts come to dominate the normal necessary flow of more important and related thinking. Special thoughts and preoccupations lead to the development of obsessive inner speech, and the person is so programmed to think in a certain way that he becomes a prisoner of his own mind.

How do you recognize the harmless obsession that troubles your thinking? Focus on the following criteria. Keep in mind that there is much ambiguity about establishing a judgment of where a productive positive thought ends and where an obsessive thought begins.

Obsessive thinking is *harmful* when:

1. There is great *repetition* and *waste* in the recurring thought.
2. It represents an *overreaction*.
3. The overreaction is particularly *painful* and accompanied by a feeling of *anxious dread*.
4. The thinker realizes that basically the thought is "*useless.*"
5. The thinking has a routinely *oppositional* quality ("You say 'yes,' I say 'no' ").

6. The thoughts are filled with strong personal needs for perfection and control.

Thinking that is not obsessional maintains *flexibility* and *internal freedom* to adapt freshly to each new situation instead of repeating the same old response.

As soon as you recognize that the nature of the obsession is really a destructive voice, you can begin to STOP the voice and work on *Switching*.

"This voice really doesn't do me any good. I can tune in on a more helpful voice."

List your three most demanding obsessions. Practice *Stopping* each thought.

1. _____
2. _____
3. _____

The Stop and Switch techniques are the fastest and most effective techniques there are for the relief of obsessions. Obsessive thinking can go on almost endlessly—if you let it alone.

CHAPTER 13

THE NARCISSISTIC THINKER
ME, MYSELF, AND I

Some recorders of the world scene have dubbed our present era "The Age of Narcissism." Evidence of it is found in phrases like "the Me Generation" and "looking out for Number One."

Narcissists are preoccupied with their own needs, wishes, desires, appetites, ambitions, pleasures, and comforts, to the exclusion of anyone else's. They usually don't see anything wrong with their behavior, since it's certainly pleasant to have your own way in everything. The people we usually see in treatment are the ones who have to deal with narcissists in close relationships: and a more baffled, frustrated, exasperated group probably doesn't exist.

We hear laments like, "He hardly knows I'm alive"; "Not once has she ever asked what kind of day I've had"; "In six years of marriage I've never picked out a movie." What the troubled spouse or friend doesn't understand is that the first sentence is all too true. The narcissist *doesn't* know anyone else is alive. Other people are allowed to exist only if they worship the narcissist.

A narcissist is like a person with a hammering toothache. He's so consumed by his inner distress he has no room for other considerations. His self-centeredness is a device built to protect him from uncertainties about himself. Over the years, it becomes impenetrable, allowing no room for outside voices. You know you're dealing with a narcissist when your own practical, social, and sexual needs are ruthlessly and consistently ignored.

There are all levels of narcissism, of course, and all of us have it to some degree. You can check to see if yours is turning into a problem by asking yourself some questions: "Am I overly absorbed with myself?" "Do people I deal with get annoyed a lot?" "Does my family feel neglected?" "Have people frequently called me selfish?"

Contented narcissists may not see much reason to change; but experience demonstrates forcefully that narcissists eventually pay for their selfishness. Without noticing what they're doing, they drive people away until they begin to feel the pain of uninvolved loneliness and a hollow life.

Narcissism occurs when a person hears only his own voice. If this appears contrary to what was urged about listening to your own voice as much as possible, note a difference here, because the distinction is critical. It is very important to be sensitive to the voices of other people as well as to one's own. If a person doesn't consider what other people might be experiencing internally, and cannot appreciate others' feelings, then a narcissistic condition may exist.

A narcissist is someone who finishes a long monologue about himself and then says to his partner:

"Now let's talk about *you*. How do you like my new suit?"

WHAT DOES THIS MEAN TO YOU?

It means that in choosing friends, dates, and lovers, you should consider how well the other person relates to you. Is he or she heavily narcissistic?

Do they relate to your ideas? Do your wishes matter to them?

Frequently, people come for therapy with a particular problem, which is a variation of this same theme. Why can't I get along with T? T may be a friend — lover — coworker — relative.

The reason may be that the person has failed to realize the extent that *narcissism* has controlled the relationship.

THE NARCISSIST'S INTERNAL DIALOGUES ARE MOST APT TO BE MONOLOGUES

See if you can recognize the source of difficulty in this problem:

Karen R. was crushed. She was a highly responsible person, and felt defeated when she came in for therapy with a failing marriage. She described her husband Ken as a charmer, a devastatingly good-looking guy who dressed to the nines. He was successful at work but neglected Karen. He would go out most evenings, and played golf the entire weekend, leaving her alone at home with the children. Eventually, Karen came to learn the sad truth that Ken could deny others everything and refuse himself nothing.

Ken didn't seem to feel embarrassed about leaving his wife and children alone all weekend, plus several nights a week. The real problem didn't emerge until a complete history had been taken.

Ken, who reluctantly agreed to try marriage counseling, admitted that he never heard Karen's voice in his head. In fact, he never heard anyone else's voice in his head. His internal speech was a preoccupation with his needs, wants, desires, wishes, appetites, ambitions, pleasures. Unfortunately, as a narcissistic personality, Ken had no interest in changing. He didn't see anything wrong with his thinking. Fortunately, however, Karen did. She saw there was reality in her belief that he never considered her needs, and that she didn't exist for him.

Narcissists, usually after some painful reversal in life, can learn that others also have their own inner speech. Unlikely as it seems from the outside, narcissists live painful inner lives. A wounded, motivated narcissist can change, one tiny step at a time. First, he needs to Listen In and hear his own words about his own emptiness—which has often prompted him to compensate by saying, "I just made it with three gorgeous women, aren't I the jock?" The narcissist can hear that his inner voice is full of himself, and it hasn't made him happy. "Listen In and Underline." Tell that to a narcissist and he will find that he has only heard his own needs, his own voice, and his own desperate longing for attention.

Through *Reorienting*, a narcissist can, with a will to change, discover other thoughts, other voices, and then a richer world.

TREVOR'S CASE

Trevor was an elegant-looking man with a grandiose sense of his own importance. Three wives had divorced him, but there were always other women at hand ready to bask in his charisma. He had alienated his children from two of his marriages. His children found that being in his presence was like being in the theater watching a master showman. But just like being in the theater, there was hardly any direct interaction between the actor and the audience. Their father only wanted the children to laugh and applaud, never to be part of the act.

After three divorces, Trevor came to realize that he had no close friends. Everyone seemed to want him at a cocktail party, but no one wanted to spend a weekend or a vacation with him—at least not if they had known him for more than 6 months.

Trevor was spending more and more time alone, and it came to be depressing for him. He was psychologically addicted to attention, but he was finding that being noticed by others was beginning to mean less and less to him. He began to notice that he couldn't stand being alone for more than a couple of hours. After that he would want to be with someone, but found it unsatisfying because he resented having to make the effort to impress someone, and he often despised the people he would choose to impress.

Finally a college classmate, whom he had known for 30 years, had the courage to level with Trevor. He told Trevor that he was suffering from more than a mid-life crisis, more than the 20-year itch. His friend described the condition as a deep inner emptiness, which Trevor had tried to fill with women, cars, boats, and fitness. None of it had filled the hunger and longing he had for self-respect and self-love.

Trevor did not react kindly to this appraisal of himself. He never had been able to take criticism, and this had cut deeply and he tried to push it away. But he was highly intelligent, and typically, he thought he could help himself better than anyone else would be able to. He read articles and books about narcissism, and arrived at his own conclusion that he would try therapy. His motivation at that time was to become *more* perfect, more powerful, more sought-after. He thought therapy would help him to become the most successful narcissist in the world. Therefore, he tried to find the greatest psychoanalyst in the world so that he would be the patient.

Therapy did not go the way that Trevor expected. He quickly became enraged at the analyst, who confronted Trevor's inner emptiness, and interpreted his desperate attempts to fill it with notoriety. Two therapists later, Trevor found himself trying Inner Speech Therapy. That was not uneventful either; but his earlier therapies had at least softened him up a bit to listen to someone besides himself. He was able to listen to his new therapist, who told him the goal of therapy was not to become more perfect, but to become more human.

The first step in I.S.T. for him, of course, was to Listen In. When Trevor tried to Listen In, he only heard that he was the greatest, the handsomest, the best lover, the most brilliant, most gifted. But was there another inner voice under the voice of bravado? Trevor listened and listened, and began to hear it. He heard, underneath, that he had woefully little self-esteem. He thought he was superficial, that he had never been able to love anyone, and had never been able to know another person deeply because he could not empathize with another person's feelings.

This first step in therapy was depressing, even frightening, for Trevor. But here his old belief that he knew best helped him out. His therapist taught him the outline of how to proceed with Inner Speech Therapy, and Trevor set out to outdistance the therapist. He came into each session with new insights based on his own use and adaptation of the five steps of I.S.T. The painful insight into his condition alternately made him want to give up, or revert back to impressing yet another desirable woman. But eventually he pushed on to find an end to the meaninglessness he had always felt in his life.

Listening In and *Underlining* were so painful for Trevor that he was an apt student of *Stopping* and *Switching*. But he had little experience in *Switching* to anything but narcissistic grandiosity. He then decided, on his own, of course, that he would make an academic study of empathy. Perhaps this would be powerful enough to draw him away from narcissistic thoughts. This proved to be the tactic that enabled him to Reorient. For longer and longer periods he was able to enjoy the fulfillment that came from knowing another person deeply. When he learned to give unselfishly more and more, he began to respect and, eventually, *like* himself—and others. He tried the same tactic in his work. Rather than going for the quick fix and the flashy show, he found it fascinating to begin to study something in depth.

Now when Trevor sees his name in lights in his fantasy world, he has an automatic thought that goes Stop, Switch, Reorient.

CHAPTER 14

THE MASOCHISTIC THINKER
THE PLEASURE OF PAIN

"Who, *me*? *Want* to suffer?"

That's what everybody says; but the truth, in many cases, is just the opposite. There are persons who actually cherish Murphy's law and secretly hope that anything that can go wrong will go wrong.

Ralph Waldo Emerson said, "There are people who have an appetite for grief." Many otherwise intelligent human beings have set themselves up to suffer to some degree or other. Some are mild practitioners of this ultimately self-defeating type of thinking; others carry it to extremes. Masochism ranges in severity from not allowing one's self to succeed to actually enjoying pain. And there are stops all along the way.

The masochistic thinker is one who confuses weakness with strength, who attempts to control others by manipulating others by his suffering. Masochists are self-critical and loaded with self-imposed guilt, most of it with little basis in common sense. If

177

you dig far enough back, you're more than likely to find a "put-down" parent whose words and attitudes the person internalized as a child. The masochistic child learned that he could keep himself safe in the family by putting himself down, or at least not thinking and acting in a way that indicated that he was happy and successful. His basic thought about himself became the belief that he was guilty and unworthy. The natural result of his sense of himself was that pain and suffering was his lot in life.

The next time you compliment a woman on her dress, notice whether or not she replies with something like, "This old bag is fifteen years old," or "Blue's not my color but it was on sale."

We do not know what thought this woman might have had between your compliment and her apologetic response. Perhaps Marcia's discovery sheds light on the need to apologize.

Marcia discovered during I.S.T. that her "in-between thought" after a compliment was "I'm not really attractive." And then when she Listened In even more carefully she found another thought that she recognized had been there since childhood. It was, "I am not supposed to think I am pretty. *That* is 'vain.' "

It is no wonder that Marcia felt uneasy whenever she was complimented, because a compliment was always paired in her mind with a parallel thought of how *vain* it was for her to look nice.

Most people have gone through life never paying attention to this stream of thinking that underlies and *determines the feeling*. People most often feel the *feeling* without connecting it to the cause of the feeling. Marcia was programmed to apologize for herself when complimented, and she did not consciously know why until she discovered the hidden power of her hidden speech.

Unfortunately, this thinking pattern can become solidly entrenched. The sufferer doesn't think himself worthy of happiness and puts obstacles in the way whenever good times threaten to come too close. The thinking goes something like this: "It's a beautiful day—perfect for the tennis matches. But the house is a mess (or the lawn needs mowing). I'd better stay home and take care of it." This is followed by a deep sigh and a surreptitious feeling of nobility. "See how *good* I am," it proclaims. "*I* don't fritter away my time. You go to the tennis matches and enjoy yourself!" Whether the other person goes or stays, the day has been ruined. The masochist, beginning with his own guilt, has successfully passed on his guilt to others.

Masochistic thinking exacts a terrible toll on both the masochist and those around him. The masochist thinks he is not entitled. He then is annoyed with others who do enjoy life. When masochism can be understood and stopped as it originates, one's self-esteem will rise; injustice-collecting will diminish; "punishments" will be replaced by rewards. After all, if we think about it, we know there are better ways to get pleasure than by feeling pathetic and sorry for ourselves.

HOW MUCH MASOCHISM IS IN YOUR THINKING?

Do you wash the dishes alone in the kitchen while the rest of the family is watching the Superbowl?

Do you chronically feel sorry for yourself?

Do you get turned on sexually by seeing yourself put down?

If you are suffering in any way, *the burden of proof is on you to prove that you haven't brought it on yourself.*

We recognize that there is enormous innocent suffering because of discrimination, poverty, war, physical and mental handicaps—just getting bad breaks through the accidents of living.

We are aware that there are self-centered and simplistic self-help writings that ignore the complexities of the problems in the world. Such real problems cannot be wished away by just thinking happy thoughts. We offer the Inner Speech Training procedures in order for any person to be more effective in the quest for social betterment. The means to eliminate needless fears and discouragement brought on by depressogenic thinking can lead to more successful thinking, and thus to greater emotional and physical stamina. Effective reformers do not come from the ranks of the completely downtrodden thinkers. The battering imposed on oneself by chronically depressed or masochistic thinking will probably make it impossible for such thinkers to contribute to the betterment of society. I.S.T. is a means of avoiding the pitfalls of that weak thinking.

Therefore, for present purposes, when thinking about *yourself*, it is best to disregard the unfortunate and unfair accidents of your history. You are ultimately responsible now for the trend of the thoughts in your mind. When thinking now about your own thinking, your time is best spent in finding the answer to this question: "What voices am I hearing in my inner speech?"

Masochists start their inner speech by thinking:

"Happiness is impossible."

THEREFORE, MASOCHISTS—

Prove to themselves that the world is not a happy place by anticipating and then provoking rejection and disappointment. They become angry that they were treated this way, feeling sorry for themselves. Masochists collect injustices. They savor a sweet sadness as they prove to themselves that the world is no damn good. They know suffering. They expect it. Masochists go on weak-thinking:

> "I am *safer* if I put myself down. If I beat them to it, nobody else can do it."

THEREFORE, MASOCHISTS—

Anticipate and expect criticism, even imagine it when criticism may not be there. Their own self-criticism beats others to the punch. They use about half their mental energy preparing for criticism. They capitulate (and give indications of weakness) as a way of life with spouse, boss, neighbors, and friends.

Masochistic Self-Defeating Thinking runs:

> "I think people will take better care of me if I suffer (i.e., don't do well)."

THEREFORE, MASOCHISTS—

Provoke guilt in other people by playing the martyr. The masochist says, "I didn't do well." The other person thinks: "Then I must not have done well either." The masochist inflicts pain on others.

MASOCHISTIC RUSS

Russ fit the stereotype so completely that it almost seemed he had studied books on masochism so he could imitate all the traits that ma--chists were known to have. He even had the same s, nptom as novelist Leopold von Sacher-Masoch—from whom the term was derived: Russ also wished that his wife would be unfaithful to him, and provoked it in strange ways, as Sacher-Masoch had done in the nineteenth century.

Russ was born a few months after his father had died. His mother was depressed and under great stress. He learned early to feel guilty for his existence, because he felt he was the cause of his mother's imprisonment in a life of drudgery. When Russ was four his mother remarried. Her second husband was much older, with four grown children. Russ again felt an unwanted child. To keep her new husband happy, Russ's mother spent as little time with Russ as possible. Any trouble he caused gave rise to rage on the part of both his parents.

Russ grew into a quiet, compliant boy who tried always to be pleasant and ingratiating. He tried never to put himself forward, nor to call any attention to himself. As a child, he literally had felt that his life would be in danger if he stood out in any way. The rage he felt inwardly at being constantly mistreated was buried so deeply he rarely experienced it. But occasionally he would have dreams of destroying the world, followed at once by a scene in which he was tortured.

The roots of his masochism are classic. Given those early experiences when his personality was being formed, he could scarcely have turned out any other way. When he was nearly 40 he married a dominating woman much older than himself. After 2 years of marriage, she grew so angry at his helpless masochism that she threatened him with divorce unless he sought therapy.

Where should the therapy begin? The answer to that was easy. It could begin with practically any thought that came into Russ's mind. His thoughts were filled with one message, "Don't make waves." His masochistic life-style was being reinforced minute-by-minute as he thought, "I will be in danger if I am assertive, or outstanding, or intelligent, or act in any way as if I am entitled to anything at all."

Inner Speech Training could have been very prolonged and difficult for Russ except for the fact that he had an extremely high I.Q., and he was eager to please any person in authority, including, in this situation, his therapist. His rage at anyone in positions of power or prominence was explored with him, so he could understand at last he had someone who wanted him to stand up for himself rather than be a doormat. His therapist and he had a good working relationship.

Listening In came slowly, because most of his put-down thoughts were so automatic that he did not attend to them. In time he heard his inner voice, and Underlined what he called his philosophy of life: to be nonexistent. His words were "Don't speak first, don't offer a suggestion; people don't like me, get away from others as soon as I can before I make a mistake and get thrown out"; and so on.

Russ found it difficult to Switch at first, because

his habits of martyrdom were so ingrained that he could scarcely conceive of any other way to think of himself or his life. He thought at age 42 he would never be able to Switch. But here he found the five-step program of I.S.T. particularly helpful because it gave him a *formula* that he could *follow*. He only had to learn how to fill in the blanks, 1, 2, 3, 4, 5. This he did, and the progress, after many repetitions, became nearly automatic. He was a C.P.A., and accustomed to following set accounting principles. He finally found it easy to change his thinking by a formula he could understand.

The most difficult inner thought for Russ was that he would be in great danger if he did not allow himself to get walked on. The classic theory of masochism is that one thinks one will be castrated if he seeks pleasure. To uproot the roots of his masochism he practiced saying sentences of entitlement: everything from, "I would like a glass of water" in a restaurant, to "I want to make love with you, Marie," when with his wife. The old automatic thought was that he would be rejected. In the presence of his therapist he could examine that thought more realistically, and recognize that the request was reasonable and apt to be met with a positive response. And, he realized, even when the answer was no, he could continue the discussion and find some satisfying options.

After practicing different thoughts, he was able to translate his thoughts into behavior. Naturally, his anxiety would rise on those occasions but, with increasing success, he felt less guilty about his needs and wishes, and more entitled to take the next step of seeing himself as a human being with the same rights as other humans in the world.

Ten years after his therapy concluded, he wrote a

Christmas card to his therapist on which he said, "I'm still throwing off the shackles of the past. I hardly ever hear that old voice that used to say, 'I'm worthless, I can't make it.' The sentence I most often hear now is, 'I am going to do some of the things I want.' Life seems good. I'm enjoying it."

Listen In. Do you feel sorry for yourself in those private inner speeches that only you can hear? And can you admit to yourself that it makes you feel a little special that you are such a self-sacrificing martyr? STOP. Why? Because your thoughts lead you on to more defeat and suffering. You are rewarding yourself for suffering. If you reward yourself for it, you will seek out more suffering. Is that really what you want in life?

Listen In and Stop the masochistic thought right at the beginning. The weak thought yields the painful feeling. Underline it and Reorient your thinking to those experiences where pain is not the primary pleasure.

CHAPTER 15

THE DEPRESSIVE THINKER
THINKING THE WORST

We're all sad from time to time. When we confront the death of a loved one, the end of a romance, the loss of a job, or even a major disappointment, we're bound to be sad. That's part of the human condition.

But when sadness is *self*-generated and becomes a *constant companion*, psychology calls it by another name: *Depression*. The most common personality problem in our culture is depressive thinking. To a depressed person, sadness is a way of life. The outlook is always gloomy. Depression saps your strength, eliminates your enthusiasm, and turns life into misery. At its most extreme, it reduces the sufferer to despair and thoughts of suicide.

There's a vital difference between a legitimate sadness and depressive thinking. The former is always related to a genuine distress. Something real, usually some loss, has happened, and it has happened recently. On the other hand, the person who is lamenting a lost love 5, perhaps even 20, years after the event, has been nurturing depressive thoughts. Rooted in a painful loss of self-esteem, this type of thinking overplays self-blame. "He didn't love me, which only goes to prove I'm not lovable" is the thought about yourself that comes to mind and, worse, stays there.

Thinking your way up from depression begins with sizing up your thinking about your life. What is your sense of your self in the world, and how do you manage yourself in it?

Your beliefs about yourself and your beliefs about how you manage your world contain the key to your sense of self. Those beliefs are worth examining, at least daily. There are certain thoughts that lead to competence and confidence. The thinking of competent people has been subjected to careful research, and how they think can be practiced and learned by everyone—if not perfectly, certainly with considerable success.

Some thoughts about yourself can and do lead to stress and powerlessness, in great contrast to the thinking that leads to confidence. For example, whenever you are thinking that the outcome of some event in your life will be negative, you are almost surely going to depress yourself.

Thought has had little systematic psychological study until recently. The latest research has centered on both *how* to think and *what* to think. It is now known *what* thoughts lead to emotional disorders. As a result, Inner Speech Training is able to describe those destructive thoughts in detail. How to change those thoughts can now be taught by a systematic process that shortens both the degree and the duration of emotional suffering.

It all starts with your thoughts about yourself. What are your thoughts about yourself?

If you categorized your thinking as depressed when you finished the checklist, then you know the overwhelming feelings of helplessness that kind of thinking produces. You think nothing excites you. You think you are bored. You think your prospects look bleak. You think you will never lose weight. You think you will always be incompetent. You think nothing will make any difference.

Experience has shown that depression responds dramatically to a restructuring of one's thoughts. Pick out the destructive words in the last paragraph: "Never." "Always." "Nothing." Those are the villains in the piece, the universalizations that bind you. They fortify your feelings of helplessness and impair your power to function. If things will *never* be right, why try?

Depressed people are the victims of distorted thinking. The depressed person accentuates the negative, eliminating the positive. Thus, they see their environment as barren and themselves as a container of shortcomings.

Fortunately, that kind of thinking can be stopped.

LIVING WITH DEPRESSING VOICES

The story is told of the man who came to see the psychiatrist, complaining of depression. "What's the trouble?" asked the doctor.

"Well, two months ago my grandfather died and left me $75,000. One month ago, a distant cousin died and left me $100,000."

"So why are you depressed?"

"This month, *nothing*!"

Depressed people will find *something*, anything to *think* about that will depress them.

Are there heavy, serious voices meeting constantly in your mental space, filling your head with ideas that cause you to feel *blue* or *sad*?—Heavy voices packed with *weakening* words and stopping you from experiencing more powerful thinking?

Are you able to connect these negative feelings about yourself and your world with recurring patterns of negative thoughts? If you Listen In, you will notice most of these repetitive negative statements about yourself are connected to a *preceding automatic thought*— a thought that enters your mental space without deliberate conscious selection.

More and more attention has been paid recently to the fact that we develop *automatic voices* even when we don't want them. Since they appear so readily, they seem to be automatic. But, in fact, they can be stopped. The negative feelings associated with the inner voices can be prevented.

Randolph felt uneasy whenever the TV weather announcer predicted that the next day would be a beautiful one. After he did some detective work on his thinking, he learned that "beautiful day tomorrow" brought on an immediate response in his thinking of "a nice day makes demands on me." What demands? Randolph was a loner, and a nice day made him feel guilty, because so many people had told him that he should be out making the most of his day: looking for a job, meeting a friend, going to the beach. As he Listened In further, he heard his inner speech becoming angry at his therapist. He had become uncomfortable about his therapy recently, and *Listening In* and *Underlining* uncovered his thought that the therapist would expect him to be more active and get more involved in life. And worse, he thought his therapist regarded him as a failure in therapy, and disliked him for his slow progress.

When Randolph marshaled these thoughts which he said just "popped into his mind," he could then look at them and discuss them more sensibly. He came to realize why he automatically "felt" badly about the prospect of good weather, and why he "felt" badly about coming to therapy. Once he knew that his feelings came from certain thoughts, he was able to do something about those thoughts.

The hidden power of his hidden inner speech was no longer hidden after he learned how to search for those automatic thoughts. The thoughts were not useful nor true, and he changed them. At that point he was able to control his feelings.

It is important in dealing with the unwanted and unjustified voices that keep causing depression to match the "down" feeling with the negative thoughts that precede it.

Keep a record. Every time you feel "blue," what is the thought behind it? Is that thought so necessary that you *have* to have it? Or would you be better off without it?

Consider the thought. What makes it so automatic? You may still think you have no voluntary control over those so-called automatic thoughts. But you can control your own mind. Is it vital to your existence to have that thought and feel bad? You can decide what to think.

Build a bridge to more positive self-esteem by learning how to deal with your own inner voice on more realistic terms. The first step is to rid yourself of the persisting negative voices in your head.

To become depressed beyond ordinary temporary sadness at a life event involves three different thinking distortions: distorting the view of your past, your present, and your future.

1. DEPRESSED PERSONS DISTORT WHAT THEY SEE (PRESENT)

Persons who chronically get "down" interpret the environment in a distorted pessimistic way to draw the maximum negative feelings into their mind.

There are several common ways that depressed people do this: They pick up mainly negative messages from their world. If it rains, they dwell on those aspects of the day that are interrupted. "It only rains when I have something special to do." "Why does the teacher *sigh only* at me?"

They have not learned to control the automatic thoughts that put themselves in jeopardy. They undo a happy thought almost as soon as it appears. "I enjoyed the Michael Jackson concert. I'll never have a glamorous career like that."

2. DEPRESSED PERSONS DISTORT THEIR OWN HISTORY (PAST)

Depressed persons can spot their faults like a scientist looking through a microscope.

They magnify their own past failures.

Their self-worth is in the state of a perpetual bear

market—falling, falling. No ability or achievement, however publicly acclaimed, is acceptable evidence of either their worth or talent. They have six plausible inner thoughts and ready excuses for why they didn't merit any good thing in their lives. "I think I just knew how to fool people." In severe depression, a person may think, "I should never have been born."

3. DEPRESSED PERSONS DISTORT THEIR FUTURE CHANCES (FUTURE)

They believe things will get worse for them.

They have been predicting a crash in their well-being for years. They will flunk the test, lose their job, be overwhelmed by life, end up needing round-the-clock nursing care. A cure for cancer may someday be discovered, but they think it will come only after they are dead. "Things are bad now, but the worst is yet to come."

These thoughts are examples of people overresponding to thoughts going on in their heads. These off-target thoughts divert the thinker from certain important data about themselves. *All three distortions lead to a dominating inner weakness.*

How many times have you overlooked positive traits in yourself to search out the negative ones when you are feeling low? Negative statements about you prevail, especially when you are already down.

"You don't understand. Things really are bad for me. It won't work out."

You have heard the story of the man who went to

see a psychologist because he felt he had an inferiority complex. After interviews and tests the psychologist told him, "You don't have an inferiority *complex*. You are *truly* inferior."

An apocryphal story, we hope, but it raises an important issue for the study of Inner Speech Training. What if you are pessimistic for good reasons—that is, you are completely *realistic* in expecting that you will fail at something? Should you be Pollyanna and deny reality? The answer is no. I.S.T. calls for truthful and accurate thinking. It can be useful to think negatively when it is factually negative. Negative thinking is an early phase in self-improvement. It provides an analysis of the problem so that a plan for productive thinking can begin.

A bad situation is made worse by thinking dominated by fright and helplessness. When panic and despair take over, the mind becomes woefully inefficient. Haven't you been almost unable to say your own name when you were acutely anxious? It is this kind of thinking that needs to be Stopped and Switched.

There is scarcely anyone who cannot better his or her own life. However bleak things are, virtually anyone can cope with the world more successfully with a thinking style that reduces the focus on discouragement and worry, and instead provides a means to be more relaxed and efficient in one's thinking. The negative thought is worth *Listening In* to, and it helps to gripe and let off some steam (up to a point). But getting it off your chest is only the preliminary exercise. The next thing is to Switch to productive and problem-solving thinking. As the Scottish poem goes, "I'll lay meself down and bleed awhile, and rise and fight again."

When negative thinking is allowed to become habitual it becomes depressogenic (depression-causing) thinking.

Listen In and start to repattern your negative thinking.

Ferret out the automatic thought that exists as a voice in your head, and occurs behind every negative feeling.

It takes work to become aware and connect the feeling with the thought that existed *immediately* before it. You will change your feeling when you become more aware of the *automatic thought* that caused the feeling in the first place.

Use the following checklist of feelings as a start in identifying those *feelings* that flow from depressogenic *thinking*.

How often do you have each of the following symptoms?

	Never	Some- times	Fre- quently	All the time
1. Feel sad, blue/ down	____	____	____	____
2. Feel lack of satisfaction in most things	____	____	____	____
3. Feel lonely	____	____	____	____
4. Feel bored/ little interest in most things	____	____	____	____
5. Decline in sexual interest or pleasure	____	____	____	____

  6. Trouble falling
     asleep or stay-
     ing asleep   ____ ____ ____ ____
  7. Poor appetite   ____ ____ ____ ____
  8. Cry easily or
     feel like
     crying   ____ ____ ____ ____
  9. Little or no
     energy   ____ ____ ____ ____
10. Easily fa-
     tigued   ____ ____ ____ ____
11. Feeling hope-
     less   ____ ____ ____ ____
12. Feeling
     slowed down   ____ ____ ____ ____
13. Blame your-
     self, overly
     self-critical   ____ ____ ____ ____
14. Withdrawn   ____ ____ ____ ____
15. Increasingly
     indecisive,
     unable to act   ____ ____ ____ ____
16. Suicidal feel-
     ings and
     preoccupa-
     tions   ____ ____ ____ ____
17. Worried   ____ ____ ____ ____
18. Overly preoc-
     cupied about
     minutiae   ____ ____ ____ ____
19. Feeling of dis-
     appointment
     and disgust
     with oneself   ____ ____ ____ ____

20. Have trouble
making plans _____ _____ _____ _____

WHAT ARE THE CHARACTERISTICS OF THESE DEPRESSIVE THOUGHTS?

In content. These thoughts overreflect the dejected mood persuasively. The common themes are worthlessness, hopelessness, pessimism, and despair.

Depressed persons take their suffering very *seriously*. They are unable to see that frequently there is a selected focus on the negative in the environment. They feel so bad that they ignore any evidence that will relieve their pessimism and cheer them up. They block out ideas that will disturb their relentless pessimism.

In structure. Starting with false premises, depressed persons draw false conclusions.

Look at these depressive sentences again. Underline all the overly negative generalizations.

"What's the use—nothing ever goes right."

Underline *nothing*.

Is it really true that nothing goes right, or have you structured your thinking so that you are going to make yourself feel that way? Try this sentence:

"I just can't cope with anything."

Underline *anything*.

Is it true; or is it again a tendency to overgeneralize in such a fashion that you feel bad because of an *exaggerated* conclusion?

Depressed people are constantly "setting up" negative circumstances to prove their worthlessness, and the hopelessness of the situation. For instance, they commonly withdraw and isolate themselves. Then they use the withdrawal to prove that:

> "No one likes or cares for me. How could they? I'm no fun."

Or they *focus on an irrelevant aspect of a problem*, such as ruminating in a guilty way:

> If *only I had* —
> " —raised my children differently —"
> " —bought that IBM stock in the forties —"
> " —taken that other job —"
> " —married him when I had the chance —"

The solution to ending your depression is a simple one; but it requires much effort on your part. And, of course, if you are depressed now, it is understandably difficult for you to try hard. But we challenge you to bring yourself out of depression by *Listening In, Stopping*, and *Switching*.

PETE'S DEPRESSION

Pete had lost the last job he held, and he felt it was because he had not done as well as he should have. He blamed himself for lack of a graduate degree, lack of drive, not being able to get along with his boss, not feeling comfortable with his fellow workers, and poor speaking and writing skills. The list was actually longer than that, as is typical of a seriously depressed person. He could list his shortcomings in excruciating and endless detail.

He had already been laid off before the stock market crash of 1987, so he had a very difficult time finding another job. The longer he was unemployed, the more depressed he became. It was hard for him to look through the papers to see what jobs were available. It seemed nearly impossible for him to send out his resume. He blocked when it came to phoning about a possible job interview.

After many months he started therapy. No one would deny that it is depressing to be unemployed. But as is the case with most depressives, he did not believe that he was causing his depression by what he was thinking. He thought he was being completely realistic in being depressed. Things were awful out in the real world. What did the therapist know about how depressing it was to be out of work? Wouldn't anyone be miserable if he had fouled up, the stock market crashed, and no one wanted to hire him?

Pete and his therapist worked on learning a new language, a language that did not produce nor reinforce depression. Pete had once studied French, and had spent a summer in France during his student days, so he could remember what it was like to speak a different language. It was this memory that helped him become an excellent student of Inner Speech Training. He used his previous language training to learn not to speak "Depression," and learned to speak what he simply chose to call, "Well-being."

This is the way Pete put it. "You have to think French words before you can speak French words. The English word occurs to you first, automatically. Then you stop that word, and switch to a French word. You have to go slowly at first because you can't come up with the French word that fast. The English word keeps going through your mind until you Switch it out. Then the French word finally comes through if you have studied the subject enough."

Pete continued, "When you are in the habit of speaking 'Depression,' that language will come up first in your mind. It takes practice; you know you don't want to speak 'Depression' anymore, so you switch it to 'Well-being' words."

Pete told this story about his experiences in searching for a new job. "I was sure I would foul up when I had a job interview. But I knew that sentence was spoken in 'Depression' — a language I didn't want to speak anymore. Those words would actually program me to do poorly. I had Listened In and heard the wrong language. I decided to speak the new language I was learning: I will prepare myself well. I will write out a few important things I want to say during the interview, and be able to say them confidently. That will help me to be more relaxed when I speak. I know that studies show that it takes about 20 interviews to get a job in my field at the salary I want."

His new language did help him to be far more self-assured. He thought something constructive, focused on what he could do, rather than what he couldn't do, and blocked out useless worry. He knew he would get a job after about 20 interviews, and he did.

As in learning to speak French, you can choose to say an English word or, with practice, you can eventually say a French word. That is a key concept in Inner Speech Training. Learning to speak any foreign language is basically the same as doing I.S.T. Most people will admit that they could take a course and eventually speak a foreign language fluently if they were exposed to it on a daily basis. But depressed people are very wary about believing that they could stop speaking "Depression," and learn to speak what Pete called "Well-being." Pete has now become something of a propagandist for I.S.T. His opening line to depressed people now is, "You always have the option of stopping the old words that have made you depressed. You can now choose to speak the words that make for well-being."

CHAPTER 16

THE DEFENSIVE–DETACHED THINKER
THE OFFENSIVE DEFENSE

In the classic story, a traveling salesman gets a flat tire on a dark, lonely road and then finds that he has no jack. He's delighted when he sees a light on in a farmhouse along the road, and he starts walking toward it. As he walks, his mind churns: "Suppose no one comes to the door." "Suppose they don't have a jack." "Suppose the guy is unfriendly and won't lend me his jack even if he has one." "I should have had my own jack." The harder his mind works, the more agitated he becomes, and when the door opens, he punches the farmer in the face, yelling, "You can keep your lousy jack!"

That story stays in people's minds because it represents a common type of thinking, something we all indulge in from time to time: defensiveness, and staying away (detached) from other people. This inner speech script is one in which we play two parts—our own and the other person's. Our Inner Voice plays a large part in the dialogue we invent. And so, in our script, the other guy is always unfriendly, angry, or accusing, and we're always justifying our behavior, defending ourselves, and thinking we should have stayed away from him in the first place.

We may not punch anyone, but we assault people verbally with a barrage of defenses. If you're a defensive thinker, you spend a lot of your time reacting to imaginary conversations. You think someone else's voice is always in your head, berating you. And you fill your mind answering the recriminations. "I couldn't help being late. There was an accident on the highway." "I didn't forget your birthday. The store was out of the right color in your size. They have to order it." Sometimes the excuses are in response to an actual complaint, sometimes merely to the voice in your head. Finally, you get exhausted and decide "People aren't worth it."

Defensive thinking is characterized by excessive explaining, in which your mind is forever justifying what you did or what you're about to do. It originates in defensive–detached persons because they think it is a hostile world out there, and they have to be ready at every moment to defend against the attack that is bound to come. Part of their defense is to be ready to justify everything they ever did. Part of the defense is to cover up and stay away from the supposed attackers. The effect of this defensive thinking is that the person refuses to be direct or to deal with the matter at hand. All this defending weakens a person rather than defends him. The very act of constructing excuses and explanations tires one out, and also makes one *look* weak. It's a case of "The lady doth protest too much."

THE OFFENSIVE DEFENSE OF RUDOLPH

Rudolph was a brilliant scientist by the time he had graduated from college. His potential had been recognized when he was fourteen months old actually, when his parents discovered that he somehow could read the "Stop" and "Slow" signs in the street. He was placed in special schools for the gifted, and did brilliantly in every subject, but especially math and science.

He developed a personality that could readily be seen as defensive–detached. His relationships with his parents and also his siblings were distant and uninvolved. He developed a quiet aloofness, and seemed to others to have virtually no feelings about anything. He had an incredible command of the English language, and could fend everybody off with extremely logical arguments about why he was doing what he was doing, and why everyone else should leave him alone. In everything, he attempted to be entirely self-sufficient. He devised any number of schemes to insure his privacy. When he was urged to take up a sport, he studied all that were available, but was drawn only to individual rather than team sports. He settled on tennis. Then he decided to hit the ball against a blank wall rather than play with another person. With his mathematical mind, and his inner need to stay detached, he realized the ball would only go half as far if he hit it against the wall, and would come back to him in half the time, thereby allowing him to hit the ball twice as many times in a half-hour period. He could rationalize all this by saying that the purpose of exercise was to *exercise*, and he was only interested in doing it with optimum speed. Only much later was he able to see that his "efficiency" was essentially a defensive mechanism by which he avoided any involvement with another person.

Rudolph's personality had developed into a defensive–detached one very early. His parents often told the story that at the age of nine months he had thrown his bottle over the side of the crib in anger, and never sucked on a nipple again. He toiled-trained himself also at about nine months, and never wet a diaper or the bed again.

The origins of his patterns came about by an engulfing mother and father, probably from the time Rudolph was born. An older sibling had died in his crib before Rudolph was born, and the cause of death was never completely ascertained. When his precocious intelligence became known, he was hovered over even more, and he fought his parents off with an iron curtain of detachment and rapier-like responses. Generally, he tried to avoid verbal contact of a personal nature, because he felt he then stood less chance of getting pushed around, and he would suffer less.

After Rudolph finished graduate school, he started work in a research center. Even though his colleagues respected him, and recognized that he was a loner, certain demands were made on Rudolph to be a team player and communicate among peers during staff meetings. These were demands that he had largely been able to avoid throughout his life. As a result of his successes in navigating his way through life in a detached way, he had few social graces, and almost no ability to make small talk. He was inhibited, bumbling, often rude, and beneath it all, terribly fearful. As bright as he was, he knew that there was something seriously odd about him. He suffered less when he could make his detachment work for him, but he was extremely sensitive when he experienced how little basic self-esteem and self-confidence he had.

His inner turmoil and pain made him decide he had to do something about his condition. He wanted to do it all alone, as he had done most things in life. He read a number of books on neuroses, and diagnosed himself correctly. Next he wondered what kind of therapy would be best for him. He rejected anything that he considered "soft." He was a hard scientist himself and wanted a form of therapy that had been developed in the laboratory, or at least in universities and research centers. He decided cognitive restructuring fit his needs.

The basic thought in Rudolph's mind, the one that frightened him and produced the detached defensiveness, was the inner thought that contact with people would be destructive to him. Therefore, he had detached emotionally so he would feel less of the pain and danger connected with relating to people. The trauma of the original parent–child pattern was his expectation whenever he became involved with anyone, even another tennis player.

Listening In became a listening for the inner voice that said, "Don't tread on me." Any contact with another person, especially any advice, would cause him to become anxious. He did not know at first that there was a thought that preceded and caused the anxiety. When asked to find the thought that came first, he approached the task with the tools of a research scientist.

Soon he heard in his inner speech center, "Don't listen. They will take you over." He then learned to Underline "take you over." Then he Stopped that inner voice. He Switched to a phrase familiar to a scientist. He would think to himself, "Keep gathering data." That enabled him to keep his mind on what the other person was saying—the data—and he would remain objective long enough to withhold his anxiety. And then he would in time Reorient. He chose to Reorient by thinking that he was engaged in a 6-month research project to see if people were indeed as dangerous as he had felt them to be during his childhood. He had never really tested that hypothesis and decided that now was the time to do it.

He further Reoriented by deciding he would test his therapist, and his therapist's methods. He would put every Inner Speech Training Technique to a test. He was sure he could try each of the five I.S.T. techniques 20 times, and decide if they proved workable and useful. If he found that they worked more than half the time, then he would decide they were worth continuing. He held his therapist to very strict standards. The instructions he was to follow had to be specific and testable. Rudolph's I.Q. was probably about 30 points higher than his therapist's, but together they probably improved some of the methods that are now presented.

As Rudolph began to use I.S.T. successfully, he became more collegial and friendly. His detachment dropped away bit by bit with the therapist, and also with his colleagues, and eventually with the world at large. He met many turning points that helped him progress, but the basic leverage that he gained against his neurosis was when he realized that his anxiety and hypersensitivity were caused by an inner thought. This thought, he realized, continually worked to make him fearful of close encounters. When he discovered that he could challenge that thought, and that the thought was not necessarily accurate, he was on the road to changing his thought, then his feeling, and finally, his behavior.

CHAPTER 17

THE MEN'S PERSPECTIVE/
THE WOMEN'S PERSPECTIVE
OLD AND NEW THINKING FOR
MEN AND WOMEN

How do women and men think? And what do they think about that is important to their happiness?

Men and women have two major thinking preoccupations in common: Love and Work.

Women and men have two major emotional problems: depression and anxiety. Depression is a feeling of helplessness. ("Woe is me, all is lost.") Anxiety is a feeling that I am in danger of losing something I value as a human being. (Shakespeare wrote, "He who robs me of my good name—leaves me poor indeed.") In briefest summary, loss is at the heart of the feeling of depression, and danger is at the heart of the feeling of anxiety.

The origins of anxiety and depression are different for each person. However they may have been started, it is the thinking of the individual that now perpetuates those emotional problems. Men and women make the same type of thinking errors that can exaggerate and extend the depression and anxiety. Whether it is a man or woman, the anxious person is allowing thoughts of danger to fill the mind, and the depressed person is allowing thoughts of helplessness and hopelessness to fill the mind.

Many studies indicate that social factors—that is, receiving and giving *love*—are the major ingredients of happiness in both men and women. That means that two of the most damaging inner speeches one can have are, "I do not love" and "I am not loved." Those thoughts are danger signals.

An effective thinker will go to work with the intent to change and correct them. If you think that you are living a lonely life without love, it's time to Switch to different priorities: to learn to love, to find time to be with loving or potentially loving people, to enjoy sharing your inner speech. Loneliness has been described as the inability to share your deepest thoughts and feelings.

Working with this book you are becoming more aware of your deeper thoughts. Practice sharing them, and your intimacy with others will grow.

The second major thinking pattern that women and men share is *work*—or specifically, job satisfaction. It is a crucial component in the happiness of both men and women. Job satisfaction means primarily that a person values her/his work—whether it is inside or outside the home. Job satisfaction also includes freedom of work opportunity, a good income, growth potential, and vacations.

All this means that you will do well to Listen In to your Inner Speech and Underline when your job thoughts are a primary focus of grumbling and complaining. Monitor the job channel in your mind. If you hear words of misery, you are apt to be miserable. Given the importance of your work in your life, it is time to change—either your thinking or your job or, more probably, a combination of both.

So much for basic similarities in the thinking of men and women. What about the differences? While recent social developments have tended to lessen the role differences of the sexes, there remain both physiological and cultural differences between males and females that can lead to different styles of thinking. (Keep in mind though, that men and women use the same basic mechanisms. Therefore, the five basic I.S.T. methods work equally well for both women and men.)

For instance, research has demonstrated that females have more left-brain dominance. The left hemisphere is in charge of language, logic, and labels. Girls begin to think earlier and find certain school subjects like English and literature easier than boys do.

Further, the bundle of fibers that connects the two halves of the brain—the corpus callosum—is thicker in females than in males, suggesting that women may have a greater capacity to integrate the two hemispheres, combining right-brain visual and spatial abilities with left-brain verbal skills. Some people believe that this may form the basis for the greater intuitive skills in women.

Yet other research has shown a male–female difference in the control of aggression. After eighteen months of age, girls seem to gain better control over their tempers than boys. Of course, it can be argued that aggressiveness in a baby girl still shocks adults, whereas it may elicit approbative amusement in a boy— "What a little tough guy!—Hey, Slugger!" This may form the basis for the better verbal stress-coping strategies seen in women, as opposed to men, who are more likely to react to stress with physical aggression.

There still remain important differences in the social learning of girls and boys that lead to differing
thinking patterns between females and males. No matter how much of a new woman, or a new man, you feel
yourself to be, you will probably still see yourself in
some of these familiar stereotypes.

Here are five popular stereotypes of what many
men think about:

A man thinks—would *you* call it narcissistic
thinking?

> "To prove I am a *man*—I *must* be stronger,
> smarter, richer, and more sexually experi-
> enced than a woman."

What would *you* do if you were a man and you had
a thought like that? You might begin by *Listening In* to
what you are saying to yourself. An accurate appraisal
of that sentence would surely cause you to Stop and
Switch—to anything—anything to take some of that
stress off yourself. *Reorienting* calls for you to picture
yourself as a fuller person, dreaming other dreams, remembering pleasures in your life that didn't mean you
had to outdo the woman in your life.

Don't be a victim of the male stereotype of the ma-
cho man.

A man might think—would *you* call this detached
thinking?

> "I *must not* depend on anyone for anything
> important to me—"

Underlining the *must not* will certainly point out
that such thinking will ruin a relationship and make

intimacy impossible. Such thinking could be subtitled "How to Grow an Ulcer."

Men do have many more ulcers than women. Since men think they should not depend on others, they go to a doctor less often than women, and when they finally do get to a doctor, their illnesses, on average, are more advanced than women's. As a result, a man's stay in a hospital averages 4 days longer than a woman's.

A man might think—would *you* call it obsessive thinking?

> "I must remain very rational. Stay cool, unflappable, self-contained."

Wrong? Wrong! Get off it by *Switching*. Remember the joy of losing control in an orgasm—merging with your lover. That wasn't a "self-contained" moment.

New research is finding that men who are able and willing to share their feelings with others, and especially with women, have less heart disease and cancer. That "cool, self-contained" thinking style is costly when it comes to medical bills.

Some men think—would *you* call it defensive thinking?

> "I have to show them" ("them" meaning the *men* in the world out there).

So what really counts is getting your name in the paper? And what happens when your name isn't in the paper tomorrow or the day after? Who or what are you then? No one said it is easy to be a successful male or female these days—but look at the pressures you may be laying on yourself. Does your inner speech also go on to say something like, "It's the world out there that really counts. I am worth something when the world values me—with more acclaim, professional reputation, a larger income, more prizes. What I'm like inside the four walls of my home is pretty much hidden from the real world out there—so my private life doesn't count for as much."

Perhaps it is those thoughts about "I'll show them" that leads to the male style of aggressive driving on the highways. And what does it get men? Twice as many 20-year-old men are killed in auto accidents as 20-year-old women. And what about other forms of violence? Men are five times more likely to be murdered than women. And men, far more often than women, commit those murders.

Stop. What is there inside you that gives you pleasure? Try this exercise. Think for a few moments. Name the three most personally fulfilling experiences you have ever had. Not what *others* thought—but what *you* in your innermost self thought was truly fulfilling.

1._____ _____ _____
2._____
3._____

Think about those things.

Some men think—would *you* call this anxious thinking?

"I need to get ready for what's coming up."

Maybe you are one of the many males who is nearly always thinking, "I must prepare myself for what lies ahead. It doesn't matter how I feel right now.

It doesn't count whether or not I am enjoying myself now—it's piling up experiences for some future testing of me that really matters." Many men hardly live in the present at all—what really matters is how things are going to turn out, or so they think.

Men live 8 years less than women. There are many reasons for this. But certainly the man who thinks he must be tougher than others, not dependent on others, unfeeling, aggressive, is unwilling to live in the present and thinking primarily about the future—is setting himself up to die earlier than he would need to.

It's time to Reorient: Listen In to your best inner speech as you answer this simple question: "What do I really want?"

Now let us look at five of the old familiar thinking patterns among women.

Some women think—perhaps it is depressed thinking:

"What if I never meet anybody?"

Listen In to that one. It sounds like that woman (or is it a man?) is putting the source of her security outside herself, in someone else. What if? What if? That is risky, isn't it? Time to change, perhaps to something like, "I will become secure personally—inside myself. Then I will share that security with another person who is also secure."

Some women think—does it sound like masochistic thinking?

"I have to put him first."

Have to? *His* career, *his* well-being, *his* thin skin? Put them first?

Years ago little girls were raised to believe that they were to drop everything else when a man came along. It cost women the potential for their own strong identities. And it made men out to be the weaklings who couldn't survive without the "little woman" holding them together. How does this newer description sound to you? "We are equal and different." Have you Reoriented?

Some women think—might it be anxious thinking?

"I'm afraid I'll lose her as a friend."

That was said by a brilliant scientist, Wilma B., after she was offered a promotion. It meant leaving the lab where she and her colleague Ruth had worked side by side for three years.

Women have often felt that when they began to succeed in the marketplace they would become as competitive as men, and lose their valued relationships with their female friends. The old image of the "real" woman was that she was not to appear eager for success—it wasn't feminine. Underline your thought. Was it appropriate for, say, the Victorian era? Switch. It's a hundred years later. "I like using my brains, and it's great to be rewarded for how well I can do."

Some women think—does it sound like narcissistic thinking?

"I have the most beautiful body at this party. But what will happen to me when I am older?"

This woman is thinking "a woman is her body." That is not unusual in our society. Never before has the exposed female body been so powerful. Glamor has become a woman's major asset. And many women have been taught to think that as their glamor fades, so does their identity. The culture of the time has dictated what kind of body has attractiveness and power: the fullness of the Renaissance, the hourglass shape of the Late Victorians, or the flatness of the current high-fashion magazines. In all of these, women were told how to shape themselves so they would have the "right" to think well of themselves.

It is time for this narcissistic woman to rethink her worth. Can she think she is more than the appearance of her body? Can she Switch to her inner self as a source of worth? The fashions will change. What catches a man's eye will change. The literature written now by thoughtful women provides valuable sources for a healthy sense of self based on talent, values, assertiveness, integrity, wisdom—all aspects of the self that grow with the passing years. They are assets worth thinking about when she prepares for the next party.

Some women think—does it sound like obsessive thinking?

"I'm not as good a wife and mother as my mother was."

Are you sure it is "not as good"? Could it be that more correctly you are a *different* wife and mother than your mother was?

More than 50 percent of wives are working outside the home today. Of course they will not do the same things their mothers did when they were full-time homemakers. Change your thinking to what you as a career woman can now offer your children, for example, in terms of a role model.

We could go on with these examples, and so can you. "I mustn't let anything compete with my loyalties at home. —I wish someone would take care of me. — How long can I go before I call him? —Do you think I said too much? —Was I too assertive? —Am I going to have to take care of myself all my life? —I never have enough time. —I wonder what others will think if I don't work outside my home." —Guilt. Guilt. Guilt.

Men's damaging inner speech most often occurs in relation to their position in the world, while women's inner speech most typically occurs in how they evaluate themselves in relation to their position with other people. (That is not the case for *all* men or *all* women.)

Listening In to women will help you underline how women often think about being a super-relater — succeeding in their relationships with both men and women (but especially with men) as a sign of self-worth. *Listening In* to men enables the listener to Underline the fact that men typically think of their self-worth in terms of how they succeed in the outside world. Witness the women's magazines: "Can This Marriage Be Saved?" And the men's magazines, "How I Shot the Big-Horned Elk."

What do these differences between men and women mean in relation to thinking?

The surprising answer is, not very much.

Thinking techniques work exactly the same for both sexes because both sexes think the same way. For women and for men, your awareness of your inner voice thoughts will help you effectively monitor your internal speech. You can Underline the weakening trends and Stop them. Thoughts and thinking are produced in both men and women in *the same way* — in words. You can hear the words. Decide if they are producing fear or depression. If they are, decide to change them to useful thinking. Change the words. Not falsely, but accurately in words that are helpful to you. Change your words and you change your feelings. Try it!

THE "HOW CAN I" TECHNIQUE FOR BOTH MEN AND WOMEN

Here is an effective technique that in a simple way will enable you to eliminate weakening thoughts.

Start by making a list of 10 of your most damaging thoughts. Some examples:

1. Things just don't go right for me.
2. How come I can't ever find the right job?
3. Nothing is ever enough.
4. I'm not relaxed with people.

Now you add some of your own special brand of damaging thinking.

Next, immediately switch these thoughts by adding just three words at the beginning of each sentence. The three words are "How can I."

"Things don't go right for me" becomes *"How can I make* things go right for me?"

"How come I can't find the right job" becomes *"How can I find* the right job?"

Do you see how you have Reoriented yourself from a helpless statement to a planning statement?

Finally, add two or three answers to each of your new "How can I?" questions. Don't stop with the questions. Add some answers that help you start doing something productive.

What are your answers to those four questions above?

I can...

I can...

I can...

I can...

CHAPTER 18

BETTER THINKING AND YOUR EVERYDAY PROBLEMS
STRESS, COPING, MIND-RACING, SEX, AND HEALTH

Whether you are a woman or a man, whatever type of basic personality you are, you face important everyday problems that require you to be at your best.

This chapter describes five important issues of daily living. To practice your thinking right now, try, as a case history is recounted, to devise your own solution before you reach the one suggested.

STRESS

The successful management of stress has become a major theme in our society. What you *think* can be either the greatest agent of stress or the greatest stress-reducer in your life.

Edgar's house burned down in the middle of the night. It was a frame house, and it burned to the ground except for the chimney. He and his family had been able to escape without injury, but the house burned so fast that they had been able to get nothing out of the house except four family photograph albums. It is difficult to imagine greater stress than to be awakened in the middle of the night by the sounds and heat and smoke of the house on fire, fearing for the lives of everyone in the family.

The next day Edgar was walking through the ruins of his house, suffered a heart attack, and died immediately.

The newspaper account said that he had spent the night at a neighbor's home and had left that house alone early the next morning to inspect his burned-out house. He was found dead a short time later. Police surmised that Edgar, a writer, had been surveying the charred remains of his books in what had been his study, where he usually wrote. It was there that he fell stricken, and his body was found.

We want to comment on this newspaper story (details have been changed) with caution. While we will never know what Edgar may have been thinking before he suffered a heart attack, we want to call attention to the fact that he survived the worst of the *physical* stress. That is, he escaped the fire of the night before. The next day, when he was inspecting his former home, it is likely he was thinking thoughts that caused him to experience enormous psychological stress. The heart attack came after the physical stress, but—again, this interpretation is just a possibility—perhaps during the worst of the mental stress.

A possible lesson to be learned is that in the midst of great external stress, such as the trauma of a fire, and following that stress, it is vital that one should Listen In to one's thoughts, so that those thoughts can be directed to center on comforting, quieting, and soothing measures, as far as that is possible to do. What you *think* is the *greatest stressor of all*; or, it can be a balm to you.

Students of I.S.T. have learned to think of themselves in a special way. They do not sneer at themselves. They do not stay mad at themselves. When they make an error, they encourage themselves. They remember that they did their best, given who they were at that moment. They weren't trying to make mistakes deliberately. Their thinking moves them ahead. They expect to build a more competent life.

HOW TO CONTROL YOUR INNER DIALOGUES TO REDUCE STRESS

We live in a tense age. Stress permeates our lives in so many different ways that it is unusual when we aren't feeling some stress. Whether it is performing on the job, at a test, winning a game, or being in a relationship, we are surrounded by stress.

WHERE DO THESE DEMANDS COME FROM?

The answer to that question should now come to your mind at once: from internal voices. These internal voices demand, demand, demand.

HOW MUCH STRESS ARE YOU UNDER?

Answer these 20 questions and you will get an effective measure of your reaction to the stress in your life.

Check the appropriate box:

1=Hardly ever
2=Occasionally
3=Regularly
4=Very often

Do you	Hardly ever	Occasionally	Regularly	Very often
1. Feel irritated or annoyed?	_____	_____	_____	_____
2. Get angry about little things?	_____	_____	_____	_____
3. Fly into a rage?	_____	_____	_____	_____
4. Forget things?	_____	_____	_____	_____
5. Have poor concentration?	_____	_____	_____	_____
6. Take too long to make a decision?	_____	_____	_____	_____
7. Perspire a lot?	_____	_____	_____	_____
8. Feel your heart pounding?	_____	_____	_____	_____

9. Experience that your muscles are stiff/tight? _____ _____ _____ _____

10. Feel faint? _____ _____ _____ _____

11. Find your hands trembling? _____ _____ _____ _____

12. Have an upset stomach? _____ _____ _____ _____

13. Feel nervous or tense inside? _____ _____ _____ _____

14. Avoid some things because of your fears? _____ _____ _____ _____

15. Feel you are losing interest in things? _____ _____ _____ _____

16. Have trouble sleeping and/or eating? _____ _____ _____ _____

17. Feel hopeless about the future? _____ _____ _____ _____

18. Feel lonely? _____ _____ _____ _____

19. Lack much sexual desire? _____ _____ _____ _____

20. Feel down? _____ _____ _____ _____

How to Score Your Answers

Now add your total score: If you had a "3" on the first question, and a "2" on the second question, your total score to that point would be 5. Continue until you have added the points for all 20 times.

If your total score was 20, you are kidding yourself.

If your total score was 80, we don't believe it. Someone with an 80 does not have the inner strength to be able to read this book and get to the end of a 20-item questionnaire.

But if you scored between 30 and 40, you are experiencing little stress in your life.

If you scored above 45, you need to think through what you are doing to yourself. Depending on how much above 45 your score went, you are in considerable distress, and even in danger of losing control of your mental health.

How you think about it determines the amount of stress that you experience.

Stress can be overwhelming at times, *but the essential and important difference is how you cope* with the stress. Stress does not necessarily lead to strain.

If you can control and handle your internal voices, you will be able to cope. It is very important to learn that halfway between the external stressor and your internal response, there is a *midway* point—a point where the stress can be handled, and where the real action is. The outcome of the midway battleground leads to productive living or it leads to anxiety and depression. Midway is where the voices are locked between the external stress—and what you think and do about it.

Outside stress eventually is changed into a *verbal*

thought in your mind. The stress comes to have a separate existence that you can perceive in your head.

But you can learn to *cope* with these verbal thoughts, these stressors, through improving your thinking techniques.

COPING

How often have you heard your own thoughts telling you unkind things?

"I don't think I want to try. I'll probably *fail,* then I'll just feel worse."

Like most skills, thinking takes practice. The skill that will help the thinker above is *Reorienting* to: "I will learn from the experience, even if I don't do it a hundred percent."

When your inner voice says

"Why go through with it? It won't make *any difference . . .* "

you are experiencing difficulties in your thinking.

Underline all the weakening words that are getting you into trouble. They are the words that rush to false conclusions. Your thoughts are actually *misrepresenting* your case—giving you *false information.*

It is time to Switch and think:

"Some things seem very difficult to me."

Now you have stopped thinking you are helpless. Now you can work out the several specific operations to be done to obtain a better rate of success.

Do you ever misinform yourself? Take Anita, a weekend tennis player who went out to hit the ball after looking at the professionals play at Wimbledon. An "easy" shot went out of bounds and Anita thought, "What's the use? I'll never be a tennis player!" Can you find the false information in her thought? Doesn't she really mean that she'll never control the ball like a champion? The pros practice three to five hours a day and have intensive coaching in each minute detail of the game.

Anita will feel better when she Switches to "I know I will play better if I take my racquet back sooner and have more time to stroke the ball."

Coping is defined as the way that you manage your problems. Your style of coping is the way that you deal with life—whether it is a flat tire, the death of a relative, or a rude waiter.

These styles of coping result from your mental patterning in the brain. They are developed originally early in your life to keep you feeling safe, secure, and comfortable. Your patterns of coping came primarily from how you learned to live with your parents and siblings. For the most part, you tend in adulthood to keep the same mental patterns and style that you used to get along in your childhood.

People cope in different ways and you can change your thinking to cope better.

If you want to see coping styles in action, watch a person with a flat tire during the rush hour on the San Diego Freeway (or the Northwest Tollway or the Long Island Expressway).

The Dependent Coper has his flat tire and sits in his car waiting for help to arrive.

The Submissive Coper waits, and when the police car arrives, he says to the officer, "Oh, officer, you police are the most wonderful people! Tell me what to do."

The Guilty Coper waits in his car for help to arrive. He then tells the arriving police officer, "Oh, officer, I have known this would happen. As you can see, one headlight is out, the brakes need relining, and I've only got one contact lens on. I mean, I'm a menace on the road."

The Dominating-Aggressive Coper strides to the nearest phone and calls the American Automobile Association, the highway patrol, and the state highway department. His shouted message to all three is, "You better get your trucks over here fast before I call the Governor. I pay my dues and taxes. These roads are a disgrace. Your service is outrageous, and your people are incompetent. I demand my rights."

The Withdrawal (Detached) Coper isolates himself. He abandons his car, climbs the fence to get out of the turnpike area, and walks home alone.

The Self-Image Expander announces to the policeman when he arrives, "My chauffeur was sick today so he couldn't drive me in my limo. My personal Mercedes is being delivered next week. So I borrowed this lemon from the dealer. And right away the tire blows on me. I've never been in a situation like this in my life."

The Healthy Character does whatever is appropriate safely to fix the tire and get himself on the way to his destination without undue delay or bother. He has a healthy self-regard which allows him to think that he can be interdependent with others and have the best of both worlds. Flat tires are a fact of life, and he knows he will manage.

Thinking underlies all these coping patterns. You gain power in your coping by *Listening In* and understanding which of these styles you typically follow.

You can gradually change your character pattern if you recognize it for what it is: a habitual mode of thinking that leads to habitual ways of acting.

You are about to have a job interview. Anxiety is normal at such a time. Here are ways to manage your thoughts:

Weak thinking	Inner Speech Training
"I *should have* dressed more conservatively. I *should have* looked up the history of this company."	"The job interview is today. I'll have an opportunity to discuss the situation and see if I want the job and if I'm suited to it."
Comment: Underline the weakening phrase, the critical voice.	*Comment:* This is a Switch to a productive thought.
"I'm *no good* at these job interviews. I *can't think* on my feet. I act like I'm *scared to death.*"	"I learn something from every interview. By the time I've had 20 interviews, I will really know how to handle these situations."

Comment: Listen In. Is your inner voice critical or friendly? This voice is beating up on you.

Comment: Stop, Switch, Reorient. It's okay to admit you're still learning.

"I wish I knew how to relax...."

"Tensing up is a problem for me when I am interviewed. I know I will be anxious. I will just keep taking deep breaths, and think the word, 'relax.' To focus on the anxiety does not help me."

Comment: Listen In. Helpless thinking here. It provides no channels.

Comment: Nice Switch here. Start tackling the problems one at a time. If you know anxiety is the toughest one, concentrate on how you will handle the anxiety.

Many popular newspaper and magazine articles on stress write about *managing* stress. Rarely do they write about an in-depth understanding of the *causes* of stress. Economists are now recognizing that stress is a factor in many illnesses, in absenteeism, alcoholism, and drug abuse. It is estimated to cost our economy billions of dollars a year. Stress management programs in business and industry are increasingly popular, and millions of dollars are being budgeted to finance them.

Recently surveyed articles and programs on stress

management advocated throwing balloons around a room, attending lectures, telling jokes, eating a healthier diet, stopping smoking, doing aerobics, and walking away from the stressor. All of these suggestions are helpful in managing stress.

What all of these external activities miss is that stress is an internal condition which is primarily caused by the internal act of thinking. It is not the event, it is *what you think of the event* that causes, or does not cause you to experience stress in your body. Aerobics will get your mind off the stressors for a brief time, and that is important. Aerobics will also give you a physical feeling of well-being, and that is valuable. But no external activity will teach you how to Listen In to how you are converting an external stressor (e.g., the boss's angry memo) into an internal thought of helplessness or danger.

Reread the three dialogues above, which begin with weak thinking and then Switch into productive thinking. It may seem too simple; but it requires practice to make it effective. The point is not to deny that the boss wrote an angry memo. The next step is to take responsibility for your own thoughts in response to the boss's memo. You can think helplessly or constructively. You are then doing much more than "managing" stress, you are *reducing* it, and learning how to cure yourself of *allowing stressful thoughts* to run rampant in your mind.

The next time you read an article on stress, we suggest you add the techniques of Inner Speech Training. You will then work to eliminate the *cause* of stress in your inner speech, and develop those satisfying thoughts that help you gain control of your thoughts, your feelings, and your behavior.

MIND RACING

If you are going to cope better, one area to learn to manage is mind racing.

Everyone has experienced *mind racing*—when you can actually feel your thoughts speed up and pressure your mind. You can't prevent those thoughts entirely. They keep recurring. Mind racing can occur as your thoughts race backwards, trying to justify your actions of yesterday.

Things didn't go right yesterday. Your mind keeps trying to redo and undo the past. You keep hearing different alternatives.

"What if I hadn't?"

"What if I had just...?"

You can't let it go and you can't improve on it. Your racing mind is keeping you awake—painfully.

If you learn to control your thinking, you can fall asleep and not endlessly relive the pain.

Or even more exasperatingly, you have had a good day and have the prospect of an even greater day tomorrow—but you were so keyed up that your mind started racing, preparing for something that hasn't happened yet, until it was again the middle of the night and you couldn't fall asleep.

You have an important meeting tomorrow, but your mind keeps racing ahead, trying to anticipate how you will manage.

You think,

What will I do if...?

What will I do if...?

What will I do if...?

No matter what you do, you can't seem to shut down all the possibilities. Your mind keeps going, trying to solve a yet unborn world. And then, the next day you may be too tired to enjoy anything.

Of course, not all mind racing occurs at night. It's just that voice thoughts are more noticeable when your surroundings are relatively quiet.

All of us have shared the experience of accelerated thought processes, which occur in many ways under different circumstances. Occasionally they flood us with waves of creativity—too often escalating to the point where our thoughts become unmanageable.

Can you recall an instance when your mind racing prevented you from fully enjoying something?

Do you remember being like Althea D.? She was intellectually brilliant, but so busy worrying obsessively about the amount of work that she had to do for her examination that she kept on getting further and further behind. She thought about all the studying she had to do, rather than actually studying. Her mind kept going faster and faster until she was so out of control that she ran out of time to study for her examination.

Maybe you too can recall an instance when you had to juggle so many things in your mind that you ended up doing nothing right.

Whoever you are, whatever you do, you are probably victimized at some time by an inability to control the *speed* of your thoughts, to concentrate on any one task for an extended period of time.

Which of the following circumstances do you associate frequently with mind racing? We offer some examples. You may have some of your own.

	Never	Seldom	Fre-quently
1. Depression (I'm hopeless.)	————	————	————
2. Self-criticism (How stupid can I be?)	————	————	————
3. Anger (I hate, hate, hate.)	————	————	————
4. Sex (I can't get the memory of that time out of my head.)	————	————	————
5. Self-hurt and rejection (What's wrong with me? Men always leave me.)	————	————	————
6. Morbid pre-occupations (I'll probably die an early death.)	————	————	————
7. Free-floating anxiety (What if I can't breathe?)	————	————	————
8. Work situations (I'll never finish.)	————	————	————

9. Obsessions
(Should I or
shouldn't I
call?) _____ _____ _____

10. Performance
anxiety
(What if I
don't pass?) _____ _____ _____

11. Recurring
fantasies (I'd
like to tell him
where to go.) _____ _____ _____

12. Fear of failure
(I won't be
able to do it.) _____ _____ _____

13. Decision mak-
ing (Should I
change jobs
now?) _____ _____ _____

14. Premenstrual
tension (I'm
so sensitive to
everything be-
fore my
period.) _____ _____ _____

15. Excess stimu-
lants (coffee,
diet pills)
(I have a buzz,
or I can't stop
my thoughts.) _____ _____ _____

16. Sleep depriva-
    tion (insom-
    nia) (I'm
    exhausted. I
    can't control
    my mind.)   _____   _____   _____

THE PSYCHOLOGICAL CAUSES OF MIND RACING

Mind racing may be a manifestation of a particular style of personality. For example, an obsessive style is a type of thinking that won't let anything go.

When a particular drive or feeling isn't expressed adequately, a feeling of internal pressure develops. It is unfinished business that can cause the mind to race and obsessive persons often won't let anything get finished. What residues of frustrations continually plague you and weaken your power to think? Pinpoint those circumstances that are most chronically frustrating for you.

When a choice exists between two opposing forces, *conflict* develops. Certain situations can cause repeated conflict in the mind. A good example is family conflict. The person may be "caught" between the spouse and the parents. If this happens to you, you are the unwitting victim of two opposing forces that are using *you* as their battlefield. It is important to stop the battle.

Don't let yourself be a victim. Try to Brake and slow down the two or more different voices in your internal speech. After they are slowed down and more controllable, train yourself to stop them completely by substituting your *own* voice whenever possible.

Any mind may race when anxiety overflows—

either from an external crisis or an internal pressure. Anxiety registers in many different ways. Racing thoughts often lead to muscular tension. If you feel tension and stiffness in your muscles, alert your body's biofeedback mechanism. Use the *signal* of the muscular tension to alert yourself to slow your inner speech.

Visualizations (close cousins of *Reorienting*) are a useful technique to use with anxiety. Picture the anxiety-producing situation. See yourself in your mind as you handle it, coping with calm confidence.

A special type of mind racing occurs when your inner speech is in the form of a dialogue with *two or more voices* in your head fighting with each other. One frequently is the Superego—the attacking voice, full of self-put-downs. Another inner voice, we hope, is more reasonable. This raging between two parts of yourself can be controlled by changing your internal dialogues.

The young executive:

"I worry constantly if I should deduct more business expenses."

"Everybody does it."

How to Prevent Mind Racing

The First Step

Identify the sources of your mind racing. Eliminate those precipitating ones that can be readily changed by physical means—like lowering coffee intake.

THE SECOND STEP

Be active. Challenge the problem. For example, if you find your mind racing chronically when you become angry due to repeated *frustrations*, try to work through the anger. Don't let it sit there. Be aware of it. Express it in a way that does not hurt others or you. If that is not possible, *displace* it onto something harmless—like ferocious exercise (an around-the-park run). It may then be easier to use I.S.T. You probably feel stronger after exercising. Then Underline and Switch the Weakening Words. Select more powerful words to control your emotions.

"He can't do that to me."

becomes

"How he treats people is *his* problem."

THE THIRD STEP

Decrease your muscular tension and you can relax and control your thinking.

The hidden principle is simple.

Tension (anxiety) is a state that is perceived and felt in the muscles of your body. If you can relax your muscles you can decrease the feedback from your body that fuels the pressure and the anxiety that you feel in your mind. People are frequently unaware that relaxation also travels *backwards* from your relaxed body back to your mind. Just as a relaxed mind helps to relax your body, so relaxed muscles will relax your mind.

SPECIALIZED WAYS OF REDUCING TENSION

1. CREATIVE EXERCISE

You've seen the joggers, the legions of runners. They know that proper exercise can be invaluable. It is one of the most important means of reducing tension, depression, and stopping your mind from racing. Today people are getting better faster by exercising properly. It doesn't have to be jogging, of course.

If you really have tension and want to get rid of it, you need to exercise—and exercise strenuously. No matter what else you do, you won't feel completely well until you exercise regularly.

The exercise needs to be strenuous enough to involve your cardiovascular system to the point that you increase your resting pulse rate. (The resting pulse is the pulse that is obtained 2 minutes *after* the exercise is completed.) The exercise should last 20 to 30 minutes, at least two to three times a week.

The remarkable, *paradoxical* fact is that the fatigue produced by exercise will make you feel less tired, rather than more tired. Finish your exercise with a few moments of I.S.T. Hear any weakening inner thoughts? Switch them. Exercise helps, but it will not keep you relaxed, unless you change your thoughts which produced the stress.

2. DRUGS

Drugs are only a *temporary* source of relief. They can help you bridge crises and stressful anxiety. They will not, however, make you think and feel better by themselves. (Note the sequence, thinking produces the feeling.) You need to work at it. This is especially true of tranquilizers that bring relaxation; after awhile they tend to lose their effectiveness. Used properly, they can be vitally important if you need a bridge—when you need to remember just how it feels to relax.

If you are using a tranquilizer, notice how you are able to get a little more "distance" on your problem thoughts with the help of the tranquilizer. You probably are still thinking the troublesome thought, but somehow it does not seem to be so terribly painful. If you can get some distance from your worries *with* a tranquilizer, you can learn to do it *without* a tranquilizer. Remember how you thought when you were on a tranquilizer? Then do the same thinking when you are not using the tranquilizer. It will give you a feeling of greater self-confidence when you can learn to quiet your thinking without resorting to any chemical help.

3. SPECIALIZED PSYCHOLOGICAL TRAINING

You can train your body to relax. Did you know that you can actually decrease the tension in your body?

Today, using advanced technical machines, you can feed back information from different parts of your body to your mind and train yourself to regulate those parts and functions of your body through the process called biofeedback.

Most of the work done today in biofeedback is in the area of muscular relaxation. This is the most important means of retraining your body to deal with a variety of dysfunctions like severe headaches, backaches, and colitis. It can be enormously effective if used properly. Biofeedback can help a wide range of disorders from your head (ache) to your toe (spasm). The biofeedback machine is signaling you when you are thinking the most useful thoughts to relax your body from head to toe.

The basic operation calls for a sophisticated machine to record and monitor the electrical activity of your muscles. You are given an electrical signal via feedback readings that tells you when your muscles are relaxed. Your mind then operates in a cycle with your muscles. As your muscles relax, your tension subsides. Your mind and body are being taught to work in a healing cycle.

Special training enables regulation of brain waves (alpha training), sweat glands, blood pressure, and heart beat.

4. SELF-TRAINING EXERCISES (SELF-RELAXATION
   EXERCISES)

Biofeedback is not the only way. Some of the same results can be produced with simple self-taught exercises. Nearly every self-help book includes them. Here is a basic example of an amazing 10-second exercise to relax and feel better.

> Ready...Flex your arms and your legs. Tighten *all* the muscles in your body and hold them for a count of 10. Then count backwards from 10 as *slowly* as possible, gently releasing your muscles. You will immediately sense a

wave of relaxation spreading over the muscles
of your body.

Repeat this exercise several times. Each time, you will
feel more relaxed. The incorporation of such a simple
exercise into your daily routine will decrease the tension you feel. Do it several times every day! Couple the
exercise with Inner Speech exercises. Learn to Switch
to those relaxing thoughts.

Everyone has been told countless times "just relax," in the dentist's chair, when starting a new job,
when walking down the aisle to be married. But like
the weather, no one has *done* much about relaxation. It
has not been scientifically possible to teach people how
to relax so that it became a lasting response. Saints and
geniuses throughout history have mastered the techniques themselves, but their success may have been
due to their special gifts.

Now relaxation is getting a lot of much-needed research, and for good reasons. Relaxation improves the
body's immune system, lowers the heart rate and blood
pressure, slows the brain waves, reduces pain in most
instances, and often relieves gastrointestinal discomfort.

In keeping with the focus of the present volume,
we want to alert you to the importance of your thinking
in promoting your own relaxation. It is what you think
about that relaxes you, or prevents you from relaxing.
The thoughts in your mind make it happen. It is crucial
for you to Stop and Switch from your everyday worries,
concerns, and preoccupations if you want to learn to
relax. Then you can allow space in your mind for those
quieting, calming, tranquilizing thoughts that block
the chemicals in your brain that pump up your stress
level.

Choose right now, as you think about learning how to relax, a short phrase or word that is very calming to you. Say or think the phrase to yourself several times. Now exhale rather slowly, and repeat those calming words as you exhale. A helpful phrase will be one that reminds you that you are safe, secure, and stable. Pick a phrase that confirms that you are all right, that your future is going to be all right. Many people choose a meaningful phrase from their religious tradition. Be sure that for you they are words that connect and resonate deeply within you. Combine those words with a quiet breathing out. It is breathing out that relaxes you, far more than breathing in. Slowly, easily, think and breathe. Think and breathe.

An effective way to Stop and Switch from your tensions is to picture your muscles systematically relaxing. Start at either end of your body and think your way to the other end, naming the sections of your body and thinking about them relaxing. Thinking about your muscles relaxing will silence the static in your mind, and enable you to Switch to your thoughts and your body working in concert to bring on the feeling of wellbeing.

Keep out the bothersome thoughts by concentrating on affirming thoughts. Breathing has an automatically calming effect, but much more so if you combine it with a quiet thought reflecting a solid, strong integration of your best self.

This form of systematic relaxation will be more effective as you practice it. Intruding thoughts will occur, and you will discover how you can let those interruptions pass right on out of your mind without becoming upset about them. As you enjoy the calming effects of your systematic relaxation exercise, you will find that relaxation can be even more calming than sleep some-times is. Sleep can, at times, even interfere with relax-ation when it is a sleep troubled by unpleasant dreams. You probably have had occasions when you awoke and felt you had been working hard most of the night as you slept. Relaxation can be under your own control, whereas some sleep is not under your control. That is why we know that relaxation exercises can contribute a special benefit to you. Try it, 10 minutes a day and find out for yourself.

SEX

You are only as sexy as you think. As unlikely as it seems, your mind is the main sexual organ of your body. Thinking is what produces sexual arousal. Or-gasms are not caused by the genitals, but by the cere-bral cortex.

Your sex life is that part of your life that is probably the most convincing proof that what you think causes what you feel. You know what it is like to feel sexy. Try this exercise: try to feel sexy as you reread the previous paragraph. Just keep reading. You are reading a section of this chapter that is about sex. Now stop the exercise. Did you start feeling sexy? Probably not. You were reading sentences about sex, but these sentences were not sexy. Feeling sexy is a by-product of thinking sexy thoughts. Now think some sexy thoughts. Take a few moments and think of one of your favorite sexual fanta-sies. Let your fantasy go on for a few minutes. Now stop the exercise. If you were able to get into your day-dream, you probably began to feel sexy.

You have just read the key to a better sex life: think sexier thoughts.

You can have intense sexual experiences from reading erotic literature through thought. Visual stimulation can lead you to feel sexual pleasure. Strong fantasies and daydreams can induce an intense state of sexual arousal even without physical stimulation.

On the other hand, thoughts can stifle sexual arousal.

> "I'm so afraid that I won't come that I don't even want to have sex."
>
> "He (She) turns me off."

STOP!

Only you can turn yourself off...Here is one way to fail:

> "*Nothing* makes me feel good sexually."

Your body has sensitive nerve endings which are concentrated in the sexual erotic areas.

You *can* feel, but your thinking may Switch to produce anxiety, rather than sexual pleasure.

If during lovemaking you keep thinking about how you are "performing," your thinking will almost certainly cause sexual problems. Thoughts like, "Does he like what I am doing?" or "Can I hold out long enough?" will cause you (and maybe your partner) to "turn off." If you think: "Does he (she) like me? or "My penis (breasts) are too small," your anxiety level will skyrocket and sex will be no fun. While you need stimulation of your sexual organs and other erogenous zones to achieve orgasm, you also need to have pleasurable, exciting thoughts during sex and to eliminate weakening thoughts.

Switching from your present sexual distracting thoughts can produce a wider and more intense sexual world for you that may have eluded you previously.

Listen In to the natural flow of the body. Concentrate by *Reorienting* the focus onto the sexual language of the body and mind. The capacity to be aroused fully is in you. Let your mind just listen to your body. Think about what your body is saying.

An important question you can ask while making love is, "What feels better...?" Keep asking yourself if there is a way that your lover can interact with you to make you both feel *even* sexier. Then do it.

Reorienting is a natural, and loving, lovely way to enjoy sex—if you leave yourself free to concentrate to do it. Use a number of reorienting questions to help you.

For example, ask yourself, "What thoughts are sexy?" Ask yourself, "What feels good?"

Hear the answers from your own mind and body. A mutual exploration will then lead you to develop a *style of lovemaking* that will enable you to reach greater sexual arousal and fulfillment. By "mutual exploration" we mean *talking* out your sexual preferences as well as acting them out together. With all the courage you can muster, tell your partner what you like best about being together with him/her sexually. Be tactful. Don't criticize; say, "I really like doing this, let's do it longer. And let's add some more of that." Express your appreciation of your partner's sexiest efforts. Compliments are always a stimulant. The greatest aphrodisiac is the warmth of a lover's responses. Human love can speak as well as show itself.

Your specific sexual interests are as unique as your thumbprint. No one else in the world has exactly your version of your sexiest daydream. There is no way that your partner is going to be able to guess what is the best way to turn you on—unless you have the openness to tell him/her.

Susan discovered that when she was getting very close to a climax, she wanted her husband to be completely motionless, and just hold her. When he did that, she almost always let go and had an orgasm. The point of this particular case illustration is that her husband would never have known exactly what she needed for sexual fulfillment unless she had told him. If she had not asked for what she wanted, she would probably have continued to feel frustrated and perhaps angry at her husband, and he would have felt that she was an unresponsive lover. Gently, lovingly, tell your partner about what is sexy for you in your thoughts.

A technique that will help you Reorient your sexuality is the *visual walk-through*.

Here is the way you do a sexual walk-through: You are now going to be the producer, director, author, and actor (and the entire audience) in the most erotic sexual encounter that you can imagine.

Start out by seeing a picture of the beginning of an ideal sexual encounter—anything you want. You have complete control. You are going to be able to do everything you have ever wanted to do. Now let the cameras roll. Add the details that excite you. Redo the scene if you would like to intensify a part of it. Keep going. You are being told how marvelous and exciting you are, that your lover has dreamed of this. As you continue with this fantasy of yourself making love, you are developing new thoughts that free you sexually.

Keep at these sexual walk-throughs. Add to your script. Make it more loving, more exciting, more fun. You will enjoy *being* a better lover as you mentally rehearse how to go about being a satisfying and satisfied lover. By doing these sexual walk-throughs you are grooving your mental pathways, so they will roll that much smoother the next time you make love.

Remember to Switch.

If you keep yourself aware of your internal speech and listen carefully to your thoughts, you can Underline the negative, critical, and irrelevant thoughts. If you keep hearing an obstructing voice cutting into your pleasant thoughts—get rid of the takeovers. Switch back to your most erotic thought-stream.

BARBARA, GENE, AND SEX

Barbara R. was 28 years old, had been married for 5 years, and was dissatisfied with her lovemaking. She was not only very tense and anxious while making love, but very angry at her husband, Gene, about her lack of sexual fulfillment. She felt that he had failed her, and that she had failed herself.

Her lovemaking did get worse as her thinking worsened. She grew angrier and more upset. When she had a sexual feeling, almost immediately she would think *negative thoughts* about Gene and their attempts to make love. Angry thoughts about past wrongs automatically intruded on her.

She knew that her angry thoughts were interfering with her sexual pleasure, but she felt that her thoughts got control of her and there was nothing she could do about it. She became very self-conscious when she tried to make love. She tried as hard as she could to do everything right. Books on sexual technique helped her some. But the harder she tried, the more she kept thinking about how she was doing. She developed performance anxiety. She had read a lot about performance anxiety, but she did not seem able to stop thinking about how she was performing in bed. She felt trapped. The more she thought about sex, and studied sex, the less sexy she felt when she got into bed.

She wanted to change. She was sophisticated enough to know that it wasn't all her husband's fault. "It takes two." She had read that often enough to know that it had to be true.

In time, she learned to Switch the voices in her head. She Stopped thinking about sex, and began to think sexy scenarios. She practiced and eventually succeeded at *Stopping* and *Switching* out the angry thoughts about her past sex life. She decided it was of no use to remember angry memories about Gene when what she really wanted to do was to make exciting love with him. He wanted the same. They both knew their marriage was not perfect, but they loved each other underneath the accumulated anger of their years together. And so they realized they were seriously shortchanging each other by bringing their anger into the bed.

Two changes in her thinking were the keys to Barbara's increased sexual enjoyment. She listened to her body, and this helped her Switch to sexier thoughts. And she developed new thoughts. Anger at Gene during sex had become a habitual, automatic thought. While her anger did not immediately subside, she realized she could stop the angry thought when it rose to her mind. She learned to Switch to some things about her husband that she *liked* when making love: Gene had an anxious, hopeful way of looking at her that was sweet, he had wide shoulders and a good tight midsection. When she did that, she learned to think about more sexy thoughts, and then grow progressively less angry at Gene, because she was enjoying more sexual pleasure. As their sexual life improved, they found it was worth the effort to try to develop improvement in other areas of their relationship as well.

You can rewrite the script of your sex life. Just work with your most important sexual organ—your own mind.

PHYSICAL HEALTH

Can happy thoughts make you physically healthier? The mind affects the body, but does the mind control the body? The answer is growing more affirmative, as science discovers how the mind, and especially thinking, exerts its influences on disease and health.

The relation of stress to illness has been widely known since the discovery that the blood cells that counteract disease cells are less active in the bodies of persons who have recently lost a spouse. The body is physically less resistant to illness (in a biochemically measurable way) following a stress that involves an important loss (a loved one) and puts new pressures (the prospect of living alone) on the survivor. Since the original research on widows and widowers, other studies have added information that many of the traumatic events in life (loss of a job, failure in school, loneliness) decrease the activity of the immune system, and lead to more illness.

Stress, of course, is in the mind of the beholder. What may be stressful for one person is fulfillment for someone else. A politician may be distressed when he has no opportunity to speak in public. The new president of the P.T.A. may be panicked when he or she must give a speech at the first public meeting. Again, it is not the event, but what one thinks of oneself in the face of the event that determines the degree of stress. If one thinks of oneself as capable and competent, the stress response is minimal, and the immune system is little affected.

So stress, like relaxation, is a response produced in large measure by what one thinks about. A generally stressful event, when it leads to panicky thinking like "How am I ever going to manage now?" will make one prone to illness.

What about the reverse? Will thinking cure an illness already in progress? The evidence now is strong that one's thoughts and attitudes can affect illness, and increase the effective activity of the immune system. However, only a few scientists who have studied statistical data carefully are fully convinced that thoughts and attitudes will cure a serious illness already under way. Nonetheless, nearly everyone has heard stories of recovered patients who attribute their health to their own resolve to fight their disease with a combination of psychological measures in cooperation with their doctors.

There is some research that has indicated that people can strengthen their immune systems by visualizing the white blood cells engulfing the germs in the body. People who have been taught systematic relaxation, followed by imaging themselves more strong and fit were able to increase the effectiveness of the immune system. Women who are angry about their breast cancer, for example, and fight it, also increase their chances of survival because their attitudes seem to mobilize their immune functions. More research is under way, and the results are promising.

There are many ways to treat an illness, and years ago they would not have been considered part of the medical treatment. These extra treatment methods go by the name of complementary medical care. Under medical supervision, these methods may include some or all of the following: a healthy diet, appropriate exercise, nutritional supplements, the use of humor, psychological counseling, relaxation training and possibly biofeedback as well, meditation, medical and spiritual support groups, and imaging.

The thought that one has some control over one's life circumstances gives hope, and hope leads to motivation. The expectation of success increases the chances of success. A study of the elderly in a nursing home found that those persons who had a hand in choosing their menu, their clothing, even the color of their rooms, would live longer than those who had no such control of their daily lives.

It's not all in the mind, of course; but the active participation of the patient in the healing process will probably influence the quantity of the patient's life—and it undoubtedly will help improve the quality of that life.

Perhaps you cannot think yourself completely well, but you can think yourself better.

CHAPTER 19

THE ACCOMPLISHED THINKER—YOU
PRODUCTIVITY AND CREATIVITY THROUGH YOUR OWN THINKING

You have discovered that it is possible to change your life by changing your thoughts. How you *think* about your life determines how you *feel* about your life.

You have an internal dialogue that is alive and active every day. This dialogue is composed of your thoughts. Your thoughts judge your thoughts, they judge you.

Although it is outside the scope of this book to describe where and how in early childhood you developed your own unique internal dialogue, you as an adult can take charge of that dialogue.

Near the end of his life, Winston Churchill said, "All the dreams of my youth have been realized." Even Churchill could have chosen to think, "I am no longer virile and strong, I am about to die. It is the end for me." Both statements would have been true. Which thought he chose to think made the difference in what he felt.

You can be conscious of what you think.

When you learned to drive an automobile, you thought of every move you made. Now you rarely think consciously when you drive, because it is so easy for you.

But if you went to England, and drove a car with the steering wheel on the right side, and drove on the left side of the road, you would be very conscious of your thinking again.

You can become conscious of your thoughts. If there is some part of your life that you want to change, change your thoughts, just as you would change your thoughts to drive a car in England.

If anxiety or depression are what you want to change, concentrate on hearing internal thoughts of danger or significant loss that lead you to be anxious or depressed. It's Technique #1: *Listening In*.

PRACTICE THINKING IN SLOW MOTION

You will then hear your voice thoughts more clearly, become more aware, and change your thoughts when you want to. If you practice thinking more slowly, you'll be able to separate each word as it goes into forming your thought. This ability to separate the components will give you more powerful thinking. It's Technique #2: *Underlining. While many thoughts are true, only some are helpful*.

You have the choice of avoiding many truthful thoughts that are of no present value to you. It's Technique #3: *Stopping*.

WHAT IS USEFUL TO THINK ABOUT?

As you think about the words on this page, it is not useful to dwell on every conceivable danger that could possibly befall you: cancer, nuclear fallout, a stock market crash.

If you are actively working on those problems at the moment, of course it is helpful to think about them. But if your present task is to tuck your two children into bed, then choose the best framework of useful thoughts of wanting the best for those children, and helping them to attain it.

It is not useful to regret the past, if you dwell only on the regret.

It can be useful to think of your errors if you focus now on what you can do and will improve next time.

Habitual self-critical thinking becomes a self-fulfilling prophecy. A person will develop a sequence of self-attacks that are almost as familiar as the sequence in brushing one's teeth. "I have trouble with math," is probably paired with thinking, "I have the worst time balancing my checkbook; I'm no good with money when it comes to figures; I'll never be able to understand the stock market; I'll never be rich." You can see how one thought leads to another in this chain of put-downs centered on numbers. Self-critical thinking can be an expensive habit!

Whether your boss bawls you out, or your inner speech bawls you out, the inner response is much the same: blood pressure rises, acid in the stomach flows faster, arteries tighten. This is the body's normal reaction to stress. If the stress lasts long enough, or switches on and off enough times, exhaustion occurs.

It may save your life to stop the self-critical thinking that produces your stress reaction. That takes some changes in your thinking, but the stress and exhaustion caused by your internal attacks on yourself are worth learning to avoid.

In general, it is *not useful to worry*. Worry has a future orientation and you are living in the here and now.

Albert Einstein said he had his most creative thoughts while shaving in the morning. How do you do your creative thinking? Each of us thinks creatively in some particular way every day—probably not the same way Einstein did.

Too often we are put off by the seemingly facile way in which outstanding creative people seem to operate. They make it seem too easy.

"Just as I was boarding the morning bus, the theory explaining the ultimate quantification of the universe based on a twelve tonal note system came fully into my mind—I stopped to jot it down on my bus ticket."

This fools us by somehow hiding all the months of hard work that preceded the breakthrough.

But even though you may not make an important discovery of public importance, you can create the shape of your own life—and that is no mean feat.

Stretch your imagination and develop your capacity to be creative in numerous small ways—a better route home, a new diet, changing a color scheme, terrific lovemaking. This is Technique #5: *Reorienting*.

How can you help yourself creatively in terms of your daily life? Here's an example: Instead of being trapped by the same boring routine everyday traveling to work, your imagination can create rich, vivid stories about the people and places you pass.

Train yourself to practice by making up the wildest imaginable story about the most colorless person in your day.

Try it several times a day. Has your day suddenly become more interesting? Go a little further. Imagine more interesting people. Let yourself have imaginary conversations with them.

WHAT IS CREATIVE THINKING?

Creative thinking is thinking that goes beyond established order and views the universe, or some part of it, in a new and different way.

Think thoughts that get behind the surface appearance of things. Some people think, "I hate the city." Someone else thinks on a more creative level like this: "I dislike the city because it limits my chances for outdoor exercise." This thought is specific, it indicates what the problem is, and points to a possible solution. The next thought might be, "I will investigate one different city park a month for the next year, and see what I could do that would be fun in those parks."

Leave your options open as you think. "I don't think I will ever be able to afford a trip around the world." That certainly is not a useful thought and, besides, it probably isn't even true. Try this more creative thought: "With air fares coming down, with more charter flights and vacation club plans, some day I might be able to make a round-the-world trip."

Too many people choose thoughts that eliminate even the possibility of creating a creative thought.

Thinking creatively is the ability to express yourself freely to a fuller potential, both internally and externally. It begins with your thoughts.

WHY SHOULD YOU BOTHER TO LEARN HOW TO THINK MORE CREATIVELY?

The process of thinking creatively leads to a deeper feeling of living a fuller and more satisfying life. Or being totally absorbed, losing a sense of time, having the freedom and capacity to see a different world and to be different.

Take every opportunity to be creative even when it is only in the most minor way in your everyday life. Seeing something familiar differently—a flower, a tree, a building, and reorganizing your everyday associations.

The important news is that thinking can be designed to allow more creativity. Thinking creatively involves far more manageable processes than waiting for that bolt of lightning. Creativity can be improved with practice and awareness in stages.

THERE ARE SEVERAL STAGES

1. *Observations* of the *need* for something new and different—"I read that the world may run out of oil in the future."
2. Now the *need* has to be *analyzed* and different patterns observed—"Can our present supply be used more effectively or do we need new types of fuel?" Then the person needs *to find the clue* that suggests where the answer can be sought. This step works best when the seeker actively *challenges* the existing material.

   "Engines are grossly inefficient. Is there a *new* way to build a more efficient engine with less heat loss?"

3. Finally, when the imagination begins to flow, the thinker comes up with what is termed lateral thinking—thinking that doesn't close down any associational possibilities. It's Technique #5: *Reorienting*.

At first, "brainstorm"—considering, perhaps even writing down, any solution that comes to mind, no matter how zany or farfetched. Then eliminate what is impossible. What you have left is the "possible." Choose the best and try it out. Disconnect old habitual thoughts and feelings so that new associations can form more freely, and try to see all the new connections (although some of the process seems to be below the level of conscious inner speech). Mixing hard-nosed research with free-floating divergent thinking is the best use of creative time.

DON'T SELECT THE SAME THOUGHTS OVER AND OVER AGAIN

If you are thinking about a problem and find yourself coming back over the same thoughts, *reroute your thinking*. When you Listen In and hear repetitions, it's a sign that you are not advancing; *your choice of words has trapped you* in the same spot.

Train your inner speech not to use clichés, because they indicate that you are not thinking *actively*. As soon as you discover that you are covering the same ground again by using the same words, let it be a signal to you to *select* a different set of thoughts. This will ensure that you have new ideas. Obsessive, ruminating, circular thoughts are a diagnostic sign of rigid thinking.

Rigid thinking ultimately becomes self-defeating thinking.

Inner Speech Training emphasizes this principle: As soon as you realize you are having weak thoughts that you had before, accept the fact that (for the present moment) you are not making progress. Select new words and thereby change the subject in your mind, or take a break and come back to the problem later when you have a new mindset. You may think it is avoiding the issue. This is not so. Repetitious thinking means that you are not getting anywhere. It is more efficient to Reorient yourself and come back to it later. In the meantime, your unconscious will be working for you. Your unconscious is incubating new thoughts.

How Can We Work with Our Inner Speech to Enhance Our Creative Abilities?

1. *Change your voice thoughts to decrease your inhibitions and take a new look at things.*

Stop those Weakening Words that lead to negative self-criticism. "Oh, I'm no good at that." What possible value does that negative commercial have? None. It is both boring and useless.

You don't need all those voice thoughts that tell you you can't do something.

If you think, "I *won't* take a vacation this year," you change your whole viewpoint from what it would be if you thought, "I *can't* take a vacation this year." You will feel more powerful if you *create a choice*. Use words that indicate *you are never finished*—that *your possibilities have not come to an end*.

A powerful technique that is frequently used in

groups is to change "I will try" to "I will." This is a basic change in cognitive style that keeps the potential alive.

Practice thinking

"What can I do?"

Practice Switching when you hear...

"I don't know if I can do that..."

What would you Switch to?

"I can..."   "I will..."

It is important to realize that what you do is a choice, not a "have to."

As soon as you train yourself to select a thought that indicates to yourself that *nearly everything you do in life is a choice*, you will experience new creativity in your life and not be imprisoned by weakening thoughts, words, and actions.

2. *Build up your creative courage.*

There is a newness and challenge to every creative encounter. Erich Fromm speaks of "creative courage" as that quality that allows one to reach out and encounter change. Remember that freedom is victory over fear.

To be creative in your thinking, reach out *actively* and focus on what you want to encounter.

3. *Take a creative break.*

Devote a part of your day to creative thinking. Call it daydreaming if you prefer. Think out loud if that helps you.

If you want to be an astronomer, practice thinking about the skies and the galaxies—not the rent.

Internal stimulation is the knack of *using your own thinking* to think about the things you want to do. A potential scientist can't linger all day thinking about where she parked her car. A new office manager can't be creative if he worries all day long about whether that day-old cough is the first sign of a fatal disease.

List the *potentially* creative people you know. Can you spot their creative blocks? How do they frustrate themselves? What are the weaknesses in their thinking? Any similarity with your own procrastinating? Learn from watching.

> ...Creative job shapers

> ...Creative planners

> ...Artists, sculptors, fledgling novelists

> ...The plain person with the good mind who seems to find a way to solve problems at work. How does she/he think?

4. *Remember that the imagination is the outreaching of the mind.*

Don't be threatened by strange voices or new directions in your thoughts. Practice visualizations to expand your imagination. Try to put together visually the wildest, most discordant elements—grass in the middle of skyscrapers, a television set placed in the middle of the ocean. And then practice uniting these thoughts with a discovery—a particular pattern. Your imagination can be expanded with practice.

5. *The too-bad-we-were-overtrained theory.*

Too much of our adult world is overcontrolled and overmanaged. Too much fun has disappeared—a victim of "overtraining." Frequently, the most creative periods of our lives are during adolescence, when our thinking was flowing and we were less inhibited by a sense of the way things ought to be. We hadn't yet learned all the "musts" or "buts." Our thinking hadn't become: "We never did that before, so let's not do it now."

"It's no use—nothing creative happens."

STOP!! SWITCH!

"I'm learning to become more creative."

Fear forces your thoughts to march in the same old ruts. Go beyond your old self.

"It's never worth the time."

STOP!!
SWITCH!

"I'm going to invest some time in this. It may prove worthwhile."

6. *Don't use the thoughts "all," "nothing," "every," "none," "never," "always."* The rule is to avoid *universalizers* and *generalizers* in your vocabulary.

"I lead such a boring life, I *never* do anything creative." Do you *really* mean that you don't do *anything* creative?

7. *Don't use tyrannical imperatives.*

Simply eliminate from your vocabulary *"should/ must/have to."* Those words tyrannize you, and tyranny doesn't work. It breeds resentment, rebellion, and obstinacy. That may stop you from having the fun of being creative.

Negative internal voices erode the power in your

mental processes and prevent you from realizing the unique, exquisite pleasures of being creative. Negative voices limit freedom by condemning the proposed goal before it is even born.

Don't subtract from a positive statement ("butting in").

Therefore, rarely use the words, "but/however/except/on the other hand."

Don't "butt in" and interrupt a positive statement by compulsively linking a negative statement.

"I got good grades—*but* I was really lucky."

"I enjoy getting out into the country; *however*, I don't do it often enough."

"I love good music; *however*, I should really have learned more about it."

"In one way, I'd love to do it; *on the other hand*, it could present problems."

People with weakening ambivalence in their inner speech won't say something positive about themselves *without* following it with a subtraction. Some people can't hear a compliment without changing it: "Your hair looks great today." Their inner speech follows with, "It looked stringy yesterday."

If you will carefully avoid certain roadblock words like "but/except/however," your inner dialogues will lead to less self-defeat and to more creative options. Don't "undo" the first half of a creative sentence in your mind. You can keep your creativity flowing like a river, if you do not dam it up with a "but."

Thinking is a thrilling and exciting endeavor in and of itself, when you don't cut it off with some sabotaging thought. Your thinking is the royal road to creativity: let it *flow*.

INNER SPEECH TRAINING
REVIEWED
FIVE STEPS TO HEALTHY INNER SPEECH

By now, you have started to notice how people around you handle their thinking. Ask yourself which ones make repeated errors—think thoughts that weaken their lives. Even more importantly, try to notice the positive people in your life. How do they think? Just what is it that makes them so chipper, so stimulating to be around? Try to figure out exactly what great thoughts are in their inner speech. *Ask* them.

Ask some friends if they notice what causes their feelings to *change*. Do people around you know that they begin to feel morose because they just had a thought that they lost or are missing something in their lives? Do they know that a sudden panicky feeling was brought on by their thought of some danger they thought they couldn't handle? Comparing notes can be a great mind expander.

Right now is a crucial time for you. For this system to be of maximum value in your life, you need to keep thinking about it. Keep LISTENING IN, UNDERLINING, STOPPING, SWITCHING, REORIENTING.

Remember that how you think can weaken or strengthen your whole life. So keep referring to these ideas. They can come to have more and more meaning for you. Select and underline passages most helpful for your thinking. Check the ways you have already improved. Make a note to yourself about the problem areas that remain.

And this is only the start of your new thinking. As H.G. Wells reminded us, "The past is but the beginning of a beginning."

INDEX